ENDLESS LOVE

Michael's eyes were locked on Terra's face, and he was waiting for her to look at him, but she kept her lashes lowered. Slowly Terra's hands spanned the breadth of his muscular back and the depth of the center above his spine.

She moved up to his neck and with her hands familiarized herself with the cords and muscles.

Mike was sure he'd lose control if she didn't kiss him soon. But she surprised him with those same gentle hands when she cupped his face and brought it close to her lips. "Please kiss me," she whispered.

Their mouths met like the clash of cymbals. Teeth and tongue met and danced a wild coupling as his thumbs caressed the columns of her neck.

ENDLESS LOVE

Carmen Green

BET Publications, LLC
www.bet.com
www.arabesquebooks.com

ARABESQUE BOOKS are published by

BET Publications, LLC
c/o BET BOOKS
One BET Plaza
1900 W Place NE
Washington, D.C. 20018-1211

First Printing: September, 2000

10 9 8 7 6 5 4 3 2 1
Printed in the United States of America

Acknowledgments

Life is a tricky road, that if left to navigate alone, can lead in a direction where you might miss its simplistic beauty. Thank you Margaret Johnson-Hodge for reminding me there is beauty in each and every day.

Ruth Kagle, you are a wonderful agent and a great person.

To Monty, Jeremy, Dani, Tina, Stacy, Christopher, David, Ashley, Kacy, Mom, Grandma, Ms. Sarah and Dad, Ken, Bryant, Whitney, Yvonne and Carl, you are a blessing.

Thank you Karen Thomas for asking me to write the story that was on my heart.

Jacquie Thomas, Brenda Jackson, Donna Hill, and all the Arabesque women who've wished me well and prayed for me, every kind word touched my heart.

To my Heavenly Father, through you, all things are possible.

One

As Michael Crawford stood beside his client and faced the stoic calm of the Honorable Keith Rathborne, he wondered if his recent penchant for bad luck had finally run its course.

Choked up in his judicial robe, Judge Rathborne turned his shiny bald head toward the district attorney of Fulton County, Georgia, and grinned. The judge never smiled.

Michael's luck sank to a new all-time low. He and his client would probably end up sharing a cell before the day was over.

"Ms. Pearsoy," the judge said, "I want to commend you on presenting one of the best, if not *the best*, summation I've had the pleasure of hearing in my twenty-nine years on the bench. Nothing short of sensational. Good work."

Michael didn't dare look at Mary Beth Pearsoy. From the corner of his eye he could make out her frozen form and that was enough to communicate her surprise. Her close had been decent. Certainly nothing to write home about. But his case had been stronger. Gary Tarow, the wealthy admitted jewel thief, had been busted in a pawnshop with a pocketful of jewelry. Not the brightest guy in the world, but the prosecution hadn't proven the jewels weren't his mother's, as he claimed.

A dismissal would have been prudent days ago, but Judge Rathborne and his pigheadedness overshadowed reason. He'd practically marched Michael around the legal circus corral, making him jump through hoops of overruled objections and denied motions. Now he and Gary waited for the jury, then the judge to decide their fate.

Unnerved by the judge's statement, usually cool Gary was quickly losing his composure. His lips were compressed into a thin line, and he trembled so much that his knee hit the table. Michael motioned with his left hand for him to be still and returned his attention to the judge.

Suddenly Rathborne's short neck shot beyond the neckline of his robe, and he glared at everyone in the gallery. "What is that incessant tapping? Silence! Mr. Crawford," the judge barked, "your work has improved marginally over the past ten years, but it's still a showcase of the grandiose. I also found your close repetitive and amateurish. A sophomoric attempt at law at best."

"Glad I could oblige."

"What was that? Speak up!"

Michael stared the judge down, unwilling to take the bait. Rathborne had held him in contempt twice this year and four times since he became a lawyer in '91. Not only wasn't he trying to go to jail and pay a fine, he refused to give Rathborne the satisfaction.

Being that it was Friday, the judge might not have him held; nevertheless, he had better things to do than sit with inmates and talk about how lawyers were scum.

"Your Honor is free to have his opinion."

"You're correct there, Mr. Crawford." The judge studied his hands, then locked gazes with Michael. "As brilliant as Ms. Pearsoy was," he handed the decision to the bailiff who passed it back to the jury forewoman. "The jury has spoken. What say you in the case of the *State of Georgia* v. *Gary Tarow?*"

"Not guilty."

Turning to his client with a proffered hand, Michael withdrew it when the man wet his pants, then fainted.

* * *

Michael entered the law firm he owned with his brother Julian and stopped short. The light was still on beneath his brother's door, although it was the last Friday of the month and after six.

Keisha, Julian's wife, was a stickler for what she'd named their monthly honeymoon getaway. Something important had to have kept Julian at work late on such a special night.

Resting his briefcase on the clean maple surface of his secretary's desk, Michael tapped on the door before entering.

"What's got you here so late?"

His brother stood beside the picture window overlooking downtown Decatur, lost in thought. Cars packed the roads and anxious people hurried to the MARTA station. "I hear we won," Julian said blandly.

From the small kitchenette off Julian's office, Michael helped himself to a Diet Coke, his brother's latest vice, and took a deep swallow. He wiped his mouth with his hand and with the other yanked his tie free.

"Grudgingly. I got a lecture on how incompetent I was. When Rathborne shouted, 'Stop that incessant tapping,' I thought he'd heard my heart beating. Got smart since the last time, though. I packed my toothbrush."

Julian looked at him sharply. "We should turn him over to the ethics committee. Whatever happened between him and our father forty years ago was between them."

Michael swallowed more soda and shrugged. "What can I say, he's crazy. What are you still doing here?"

Julian slowly started for his desk. He nudged aside two stacks of papers and pulled out a long envelope. "Waiting for you."

As he looked at the back of the plain manila envelope that resembled the type his company used for confidential interoffice mail, it suddenly dawned on him why Julian stayed late. "I know I'm late on my expense reports. I'll get them to Hilary tomorrow." He downed the remainder of the soda and headed for the door, already planning what'd he say to convince April to give their marriage another try. They'd been separated for ten months, but maybe the saying "Absence makes the heart grow fonder" would be true for both of them. Although he didn't feel the same passion he once felt and wasn't even sure what he felt was love, he was committed. And until they decided otherwise, they were still married. Maybe a trip to Puerto Rico would help rekindle their lost love. He made a mental note to check the flights and opened the door to leave. "I'll check you later."

"I need to talk to you." Julian maintained his post at the desk.

Anxious now to get on with his weekend, Michael turned around, annoyed. "I can't believe you stayed just to get on me about my reports. The end of the month technically isn't until next Wednesday." Julian didn't respond. "What's wrong with you?"

The closer Michael got to his brother, the better he could see how pain colored his eyes.

He sank into the chair. Something terrible had happened. No matter how he tried to prepare himself, he couldn't forestall the pain. He sent an urgent prayer to heaven and braced himself for the worst. As his prayer list grew to include his parents, brothers, their wives and children, family friends, neighbors and colleagues, he began to sweat. It could be anybody. "Who died?"

"This came for you today."

The official-looking envelope hung from Julian's hand. The mirrored reflection from the windows hit it and that's when he read the name. Blount and Blount, Attorneys-at-law. His stomach settled down around his knees, and the urge for something stronger than diet soda took hold.

Reading his mind, Julian set a tumbler of rum and Coke on the desk in front of him. Michael took a deep swallow and wished his luck would turn.

He opened the envelope and slid out divorce papers, signed in his wife's bold script. Puerto Rico was definitely out.

"So this is it." His voice echoed in the tight silence, and he looked up at his older brother. "Nobody died. Just my marriage." He fingered the legal documents, never fully comprehending their meaning until now. His marriage was over. Done.

"She wants out. What are you going to do?"

The shreds of his heart managed to bind together enough to beat against his rib cage. "I was thinking Puerto Rico. Not divorce court."

"What are you going to do?" Julian asked again, in a voice filled with sympathy.

Michael thought of the five-year emotional war he'd fought with April, of the begging and pleading on both their parts, of the numerous tests and the agonizing failures at making a baby and of the reconciliation of knowing that at this one thing, he was an abysmal failure.

He reached for his brother's Cross pen. Funny how a piece of paper had affected his life twice in one day. One good. One bad.

Not the paper, he corrected himself. But the words written on the paper.

"Michael?" If he didn't answer, Julian's concern would make him call their four brothers and they would come add their two-cents worth of advice. He didn't need it. He'd just lost the war.

"Your question, counselor, is a good one. What am I going to do? I've been married for more than ten years and during the last two years, the marriage in question has disintegrated into a pile of days of one of us trying to remember why we were mad at the other."

On his brother's credenza were photos of the family, couples and children. Michael selected his from among the other smiling faces. "This," he shook the photo, "is a lie. We were young and didn't know how much pain we could inflict on each other."

"Mike—"

He shook off Julian's hand.

"I thought we married forever." The rum and Coke tasted bitter but he swallowed the rest and spun the glass on the desk. It teetered in a wobbly circle then clattered to a stop.

"Forever is the blink of an eye. Forever is the time it takes sperm to die inside the woman you thought loved you. Nothing is forever, Julian. Love isn't. Marriage isn't." He dropped the picture atop the divorce papers. "Lucky for me, failure isn't forever."

When he looked up, tears were in his brother's eyes. "I'll never be able to have children, Julian. Can't change that for anything in the world. Not going to try anymore. My life is my life now. And April's is hers."

He scrawled his name on the documents then left the office.

Fresh from the shower Saturday morning, Michael dried his hair and slipped into boxers and sweatpants. The August day promised to be long and hot. Everything in the room was packed except the computer. He hit a series of keys and pulled up his voice messages.

"Michael, this is April." His ex-wife's voice stopped him from pulling the T-shirt over his head. "Um, I know you have to get your things from the house, and I don't want to make you uncomfortable by being there. I'll be away for a few days this week. Today, Wednesday, Thursday and Friday. You can pick up whatever you need then." Strain made her voice crack and she giggled. Something she'd always done when nervous, except there was no joy behind the laughter. "Take care."

The beep sounded indicating the next message. "Michael, come to dinner tonight. Your mother wants to know why you rented an apartment instead of moving home." His father's voice faded then came back. "I'm so sorry, son."

Sitting in the chair, he forced himself to answer e-mail and respond to Hilary's mail listed as urgent.

The monotony of completing his expense reports kept his

thoughts focused on work and away from the sound of April's voice and the inflections in her tone.

Was she happy it was over? Relieved to be free?

He shook himself, forcing pen to paper. Divorces happened every day. Life went on.

The file for a civil case against Blount and Blount rested atop a stack of legal pads. What had the scandalous law firm done now? Taken candy from small children? They were known for getting large settlements for their clients, and he initially had been surprised that April would use them. But she hadn't known of their proven record of using unscrupulous tactics to get opposing parties to back down from their clients.

He had to admit they tried hard to shake him down for money, threatening to air his infertility, but April had put a stop to their tactics and they had an equitable settlement. Now as far as he was concerned, Blount and Blount had better watch out. His clients had a good case, a tough case against them, and if the judgement was found in his client's favor, Blount would be liable for millions. He opened the folder, smoothed the seam and read until he'd absorbed all the information.

From memory, he jotted points of law for his paralegals to research and numbered the order of his first motions, placing two question marks next to the word *discovery*.

These attorneys who specialized in being women-friendly divorce lawyers were in for a fight.

Divorced. You're divorced. I'm divorced. The words played in his mind until he lost focus and shoved the briefs away.

The air conditioner clicked on and ruffled the blinds at the Extended Stay Hotel, and he glanced at the white-faced clock. In a couple of hours, he could pick up his keys for his new apartment and move in.

Now that everything had been decided, he would no longer be calling the Melbrook Lane establishment home. Dismantling the computer took only minutes, and he secured it in a box by the door. He grabbed his jacket from the back of the chair and wrestled another stack of boxes into his arms. Instead of waiting until next week, he'd get his stuff from his old house now.

The phone rang just as he turned the knob. Propping the boxes against the wall with his knee, he snatched up the receiver.

"Michael Crawford."

"Mike? Mike? You there?"

The voice of his cousin Drew filtered through the phone. Michael squeezed his eyes shut. "What do you want, Drew?"

"Hey, cousin! I heard your bad news and thought I would call to say how sorry I am."

Drew, sorry? That was an oxymoron if he'd ever heard one. Drew was a walking screwup from the word *go*. He'd burned family bridges like Georgians burned wood. Still, curiosity made Michael stay on the phone. "How did you hear about it?"

"Well, you know how it is. I had to leave another job and was down on my luck and your daddy is a good man. He let me stay with him and your ma."

A knowing feeling settled on his shoulders. Was it possible to be a leech and be almost thirty? For the past ten years, Drew hadn't held a full-time job for more than five or six weeks tops. He'd disappear for extended periods only to reappear months later. As far as Michael knew, no one had ever been able to pin down Drew's whereabouts, but that didn't mean Aunt Celia didn't try.

"Mike, you still here?"

"Still here," he said, rubbing the back of his neck. "Listen, Drew. Today I've got to move out of the house so if I don't get started now, I won't ever get finished. Thanks for calling—"

"Why don't I help you? I've got the whole day free. I know you could use another strong back."

Michael cursed himself. Today he wanted quiet, time to devise a plan for the remainder of his life without his wife. He didn't want his talkative cousin under foot telling corny jokes and filling his head with nonsense.

"I've got movers for the heavy stuff," he lied. "But thanks. I think I've got it under control."

"Mike, you saying you can't use a hand to help pack a life you've had for ten years? I've been divorced. I know," his cousin said plainly. "I'm just trying to help."

Ashamed, Michael pinched the bridge of his nose. "Okay. Do you know where I'm staying?"

"Your father gave me the address this morning. Open the door and I'm ready to go."

"I'll be down in a minute," he said and had to laugh.

The new apartment looked different in the daylight. He'd looked at it one evening two months ago when his practical side told him to make arrangements should his last attempt at reconciliation fail. At the time, there'd been a long waiting list of people interested in the ultramodern facility and little chance he'd get it but he'd submitted his application anyway.

The building had been built in the early seventies when single people valued living space instead of cost-cutting efficiency apartments. Wide and spacious, the apartments had been updated early in the millennium year with touch-pad and keyless locks for the door, motion-activated water faucets that recognized when an object was placed underneath and computer-operated showers. The conveniences were nice perks, but he just hoped he liked the place, which had been recommended to him by a friend, Professor Regina Clinnell at Emory.

At the time of the tour, the apartment had been occupied so he only got a view of the large living room encumbered by the last tenants' overbearing furniture.

The bare wood flooring had been waxed to a high shine. He appreciated the airy studio feel and immediately knew he wouldn't cover the solid wood floor.

The bedroom and guest-room floors had been treated to the

same glowing finish, and he liked what he saw. Before he could start his inspection of the office, bathrooms and closets, a knock on the half-open door brought him around. "Mr. Crawford? It's Terra O'Shaughssey, the building manager. May I come in?"

"Yes, please come in." He strode toward the entrance and with his foot pushed a path clear for the arcing door.

"Hi," she said.

"Hello."

She stood quietly in the doorway, her gaze flitting to and fro, never meeting his. "Excuse the mess. I'm Michael," he said.

He was rewarded with a quick look. Beautiful eyes, his brain registered. "What can I do for you?"

"Oh. Here is the electronic key for your door. You get two sets and I have one. The key works easily. Push the button, and when you hear a soft bing, you can enter. As you already know, this is a test system, so if you have problems call me. Your door is also self-locking once shut. Oh, here is the lease agreement with a set of building rules.

"All mailboxes are on the first floor. Your mailbox is ten-ten, and here's the key for it. My apartment is forty-twenty. Drop your rent off in the box outside my door on the first day of the month. Anytime after the fifth, a twenty-five dollar late fee is assessed. I think that's it. Any questions?"

"Yes."

He was rewarded with a panicked look. This time she didn't look away so quickly. "What is it? I mean, what is your question?"

"Can I have the paperwork?"

She blushed bright and pretty, but that was the loudest thing about her. When she spoke, her words were delivered soft and low in a genteel manner. He noticed how she clutched the brown clipboard to her chest as if it were an invincible shield.

A grin worked his jaws when she said, "Sure," and gave him the documents. "I think that's it. I do have one question.

Is the guy sitting on the steps with you? Because if he's a vagrant, we can call someone and they'll take him to a shelter."

He stalked to the window and looked down, noticing Drew on *his* cell phone. "He's not a vagrant. He's my cousin. Come to think of it, I don't know if he's a vagrant or not. But he's perfectly harmless." Michael held back his grimace. He hadn't known Drew was living with his parents. He didn't know why the judge hated him. Lately he didn't seem to know anything.

The past year blended into a haze of events he'd attended and missed. None of which he could honestly say he remembered.

"Would you like some coffee?"

Michael turned and realized he'd missed Terra O'Shaughssey leaving.

TWO

Terra O'Shaughssey shut out the world when she closed her apartment door, and wished also to block thoughts of Michael Crawford. Her natural curiosity about people kept returning her thoughts to his expression as he'd studied his cousin.

Care, concern and love were reflected in his serious gaze, and they warmed her. Michael possessed a yearning that she innately wanted to respond to and she couldn't understand why. He was a stranger. A tenant. A recently divorced man, according to Regina Clinnell, the woman who'd recommended him to this building.

Something about him held her captive as she'd walked down the four flights of stairs. And she didn't want it to.

Terra slid her clipboard upright on the bookshelf and strolled out to the living room. The apartment was cool, bathed in a summer breeze that blew in from the screened-in patio. Nice weather had encouraged a beautiful array of flowers and fruits to grow and this morning she and a few neighbors had enjoyed exchanging them.

She deposited garden-raised carnations, roses, pansies and petunias in glass vases around the room, dropped the fruits in the crisper, poured herself a glass of apple juice, then retired to her favorite chair on the patio.

This is contentment, she thought as she sipped juice and watched squirrels race across the top of the fence that divided one property from the next.

Did Michael Crawford have contentment in his life?

She thought back about a hundred years and recalled her own divorce. For her, it had been the start of a brighter and better future.

However, Michael seemed to be stuck in limbo. She couldn't rightfully stop him from living there; his credit was worthy and his references glowing, in addition to being the co-owner of a respectable law firm. Who wouldn't want him as a tenant?

His sullen face wavered in her memory. Perhaps he hadn't gotten what he wanted out of the divorce.

Perhaps he hadn't wanted the divorce at all. Something told her she was right.

Her textbook *Interpersonal Communications Skills* lay on the table. She needed to review the ten points of settling conflict, but didn't feel up to the mental challenge just yet. Her life would remain conflict-free if her siblings stayed in Brunswick.

She reached for the romance novel she'd been reading before having to deliver the lease and keys, and picked up where she left off. Since she was fairly close to the beginning, the hero was acting indifferent to the heroine and she to him. Tempted to read the last chapter now, Terra resisted.

The salesclerk had assured her that although the couple initially fight their attraction, they overcome obstacles and get together in the end. When pressed for more details about the story line, the clerk simply smiled and quoted the price.

Terra rubbed the page, careful not to break the spine. She didn't need to immerse herself in fiction. Her shelves were filled with autobiographies and historical books as well as books on poetry, gardening and self-improvement. But reading a good romance novel gave her pleasure. It allowed her an opportunity to explore other people's lives without intruding on people she knew personally.

Terra read a few pages and stopped. Coincidentally, the hero's name was Michael. Luckily this man looked nothing like the new tenant. The fictional Michael had a scar across his jaw and was dark-skinned. The real Michael, although clean-cut and good-looking, didn't have scars she could see except for the sadness that surrounded him.

Shorter than the average man, the fictional character had dark smoldering eyes, while the real Michael had hazy gray provoking eyes that shuttered if you looked too close. He'd made it clear through his demeanor that he wanted to be alone and she was pretty sure that included being free of the nosy musings of his landlady. She shook her head to clear it, took a sip of juice and began to read.

Terra noticed that an hour had ticked by when she flipped on the ceiling fan to cool herself from the afternoon sun. She toed off her shoes, sat back down and kept reading, the textbook forgotten.

The doorbell interrupted the first kiss. She hopped from one sleepy foot to the door. "Who is it?"

"Michael Crawford. We've got a problem."

Catching herself smoothing back her short black hair, Terra breathed deeply and concentrated on calming herself.

He knocked again.

Her heart rate kicked up and she opened the door. "Mr. Crawford," she said, faking calm, "what's the problem?"

Keeping her eyes focused on the center of his chest wasn't a problem, as she stood a little shorter than his more-than-six-feet height.

"The problem is that none of the keys work."

"How strange," she said softly. "They worked yesterday. Maybe I should try them." Go away, she wanted to say. Michael and Sylvia were about to kiss. Instead she looked down the hall and in her peripheral vision noticed him following her gaze.

"Can we do this now," he said with forced patience.

"Of course." She glanced up and felt her heart flutter into overdrive the longer he looked at her. Pretty soon it would grow legs and skip right out of her chest. "My keys," she said, reaching a hand inside the door to the wall.

"No shoes?"

Terra looked down at her bare toes and the bright-red polish her sister had insisted on giving her for her birthday last month. The door clicked closed behind her. "I'm fine. This'll just take a minute."

"Suit yourself. Let's start with the door to my apartment."

Terra turned for the elevator and Michael for the stairs.

"Good for your heart," he said.

She gestured toward the elevator. "Easy on the feet."

"Point taken."

They rode the four flights to his floor, and she hurried to the door. Take charge, her inner voice commanded. Terra pressed the hand-held keyless entry device once and waited for the click to indicate that the door had locked. Nothing. No matter how often she pressed, the door wouldn't lock. A test item, this door and her door were the only two in the building fitted with the locks.

Shaking in frustration, she stared at the remote and the lock. Just to be on the safe side, she pressed the button really fast, then slowly.

"Didn't work for me either," he informed her matter-of-factly.

She gripped the key pad in her fist and resisted the urge to lower herself to keyhole level and stare at the dark screen. While getting a good look might work for motorists stranded over the open hoods of cars, she was nearly positive it wouldn't now, especially not with Michael Crawford standing over her!

Terra buoyed her flagging confidence. "It appears we have a situation. I'll go and write this up, and we'll get someone right on it."

Michael leaned back against the wall and folded one muscular arm over the other. "What will writing it up do?"

"A record is kept on all building maintenance."

"Then what happens?"

"When?"

"What happens after we write a report?"

"Then . . . then . . . I . . . well . . . nothing. I mean, we've never had to write this sort of report before, so I don't know."

"You mean to tell me the locksmith god doesn't fly down from cloud lockedout and give me the golden key?"

His sarcasm wasn't amusing. In fact, she felt worse with every passing moment. She put up her hands. "Mr. Crawford, I can make this right. This has never happened before."

A stream of nervous perspiration dribbled down her forehead, and she wiped it. Pulling her hand away, she stared at the moisture on her finger. Glancing up quickly, she caught a look of impatience on his face. "We're close to a resolution," she said. "I'll take care of this right away.

"I hope it's *very* right away, Terra. I wouldn't want you to have to patrol these halls until it's made right." He walked inside his apartment and closed the door firmly in her face.

Shocked, Terra stared at the thick walnut door and wanted to cry. She walked back to her apartment, wondering what could have happened. Yesterday the keys had been delivered and when she'd tried them, they'd worked. Methodically she retraced her movements and ended up back at her desk with the extra set.

Maybe they would work. She hurried upstairs only to return to her apartment more frustrated. Neither card worked. There was a control panel in the basement so that in case of a power outage, the locks could be disengaged and the tenant could enter his apartment and the door would automatically lock behind him. But that wasn't the problem. The door simply would not lock.

She rested her face on her hand and stared at the keys as if waiting for an answer to magically appear.

Terra reached for the phone and dialed the corporate office, then realized it was after 4:30 and all the company bigwigs had left to attend a seminar. She dialed the administrative assistant's number and left a message, then tried the locksmith and received a recording that he'd be out of town and unavailable until Monday at ten o'clock.

Her heart sank. It had been forever since she'd pulled an all-nighter, and she didn't relish the task with the peevish Michael Crawford as her charge. But she had promised a resolution and a resolution he would get.

This would go over well in her management-theory class. If this incident was reported to the wrong person, her 4.0 grade-point average could easily sink and along with that her chance at the ultimate job—managing the new homes in Vanderbilt Manor Chase Estates in Cobb County.

Not only would the lucky manager have a customized home on the property, but a company car, stock options and a great medical package. All fifteen students in her class were vying for the job. If keeping tabs on Michael Crawford's belongings for a weekend meant a squeaky clean record, it was a small sacrifice.

"Terra?"

Her best friend Margaret's voice rang through the apartment.

"I'm in the office. How did you get in?"

Margaret Sexton appeared in the doorway, bright and cheerful. A plus-size model, Margaret managed to look gorgeous all the time. She billowed in a hot-pink top and dark jeans with leather ankle boots strapping her feet. Her hair was done up six inches off her head and Terra often wondered how a woman nearly six feet tall with six additional inches of hair cleared doorways. Another of life's mysteries, she guessed.

The sun had set, bathing the apartment in a dusky glow from the streetlights. She turned on the lamp beside the stereo and closed the patio door.

"You left the door unlocked," Margaret accused gently. "What's up with that? For all you know I could have been one of your brothers or sisters."

"I know. I wasn't thinking." Terra pushed past Margaret and made sure the door was now locked. "Margaret, I need a big favor."

"What is it?" Electronic organizer in hand, Margaret pulled

up the date. "I've got a meeting tomorrow at two, a look-see at three-fifteen and a shoot at five. I can get you in at eight."

"Tonight. I need it tonight."

The electronic pencil zipped around on the calendar in Margaret's capable hand. She shook her head. "No can do, sweetie. I've got a date."

Terra stopped fiddling with the keys and stared at her friend. "You're kidding. With who?"

"His name is Caesar Bellamy and, honey, while he might sound Spanish, he's one-hundred-percent black male. I met him at the opening of Justin's, Puff Daddy's restaurant, but that was years ago. He just called right out of the blue and asked me out. So I said, 'Why not, Margaret? You're not doing anything else.' " She talked a mile a minute. "So I said yes. I'm as good-looking as Elle and can't get a man with a hundred-dollar bill taped to my breasts. He'd take the money but leave me." Margaret quirked her mouth, rolled her eyes, walked over to the sofa and sat. "Goodness gracious. Don't you ever get tired of listening to that whale music? If you were meant to understand all that squealing, guess what?"

"I'd be a whale. Yes, I know. You say that all the time. If it's bothering you, I'll turn it off."

Margaret grew more perturbed. "Terra, this is your place. Tell me to go to hell and keep talking. How's your interpersonal class coming?"

Terra felt the large lump of her romance novel under her left buttock. "Great," she said softly. "I'm learning how to resolve conflict."

Margaret grinned at her. "The next class you need to take is how to lie like a Wall Street broker, sugar. I saw the romance book when I came in."

Terra's cheeks grew hot. "I had a new tenant move in today, and I took a break and decided to read for pleasure. But you're right. I need to be studying."

Margaret leaned forward. "I can blow what's-his-face off tonight. What do you need?"

"Oh, no." Terra rose. "I don't want you missing the first date you've"—Margaret cleared her throat loudly—"had in eight months."

"But I can't leave you in the lurch. What did you need?"

"It's kind of a baby-sitting—"

A loud pounding startled both women. "Ms. O'Shaughssey? Terra? Are you in there?"

The door rattled and Terra pushed past Margaret and pulled the shaking wood open. "Yes, Mr. Crawford? What's the problem now?"

"You said there was a resolution in my future. I'd hoped it'd be today."

"It will be today. I promise." He looked past her and gave Margaret a perusing glance. "Is there anything else?" It didn't matter that Margaret was much bigger than she, Margaret was gorgeous and men couldn't keep their eyes off her.

He extended his hand and dropped another key in her palm. "The mailbox key doesn't work either. So far we're oh for two."

"Things will get better. Can I come up in a few minutes? I just need to take care of something."

Michael finally looked at her with gray stormy eyes. She blinked twice and was positive she didn't want to face him in a court of law.

"Quickly."

Terra closed the door and met Margaret's shocked stare. "Who was that monster?"

"Mon . . . monster?" Terra chuckled in disbelief. "I thought the gray-eyed, brown-skinned, muscular hunks were your type."

"*Quickly,*" Margaret imitated. "Who does he think he is?"

"The man who rents the penthouse apartment for fifteen-hundred dollars a month and doesn't have keys that lock his doors."

"Oh." Margaret made a sympathetic sound. "Girl, you got a problem. Who are you baby-sitting tonight?"

Terra looked at the door and pulled her mouth into a straight line. "Him."

They both looked at the door where Michael had just stood. "Good googamooga. You've got your hands full."

Hit with inspiration, Terra turned on the radio to a jazz station and ran into the kitchen and tore through the pantry. She found what she was looking for and ran back to Margaret. "Please stay with me?"

Margaret's gaze took in the white wine, chocolate and microwave popcorn. "We can have a feast," Terra said. "Me and you and any kind of music you like. Even r-r-r-rap."

Her best friend laughed and then looked pitiful. "Terra, it's my first date in months. Nearly a year. Come on. You're putting me in a bad position. You know I can't say no, but if the shoe were on the other foot, would I ask you to do this?"

Terra contemplated how long it'd take her to drink the whole bottle herself. "You're right." She dropped the goodies on the counter and hugged her friend. "I wouldn't have lasted with the rap going anyway."

Margaret laughed and with arms linked around each other's waists, Terra walked her friend to the door. "I knew you wouldn't be able to. I almost forgot. You promised to go wig shopping with me. You're still going, right?"

"Wig shopping? Do you really need me, Margaret?"

"Terra, I need a long piece for a photo shoot. Lunch is my treat. Come on. Girls day at the mall on Sunday."

"All right," Terra said, caving in. What was the harm in doing a little shopping? She so rarely treated herself anyway, it would be a good time to shop for end-of-summer bargains. Maybe she'd get some new sheets.

She and Margaret stopped at the front door. "How about when I get home tonight, should I stop up? I won't be late."

"Are you sure?"

Margaret gave her a sassy grin. "He's not getting that lucky. See you later, sugar."

After checking to make sure the door was locked, Terra repaired the pantry then gathered her textbook, flashlight, snacks, sleeping bag and just to be cautious, her baseball bat and can of Mace. She slipped her feet into sandals, glanced at her romance novel and shook her head. "I've had enough trouble for one day." Flipping off the lights in her apartment, she wondered what the fictional Michael was doing tonight.

Three

Michael read the back of the box of rice again. "Boil for ten minutes or until soft." Without measuring cups, it was hard to gauge how much rice he'd poured into the five-quart saucepan, but a couple of fistfuls seemed sufficient.

Only now there seemed to be too much water in the rice. He laid down the spoon, the only piece of silverware he'd found in the endless boxes, and headed back to the living room and the new stereo system.

As he read the directions for installation, he heard the floorboard outside his door groan again. He'd been told that two years ago, the top floor of the building had been converted into living quarters, now his apartment. For him, the selling quality of the apartment had been privacy, but somebody was intruding and he wasn't going to stand for it.

Michael U-turned, snatched the door open and pulled up short. "What are you doing?"

Terra stood outside his door, a pleasant smile on her face. "I'm your bodyguard for this evening." She spoke softly. "Have no fear, I'm here to protect you and your belongings."

He found himself wanting to laugh and fought the urge. "You protecting me? That's funny."

A determined expression crossed her face, but she said nothing and sat down opposite his door. That's when he noticed the sleeping bag, flashlight, baseball bat and Mace next to a textbook. "You're sleeping outside my door?" He couldn't keep incredulity from his voice. "Are you nuts?"

"Most people just say I'm quiet. Nuts has never come up." She opened the textbook and flipped to a page, then looked up at him with thoughtful black eyes.

Michael felt a quickening in his stomach. Hunger, he thought, looking at the determined, calm woman. "You're strange."

"So you've implied." She began to read, then fished a highlighter from her pocket. In nice even strokes, she highlighted lines of text.

For the first time in his life, he didn't know what to say to a woman. "How long do you plan to stay out here?"

"Until corporate opens on Monday."

"You're kidding."

She just shrugged and went back to reading.

"I can't have a woman sitting outside my door guarding me." Michael laughed. What if something happened to her? Everyone would blame him. She didn't look strong enough to handle a baseball bat and wield a can of Mace at the same time.

There was no humor in her voice when she asked, "Are you saying I can't do my job?"

"No, I'm saying I can't have a woman guarding me."

"You asked for a resolution, Mr. Crawford. This is it. Good night."

He ignored her attempt to dismiss him. "Do you want to come in?"

"It kind of defeats the purpose of being a deterrent to crime. I'd like to stop the criminals *before* they cart your property away."

"For goodness' sake, lady! The downstairs door is locked."

She gave him a knowing smile. "Your apartment is smoking."

Michael turned around and sure enough, gray smoke billowed toward the ceiling. As he let the door go, the smoke detector started to buzz.

Everyone on his block was asleep. The apartments were black except for the soft glow of a few night lights. Michael felt like a security guard charged with keeping the peace. Only peace wouldn't be his tonight. His night had been filled with what-if thoughts that spanned ten years.

What if he had been able to give April children? What if they'd adopted a child? What if they'd gotten a troubled child? Could they have handled it? What if they'd stayed married? Would she have resented him for the rest of her life? What if divorce was the best thing for them?

He fell on his bed as his thoughts strayed to the unmarried women in his life. There were only a few. The most recent single woman was Terra, and he had to admit, her beauty attracted him as well as her unassuming strength. A rare quality, he realized as he dissected his attraction to her.

Then how could he let her sleep in the hallway? The front door opened and closed, and he listened intently to the movements of the intruder as he advanced toward the master bedroom. Michael rolled to his feet and searched for a weapon.

His foot landed on a shoe and he grabbed it.

"Mike? You awake?"

Relief hit him in the chest. "Yeah, Drew. I'm still awake." He slipped into his sweatpants and tightened the drawstring.

Drew turned on the light in the hallway and stuck his head into Michael's room. "Who's the chick sleeping in the hall?"

"She's not a chick. She's Terra, the building manager."

"What's she doing out there?"

How could he explain this? "Guarding me."

"What kind of nonsense is that?"

"Her idea, not mine."

"You couldn't talk her out of it?" Drew's disbelief challenged his manhood. "You're an attorney. You're supposed to be able to talk people out of anything."

"I'm going to take care of her right now. How'd you get in?"

"That front lock is child's play. I pushed hard and it gave."

"I feel safe," Mike said sarcastically. "Are you staying or what?"

Drew wiped his head with his hand. "I thought I'd crash here for a while. Is that cool?"

Why not? he thought. He'd been so detached from everyone and everything, so involved with his own problems, he hadn't paid attention to the needs of the family. The Crawfords were a tight bunch. And if Drew need a place to stay, he'd help him out for a few weeks.

"If it's too much trouble, man—" Drew started for the door.

"No trouble at all. The spare bedroom is already made up. Towels under the sink."

"Thanks, man. Good night." Drew disappeared behind the door and seconds later, started the shower.

Michael would never admit the sound made him feel more comfortable, knowing he wasn't alone. That admission would never cross his lips. But he breathed easier as he strolled up the hallway barefoot, through the living room and to the front door.

Carefully he opened it, shoving aside an empty box in the doorway and took a moment to absorb Terra's private sanctuary. His hallway. Hugging the bat, she slept on her side, curled into a loose S on top of the folded sleeping bag.

He thought of waking her, then changed his mind. If there was any guarding to be done, he would do it.

Gently so as not to rouse her, he extracted the bat, scooped her into his arms and carried her inside. Her right arm hung by his side, but her left hand tickled his waist. She sighed deeply as he made his way down the hall to his bedroom.

His sheets were already mussed but clean, and he laid her on the king-size bed. She moved with the grace of a cat as she settled into a comfortable position and resumed her deep slumber.

He placed his knee on the bed, caught himself and stepped back. Twice. What was he thinking?

That he wanted to join her. Be held in her arms. He wanted to connect with another human being on a physical level and feel loved.

Even as these were his thoughts, his feelings ran deeper, like the roots of a two-hundred-year-old tree.

As a lawyer, his job entailed chasing the truth, no matter how elusive or difficult. As he stood over Terra, whose frame was covered in a T-shirt with *Emory* emblazoned across the chest and denim shorts, her feet bare and her toes painted red, her dark hair highlighted by the moon, he wanted to connect with her.

He didn't know this woman, except for the fact that he now occupied a space in her building, but they were here, for all intents and purposes, strangers connected by circumstances.

Her chest rose and fell, and he reached out and drew his fingers lightly over her forehead and smoothed back her hair. She barely stirred.

Suddenly a deeply buried engine inside his soul kicked to life. He took another step back. His actions were about to become highly inappropriate.

Gently, he removed the extra pillow from the bed and a blanket from the hallway linen closet, made up the living room couch and laid down.

The what-ifs started again, and he decided to indulge them. What if he and Terra dated or even got married? Would they be happy? What if she wanted children? What if she didn't? Would he ever know an endless love?

He finally closed his eyes, and when he dreamed, for the first time in a long time, he dreamed of a woman who wasn't his ex-wife.

* * *

Michael sat straight up out of a dead sleep. He shook his head to clear it. Was his dream that Terra was in his bed real?

Throwing back the gingham cover, he untangled his legs and tiptoed down the hall. He debated knocking, then ruled it out as unnecessary. After all, the door was his and what if nobody was on the other side?

He cracked it open and looked inside. Sure enough, Terra lay spread out all over his bed in an open invitation for him to join her. He quietly shut the door and headed back to his makeshift bed and fell asleep smiling.

Awakened by the aroma of cooking food, through sleepy eyes, Michael woke an hour later and could see Drew in the kitchen. "Hey."

"Hey, man. You can use my shower, I mean your shower," Drew offered.

Michael sat up and wiped sleep from his eyes. Terra was in his bed, and Drew was cooking in the kitchen. So far the morning was going well.

He stepped into the guest shower to wake up then dressed in his office and acknowledged his stomach's groan for food as he headed toward the kitchen again.

Groceries. Something else he'd have to remember was now his responsibility. When Drew opened the oven and Michael caught sight of fluffy golden-brown biscuits, he sank onto a barstool. "Where did the groceries come from?"

"There are four stores within three miles of your building, and a farmer's market is a fifteen-minute bus ride away."

Maybe having Drew around wasn't such a bad idea. But in the divorce, he hadn't counted on losing a wife and gaining a roommate. "Drew, where did you disappear to yesterday?"

His cousin looked away. "I had some business to take care of."

The lawyer in him couldn't resist asking the question. "What kind of business?"

Drew slid two perfectly poached eggs onto a plate and surrounded them with fresh biscuits and thin slices of bacon. The bacon didn't look greasy and seemed different than pork, but he was game to try it based on the delicious smell. His stomach growled in appreciation. "What kind of bacon is this?"

"Turkey." Drew drizzled a crushed fruit sauce over the biscuits. "Go ahead and eat."

Michael dug in and closed his eyes. "Man, this is great." His cousin looked pleased but embarrassed. "Where did you learn how to cook?"

He shrugged. "Picked it up here and there." Drew busied himself straightening items on the counter. A box of spices, dishcloths and magazines.

"Well, it's certainly delicious." The compliment triggered another bright smile.

"You know, I was thinking, Mike." Drew stopped.

"What about?"

"When I got divorced, I was depressed, lonely and pretty pathetic."

"And your point would be?" he said, growing defensive.

Drew stared at Michael with the eyes of Drew's father, Jedidiah Crawford. Uncle Jed had been dead for nearly fifteen years, but it didn't stop Drew from being his spitting image.

"Mike, you could be me. My life seemed like it didn't have any direction, you know?"

And it does now? Michael thought but kept it to himself. "I was thinking you should throw yourself a party. An I'm-single-and-ready-to-mingle party. Change your name to Mike. I call you that, 'cause Michael is so long and formal. Look around, man. This place is big enough, in a nice area. You know, celebrate your newfound freedom."

Michael shook his head. "I'm not twenty-four. I can't throw a house party and have people pumping it up." He laughed at the image of himself in baggy pants and Timberland boots. "That's not me."

"I'm thirty, Mike. You're never too old to pump it up."

Michael bit into a biscuit and savored the rich buttery flavor.

"I don't know. Who would I invite? Everybody I know is part of a couple."

Drew became animated. "Make new friends. Buy new clothes. All those suits can't be comfortable, let alone something you want to wear to a party. I'll tell you what. You buy the food and liquor, and I'll take care of inviting the people."

"Who do you know, Drew? You're never in one place for very long. When do you have time to make friends?"

Drew backed away and started putting dishes in the sink. "Never mind."

Michael felt terrible. This was the first time in years he'd spent any time with his cousin, and here he was challenging whether he had friends. Mike took a hard look at himself and realized he hadn't fostered many relationships independent of his marriage. Golf was a sport he'd learned in order to feed an intrinsic need to relate to his peers away from the courtroom. But he reserved his energy and real enthusiasm for the basketball court and his "around the way" buddies.

Whatever happened to Tommy LaPage and Floyd, uh, what was Floyd's last name? Martin? Yeah. In law school they had been his best friends. They'd gotten together for a few years after Mike's marriage, but Mike didn't fit into the single life anymore and they'd drifted apart.

In a way, he was worse off than Drew.

"The party sounds like a great idea. I'll think about it?"

Drew looked relieved. "Great."

Michael ate another couple of forkfuls then asked, "Do we have enough to share with . . . the sleeping bodyguard?"

"Coming right up."

Drew handed him a full plate, then went about fixing another poached egg for himself.

Terra stirred as Mike opened the door. He stood by the bed and just watched her sleep. How rare to watch a woman sleep and not be curled up with her. Terra made sleeping look like an art form.

"Wake up, sleepyhead."

She rolled to her back and her eyes slid open. "What are you doing in my room?"

"This is my bedroom. *Bodyguard.*"

The word made her sit straight up. Michael put a hand out to steady her. Her body was warm and her hair sleep-tossed, but she still looked beautiful.

"Is everything okay?" She sounded uncharacteristically panicked.

He nodded. "I brought you some breakfast."

"Oh, oh. Mr. Crawford. Michael," she scrambled to get out of his bed. "I didn't mean to fall asleep. Breakfast." She stood up, and he supported her weight until she got her bearings. "Thank you. I can't."

"You've slept in my hallway and now in my bed and you can't eat my food?"

"It smells delicious, but no thanks. Will you be here for a little while?"

He held up the plate as she dashed around the room gathering her shoes and book.

"To go—?"

"Anywhere. I'd like to take a shower and freshen up. Plus, I need to let the tenants know where I am, just in case there's something I need to attend to."

He'd spent a sleepless night worried about the woman who'd slept outside his door, and now that he offered her breakfast, she didn't want it?

He took hold of her elbow. "You can do all those things after you've eaten."

"No, thank you." Her quiet but firm tone cautioned him to release her arm. She blushed and his stomach did that flipping thing again. "I'll be back in an hour."

"Fine."

Michael watched her walk down the hallway, say a brief hello to Drew, then slip out the front door without so much as a backward glance.

He followed her, plate in hand. He and Drew shared quizzical stares as he closed the front door. "What are you thinking about now?"

"I'm wondering if she'll come back like she said."

Drew turned from washing dishes. "My wife never came back to me. Women aren't liars when it comes to that. They say they're leaving, and one day you look up and they're gone."

Drew finished the dishes, leaving Michael alone.

He went to his room and yelled up the hallway, "But if she's says she's coming back, you got a fifty-fifty chance."

Broken promises filtered into Michael's thoughts as he finished up his meal and began the tedious task of unpacking the master bathroom and putting the finishing touches on the stereo.

His wife had promised to love him forever. He'd vowed to do the same. *In sickness and in health.* If the inability to have children qualified as a health issue, he had her on a technicality. She'd breached a contract to love him. He could sue her.

Judge Rathborne would love to sink his shark teeth into a case featuring members of the Crawford family.

Michael pinched the bridge of his nose. He wasn't supposed to think like this. If the men in his family found out, they'd rib him until the day he died. He was a Crawford. A strong family man who was proud and honest and decent to women, children and small animals. Strengthened by the reaffirmation of his manhood, he went into the kitchen and refolded all the dish towels.

Four

Terra's feet had barely cleared the bottom stair when she heard her brother's voice. "Where have you been?"

Staring at Jack, her twin and older brother, she tried to gauge his mood. A bad seed, he'd caused her parents enormous pain, yet after so many years they still searched for his good side. Her gaze wandered to the fists that had too often touched her skin, leaving bruises and bone-deep scars.

I'm too old to get hit. If it's a fight he wants, it's a fight he'll get.

"I've been around." She made no move to open her door, but clutched the sleeping bag tighter. "How did you get in?"

"I can't visit my sister? What? You too stuck up for your own family, *Ms. Grad school?"*

Yes. *Yes!* "I've got a long day ahead, Jack. What do you want?"

He smiled, his attempt at charm pathetic and transparent. That might have worked fifteen, even ten years ago when there had been hope for a real relationship between them. Yet at almost thirty, Jack had been on the wrong side of life for a long time.

His resentment of her life and choices had been the fuel of many family fights. Generations of their family had chosen to work in the chicken factories, the only source of real income in their small hometown. Fathers and sons. Mothers and daughters. Cousins and more cousins. She'd chosen college.

The choice had been tantamount to a seventies Cuban defection. Instead of their being happy "she'd made it out," they felt anger. Anger, like wool-eating moths, destroyed the fabric of family.

Each visit home became more difficult. Jealousy and condescending reminders to "keep it real" flew about like hungry flies. And Jack was her worst critic.

He'd gone to UGA on a basketball scholarship for two years, then flunked out. She'd gone to Georgia Tech for her bachelor's and graduated summa cum laude, and was now attending Emory for her master's.

She looked at her brother and felt emotionally empty.

Jack stared, his face sunken and chalky, his lips black and cracked from drugs. His clothes could have come from a garbage dump the way they smelled and looked. His eyes were vacant of love or repentance but filled with evil determination.

There was no way into her apartment other than around him, and she had no intention of letting him inside her home.

A door closed at the end of the hallway. "Julianna, is that you? Hold on." Terra pushed past her brother's tall frame and felt him tense. He stank of fear. She quickened her steps.

"I was visiting Rusty, and he asked me to drop off your sleeping bag." She stopped at her neighbor's door and Julianna gave her a confused stare.

"Terra, are you all right?" she whispered.

"Just fine. Ready for my morning walk. You going too?" She felt her brother's presence behind her and prayed he didn't embarrass her. Or worse, hurt her or Julianna.

Julianna's pale-blue eyes landed on the stranger, and she caught onto the charade quickly. Instantly she opened her door and yelled, "Chris! Get out of the bathroom and let's get to walking. Terra's waiting." She stared at Terra, her eye cautiously flitting to Jack.

"You know how Fulton County detectives are," Julianna said. "Staying up all night solving crimes and busting criminals so they can sleep late the next day. Go figure."

Jack's hand froze near Terra's neck and her silver necklace. *Please, don't.*

The door suddenly opened. A big, blond man, muscular from his temples to his toes, stared out at them. Steel-blue eyes rested on Jack. "Jules, I'm ready. Why all the shouting?" Terra stared at a man she'd never seen before in her life. "Hi, Terra. Who's your friend?"

Tension filled the air, and she noticed—as she was sure Jack did—the gun at Chris's waist. Her voice came out a whisper. "My . . . brother."

"I'm out," Jack said and bumped into her. She in turn bumped into Julianna.

"Hey, pal? You bumped your sister. What are you going to say?"

Out of the corner of her eye, she saw Michael Crawford descend the last stair, a plate in his hand, his gaze on her brother.

Jack froze, the look in his eyes murderous. He maintained remarkable balance at the top of the stairs as he swept his raggedy coat away from his side and bowed. "Excuuu-se me, oh queen Terra-rist!"

He jumped down the remaining three stairs, burst through the door and started to run.

Tears sprang to Terra's eyes, but she refused to let them fall. "I'm sorry. My brother wasn't always like that."

"Are you all right?" Michael was beside her, his chest a protective wall from Jack's last performance.

She nodded.

"Michael Crawford. Fourth floor." He shook hands and stepped back.

"Chris Weaver, and this is Julianna Shelly."

Terra composed herself and damned the shaking in her bones.

Julianna rubbed Terra's arm. "You don't owe us an explanation. But if you don't mind my asking, how did he get in?"

"I don't know," Terra answered.

"My cousin said you only have to apply a little pressure and the door opens."

Terra nodded. "I'll have maintenance look into it." She focused on Chris. "Thank you for being . . . a cop."

He laughed. "You don't hear that often. You're welcome. Let me know if you need any further assistance. I'm here mostly on the weekends." Julianna smiled up at the big man.

"Let's go walking. Terra, Michael, you want to join us?"

She backed toward her apartment. "No, but thanks. I've got some studying to do."

Hurrying down the hall, she felt Michael behind her and was inside her apartment in a flash, hoping he wouldn't come in.

He pushed open the door, and it clicked closed behind him.

"Terra, are you all right?"

She thought of lying, but as she'd been told all her life, her eyes were her most expressive feature. They were filled with tears, and she felt ravaged. She dropped the sleeping bag and wiped her eyes.

"I'll be fine after a long hot bath. It was nice of you to bring the food." Her breath hitched on a small hiccup. She was still upset but trying hard to disguise it.

He stood without moving. "Was I just dismissed?"

"I believe you were, counselor."

"Rule number one."

She cocked her head. "Rule one?"

He placed the plate on the counter and walked toward her. "Don't call me counselor."

"Why?"

"From your lips, it sounds very sexy."

She rubbed her hands together, then folded her arms over her chest, rocking on her heels. Michael wished she'd look at him. "So noted. You're still here."

"I never could stand to see a woman cry."

She leaned away from his hand, and her heartstrings tugged when she saw what he held. A plain white handkerchief. Her grandfather used to carry one, and he would soothe away all her hurts. Unlike other family members, he never found fault in the fact that she was bright. In fact, he encouraged her to press the limits of her intelligence. On his knee she learned black history, and by his side she learned ethics and morals.

If she was different from the rest, her grandfather had been a big part in it.

She loved Henry O'Shaughssey with all her heart and when he died in '85, a part of her died too.

The deep pain Jack caused made tears slide down her cheeks, and Michael caught them on the soft cloth.

"There," he crooned. "I have brothers, too, and they can be a pain."

Michael Crawford was being too kind. Never one to indulge in self-pity, Terra realized it would be easy to lean on his strong shoulder and cry until years of pain melted away. She also recognized what a threat he presented to her vulnerability. She didn't need his sympathy. One look at the way he dressed, his expensive furnishings and his shiny black truck told her he would never fully understand her background or her dysfunctional family.

Terra squared her shoulder against what he represented. He didn't back away as she expected, but stood his ground and forced her chin up so she could look at him.

"I don't want to talk about it," she said.

"If you ever do, I'm upstairs. And don't pull another stunt like trying to sleep in my hallway. I'll take care of my own security, and we'll get the problem resolved on Monday. If I catch you up there tonight, I'll consider you a trespasser, and you don't want to know what I do to those types."

The muscles in her cheeks tugged and she smiled, the handkerchief clutched tight in her hand. "So noted."

He backed away and she breathed again, grateful for his understanding.

"Where's the nearest mall?"

The shift in topic gave her a chance to regroup. She walked

into the kitchen and pulled out a pen and paper and drew as she talked. "We're not too far from South DeKalb Mall. It's off 20. It opens in about an hour. My friend Margaret and I are heading there around two." *Why did I say that?*

"Drew and I are going. Maybe we'll see you there."

"I doubt it. We're just going to exchange some things and leave."

He nodded. "Okay."

"Well. Thank you."

"You're welcome." He made no move to leave.

"Good-bye."

After one last lingering look, he opened the door and walked out.

Terra double-checked the locking system on her door and was assured by the series of beeps it was in working condition.

She straightened the oversize loveseat cushions and stowed the sleeping bag in the back bedroom closet, then sank down and picked up Michael's handkerchief. She looked at the neatly folded cloth and took her time unfolding it until it was a nice flat square. Holding it in her palms, she pressed it to her face and inhaled deeply. Her eyes closed and an image of Michael filled her mind. Tall with sugar-brown skin and slate-gray eyes, he was handsome in a rugged way. He didn't strike her as a desk type with his skin kissed by the sun and his large work-roughened hands.

His body size seemed contrary to his occupation. She imagined him as an outdoors-type man at home on a farm or in the yard instead of a courtroom.

She refolded the small sheet as she silently chided herself for giving Michael a new life in her imagination. He was simply being kind. In his line of work, he saw his share of tragedy and sad stories. Hers with Jack was no different, therefore Michael was demonstrating a normal level of caring—nothing more.

Terra rose from the couch and started running her bath, her mind still replaying each event from the time she'd awakened to the moment she'd noticed that Julianna had locked her door. Never sticklers in the past, the tenants knew one another and trusted one another to watch out for the other. And although they practiced reasonable measures of safety, no one had ever had a break-in or anything stolen.

That's why she hadn't been worried about sleeping outside of Michael Crawford's door. But in the blink of an eye, Jack had changed the dynamics of her home.

The distance from Brunswick to Atlanta had seemed far when she was twenty, but now, nearly ten years later, it didn't seem far enough. Her family was doing it again, and she wouldn't allow it. They'd ruined her marriage, and she'd taken care not to get involved again and repeat that mistake, but now they were encroaching on her home. And where there'd been one, others were sure to follow.

She inserted a CD of soothing piano music in the player and relished the serenity of her apartment: the fresh flowers from the roof garden that filled bud vases on each flat surface, the couch covers that she'd sewn herself, the drawings she'd made of some of her travels around Atlanta. This was her sanctuary—her home—and nobody was going to invade it without her permission.

The plate of food caught her eye, and she put it in the refrigerator, then cut off the bathwater.

Thoughts of Michael Crawford's compassion worked into her, causing her to wonder about the man who'd wiped away her tears. And made her sleep in his bed without strings, without him.

Was he the last of a dying breed? Where had he come from?

She stripped and stepped into the warm bath. The bath salts relieved the tension and helped her relax. As she leaned back against the fluffy plastic bath pillow, she wished again that she had a skylight. Then that tiny, quiet corner of the world would be hers alone.

The bathroom's small window was big enough for a small

child to slide through, but nothing to worry about in terms of an entry for a criminal or Jack.

She sank deeper into the water and let her mind wander.

Her thoughts returned to what she'd seen when she opened her eyes this morning.

When was the last time a man had offered her breakfast and brought it to her? Too long to recall. When Michael stood close, she'd wanted to be in his arms. How long had it been? Years, she noted, embarrassed. At least two since a man had held her.

Mr. Sakimoto at the corner grocery store didn't count because she'd fallen off her bike.

The ledge of the porcelain garden tub was filled with lit scented candles. Deciding against the stimulating pulse of the Jacuzzi jets, she moved her finger along the tub edge and came upon her novel she'd brought into the bathroom earlier. A smile tickled her lips and she picked up the book.

When she'd left off, Michael had been about to kiss Sylvia. Drying her finger on her favorite pink fluffy towel, Terra opened the book and picked up where she'd left off.

The fictional Michael seemed to have it going on as he kissed the heroine for the first time. He didn't swallow her face, like the last man Terra dated, but he kissed her slow and steady, his tongue playing a game of seek and find with hers.

Looking at the cover, she decided that the couple seemed like an odd match.

The water mellowed her anxious mood, and she slipped lower. Eyes closed, she visualized herself as the heroine of the story and Michael Crawford as the hero.

His lips were strong but gentle, moving against hers at a summer-slow pace. They grazed her cheek, down her neck, then up again, where his teeth caught her chin.

Warm water became his lips and touched the cleft between her breasts, then the tops of her shoulders, while her feet danced—with the control panel. Cold water splashed down her leg, and she jumped, dropping the book to the floor. "I'm crazy."

She hopped out the tub, drained the water, cleaned up and got dressed. Daydreaming about the new tenant wasn't healthy. He needed to view her as a professional. Even if the whole building was falling down around her ears, he didn't need to see the runs in her knee highs.

She'd solve his problem and leave him to his life.

Michael walked into South DeKalb Mall and felt like a virtual stranger. He hadn't been to the mall in years. How had he let Drew—homeless, directionless Drew—talk him into going to the mall to shop for a new wardrobe?

"Drew," he said, coming to stand beside his cousin who gazed at nugget rings in the jewelry store window, "this isn't for me."

"Take it easy. It's only shopping. Not a Supreme Court case."

Unaware, Drew attracted the stares of many of the female shoppers of all ages. Michael looked around.

There were lots of women in the mall. In the stores. In the halls. On the phone. At the food court. Everywhere. Women.

He executed a three-hundred-sixty-degree turn.

He and Drew seemed to be the only men.

"What kind of place is this?" he asked beneath his breath.

As tall as Michael with slightly less muscular build, Drew grinned and adopted a slight but noticeable dip to his step. "A babe factory. Come on."

Watching his cousin dip and slide instead of just walk was enough for Michael to know there were downfalls to being single.

Drew had chosen to dress in his b-bop attire. He wore a white T-shirt covered by a plaid shirt that hung open, baggy jeans and thick-toed boots. He'd started doing something to his normally midlevel Afro so that it looked like individual twists jutting from his skull.

In JCPenney's window, Michael checked his low haircut. It was fashionable. Clean-cut. Professional. Just the way he liked it.

Drew's face appeared next to his in the reflection. "You should grow it out some. I like the beard. Let it grow in, man. Try some different hairstyles. Women like that."

Michael regarded the statement with interest. "They do?"

"Yeah, man. You been hooked up too long. Stick with me and I'll bring you into the twenty-first century."

The collar of Michael's light-blue, short-sleeve polo shirt suddenly looked outdated. Maybe he did need a change. He wasn't the man he used to be. And the life he once knew no longer existed. Why not go along for the ride? He clapped his hands together. "Where do we start?"

Drew grinned, pointed down the mall and they started walking. "I know the perfect place. There's a boutique down here that sells slammin' pants. You need some leather."

"As in sofa?"

His cousin threw back his head and laughed. "A little different than that, but you got the idea."

Women streamed by them in all states of fashion, and Michael took notice. The summer heat had driven everyone to sandals, and toes stuck out everywhere.

Am I a feet man? he wondered, as he stepped into a tiny store behind Drew, and noticed the woman in the store. About five-five, her multicolored toenails led to long shapely legs that stretched over nicely rounded hips to a bare torso. Michael openly stared.

The woman had two rings in her navel. His gaze ricocheted to hers. In her midtwenties, she brushed aside hair so long he doubted its authenticity, and eyed him with equal interest. Long nails curled from her fingertips, and her pointer finger landed between pretty white teeth.

"Hello," he said.

Her eyes traveled over his hair, shirt and belted navy blue trousers.

"Hey, pops." She brushed past him. His chest tingled where her breasts slid. "Hope you enjoyed it." She swayed out of the store.

"Told you." Drew fairly giggled, then engaged in a discussion of fashion with the clerk, whose eyebrows were pierced.

Michael rubbed his chest. What had just happened? Were these people from the same planet as he?

Watching from the safety of the store, he counted the bare midriffs that flowed by the open door. Stopping at thirty, Michael wiped his mouth to cover his shock. When he was young, you didn't see a midriff until you married it.

"We've got a few pieces for you to try on," the clerk said. "But we have to wait on a dressing room."

Michael tapped his cousin on the shoulder. "Women have belly buttons." He knew he sounded like a total idiot.

Drew grinned, laughing and stomping his foot. "I know, man. It's, like, I didn't know until I got divorced. You've missed a lot." His cousin draped his arm over his shoulder, and they stared into the mall together. "You can have any one of those."

Two beautiful women had stopped at Victoria's Secret across the mall. They held up bras to their chests, chatting and laughing.

Michael wouldn't have thought he would add *voyeur* next to *divorced* on his personal résumé, but his body warmed watching the two attractive sistas decide on panty-and-bra sets.

He'd shopped for gifts for April, but she made a list, he ordered the items, had them wrapped and presented them to her. That was their agreement and it worked for him.

Nothing he'd ever bought looked as sexy as the lingerie the women were holding.

"I like the big one. The one with the backside out to there," Drew said, pointing to the shorter of the two. Dark with a cherub face and a pretty smile, she was the more animated one, holding up leopard-print panties and talking a mile a minute. Like April, Michael thought, then shook himself. Today is a day of change. No thoughts of the past allowed.

"She's cute," Michael agreed, trying to make the mental adjustment to his newfound freedom. "But, uh." He felt heat rising and forced the guilty I-shouldn't be-doing-this feeling away and caught himself smiling. "I think the one with the red hair is attractive. You know, she looks intelligent, probably a career woman. You think she's single?"

"Can't hurt to ask."

Just then the women spotted them and turned interested eyes their way. Drew waved them over.

The short woman cocked her head to the side and pointed to herself. Drew nodded. The tall redhead gazed at Michael with bedroom eyes and pointed to herself. She smiled and Drew started mumbling. "This is our lucky day. Come on."

They started forward, then froze. The redhead gathered the blouse of the short woman in her hands, tipped her head and French-kissed her long and slow. Tongue was everywhere!

Michael felt his mind and body rejecting everything he was seeing. His jaw unhinged and his mouth hung open. His body spasmed, and he jumped back, holding on to a rack for support.

"Oh, my Lawd. Do you see that? I can't watch," Drew said loudly, his hand covering his eyes as he stared between his fingers. "Just a waste of good woman. A doggone waste."

The women turned back to them, smiled and left the store.

"They're everywhere," the clerk said in a breezy tone in Michael's ear. Startled, he turned. The man's eyes were darkened with some type of makeup and a skintight Spandex shirt molded his chest. His blond hair was spiked toward his forehead and his belly button was showing too. A tag with the name Barry hooked onto his hip-huggers.

Michael tried not to flinch and wasn't successful. "They are?"

Barry pursed his lips. "Everywhere. Women *and men,* honey." He sounded delighted. "Your dressing room is ready. Come with me." Drew had taken up a women-watching post by the front door, giving Michael little choice but to follow Barry. Once behind the closed dressing room door, Michael wedged his foot against it and stayed there for a long time.

Four hours later, exhausted and irritable, Michael headed for the food court, his wallet lighter than it had been in a while. Shopping bags from stores he'd never heard of weighed him down. He stood in line for a soda while Drew commandeered them seats. Michael dropped into the chair and downed his cola in several swallows, wishing for something stronger.

Men with men, women with women, men with women, women with strollers and teens filled the corridors. Music flowed from the stores, mingling in the heart of the mall, lulling the hum of constant chatter. Michael took it all in.

"I've never seen so many people doing nothing in all my life." His new jeans scratched his legs, and he pushed at the seam. Drew had insisted he wear his new clothes, and he'd agreed. He had to admit, the cotton T-shirt beneath a short-sleeve open shirt felt more comfortable than what he'd put on that morning, but the boots were killing his toes.

Why did I buy them? The pretty salesclerk assured him once they were broken in, they'd feel great.

"My feet are killing me," he said to Drew who seemed to be in his glory, doing nothing.

"You'll get used to them. Wasn't Becky good-looking?"

"Who's Becky?"

"You know, the salesgirl at the Wild Pair."

Michael nodded. "Oh, the *very* young-looking one. The one with the degree from Tech. It seems like all I've done is see pretty faces. You can't trust that."

Drew dismissed his warning. "Those lesbians were a fluke. The ratio of straight women to men in Atlanta is ten to one. That's a lot of sex. Hey, isn't that your landlady?"

Through the throng of people, Michael picked Terra out of the crowd. She strode toward him with an easy swing to her hips and a light step. Neat blue jeans hugged her legs, and a pink button-down accentuated the color on her lips.

Her hair was pulled away from her face, drawing all the attention to her full mouth and smiling eyes. She touched her friend's arm as they joked. Terra looked young and happy.

A wave of loneliness hit him hard like a fist. Lately he didn't know what happiness was. His emotions were so skewed, so entangled in a ten-year marriage that ended years before the papers arrived, he couldn't intelligently discuss the meaning of the word.

He'd always heard that to be happy, you had to associate with happy people, but that had never applied to him before. Happiness wasn't something he sought, it just was.

But, he wondered, how could he find happiness, when he couldn't identify the road that had ruined what he thought had been a happy, loving relationship?

Deep in thought, he didn't notice Drew stand up and step in front of Terra's friend until he heard her saying, "Excuse me. I hope I wasn't in your way."

"You're not. I'm Drew."

Michael surged to his feet. "Terra, hi."

She and her friend stopped abruptly, and Terra's eyes raked his form. "Michael. Is that you?"

He tugged on his shirttail, self-conscious. "Of course it's me."

Terra's friend giggled. "You look different. Are you two brothers?"

"Cousins," Drew said, his gaze transfixed. "Can I buy you something to drink? Eat? You hungry?"

Margaret's mouth turned up in a sweet smile. "I'd like a drink." Together they walked toward the Chinese restaurant. Drew took Margaret's bag and the two held hands.

Staring after his cousin, Michael shook his head. "I think he's in love."

Terra's expression reflected the shock he felt. "She was just telling me about the date from you-know-where and now she's holding hands? What's in the air down here?"

They sidestepped a runaway stroller being pushed by a toddler and faced each other across the table. "Are you hungry?" he asked, then started to laugh at Terra's wary expression. "Nothing's in the air, I promise. Nobody's in love but Drew."

She shifted her purchase from one hand to the other and regarded him closely. "Built up an immunity?" The noise in the food court rose to a deafening level, and he considered her question. "You don't have to answer."

"Not immune," he finally said. "Just had a good inoculation."

She nodded, looking around. Their eyes met. "Divorce'll do it every time. I think I will have that drink. You hold the table. Coke?"

Michael nodded and reached into his pocket. "I've got it," she said.

"I couldn't let you pay. I offered you a drink," he said.

"For breakfast."

He nodded and within a few minutes she returned with icy sodas. They sat across from each other.

"How did you know I was divorced? Is there a neon sign on my forehead?"

She sipped her drink, thankful for the distraction. "Let's just say I've been down that road before."

"You're a divorcée?"

"It was a long time ago." At his shocked expression, she laughed. "You don't have to look so confused. Trust me, it's not a neon sign or anything. I just recognized the signs."

"Now I've got signs." He thought that was funny. "Sounds like a fatal disease."

Terra closed her eyes and purposely redirected her gaze, lest she be accused of staring. "Successful man from Atlanta. Family nearby. You're either two things: Divorced or you know."

He caught the implication quickly. "I'm not gay."

The couple at the table next to them looked over.

Michael's laughter tickled her skin like a feather. She wanted to go outside and share a breeze with him. "I didn't think so." She swallowed the rest of her soda and wiped her mouth. "About earlier today, I feel I owe you an explanation."

"I'm listening."

She stopped. "I . . . uh. Well, Jack is my brother and he's had problems in the past and he doesn't usually come by. So don't worry about your stuff." Terra looked for Margaret. She was talking way too much. "Who's watching your apartment now?"

"My nephews. Nobody'll want to mess with Tony and Majic. They're my brother's sons and they play for University of Miami's football team."

"Good. Your locks will be fixed before you get home Monday."

"Fine."

"I'd better go get Margaret. Good seeing you."

He drank the rest of his soda. "I'd better get going too. Hey, stop up next Saturday if you have time. I'm having a few friends over."

"Okay. You'll just have to notify the other tenants if you're having a gathering of more than twenty people in your apartment."

On the edge of the crowd by the pay phones, Margaret and Drew were pressed together like long-lost lovers.

Enough was enough. Michael stalked over, his toes crunching in his new boots. "Come on, man. Let's go."

"What's the rush?" Drew still didn't look at him.

"Dinner at my parents." Michael shoved some bags into Drew's hands and elbowed him in the chest.

His cousin finally looked up, but Michael ignored his annoyed expression. "Now, Drew."

He turned to Terra and a lovestruck Margaret. "Good-bye, ladies."

Five

The sun had risen early Monday morning, casting tremendous rays of sunshine across Atlanta. Helmeted bike riders rode past the apartment building on Kay Street, getting in their daily exercise and making Terra wish she could join them. Her bike remained hooked to the roof of her porch, a cast-off of her busy life, but she didn't have regrets. Instead, she planned.

One day, she'd pedal happily through the subdivision of Vanderbilt Chase Manor Estates and know she'd chased a dream and won.

Late that afternoon, the locksmith stood in the hall beside her and demonstrated the effectiveness of the electronic lock he'd just installed. The device now locked the front door to Michael Crawford's apartment, but wouldn't unlock it.

"This happens with electronic products from time to time," he said with a voice full of Southern authority. "We just don't know why they don't want to work. Everything's got a temper."

From the corner of her eye, Terra regarded the so-called expert. Hating to resort to stereotypes, she strove to find kind words for the man who was wasting her precious time. In a way, his personality reminded her of the lead character in the movie *The Waterboy*.

Mr. Achman *was* short and overweight. He wore a white T-shirt and blue jeans, which were a size too small with a red bandanna hanging from his pocket. He *was* two hours late, and he *was* charging the corporation one hundred dollars an hour to be perplexed.

He knelt on one knee and eyeballed the lock. Terra hurriedly diverted her gaze from the fleshy crack at the top of his pants. "That didn't work for me either," she informed him, suddenly getting a clear picture on the depths of Michael Crawford's frustration.

"Nice, nasty. Uh-huh," he said to the door. He pressed buttons on a handheld computer, evoking a series of beeps.

"She's one of those nice-nasty types who says things one way, but really means to be sarcastic. I went to college too. All my professors were sarcastic. That's why I quit."

Stunned at his intuitiveness, she rushed to apologize. "I'm sorry. I shouldn't take my frustration out on you. It's just that you've been here for two hours and I promised the tenant the door would be fixed by the time he gets home." She glanced at her watch. "Which will be in about forty-five minutes. Surely, Mr. Achman, you can understand my dilemma."

He looked at her over his shoulder. "You are a nice woman with a nice voice, so I forgive you. You need this working in forty-five minutes and then you want me to disappear."

Terra clapped her hands together. "That's right. Can you do it?"

He raised his handheld computer. "Achman can do anything. *If* you stop hovering over my shoulder. Go on and find something else to do and come back in exactly ten minutes."

"Done. I'll be back. Thank you."

"You are very welcome."

Taking the elevator, Terra let herself into her apartment, glad for the respite. This situation had to be resolved today. Just having slept on the floor for one night was more than any reasonable person could stand. Plus, the jeans she'd worn that night had been a tight pair that she'd since forced to the back of her closet with the rest of her too-small clothes. They'd fit but barely. Her thighs hurt as she flopped onto the couch.

Weary nerves stabbed at her muscles, and she closed her

eyes and laid her head back, imagining the class discussion at Emory later that evening.

What is conflict and how do you resolve it?

Her brain searched for a minute and formulated a simple answer. Conflict is seeing a man's pain and not being able to do anything about it.

Unsure whether personal conflict applied to the class discussion, Terra indulged the private thoughts.

By nature, women were nurturers. Taught from the crib to care, women had an ingrained sense of how to ease pain.

Terra mulled the argument a moment, then another thought developed. If she only wanted to nurture Michael, then why was she dreaming of his kisses while his hands stroked her body?

That wasn't nurturing; that was sex. And although sex felt good and awarded a temporary departure from reality, the truth was it didn't last. The pain would return for him, and she would inevitably get her feelings hurt.

Slowly Terra stood and smoothed the wrinkles from her above-the-knee floral skirt. The life she'd built in this apartment, in this city, was her comfort, her solitude and her peace.

Absently, she pruned dead leaves from flowers around the room and dropped them into the garbage receptacle, likening the task to how she'd scrupulously managed her life for the past eight years.

In a fantasy, she could do what she wanted with Michael Crawford. Kiss him, hug him, hold him, make love to him, whatever.

Fantasies were harmless, private dreams that were locked in her mind. But anything beyond that was off-limits. *He* was off-limits.

She picked up her textbook, purse and keys and took the elevator up four floors to his apartment.

* * *

The door finally locked.

Michael pressed the keyless remote and heard the locks engage. A woman of her word. Rare, indeed.

"Are you satisfied?" Terra asked, as she looked from him to the door.

"Very." Michael triggered the remote to unlock the door. "Thank you."

She smiled and reached for the knob. "All's well that ends well. Good-bye."

"Why the rush?" he asked, before he could catch himself. Why not ask her to stay for dinner? He was eating alone while Drew scoured the mall for his lady-love. But what if she already had a boyfriend? Maybe they had plans. Doubt began to eat at his confidence. Of course she had plans. A single, beautiful woman. She had plans!

"As a matter of fact, I have plans." His ego deflated like a day-old balloon. "But I'm sure I'll see you around."

Before he could form another coherent thought, she was gone, the door closing behind her.

In a courtroom, he could raise an objection before the prosecutor could finish a sentence, but he couldn't convince Terra to sit and share a meal with him.

Michael looked at the cold duck Drew had prepared with a medley of vegetables and wild rice. A feast fit for a king. Only he had no court.

The keyless remote slid easily on his key ring and he tossed the keys on the bar and entered the kitchen.

Piling his plate high, he wondered about Drew. Two days had passed since Drew met Terra's friend in the mall and now he was acting strange. He couldn't find her phone number, and apparently it wasn't listed. Drew's moping wasn't helping Michael's somber mood.

Sounds of families arriving home from the park filtered up from the front balcony. Minivan doors slammed, and laughter ensued as people filed inside their building across the street.

Another mother must have arrived because he could hear the two talking.

"*Ann, wait up for a sec. Are the kids trying out for basketball in a couple of weeks?*"

"*I don't know. We have sign-up the first weekend after school starts. We were hoping with school starting in two weeks to sneak in a weekend getaway to the ocean.*"

"*Destin?*"

"*Definitely.*"

"*We had fun there,*" the woman said excitedly. "*The boys will love the beach. Honey, before you know it, Christmas will be here.*"

The voices faded and Michael could feel isolation building in him again and opted for some music. Depositing his steaming plate on the table in the living room, he searched the alphabetized CDs, selected one and popped it in.

Reclining in the corner of the sofa, he started his meal.

The salty tones of Etta James sounded good. He'd been away for too long. One song made him smile. April had dressed up like Etta for a Halloween party once.

The food turned to dust on his tongue. Jerking to his feet he tipped his glass of wine, spilling droplets on the hardwood floor. He tossed his napkin on the liquid and hit the eject button on the CD player.

Once again at the CD case, he sorted through the discs. James Brown was out. He and April used to mimic the man after a rousing round of bedtime foreplay. B.B. King, Gerald Levert, Gladys Knight, Kenny G, George Howard, Najee, Whitney Houston, Mariah Carey. All out.

Anger surged through him like an electric current. Too much reminded him of his past. Music, food, restaurants, events. How was he supposed to build a new life if he couldn't shed the old one?

He had to do new things. Make new memories. Grabbing the tall kitchen garbage can, he threw away each CD that reminded him of any time or place with his ex. Few remained, but Michael didn't care as he returned to his cold dinner. The room silent again, he gave the idea of a party serious consideration.

What was the harm? Meet new people; make new friends. Why not? The downstairs buzzer sounded, and he went to the intercom and buzzed. "Who's there?"

"Drew, open up."

Minutes later, Drew walked in looking forlorn and lost.

"What's your problem?"

"I thought I had this job, and they gave it to someone else." He stretched out on the other full-length couch and folded his hands on his chest. He looked miserable.

"You can take the misery crap and get it out of here."

"What's with you?"

"Nothing." He had no desire to rehash his afternoon. "What kind of job was it? I might know somebody who can help you."

"Don't sweat it," Drew said, evading again. "Why is the garbage can filled with CDs?"

Michael gestured with his fork. "Housecleaning. Cleared out some old stuff."

Drew looked balefully at the full can. "That the trash?"

Michael chewed a piece of duck. "Yeah. That's got to go out to the Dumpster tonight."

"Mind if I—"

"You play one of those CDs, you find another place to live."

A knowing expression filled Drew's eyes. "I'll take it on my way out. Give any more consideration to the—"

Michael cut him off. "I think we should have a party. Don't you?"

Drew propped on his elbows. His gaze seemed to measure the floor for dance space. "I'm down with that. I've got the guest list if you've got the rest of the details covered. Food, music and liquor."

Michael weighed his options. His sanity versus depression? "I'll take care of it." He'd extended an invitation to Terra; maybe she'd come. A tingle of excitement budded.

Six

Music by Master P shook Terra awake along with a mixture of laughter and talking. What in the world was going on? What day was it? What time?

For a minute it sounded like a block party, but then she realized the music was coming from above her head and it was 2:30 in the morning. Somebody in the building was having an unauthorized party!

Dazed, she let her feet touch the cold floor and absorbed her first dose of attitude. Who was getting her out of bed in the wee hours of a Saturday morning because they didn't want to follow the rules?

Margaret! If Margaret was having another of her industry shindigs, Terra swore, she'd write her up this time. Really!

She was gathering the gray, silk robe around her shoulders and her flashlight, when she heard her front door locks disengaged. Her heart skipped a beat.

"Terra? Terra?" Margaret called, inching inside the dimly lit living room.

"Right here." Terra hurried up the hall. "Is this you?"

"I'm not this crazy," she said indignantly. "That man upstairs is out of his mind. He's been jamming like that for more than an hour."

"How come I didn't hear him?" Terra gathered her clipboard of rules and shoved the flashlight in her pocket.

"You sleep like the dead, that's why. What are you going to do?"

Confrontation had never been her strong suit. But this is good, she thought in the less scared portion of her brain. I can practice how to resolve conflict. Terra gave what she hoped was a tough look. "I'm going . . . to . . . tell . . . him . . . to cut it out."

"That's the language that stops wars." Margaret tended to be sarcastic when sleepy. She needed about ten hours of rest right now. Determination flashed in Margaret's eyes. "You tell him to quit or get!"

Terra confirmed with a shake of her head. "That sounds good. Quit or get." She leaned close to the door. "I know you went up there. What's going on?"

"The hall is filled with people. I didn't see him or anybody else I recognized." Margaret's voice dripped with disappointment.

"Has Drew called?"

Her face fell, but she fronted well. "Course not. He's just like any other man. You show you like them too much, and they run."

"You couldn't have liked him too much, you only just met him," Terra reminded her gently. "Love doesn't come easily," she advised her friend. "I know."

Margaret's gaze softened. She looked almost angelic. "I know. But we connected. Right away."

Terra drew back, feeling sorry for her. Talking about Drew would only prolong the time it took Margaret to get over him. She changed the subject. "Did you see anybody on the stairs?"

"I didn't pass anybody. But do you hear that?"

They quieted and Terra crept close to the door and placed her eye near the peephole. Tall, vixenish-looking street women strolled down the hall smoking and laughing. It was 2:43 in the morning, and it didn't appear that there was an end in sight. The large belly ring on one of the women caught the light and glittered. Looked like a side of beef wearing an earring. Yuck.

"Whatcha gonna do?" Margaret asked.

"I'm going up there."

Margaret kicked off her sneakers. "Here, take these. You never know when you might have to Reebok somebody."

Terra smiled for the first time. Violence was totally unnecessary. "I'll be fine. Are you going to be here when I get back?"

"No, I've got an early call. You can give me the gory details later."

"I'll do that."

The phone started to ring and she picked it up. "Hello, yes, ReAnn. I'm taking care of it now." She gave Margaret her most determined look. "Really, I am."

Margaret stopped at the second floor and, after giving Terra a hug for courage, pushed her toward the third floor.

Terra continued up the stairs. Sure enough, music pumped from the stereo and debris—beer bottles, pizza boxes and snack bags—littered the floor.

The inside of the apartment didn't resemble the place she'd visited days ago. The white lights had been changed to green and silhouettes of bodies hovered in corners and in the middle of the floor.

Few people danced, but the ones that did resembled wild, drunken ballerinas. Terra passed between two sweaty men and cringed when they tried to freak her. "No, thank you. No, thank you. Stop!"

"I didn't know this was a pajama party," the man with the loosest Jheri curl said. "Let's get comfortable."

"Don't."

"All right, but, baby, you missing something that's outta this world. Don't knock it before you try it."

She gave him the five-fingered stop and continued to make her way toward the spot where the sofa had been. Shoved against the wall and covered with people, she turned her flashlight on them and searched for a familiar face, knowing she never wanted to meet any of these hooligans in an alley. Pretending not to see their scowls, she headed toward the office and was relieved to find it locked. She moved on down the long hallway.

Parliament's "Flash Light" spiked the air and was greeted with cheers of enthusiasm.

Terra envisioned the cops or Julianna's Chris citing her for violating the noise ordinance. She wasn't taking that heat.

Driven against the guest-bedroom door by two couples exiting the bathroom, Terra could feel her anger deepen at the smoky-sweet smell that followed them. She wasn't looking for Drew or Michael anymore. *Only Michael.*

Pushing against the master-bedroom door, she squeezed in and stopped. A lady and a man rifled through the dresser drawers, pulling out clothes, then dropping them on the floor.

"Stop that right now!"

The man pulled a cigarette from his mouth and coughed in her face. "He lost the bet. I won the shirt."

"Who lost?"

His fingers gripped the cigarette loosely, sending ashes to the floor when he gestured. "He did."

A swell of people surrounded each other so tightly, she couldn't make out the inner core. But she didn't have a hard time guessing whom the *he* was. She flipped on the bathroom light and closed her eyes to the mess. Her concern was her tenant and the building and not exactly in that order.

Pushing through the crowd, she could smell the sharp scent of liquor. "One, two, three, drink." A slender man with glassy eyes wearing a red, polyester suit rallied the ten or so participants, and they threw back their heads, shot glasses to their lips.

A bottle of Cuervo Gold Tequila landed near Terra's foot, and she picked it up. Michael Crawford was in big, big trouble.

She elbowed her way to the center, and a collective groan sprang from them.

"He's gone. Roasted and stuffed. Can't hang with the big dog," the glassy eyed man said. "Who's next? You, baby? You want to take me on?"

"Absolutely not. This . . . this is an illegal party that must cease and desist. Immediately!"

A Frankie Beverly and Maze slow jam brought bodies together.

The couple that had been rifling through the drawers was now locked in a swaying embrace.

A hot hand cupped her ankle, and Terra jumped, wondering who was on the floor. A freak, no doubt.

She glanced down and her gaze landed on a passed-out Michael Crawford. Anger and disappointment worked through her.

He was the loser. In more ways than one.

"Get him up now."

Two men helped him to the couch.

She walked into the living room and ignoring every deceitful, sordid act, focused on the one she was about to perform.

At the window, she gathered her courage, turned and yelled, "Police! Get out! Police! Run!"

Within minutes the room had cleared like morning dew in bright sunlight. She disabled the stereo, CD and DVD player, confiscating cords and slipping them into her robe pocket.

Without the revelers, sound reverberated against the walls.

Margaret's sneakers protected her feet from food, spots of spilled liquor and one leaking cooler of wine. The stove and kitchen were covered with bottles of beer, platters of meats and cheeses, and bags of food.

The place was a royal mess.

Careful to avoid slipping, Terra locked the balcony door, and searched the junk on the counter for the house keys. She pocketed those, too. If he woke up, he wouldn't be able to get far on foot.

Turning toward the front door, a deep snore rattled the silence, stopping her in her tracks.

Terra wanted to leave. Leave the mess and the man behind, but she also wanted one last look at him. In her fantasy, Michael had been perfect. Not drunk. Tim, her ex-husband, had accused her of not facing life's truths. She walked toward the back to do just that.

In the master suite, on an expensive gray leather sofa, Michael Crawford lay sprawled in black leather pants and a gray, open-to-the-chest shirt. Who was he kidding in that getup?

A patch of curls peeked from his collar making her pause and really look at him. The truth was he *was* attractive. And he slept as deeply as she imagined he would.

His long arms were muscular with defined biceps and triceps. Arms a woman wouldn't mind being held in, protected by. His chest bulged beneath the ridiculous shirt, but a part of her wanted to strip the flimsy material and lay her head directly above his heart.

He slept with his back against the sofa's cushion, one booted foot on the floor, the other hanging over the armrest, his face away from her. He would be out for the rest of the night, if not longer, so she shed her guilt over staring and continued.

Her gaze carefully, slowly, slid down his torso and over the impressive bulge in the front of his pants. She fanned herself with the clipboard and looked at his face as if to ask, "Do you really have as much as you're advertising, or are you faking?"

He moved, startling her, and she stiffened, worried how she'd explain her presence in his bedroom. Then he sat up, his eyes wide and on her.

"Terra," he said, lucid enough to be surprised, "I'm glad you could make it."

What? "Your party is—"

"Da bomb, right?" He stood on unsteady legs and wavered as he moved toward her.

For every one of his steps forward, she took two back. "You're in trouble. There's damage to property, and I believe some of your guests were engaged in illegal activities."

"I'm sorry. I didn't want it to happen this way." He walked like he were balancing on stilts. His eyes rolled he sat on the corner of the bed and patted the side. "Sit," he said softly. "I can't see you over there. Promise," he threw up his hands. "Won't touch."

She inched over and sat a good two feet away.

"First rule for a law student," he said. "The eyewitness is rarely accurate. Physical evidence is the most reliable evidence." His words slurred, but a shot of admiration worked into her anger, confusing her. He was quoting law while being drunk. Michael Crawford was a tragedy and a comedy all at once.

"I don't care what I didn't see, I know what illegal drugs look and smell like. So my word is as good as yours, and I'm not drunk. Why'd you do this?"

He looked at her, his eyes red and tired. "Liberation."

Silence absorbed their breathing and pushed back at them. "What are you trying to free yourself from?"

"Self-pity. I needed this one night for me." The air conditioner hummed and flapped the blinds in the window. "Terra?"

"Yes, Michael?"

"When I get my life together, will you go out to dinner with me?"

"I don't think so."

"Yes or no. Can't think about it."

His eyes were half open, and she was sure he'd never remember this conversation. He looked so vulnerable, it tore at her resolve.

"If you got your life together, yes."

"Good. Will you call me Mike?"

She grinned. "Yes."

He lay down and rested his head on the pillow, his eyes closed. "Stay." Her heart skipped a beat. "For a minute."

The odd request from this extremely large, virtual stranger stunned her. Before she could make up her mind, he inhaled one long deep curl of air.

He's harmless, she realized. What would it hurt to stay for one little minute? "Yes. For just a minute," she whispered.

Sitting beside him, she watched him sleep, at first ticking off the seconds with quick hushed breaths, then slowing as the numbers climbed toward the imposed deadline. Her whispers faded in the forties, and she stopped counting somewhere around fifty-two.

He slept like he lived—all over the place. One arm was flung wide, the other resting across his stomach with his head thrust to the side. He seemed to be going in two different directions at once. And he was. This man was so different from the man who came to see the apartment a few months ago.

Which was the real one?

She wouldn't ever find out, she told herself and made a conscious decision to stand, put one foot in front of the other and walk to the hallway linen closet. There she pulled down an extra blanket and when she stood over him, covered his body in one swoop.

She thought of leaving the blue fringes on his face, but her hand moved before her brain sent the signal to stop and she peeled it away.

That's when he touched her. His hand clasped hers against his chest and held it there. The movement choked her up.

At this moment his pain was her pain, his heartbreak hers. She didn't want it. Couldn't deal with it. The price was too high.

Terra realized she was on the stretch of road between wonder and love and mentally slapped herself.

She was caught. Like a thief in the night. Like a woman to a vulnerable man. Caught. Like she was when she betrayed her husband for her family. Caught, she reminded herself, like she never wanted to be again.

She yanked her hand away and watched as he settled back into his snoring groove. His bare ring finger leaned helplessly over his chest.

This man was not going to take her *there*. He was just a

drunken tenant who'd suffered a beat down by Cuervo Gold Tequila.

Reminded of the task at hand, Terra clutched the list of rules and wondered where to post them to get his immediate attention.

A naughty thought came to mind and as she peeled the paper from the adhesive back, she hoped every second it took him to remove the sticker would be a worthy repayment for disturbing the tenants and her. For the briefest second she touched his chest and a magical energy passed between them.

Then she picked her way through his apartment and locked his door. Removing the rock from the downstairs doorjamb, she secured the building and took a minute to listen for noise. There was none. The way it should be.

Terra let herself into her apartment and went to bed.

Seven

Cotton filled his mouth, rock music thundered in his head and somebody had set fire to his muscles, Michael thought before he opened his eyes. A strange feeling invaded him as he lay on his bed. *Who's bothering me?*

A long groan seeped from his throat. He cracked open one eye then the other and winced. Gray eyes stared holes into him. Ugh. His brothers. He slowly closed his eyes.

His body ached, and his neck felt as if it had been put through his grandmother's ancient washing machine. But as he lay flat on his back, he wondered how he had gotten into his bedroom and into his bed.

He remembered drinking shots of liquor with a group of friends Drew had invited to the party. The game had started like truth or dare and ended up—he guessed from the way his body felt—with him as the loser. Vague images formed of him and the group moving the game from the living room, so people could dance, to his bedroom. Hot liquor flooding his throat. The room spinning. The mindless, endless darkness.

Florida A&M's marching band was rehearsing in his head, and this was fun? Michael swore right then he'd never have fun again.

He chanced moving his legs, only to be betrayed as they sent a fiery pinball shooting to all the pain centers in his body.

"Hurts bad, doesn't it?" He heard Nick, the Marine Corps colonel and the corporal punisher of his family, say.

"I hope you and Jade have ten daughters."

"Yes, sir," Nick growled. "That'll fix me. How about another shot of Tequila?"

Michael's stomach heaved in defeat.

His mouth remained glued shut from the liquor and bacteria that no doubt had started a party behind his cemented lips. An act of Congress forced his lips open again.

"Shower."

"Whose turn is it?" Julian asked. "I took care of Eric."

"Michael took care of him. I took care of you when Keisha thought—never mind what she thought. Michael also took care of Nick when he came back half in the bag from the plane crash," Edwin informed his brother.

Michael wished Nick would just pull out his semiautomatic and end his suffering. The more his brothers talked, the more he realized death would be a welcome interlude to their bantering.

He fell into a semisleep state as grumbles passed between the men until Eric and Justin lost.

"The rest of us men are on KP," Nick commanded. "This place needs to be cleaned by 0600."

"If he wasn't wearing that gun, I'd hurt him." Justin, ambassador to Equador, said to Eric over Michael's head. "He's still younger than I am. *I tell him* what to do."

"Go ahead." Eric chuckled. "You'd be lucky to get a punch off with that fat belly of yours."

"I still look good. That's what counts."

Michael felt his arms being hoisted, and his head swam as if it were a buoy in a turbulent sea. If he ever recovered, he'd never, ever, ever, ever drink again.

"You're getting fat, too." Eric yelled into Michael's ear, groaning under the strain of lifting his dead weight. In truth, Michael prided himself on maintaining a low body-fat percentage, but at the moment, his limbs did feel like tree trunks.

They half walked, half dragged him into the bathroom. Eric raised Michael's tired eyelid.

"You'd better get yourself out of those pants 'cause if you can't, I got a pair of scissors I use on umbilical cords. They'd be perfect for that cow you're wearing."

Through the haze, the threat registered and he knew he'd paid at least four hundred dollars for the pants. He unzipped and stripped in good time, for a drunken man.

"You know how to work this shower?" Justin shouted to Eric. He raised his glasses to his forehead and stared at the electronic keypad on the wall.

Eric walked into the room-size shower, pinning Michael to the wall with his hand.

"He had to move somewhere where they don't even have a nozzle. I think this is it."

Michael yelped as hot water stabbed him in his head. He reset the water temperature and shoved his brothers out. His colorful expletives earned him laughs that ricocheted against the shower walls.

"Shut up and your head will stop hurting," Justin advised.

Michael threw back a driving insult.

Justin looked around the shower wall. "You're going to screw me with that?"

Eric elbowed Justin out of the way and received a faceful of wet washcloth for his efforts.

He threw the cloth back at Michael. "Shut up or I'll have Nick come and shoot the both of you."

Michael's head hurt too much to complain, but he stored in a soggy memory bank that he owed Justin and Eric a punch in the mouth.

The water felt good as it poured over his head and drove the fuzz away. He stood there for what felt like an eternity until Justin began barking orders. "Wash yourself, you stinkin' bum, before we take this toilet brush to you."

Michael cracked a bleary eye at him. "Kill you in your sleep."

A clean washcloth slapped him in the chest, and he caught it before it hit the floor.

"His reflexes are returning," Eric yelled, causing Michael to hold his head to keep the pieces together.

"Shut off the light," he demanded as he made an attempt to wipe at his chest and underarms.

"Can't trust you," Eric said. "You better hurry up. I heard Nick say something about throwing away some law journals."

"What?" Michael said in disbelief. "Did the Marine Corps make him crazy?"

"Somebody spilled something on them."

Justin came up behind him and squirted shampoo all over his head.

"Quit!"

"Man, hurry the hell up."

The fragrances of fruit made him nauseated but he got over it and scrubbed his body clean.

An hour later, Michael sat in his living room swathed in a thick black terry-cloth robe, sweatpants and a wet hand towel covering his head. Peripheral movement still made him dizzy.

His brothers sat near him watching *SportsCenter* highlights that showcased wins and losses from Sunday.

When was Sunday? "What day is it?" he asked cautiously.

"Monday," Edwin answered. *"Shh.* They're about to show the Vikings and Rams highlights."

"I missed work." He'd had two depositions today, plus a calendar full of appointments. Hadn't he made an appointment to see Judge Ambrose for this morning? His brain registered only the foreboding.

"You missed it all. I had to cover for you." Julian nudged a bowl of soup across the table. His face was blotchy as if he'd overexerted himself or was angry. Mike would put ten on the latter. What was his problem? His life was going fine. He wasn't the one in the middle of a major life change.

Rivulets of steam wafted from the yellow broth. Would that kill him? Would he spend the rest of his life regretting swallowing the mixture that looked no better than dyed yellow water?

Well, if he had to go, what better way than with his brothers there to laugh him into the grave. He took several tentative sips. His head popped up. "I missed dinner at Mom's."

At Julian's disgusted grunt, Mike focused on him. As the oldest, Julian was the unquestionable leader and ran the family with the assistance of his brothers. They all had their strengths, but Julian was the boss. He was a top attorney in line for a judgeship. Never short on words, he spoke first when someone needed straightening out.

But today he was quiet. Angry. Angrier than Michael had ever seen him, and he knew they would eventually have a showdown to clear the air.

"What else are you missing, Einstein?" Edwin, the coolest, most laid-back of his brothers, asked.

"What else am I missing?" Mike looked around the apartment and couldn't decipher what was or wasn't there. He'd been there for a week and a half. "What's gone?"

None of his brothers would look at him except Nick. Good ol' Nick, who'd almost lost his wife, Jade, to a madman. Nick, who'd crashed a plane and watched their sister-in-law die. Nick, who'd been the renegade, but changed his life when he met and married bounty hunter, Jade Houston.

Nick was the go-to guy in the family. "What's gone, Nick?"

As a Marine Corps officer, he dealt with world truths every day. A slightly embarrassed expression crossed Nick's face.

The soup turned to stone in his stomach.

Nick pointed to his own chest then waved his hand toward Michael's. "We cut a four-by-four-inch sticker off your chest before you woke up."

Michael started to laugh. "You're joking. I'd have noticed it in the shower."

"Negative."

Opening the robe, Michael stared at the empty square where there was supposed to be black curly hair. "What are you, crazy! Get the hell out. This isn't funny!"

His brothers laughed at his expense for what seemed like a full two minutes. "What made you cut the hair off my chest?"

"We couldn't get the sticker off any other way."

"What sticker?" Incensed, he glared at them.

Justin pulled it from his pocket and laid it on the table. "This one."

The glaring red patch of rules seemed to leap off the table at him. "What the hell is that?"

"Looks like a list of rules, and you seemed to have broken every one."

Michael picked up the patch, his hair jutting from the back. He skimmed the first few lines that referenced rent and key replacement and skimmed down to the middle, rule number seven, was no unauthorized gatherings of twenty people or more.

Michael swore softly at the fine beside the rule. *Five hundred dollars?* That was an exorbitant price for one little party. Especially since he hadn't enjoyed much of it. The doorbell rang and Nick marched over and opened it.

"Hello," Nick said.

"I'm the building manager, Terra O'Shaughssey," came her shaky voice.

"Nick Crawford, brother of the guilty party. Nice to meet you. Please, come in."

All four of his brothers rose and watched with interest as Terra walked into the room. She wore a helmet, shorts made for riding and had gloves in her hand. Her skin glowed from being outdoors, and she seemed very uncomfortable with the six of them staring at her.

Michael eased around the table, holding up the hairy patch. She looked at the floor, shifting her feet, backing away. He'd seen fear before, but her behavior baffled his liquor-befuddled mind. It was as if she were apologizing to him. That didn't stop him from advancing. "What's the meaning of this?"

"It looks like a list of rules."

A few of his brothers snickered and Justin coughed. "I'm aware of that. What was this list doing plastered to my chest?"

"I wanted to get your attention the minute you woke up." Her eyes flamed with determination. She'd cocked her head, leaving the long column of her neck exposed and begging for attention.

"Well, you succeeded. You're the cause of this." He exposed his chest to her, and his brothers laughed until Eric nearly fell over the arm of the couch.

Dismay lit her eyes, and Mike realized their laughter shamed her and it was he who should shoulder that emotion. She didn't know his brothers were laughing at him and had gathered in this tribunal meeting to straighten out his wayward soul.

"Don't move," he instructed more brusquely than he intended, then turned to his brothers, who watched with rapt interest. "Get in the back or get out." He felt Terra wince and reminded himself to modify his tone around her.

They formed a haphazard single-file line toward his room. He didn't turn around until he heard the door close. The boisterous laughter from the other side was something he'd deal with later.

He faced his landlady, who looked liked she wanted to be anywhere else but there, yet she stood tall doing her duty.

He spoke with forced calm. "Look, Terra. I may have broken a few rules, but you had no right to violate my person."

Her voice didn't rise, but her eyebrows did. "Violate? That's the least of your problems. After what I witnessed, I could have you evicted and press criminal charges against you for not only disturbing the peace but also for allowing your guests to use illegal drugs on the premises."

A distant memory pressed forward. "I recall having this conversation. Who was using drugs?"

The look she gave him said it wasn't she who had to justify anything. "I don't know who they were. They were your guests. I know what you said two nights ago, but I know what marijuana smells like."

"How does it smell?"

Her gazed darted, full of uncertainty. "I'm not in trouble here. You are. You had a party and you have a choice." She swallowed, looking like she wanted to faint. "You can pay the fine."

"If I don't?" She looked everywhere but at him. She was scared to look at him. Suddenly he craved to have her rest her gaze upon him.

"You could be evicted." She backed up. "I came up here to see how you were doing. But it looks like you're in good hands."

"Don't believe everything you see."

"Seeing is believing. You have thirty days to pay the fine. Here are your keys."

He accepted them. "Why did you have my keys?"

"I didn't want you to drive drunk."

"Thoughtful of you," he said dryly. "The fine is five hundred?"

"That's right."

He couldn't get any more annoyed. "A bit much, wouldn't you say?"

Her smile sent heat racing up his chest. "Consider it a small price when you think of bail."

Mike leaned his head back, remorse slamming into him with a force so great, he had the urge to sit just to absorb it all. In that instant, he saw himself as she must see him: a drunken man who lacked control. "Look, I know this looks bad, but—"

Her quiet voice interrupted him. "You're only accountable to me for the property. Your personal life is your own."

"What you saw isn't who I really am."

Terra took the high road and gave him a complacent smile that tore at his self-respect. "I'm glad you're up and about."

She walked out the door, and Mike heard her sneakers hit the stairs. A few minutes later, he saw her riding down Kay Street on her bike.

The door down the hall opened and his brothers straggled

out. They draped themselves over the couches and looked at him with open curiosity. Julian glared at him.

The two oldest brothers, Michael and Julian, met each other's stare evenly.

"Are you finished?" Nick demanded.

"Finished what?"

"Let's start with not telling us you were moving. You didn't ask anybody to help. Moving. Not telling us where you were. Getting drunk. That's not you."

"Why can't I figure out my life my own way?"

"You have responsibilities," Julian said. "Have you forgotten your obligation to the firm?"

"You won't let me," he exploded. "I realize this might be difficult for a number of you, Nick, Eric, Julian," he said, shaming them. "But I've got a life. I'm not married anymore. Do you know I'm the first Crawford since the turn of the century to get divorced? Grandma imparted that bit of history on me at dinner last Sunday."

Unsympathetic, Julian snapped back. "You don't even drink Tequila. At least if you're going to get drunk stick with what you know."

His brothers gave Julian a look that would peel paint. "What are you looking at me for? He's the guilty one."

Mike sat down, leaned his head back and closed his eyes. "I got a lot going on. Just give me some time."

"How much time?" Julian demanded.

"I don't know. Fire me. I don't care."

"He doesn't mean that. Get off his back." Eric faced Julian and didn't back down. In an unprecedented act, the two stood toe-to-toe. "You've never been through what he's going through, so get off his back. When he's ready, he'll come back to work. His job is going to be there because you're going to make sure it's there."

Ever cool, Nick stood between them. "Y'all getting ready to fight?"

Mike looked at his siblings. "Sit down, you idiots. Down," he repeated when they continued their stare-off.

Finally both retreated to neutral corners. "I need to take some time off. There's a lot going on out there I don't even know about."

Julian walked to the refrigerator and came back with some cold duck wedged between two pieces of bread. "Like what?"

Mike had long since removed the towel from his head. He picked it up. "Women have midriffs."

Nick burst out laughing and Eric joined him.

"I was shocked too. Let me tell you something else," Mike paused until he was sure he had their undivided attention. "There are gay women in Atlanta."

Five pairs of gray eyes stared at him. "I saw them at the mall. Get this." He leaned into his captivated audience. "Women have pierced their navels." He shrugged. "It's very sexy."

Justin shivered. "Get the hell out of here. I saw the eyebrow and tongue thing. Grossest thing you ever want to see. But the stomach? I thought just music-video people did that."

Eric rested his head on his fist, his diamond sparkling in his ear. "When did you start watching videos?"

His brother sputtered. "I—I saw some late one night."

Mike stood. Although entertained, he needed some sleep. He put his soup bowl in the sink and walked to the door leading to the balcony.

Two ladies chatted across the street, and he could only imagine what they talked about. Probably their children and schedules.

"How are you going to fill your days if you don't come to work?" Julian asked.

"I'll find something to do."

Disgusted, Julian shoved to his feet. "You need to come to work. At least one day a week. I don't care what anybody says. You've got cases to finish, cases started." He addressed his brothers before they could protest. "Short of dying, he can't just walk away from them. Especially the case against Blount and Blount."

"Julian—" Nick warned.

"He's right," Mike said to end the brewing argument. He glanced at Eric. "I've got to get some things done, but nothing is so pressing I have to be there every day." He looked at his brother and partner for the past ten years. They'd built a successful law firm from the ground up. Now he needed a break. He wanted Julian to understand. "This isn't forever."

Silence stretched.

Julian spoke to him as if he were talking to a destroyed witness. "Isn't it a little soon for a replacement? I mean, you were just crying over April."

"Soon for what? Someone to take an interest in my well-being?"

"You got something going with her?" he demanded.

"No. Couldn't you tell." Michael's voice rose. "She was here to throw me out. But where do you get off questioning my private life?"

"Where do you get off acting irresponsibly?"

"Ease up," Eric warned.

This was so typical. Mike chuckled. Of course he was to blame. He was the reason the marriage didn't work. Only he didn't feel that way and was tired of shouldering the full force of guilt.

He strove for calm. "Look, nothing is going on between Terra and me. If she has her way, I'll probably be thrown out of here and possibly put in jail."

He rubbed his hand on his thighs. "I know this is hard on the family. Everyone embraced April like a sister, and I appreciate that. And even though she and I aren't together, there's no reason why your families can't spend time with her.

"She was part of our lives, face it. But for me, that life is over. One day, I'm going to move on."

His brothers were silent. Edwin leaned in. "We just want to be sure you're not looking for a replacement."

This angered Mike and he stewed in it for a moment. "I never wanted this. But now that it's happened, I have the right to live my life. If you don't think you can handle me moving on, then stay away from me. I don't want to hear it. Now let's change the subject."

Julian stood and shook Mike's hand. "I'm calling this meeting to order." *SportsCenter* clicked off.

Mike sat down and swallowed a couple of aspirin, chasing them with water. His headache had grown by leaps and bounds and would no doubt get worse the longer his brothers were present.

They discussed their father's retirement party and immediately engaged in a heated financial battle with Justin, the cheapest of the brothers.

Mike listened with half an ear. He appreciated his brothers' support. His apartment didn't look any different from when he began setting up for the party Saturday afternoon. But from his vantage, he could see six full industrial-size garbage bags and could only guess what they contained.

He needed time to think. Time to sort things through. What had happened to Drew? And who were all those people who had filled his place? Many had looked shady, like people he wouldn't associate with on a good day.

"Everybody send your financial contribution to Michael."

Hearing his name dragged him back into the discussion. "Me?"

"I'll collect the money until he gets his head back," said Nick, who seemed the most compassionate about his brother's troubles. "Send it to the office. Jade and I are moving from the boat."

Everyone looked up surprised. Even Michael found himself listening.

"I thought you liked living on the boat," Eric said.

"We do, but it's time." He held up his hand. "No, she's not pregnant. It's just time." When the silence grew, he said, "We're thinking about it. That's all."

"Fine. The money goes to Nick." Julian pointed to Michael. "You'll be at dad's retirement party in one month. No excuses."

"I'll be there. Now I'm going to bed." He started up the hall, and *SportsCenter* clicked on. Just like his brothers. No matter how much he said he didn't need them, they would never desert him.

An old feeling of comfort blanketed him as he headed back toward them and stopped in the doorway. "Has anybody seen Drew?"

"Drew? Our cousin?"

"Yes, Drew, Uncle Jed's son. Have you seen him?"

"I heard he was locked up in Jersey about six months ago," Justin offered from the kitchen.

"I heard that too," Julian confirmed.

"How do you hear stuff in Equador?" Eric asked.

"E-mail. Why?"

Mike decided to keep his mouth closed. "No reason. My landlady hates noise, so keep it down. This is a respectable neighborhood."

Their laughter followed him into his dreams.

Eight

Professor Regina Clinnell had turned out some of the best students Emory had to offer. Her class on management theory was tough. Few survived, but those who did went into the business world and earned six-figure salaries.

Regina Clinnell didn't waste time and if she was your advisor, you never wasted hers.

It had taken Terra three weeks to get an appointment with the professor. Three weeks since Mike Crawford's party and she hadn't heard a sound, and now that she sat before Dr. Clinnell relaying the events chronicled in her report, it all seemed tedious. And nerve-wracking.

She could feel Dr. Clinnell's frustration as she spoke about the debacle surrounding her inability to properly secure his premises. She hurried through the horror story related to the party and completely omitted the part about the suspected drug use. After all, she hadn't seen anything.

The more Terra talked, the deeper the grooves became in Professor Clinnell's forehead. At one point, Terra wondered if Clinnell's face was going to turn inside out. Terra stopped talking.

Through tight lips Clinnell said, "You have completely lost control of the tenants and the property. Your response could have compromised the integrity of the program and sullied the reputation of the university." She shook her head and her wig moved, increasing the starkness of her wide face.

"Not only is property management a learning tool, it is a business for this institution. I'm considering pulling you off this project and assigning it to a more capable student."

Anxiety choked Terra. Her throat closed and her voice refused to work. She forced herself to look at her professor and speak with what she hoped was confidence. Unfortunately, her voice broke. "I take full responsibility for what happened, but punishing me isn't going to make Mike Crawford a better tenant. Mistakes were made, but I managed the situation. It won't happen again."

"Do you know who Mike Crawford is?" The woman didn't want an answer, and Terra didn't offer one. "One of the most highly respected attorneys in Atlanta. In a sense, he's a guest of the university's and of mine. I invited him to participate." Under the professor's hawklike assessment, Terra detected an undercurrent of jealousy. *Regina liked* Mike. "I have the feeling much more went on than is written here."

Boozing, loose women and fantasies about Mike and me in compromising positions. Terra held herself still. "I assure you, Dr. Clinnell, everything is under control. Mr. Crawford and I discussed the matter and we've come to a meeting of the minds. He's agreed to never have a party again." At Clinnell's stern look she pushed on. "Without my knowledge."

Reluctantly, the professor nodded. "I'm going to give you another chance. But you're skating on thin ice, and you're jeopardizing your opportunity to interview for the Vanderbilt job. I would suggest getting better acquainted with your tenants and establishing a solid relationship with them. Then you'll know the happenings on your property before things get out of hand. Your grade for this project is a B–."

Relieved, Terra refused to beg for a better grade and prepared to leave by standing. "Thank you for your confidence and your criticisms. I won't let the university down. See you next week."

On the train ride home, she mulled her actions as she had a thousand times in the past weeks. Hindsight was always twenty-twenty. She could have called a temporary security firm to guard the apartment or just stayed awake instead of falling asleep and waking up in Mike's bed. Dr. Clinnell would have passed out if she knew that kernel of information.

But she'd wanted to handle the situation, maybe to prove she didn't need a rescuer. For much of her life she'd depended on others for her safety and welfare and had been disappointed over and over again.

While sleeping outside the apartment hadn't been her brightest idea, she hadn't been in imminent danger. A safe risk, she reasoned. And in business and life, a calculated risk made people and companies rich.

From the train, she walked the two blocks toward home. Atlanta in the fall was more beautiful than ever. Trees burst with a medley of colors, and the shouts of happy children getting in their final games of hide-and-seek filled the evening air.

This time of year always represented a new beginning for Terra. A time of change and renewal. The trees shed beautiful leaves in preparation of the upcoming rebirth. But the leaves weren't discards of life. The robust colors served as visual therapy, lifting spirits and bringing smiles to the faces of those who experienced their luster.

On impulse, she scooped up a handful of the colorful leaves and spun the stems between her fingers to form a dazzling fan.

Suddenly life seemed okay. B–? The grade was fair and, she conceded, improving her professional relationship with Mike wasn't a bad idea. He wouldn't be the reason she didn't get the job at Vanderbilt.

Terra walked into the apartment building late Monday night and listened. Blissful silence greeted her and she went into her apartment and dropped her books on the table.

Instead of turning on the harsh kitchen light, she lit candles and hit PLAY on the CD player. Sounds of the ocean filled the room.

The long, straight denim skirt she'd worn all day confined her legs and forced her to take demure steps when she really wanted to run. In a flash, she stripped and before she could change her mind about an evening jog, tossed on an Emory T-shirt, loose sweats and running shoes.

Feeling more relaxed, she strolled up the hall, taking a moment to sort the mail.

A letter from her mother slid into her palm. Terra sighed, torn between opening the letter and reading the contents or just calling home and finding out what she wanted. She opted for the letter.

Terra,

How you, baby? I know you're a busy girl and all, but I wish you'd take some time to visit. I'm not getting any younger. The family is fine. Your sister Valencia finally got a job at the Kroger and is back home with the kids. Her three kids keep up a lot of noise, plus I've still got Ronnie's four little ones to look after. Today your father threatened to move to Atlanta with you just to get away from the noise.

Well, that is the reason for this letter. Jack told us you called the police on him when he paid you a visit, and we're sad to hear that.

Jack's your brother, Terra, and Jesus loved his lost children just as he loved the righteous. But you can't be too righteous, girl. I was proud when you wanted to get that college education and now I don't know if it did any good if you're using your gift of intelligence to work against your family. That is why I'm writing, too, because we need five hundred dollars to bail your brother out of jail.

He's been in a bad way and you know we O'Shaugh-sseys stick together. You can send it today Western Union and I'll get it tomorrow. I know you'll help. Deep down, you're a good girl. Put "puddles" as the secret code. I don't want Val to get her sticky hands on it before I can get to the Kroger. Love, Mama.

By the way I heard from Sam. He said you sent him a care package and that the books were greatly appreciated. I'm glad you're close with one of your brothers and don't tell Sam, but he confided in me that when he gets out, you said he could stay with you. I knew there was goodness in your heart. Show some to Jack and send the money.

Terra gently folded the pages of the letter written on notebook paper and squeezed her eyes shut, trying to hold back tears. Despite her best effort, one dropped onto the letter and marred the hurried writing.

Her heart heavy, she continued to read.

P.S., if you could send a little something extra for Val's girls, I would appreciate it. Call me when you get this letter. Mama.

Tight fingers of stress and anxiety crept up her shoulders and neck until she felt as if a boulder were weighing her down. Five hundred dollars.

How many times had *she* done without? Sacrificed for the sake of another family member. As a child, she tried not to be selfish, but the older she became, the more she resented the hand-me-downs she got if they survived her three older sisters.

Rags by the time she'd gotten them, she'd sewn hems, lengthened sleeves and took in seams so she could look like everyone else. That she never quite pulled it off didn't matter because she knew she'd get out on her own one day and her life would be what she made it.

But her family was still trying to dictate how she was to

live. Jack was in jail and her mother expected her to yet again bail him out.

She placed the letter on the table, turned up the volume on the CD player and went in search of something to eat. Food would soothe her. The doorbell cut into a major decision between a steak, salad and garlic bread, or wine and microwave popcorn.

Dropping everything on the counter, she checked the peephole before opening the door. Her heart thundered in her chest. "Hello, Mike. Come in."

The casual greeting seemed to throw him off guard, but only for a moment. "Thank you. Can I speak to you?"

She blinked twice and registered what was different. In the three weeks since she'd seen him, he'd started to grow a beard and mustache. The rugged look made him even more handsome. After the first week had passed, she'd wondered where he'd been, if he'd left town or was maybe even looking for another place to call home. The thought had saddened her and would probably make Dr. Clinnell reconsider her for the management position at Vanderbilt. Terra had taken to looking for his black truck while on her morning walks, and on school days when she'd reach her block, her eyes would automatically stray up and search for light.

Tonight had been no different. The apartment had resembled a ghost town at midnight, but here before her in her doorway stood the lone occupant.

"Is this a good time?"

"Sure. You caught me deciding between a steak dinner or microwave popcorn." She considered asking him to join her, but the piece of meat was smaller than her palm.

Instead, she gestured to the oversize loveseat and seated herself in the easy chair. "What's up?"

He rubbed his hands together, and she longed to hear the heavy bass of his voice again. "I came to apologize for any trouble I've caused. I realize the party disturbed others, and I don't want to start off on the wrong foot with anybody. Especially you."

After the dressing down she'd taken on his behalf, reveling in his apology for a while didn't seem like such a major character flaw.

"Care to join me for a glass of wine?" she asked.

"Beg your pardon?"

Tickled that she'd managed to trip up the prominent attorney, she smiled. "What did you say?"

"I said"—he leaned back in his seat, crossed his ankle over his knee and rested his arm along the back of the chair—"you heard what I said. If you're offering, I'm accepting. Yes, I'll join you for a glass of wine."

"Good." Terra uncorked a fine wine and let it breathe while she got down the wineglasses. She prepared a small tray of hors d'oeuvres before returning to the living room.

Mike stood and took the tray from her hand and his glass the other. "This is very nice, thank you."

She didn't realize she was smiling until she looked up and saw him smiling.

"You had some good news, obviously," he said. "Care to share?"

Terra was tempted to tell him of her troubles with Jack and Regina Clinnell, but she preferred his company to watching him flee.

"My good news is that I'm still enrolled in the M.B.A. program at Emory."

"Was there a chance you were going to withdraw?"

"Not of my own free will. How was work today?"

"Whoa, wait a minute. You changed the subject too fast. What classes are you taking?"

His genuine interest warmed her. She didn't usually discuss her life with anyone except Margaret, because, she reasoned, who cared, besides herself? Her family certainly didn't.

"I'm taking a management-theory class and another on interpersonal communication. Then I'm done."

"Congratulations. I know you'll be happy when it's over."

"I don't know," she said hesitantly. "School has been such a big part of my life, I might go back and get my doctorate."

He looked suitably impressed. "Go ahead, sister. What will you do with your doctorate? Academia or president of a company?"

Terra laughed at the thought of standing at the head of a boardroom table. She still had trouble making eye contact with the clerk at the grocery store.

"If only it were so easy." She looked away from the navy, ribbed, cashmere sweater that molded his chest. What would she do if he found her attractive? Mike was good-looking, had money, a job to back it up and a reputation that preceded him. And he was in her living room.

What would he do with a hick country girl from Brunswick with hellions for siblings? Sobering reality scorched her sexy thoughts into cinders.

"So is apartment management where you want to hang your hat?"

"No," she forced herself to speak up. "No. There's a community in Cobb County that is the ultimate in living experiences. I'd like to manage that."

"Tell me about it."

"The community has everything you need within the confines of ten thousand acres of land. There are schools for three levels of education, a grocery store, cleaners, gas station, recreation centers and even two churches. Presbyterian and Baptist. I'd like to manage the personal property end."

The more he listened the softer her voice became.

"I'd be a liaison between the association and the homeowner. Help get the kids settled in schools and involved in the community."

"You like working with children?"

"Oh, yes. I don't know how people do it full time, but that would be a small part of my duties. What about you?"

"I have lots of nieces and nephews. None of my own. So what's the hold up?"

"It's not time to apply yet, besides, I've got to finish this assignment first. How's work?" she asked, keeping her gaze locked on his face instead of the hair that peeked out of the top of his sweater. Guilt still plagued her over her impulsive behavior.

"Work is good. I took a leave of absence."

She nibbled on a cracker with cheese. "Do you know what you're doing?"

He chuckled and shrugged. "I think I do," he said, his tone matter-of-fact yet teasing. "I own the firm. They can hardly fire me. Well," he shrugged, "my brother won't fire me."

He held the delicate crystal between large fingers, and Terra had to consciously move her gaze.

She could blame the wine for her loose lips, but she wasn't drunk. She was just seriously attracted to him. Everything about him spoke of charm and wit and an easy confidence that made him extra desirable.

The last time she'd seen him he'd been draped in a black robe and looked like he'd beat death in a close race. But today he seemed over the entire experience.

Unconsciously, he brushed his hand along the soft embroidered fabric on the loveseat and in her mind, the pattern became the contours of her body.

I'm getting drunk. She set the glass on the table. "What will you do with your time?"

"I'm getting the apartment straightened out, and my immediate focus is on getting an office set up. I'd like to do more work from home. Virtual offices are the trend in business. Besides, I need a good excuse to cut back a little. I called an office designer to come in and give me an estimate. I've also got to get someone in to set up the computers."

She crinkled up her nose, skeptical. "How long did they say it would take to come out?"

"Four weeks."

"I figured as much. What type of system do you have?" He quoted the latest Pentium and she nodded. "That's the top of the line. I've got something similar."

"You know computers pretty well?"

"I have a B.S. in computer science from Georgia Tech, but I've dabbled in office design a time or two. My office is through that door if you'd like to take a look."

"I'd like to see it. Your apartment is a little smaller than mine, but my office is in the same location." He walked to the back corner of the room and entered the door.

On tiptoe, Terra tried to see over his shoulder and when she couldn't, waited behind him.

"This is pretty much what I have in mind. I need floor-to-ceiling shelves for my journals and books." He half turned to her. "But this desk. I like this. Where'd you get it?"

"I had it made especially for this space, although I've seen good substitutes at the office furniture store in Commerce."

"You need three computers? They must work you hard at Emory."

"I like to keep different things on them. That's my first and I like the feel of the keyboard. The second has all the updates and the ergonomic keyboard and the third is my laptop."

He walked over to her shelves of romance novels and she braced herself for snide comments. One minute passed to two and they never came.

"This looks interesting." He'd chosen a book by one of her favorite authors. The title caught her eye. *A Man After Her Heart.*

"Good book?"

Terra remembered the story all too well. It was a chase-and-capture story, and when the hero and heroine got together, the romance sizzled off the pages. "Very good."

"Great, can I read it?"

Terra reached for it then stopped. "You want to read a romance novel?"

"What?" he challenged. "Real men don't read romance?"

"Sure. I'm sure they do. I just didn't expect you to."

She backed out of the office, and when he passed, accepted her glass from him. Anything to keep her hands busy and where they belonged. Because right now, with her favorite book in his hand and the purr of the ocean in the background, Mike presented a pretty sexy picture.

"Feeding a stereotype, are we, Terra?"

Blush heated her face. "Never. Please, take it. Is this music bothering you?" Waves crashed against the surf and the seagulls called to one another in the distance. The whales kept up their own symphonic harmony, taking her to the beach.

"It's different."

"I'll take it off. What would you prefer?"

"For you to leave the music on and finish your wine."

She sat back down and took a sip. If she didn't slow down, he might be putting her to bed. Again.

Terra leaned back and enjoyed his company. His cologne enticed her, a blend of musk she'd never before encountered. Clear-eyed, he wasn't the same man who'd passed out, the victim of Cuervo Gold. Tonight, he was just a man paying her a visit. The feelings she'd had of being caught in his spell dissipated, and she chalked them up to her dry spell without a man. Of course she'd have romantic feelings. Two years was a long time.

This was a good lesson for her. Mike so far had been her most challenging tenant. Gaining experience with him would only help her should she manage the Vanderbilt property.

"You're probably too busy," he said, "but could you come up and make a few suggestions on how to set up my office? I'd pay you for your time, of course."

Dr. Clinnell's suggestion to establish a better relationship with Mike popped into her mind. "Payment isn't necessary. Whenever you're ready, I'd be glad to."

He finished his wine and rested the glass against his knee. "Is tomorrow too soon?"

Yes. "Well, actually no."

His gray eyes asked for forgiveness. "I made a bad impression my first week here, but I hope to change that."

Everyone could change. Mike proved that. At that moment Terra decided later that week she'd call her mother and send the money she'd requested. She reached to the end table and fingered an object. "Here's your handkerchief."

"You didn't have to."

"Yes, I did. Thanks. Can I get personal for a moment?"

"Sure," he said as if he didn't have a thing to hide, but his closed features said otherwise.

"Are you the youngest of your brothers?"

"No, I have the dubious honor of being second oldest." He grimaced, yet his eyes were filled with love. "All the responsibility and none of the glory."

"You all seemed pretty close."

"We are. I guess they were here"—he had the grace to look embarrassed—"to perform an intervention."

"Wow. That's pretty incredible. You have a supportive family." Terra caught herself sounding wistful and didn't like it one bit. "Don't let my babbling keep you from doing something more interesting."

"You have an uncanny knack for changing the subject."

"I didn't realize we had a topic."

"Yes, we do." He leaned forward. "Where do you fall on the family tree? If you don't mind my asking." How could she after she'd delved into his family business?

"I'm number eight. I have six brothers and three sisters. Jack, whom you've met, is my twin."

"Night and day, I suppose?"

"We're as different as the moon and the sun."

"My brothers and I are, too. We get along, but that took years to cultivate. Some of us are closer than others. Are you close to any of them?"

Terra felt herself smiling. "My brother Sam and I are very close. He's made mistakes, but he's a good guy."

Mike nodded. As a man who specialized in mistakes lately, he understood. "He's a lucky guy to have you on his side."

"Thank you," she said.

"Where are you from?"

"Brunswick. Just down the road."

"I was there last year for a short time on a case and didn't get to relax and enjoy myself. I wish I had. There's a peacefulness to it."

She wrinkled her nose. "I prefer Atlanta. There's so much to do. To see. Not like a small town where everything is the same."

"I don't know," he disagreed. "There's something to be said for knowing your neighbors and seeing familiar faces. What brought you here?"

A better life. A chance to survive. She didn't want to get too personal, but she wanted to be honest. "You've seen my brother. I don't like to see that times nine. Not all the time."

"Bad choices?" Mike asked, sounding sympathetic and concerned at the same time.

"Pretty much. The majority are working at the chicken factory along with my mother and father."

"How did you end up here?"

Terra laughed at his perplexed expression. "I started working in the chicken factory the summer I turned thirteen. Slaughtering chickens wasn't my idea of a career choice, so I buckled down and knew college would help me better myself. My grandfather seconded my choice."

"Your family didn't want you to go?"

"My sister Paula was sick with leukemia and the treatments and the trips to Atlanta took a lot of money. I worked until I was eighteen, but when I chose college rather than work, it was seen as a step against Paula. It wasn't. I was just trying to make a future beyond that day-to-day existence. So I went to college and got my B.S., then worked for a few years to pay off loans. Now I'm back for my master's."

"Do they treat you better now?"

"In their own way they respect me. Need me," she said quietly. "Excuse me for one minute," she said and hurried from the room. A sheaf of paper fluttered to the floor, and he rose and picked it up.

Childlike block letters seemed to leap off the page as Mike slid it back onto the table, but his eyes remained riveted to the words. The letter was from Terra's mother, and while he didn't mean to read it, he did so within a matter of seconds.

The words were meant to hurt Terra and remind her from whence she came. To tear her down for choosing a different life.

Terra was fortunate not to have ended up like her siblings. Respect for her rose as did Mike's desire for her to succeed. No one deserved success more. How could a mother chastise a child for not standing up for another who was so obviously wrong? He didn't understand and maybe that's why God didn't see fit for him to have children.

Mike wanted to comfort Terra, reassure her that her instincts were those of a strong woman. Someone who'd achieve all she wanted because she was made of the right stuff. But she possessed an insecurity that appealed to him yet stifled her own freedom. He wished to help her break out and let herself enjoy her gifts.

After all, she'd done him a tremendous favor by not judging his behavior and opening her door to him. She had a kind heart and right about now, he found it very appealing.

The water went off in her bathroom, and he sank back into the comfortable loveseat. Getting her to relax and open up would take some time. If she chose, there was just enough room for her to fit on the couch, but she wouldn't.

From the hallway, Terra studied Mike for a few seconds. She hoped her eyes were no longer red from her brief crying jag. How could she be attracted to a man that stood for everything her family wasn't? Mike represented the law, something her brothers and sisters were adept at breaking. Even Sam, her baby brother.

So what if he'd stolen and given the financial proceeds to their family? A modern-day Robin Hood Sam was not. What he did was wrong even if for the right reasons. So how could she justify Mike to Sam and vice versa? The last time Sam had been arrested had horrified her. During a rare visit home, he had been tackled to the ground by a bounty hunter, who cuffed him and carted him off to jail.

Within seconds her life had changed. Just like now. Two months ago she'd have never given an attorney the time of day, much less let an attraction grow between them. If she were strong, she'd stop now before she got her feelings hurt. *We can only be friends.*

Adopting a casual air, she breezed in, placed her wineglass on the table and sat in the single chair. She didn't want to wake up with regrets. The CD ended and they were able to hear the soft patter of rain. "I guess no run tonight." Mike changed the subject giving her room to breathe. *Thank you.*

"Running in the rain is fun, but I'll save it for another night." Cautiously she said, "I'd rather be drinking wine with a friend."

She reached for her glass and he took her hand. Warmth worked its way through her skin and spread throughout her body like liquid fire. He squeezed her hand and she squeezed back. One tug and she'd be on his lap.

"I'm glad you consider me your friend." He stood. "I'm going to let you get to your dinner. What time will you come up tomorrow?"

She could barely find her voice. "Ten?"

"Good. I like to get an early start. Thanks for the book. See you in the morning."

He let himself out and Terra could hear him whistling as he took the stairs.

Her hand still radiated heat from his touch, and she turned it over, feeling him everywhere from the tips of her fingers to her wrist. "How absolutely amazing." In some ways it was better than a kiss.

Taking his glass to the kitchen, she refrigerated the steak, poured herself a half glass of wine and noticed the pink edges of the romance novel she'd been reading weeks ago.

A thrill danced up her spine. What were Michael and Sylvia up to? Terra curled into the chair and started to read.

An hour later she hadn't stopped, even though in her mind she'd substituted the real Mike for the fictional one.

She couldn't wait to see the real one in the morning.

Nine

The emptiness of the apartment bothered Mike. He was used to having someone greet him when he got home. Granted he was only coming from Terra's apartment, but the quiet unsettled him.

He and April had spent much of their adult life together. They'd dated since his early twenties and married when he was twenty-seven. He'd grown into manhood with her by his side. Now, ten years later, they'd separated and divorced, and he hadn't heard from her.

A thought triggered, and he knew what he'd been trying to do for weeks: get over her.

The music was gone and the photos, even the towels. Banished. Replaced. But could he replace the void? The party was supposed to fill that hole. Get him started on a new beginning. Instead, he'd lost more than just five hundred dollars. He'd lost his self-respect, and that wasn't something he was proud of.

Mike roamed the apartment, searching for a task large enough to occupy his mind, but he couldn't find anything. Every room was spotless. Even Drew's room. He hadn't been home in weeks and quiet inquiries hadn't turned up a thing. Drew was the most mysterious person he'd ever known.

Mike pulled open the refrigerator. The bare lightbulb reflected the emptiness off the clean surface. Man, he was hungry. A steak sounded good. A steak with a little Terra on the side.

He had to smile. She was so damned cute. And quiet. And intense. And interesting.

All night he'd alternated between making and avoiding eye contact. When she asked him a question, she'd practically stare a hole into his chest. But when he asked about her family, she'd given him his first real look at her. How could they treat her so shabbily? What she hadn't said spoke louder than what she had. They'd ostracized her. Treated her harshly because she wanted a different life. Even as much as he wanted to defend her, a bigger question haunted him. How badly was he falling for her?

As always, he tried to qualify his feelings. Was he interested because of the way she appealed to the man in him who wanted to protect her and make love to her, or was he interested because she was so different from any woman he'd ever met?

Both, he admitted. As a red-blooded man he'd be lying if he said being with Terra wasn't an interesting thought.

But what stirred deeper inside his gut went further than a quickie on her couch. She was better than that. And until he was sure where they were heading, he wouldn't make a move on her.

Her actions supported his decisions. In the past, she'd refused every attempt he made to share meals with him, but tonight the tables had turned. Upon her invitation, they'd shared wine and nice conversation.

Bombarded with memories of the night of the party, he realized she'd agreed to have dinner with him. How could he hold her to that promise, especially after his slide into the bottle?

The book. Hopping up, he retrieved the novel and turned on the light. Maybe the book would shed some insight into a woman's psyche. After all, he was a recently divorced, clueless brother who needed enlightenment. By reading the book, maybe he'd be able to figure out the secret to understanding the fairer sex. Of course all of this was part of his master plan, which was to get Terra out on a date.

He glanced at his watch. She was going to be at his door in less than twelve hours. He had a lot of learning to do.

Ten came quickly. And Mike was sure of one thing. He knew no more about women today than he did yesterday. The guy in the book was being a complete idiot and the woman was being too stubborn. They'd allowed disagreements to drive a wedge between them. Now they were broken up, and it didn't seem like they were going to get back together.

By page one hundred, he was completely annoyed with them both. If only they would talk.

The words rang in his mind as he headed up the hallway with his gray cargo pants riding low on his hips, his T-shirt stuffed into the waist and his shirt, another one of Drew's picks, hanging open on his shoulders.

We never talk anymore. April used to say that all the time.

But how many times could he say he wasn't going to have another test regarding his low sperm count? No, he didn't want to try to adopt again. Just no. The more persistent she became, the less they had to talk about.

Women were difficult. Even in books.

He ate breakfast in a hurry and was about to wash dishes when the front door locks disengaged. Drew walked in, disheveled and tired-looking.

"Hey, man. What's going on?" Drew said as if today were any other day, instead of the anniversary of his three-week disappearance.

Mike completely lost his cool. "What do you mean, 'What's going on?' What's up with you? Where have you been?"

"I've been working." He smiled. "I got a job on a cruise ship and we were out at sea for three weeks."

"Drew, I'm not putting up with lying in my house." His cousin was younger and probably faster, but Mike was sure he could throw him out if necessary.

"I ain't lying. Look at my pay stub."

As if he were checking on a teenager, Mike reached for the stub balled and wrinkled from Drew's pocket. He glanced at it with a skeptical eye. Sure enough, he'd been paid for three weeks.

"Why didn't you call and tell somebody you were going to be gone for three weeks? I was worried. Besides, we planned a party and you didn't even show up. Your friends nearly got me kicked out of here."

Dirt covered Drew from head to foot, and a distinct odor of fish permeated from his body. He needed a shave and shower and probably some rest, but Mike wasn't going to give him a break. Job or no job. He reigned in his temper.

"Look, we're family. You live here. If you're going to be gone, just call."

"Why are you trying to keep tabs on me?" Drew seemed agitated.

"You're a grown man, Drew. I'm not trying to do that, but I was worried enough about you to call Aunt Celia. She told me to wait a couple of days, and I'm glad I did."

Drew's face pinched with anger. "I'm grown, Mike. I don't answer to anyone and you shouldn't expect me to be accountable to you. Especially after *you've* been put to the curb. I would think you'd enjoy not having to keep tabs on someone else."

The reminder was an abrupt slap in reality. He didn't need to know Drew's every move, but he also wouldn't allow him to use his house as a hotel.

"Stay here as long as you like. But let me know when you're going to be gone for a few days."

Drew's red-rimmed eyes calmed. "No problem. I need sleep. We ship out of Miami Thursday at four." He started up the hallway just as the doorbell rang. "Hey, did Margaret call?" Mike shook his head no. "You expecting somebody?"

"Terra. She's coming to give me some advice about my office and show me how to set up my computers. Why?"

"Ask her why her friend is so flaky."

"Handle your own love life. As you so elegantly put it, I was just put to the curb. I've got my own problems." Mike was at the door, and Drew was still in the hallway. "Good night. Get lost."

"Ask her," Drew whined.

"No." Mike opened the door. "Sorry about that," he said to Terra.

"I thought for a moment you changed your mind."

"Never. Come in."

His reaction to her was still gut-clenching. So that much was true from the novel. In the book the man was aware of Florence's exotic scent and the way she felt with her body pressed to his. What a lucky guy, he thought, as Terra walked in.

Terra smelled like summer flowers as she passed him with a notepad and a half-dozen magazines in her hand. A white tank top covered her upper body, while she wore a white skirt that hit her right above the knee. Her long legs were smooth and shiny, and her feet were strapped into intricate sandals with strings that wound around her foot and ankle.

Was that a toe ring? Terra? He wanted to celebrate. He was definitely a foot man.

"Something wrong?" she asked.

She looked great. He thumped his stomach with his thumb and shut the door. "Not at all. The office is this way."

They strolled into the vast space that held only unpacked cartons. But without a desk, he thought it more prudent to get the important items first.

The wood floors gleamed from a fresh waxing, and he couldn't help but wonder if she was thinking of her last time in his apartment. He wanted to put that morning out of his mind.

She'd wandered over to the left window and pulled out a steel tape measure.

He watched her work; she seemed completely unaware of him. He had to break the silence. "What are you doing?"

She looked at him briefly. "Measuring the window." Then she smiled.

Was she flirting? Or did she just have a healthy sense of humor under that shy veneer? He had to find out.

"Why are you measuring when I don't know if I want blinds or curtains?"

"Because when we go pick something out, I don't want to have to come back and measure." This time she grinned and showed teeth.

She wasn't flirting. He was stupid.

"Hold this," she said and gave him the end of the tape. She walked backward toward the other end of the room. "This is a long wall. Sixteen and three quarters by—" She jiggled the tape and he let go. It snapped in her hand, and she dropped the silver tape box to the floor.

"You're bleeding." Mike panicked when she winced in pain. "Is it bad?"

She protected her finger from him as he tried to get a close look at the wound. "I'm free of anything contagious, but I don't think you should touch it. It's not deep," she said calmly, quietly. "If I rinse it, the sting will go away." She dropped the notepad and was heading toward the hall bathroom when Drew opened the door.

She executed a quick turn and ran smack into Mike's chest. His arms automatically closed around her.

Drew walked into the hallway naked as a jaybird.

"Are you crazy?" Mike yelled at him.

The door snapped shut. He could hear Drew's panicked voice from the other side. "I forgot my towel. I thought you were in the office and I could sneak to my room. Sorry, Terra."

"S'okay. With six brothers and a father, you see a lot of things you shouldn't." She stepped back from Mike but not far. Hmmm. He refused to let her go completely. His body tingled from the full-length contact.

"May I use your bathroom?"

"Of course." He escorted her through his room to the bathroom, closed the door, came out and pounded on the hallway bathroom door. Drew opened it a crack and Mike threw a towel in at him. "You're going to give me a bleeding ulcer."

"Sorry, man. Won't happen again."

"It better not. Now get in there and don't come out until all your body parts are covered."

With Drew safely in his room, Mike headed back to his bathroom and knocked on the door. "Is everything okay? Is your hand still bleeding?"

"No. I'll be right out."

"Take your time. Band-Aids are under the sink. I'll be in the office." He noticed tiny dots of blood on his shirt and quickly changed into another before heading up front and opening the balcony door.

Outside, children raced their bikes up and down the sidewalks, laughing and chattering away, but their happy noise faded as he replayed how it felt to hold Terra in his arms. Pleasant and different. But not in a bad way. She was small and with his arms around her, he felt strong, like her protector. Just as he'd wanted.

Of course the entire incident had been an accident, but still, he'd held her longer than necessary and she hadn't moved away.

"Is it safe?" she asked from behind him.

She *was* kidding, he discovered from the blush in her cheeks and her playfully suspicious eyes.

"You're safe." *For the moment.* "Is your hand going to be all right?"

"Surgery won't be necessary. But I think I'll be watching it from now on. Shall we finish?"

Mike stepped inside and had a hand on her waist when they both heard Drew's door open.

"Terra," he said from down the hall.

"Yes?"

"Sorry for flashing you."

She laughed. "You're forgiven."

"Have you seen Margaret?"

"No, she's been out of town. She wondered what happened to you."

His voice grew excited. "Why hasn't she called me?"

"I don't know, but you could ask her. She lives downstairs. I know she'd be glad to hear from you."

This brought Drew from his hiding place. Scrubbed clean, he ducked his head around the corner and looked at them. Mike rolled his eyes. The boy would have to take a lesson in restraint.

"Downstairs all this time and I didn't know." He looked amazed. "What floor and what's her apartment number?"

"Third floor, apartment 3026. Stop by. I know she's there. I just talked to her."

The front door closed leaving Mike and Terra alone. "That was nice of you," he said sarcastically.

"What?"

"To fix up my cousin. As you can tell, he's a little different."

"And?"

"You're setting him up to get hurt."

"He seems quite capable to me."

"He isn't. You don't strike me as the type to play match-maker."

"I'm not."

"Then what do you think you're doing?"

She looked deep into his eyes. "Nothing. I'm going to finish measuring, and you can look at some catalogs I brought up."

Speechless, he watched her go. Was that the end of the discussion?

He walked back to his office and leaned against the door frame, shoving his hands in his pockets. "Is that how you end most conversations, by walking off?"

"What?" She had a Southern drawl that made his heart skip a beat. *What* sounded like *wuuut*.

"You heard me," he said, just as softly. She measured from the ceiling to the floor and drew on her notepad. She walked the room as if getting a feel for the place. "You have some very bad habits."

She chuckled at this. "I do?"

"Yes, you do."

Terra leafed through two magazines and held the paper up to the wall.

He tried to stop himself from smiling but gave up. "Don't you want to know what they are?"

"If I have them, it stands to reason I know about them already. How do you feel about lavender?"

"You're doing it again," he said.

"What?"

"Do I have to make up a new rule?"

A full minute passed before she responded. By then he was hungry to hear her voice again. "You have too many rules if you need them to have a conversation."

"Is that so?"

"Uh-huh."

She sucked in her lower lip and stuck out her tongue as she concentrated. The little pink tip roused long dormant desire. He moved closer then stepped away.

"I don't want to talk about my faults, Mike. While that may seem fun to you, I hardly know you well enough to reveal all my"—she shuddered and dropped her voice—"bad habits. Sorry."

He felt his eyebrow land somewhere near his hairline. When he finished laughing he looked at the paint wheel she'd pulled from the back of one of the magazines. "Lavender sucks."

She turned and smiled at him. Flirtation lingered in her eyes. "You're right again. Lavender doesn't suit you. You're a purple man."

He laughed aloud and sat in his office chair. His half of the desk settlement. "What suits me?"

"Red."

"I like red. Not fire engine, but something darker. Bolder."

"Exactly. That says a lot about you."

"Enlighten me."

"Red is daring and lacks fear. Red's a good color for an attorney. We'll go brick if that's okay."

"Sounds fine."

She flipped to a dog-eared page. "Look at this desk."

She slid the magazine in front of him and kneeled by the chair. "I can imagine this entire outfit in here. You have the desk and the computer sits on top, but you get the moving keyboard tray, then look," she turned several pages and Mike had a hard time keeping up for just looking at her.

She shook the magazine to divert his attention. "Check out these bookcases. The ladder comes with the unit. Then if you add the tables that attach to the desk, it enlarges your work-space one hundred percent. What?"

That drawl was luring him in. It sounded like pure music. How could he convince her to spend more time with him?

"You don't like that one," she filled in and grimaced. "It is pricey at forty-five hundred dollars."

"Let's definitely pick something less expensive."

Warmth faded from her eyes. She looked at the magazine and closed the pages. "I can leave this to you and you can handle the rest."

What just happened? "I said the price was high, not that I can't afford it."

"That's not it. I'm not trying to spend your money." She spoke with such furious control, he tread carefully.

"I know you're not. If you were, you'd be charging me by the hour."

"I'm glad you understand. You'll be fine." She stood and walked to the door.

"I know that. But your opinion matters."

She acted as if the words were delivered on the tip of a sharp arrow. "Mike, I'm hardly qualified to give you advice. I've worked on all of three offices and one of them was mine. I've got studying to do." She was at the front door before he got to the hallway.

"What just happened?" Her rejection stung, especially since he had no idea what he'd done.

"Nothing. You got a good head start. I hope that helps."

"Be honest with me, Terra." She stopped trying to leave. "Did I do something to offend you?"

Her shoulder slumped in silent defeat. "No, you didn't."

"Can you say that and look at me at the same time?"

It took a long time but she met his gaze briefly. "I have to go."

"What is it?"

"You're making me do things I haven't done in a long time."

"Such as?" He walked toward her.

"I feel vulnerable around you. Like if I trip, you'll catch me. If I cry, you'll wipe my tears. If I smile, you'll smile back. I'm feeling a little loose around you, and I don't want to feel that way. When you said, 'Let's pick something else,' I had this feeling." She shook her hands around her stomach. "A comfortable feeling. I don't want to feel that way. I'm your landlady and you're my tenant. We have a professional relationship, and I'd like to keep it that way. That's why I have to go."

He took her hands in his and tugged gently. She took a step toward him. Sexual, sensual tension flowed around them, drowning out the sounds of the children outside and the elevator in the hallway.

She took another step toward him. "How loose?" he asked.

Her voice was a whisper against his cheek. "Like if you tried to kiss me, I wouldn't stop you." Her lips were full, waiting to be kissed, and he angled his head to taste her.

Screams of alarm rang right before a loud crash of bicycles broke the silence. Worried parents shushed the crying children, and Terra seemed to fade. Her hands disentangled from his and she backed away. "We're professionals. Let's keep it that way."

He gave in for now. "Whatever you say."

She left and he wondered why he let her go. Why, with her lips begging to be kissed, had he not obliged? Did he feel a misplaced sense of commitment to his ex or was he just scared of rejection?

Drew walked into the apartment and passed Mike before coming back to stare in his face. "What's wrong, man?"

"Nothing. What are you doing back? I figured you'd have moved in with her by now."

"Funny. Terra came down and they gave each other the 'we need to talk, girl' look, so I split. Margaret will stop up later. She has a shoot today and invited me to go along with her. She's a model, you know."

"No, I didn't know. I didn't even know she lived here until Terra said so earlier. Come to think of it, I don't know any of my neighbors."

"Knowing Margaret is good enough for me." Drew headed toward his room, whistling. "By the way, Margaret and I want to go on a date, but she won't go if Terra doesn't go. I suggested a double. Can you come?"

A picture of Terra's face from moments ago flashed through his mind. "I don't think Terra would appreciate that."

"I guess I could ask Jimmy."

Mike's eyebrows shot up. "Is your brother still a stripper with Chocolate City?"

"He's an artist but, yeah. He'll do it." Drew headed back toward the phone in the kitchen. "He'll need some advance notice. You know how he likes to pick up a woman every night."

"I'll go."

"Are you sure? Jimmy'll do it. It won't take much convincing. Terra's a beautiful lady."

Mike pushed the button down and growled at Drew. "I said I'd do it. Now the subject is closed."

"No problem, man. Don't have to get stressed."

"I'm not stressed." Even as he made the claim, he could feel knots working in his neck. "I'm going to listen to some music. You going to sleep?"

"I'm going to try, but I won't mind the music. Wake me when Margaret comes up. What else are you fixin' to do?"

"Lift some weights, then get the oil changed in my truck. Why?"

"Just wondering if you were going to be sitting around depressed or if you were going to do something about Terra." Drew yawned. "You got that I-don't-know-what-to-do look."

Was he that transparent? "Oh, really?"

"Yep."

"I'm not going to do anything about her. My life is confusing enough as it is. Get some sleep."

Mike picked up the CD remote and pressed. Nothing happened. Not a blink of light or a blip of sound. He checked the batteries, then the cords; all were inserted into the sockets. Still nothing. He tried the remote again. Silence.

He moved the system away from the wall and one by one followed the connections to the receiver. The connection cords were gone. He searched the floor to no avail.

The cords were definitely gone. They must have gotten stolen along with half his wardrobe. Mike grabbed his keys and wallet and threw gym clothes in a bag.

The phone rang just as he was heading out the door, and he stopped to listen to the message. "Mike. It's Julian. Pick up." A few seconds of silence passed. "You're never going to believe this, but your old buddy Judge Rathborne was arrested last night for assaulting and raping the wife of a defendant. One guess as to whom he wants to defend him. Call me."

Ten

Terra flopped onto the soft fabric of Margaret's Pier 1 couch and looked at her dreamy-eyed friend. She'd found her man-love and was in man heaven.

Unfortunately for Terra, watching Margaret sashay around the kitchen as she fixed tea and opened a box of cookies made her sigh. "Where'd Drew say he's been all these weeks?"

"He was working. On a cruise ship."

"Don't tell me he's Isaac on *The Love Boat*."

"No. He's a cook."

"Did he go to culinary school?"

"No. He learned to cook in jail."

Terra choked on the thin buttery wafer and sipped her tea until the offending confection dissolved. "Jail? Margaret," she admonished. "He had to have been joking."

"We have a policy of total honesty."

"Policy? You just saw him again for the first time in three weeks. How can you have a policy? Besides that, you're the catch! Not him."

Margaret looked at her, completely stunned. "Terra, I do believe this is the first time I've ever heard you raise your voice. Congratulations, girl. There is a backbone in there some-where."

Terra wouldn't be dissuaded from her cause. "Jail? For what?"

"Now keep in mind he was young and directionless. You know how many of our young men get caught up."

"Caught up in what? Gangs?" The word scared her as much as the offenders. All the gang members she'd known from around the way in Brunswick were either in prison or dead. They didn't learn that you never grew to be an old drug dealer. Again her thoughts turned to Sam. He'd gotten five-to-fifteen for his behavior.

Margaret knew a lot about her, but she didn't know that Terra, at one point, had more siblings in jail than out. Nobody knew. And she meant to keep it that way. "Are you sure he said gang?"

"Well, not in that sense of the word. Drew made drops for a drug dealer and got caught. Two years, he said. The worst years of his life. But that's behind him now." Margaret's face brightened. "I like him, Terra. He's nice and honest, and he's not trying to kick some game. Honest to God, he's not."

"Does he know you're a model?"

Margaret pointed to the wall above the couch. Hanging was a six-foot-long painting of Margaret dressed as a queen. Mounted photographs of Margaret and nearly every famous black actor in show business covered all the flat surfaces. Only someone dense wouldn't guess.

"He was dumbstruck when he first walked in. I told him and he doesn't mind."

"I'll just bet."

"What's up with you? I've never seen you this way."

"Those Crawford men are a bunch to watch. I met the whole lot of them and, my gracious, are they . . ."

Margaret leaned forward. "What?"

Terra pushed to her feet. "They're the most handsome men I've ever met! Gracious, Margaret. Six of them. Standing there staring at me like I was chicken on a bone. Have mercy," she whispered. "I wanted to crawl into a hole. They're all tall, gorgeous brothers with these remarkable gray eyes and beautiful brown skin."

"Did Mike see you checking out his brothers?"

"I wasn't checking them out." She felt the admission building in her. "I—I went to see him. That's probably why I took his keys the night of the party and why I volunteered to help him set up his office," she whispered. "I wanted to see him."

Margaret fell off the couch, laughing. "Good googamooga. He's got you. I can't believe it. He's been here all of what, a month?"

The fantasy was stripped away with each peal of Margaret's laughter. Terra sipped her tea and watched her friend through squinted eyes. "What are you babbling about?"

"You get so Southern when you know you're caught. *Wuut 'r 'u babblin' 'bout?* Ha!" She laughed so hard she started to choke. Terra debated saving Margaret, then patted her on the back until she recovered.

"Do you feel better? Are you through?" When she spoke, Terra made sure to tuck her accent into proper English pronunciation.

"I see the old Terra is back. Yes, I'm through. It's nice to see you in lusting."

"Get over yourself. That's you, not me."

"You've never told me to get over myself." Margaret got over her shock and burst out laughing again.

Terra stood and started for the door.

"I'm sorry, Terra. Terra." Margaret grabbed her hand. "Come on. Don't leave. Please?"

Terra reluctantly took her seat. "Can we change the subject?"

"In a minute. Look, Drew and I want to date. We know we're in love, but we want to formally have one official date before we consummate our relationship."

"What were they feeding you in the Sudan last week? You're under the influence of something positively foreign."

"I lost five pounds over there. The food is different from ours. It's very spicy. Anyway, you have to help because Drew doesn't drive."

"Margaret?"

"Yes?"

"How old is Drew?"

"Thirty."

"He doesn't drive or he can't drive?"

"He doesn't. He's dyslexic. He has a hard time reading signs. He can read, but it's slow. He read me a poem he wrote and, Terra, it brought tears to my eyes."

Ever the crier, Margaret reached for a tissue from a handy box situated like a decoration on the coffee table.

"I'm sorry for implying he wasn't smart. I had no right."

"That's all right, honey. He said very few people know. His mother, of course, but Mr. Intimidator he lives with doesn't. He said they always said he was different."

The conversation she had with Mike resurfaced. "He didn't mean that in a bad way. In fact, Mike asked me not to fix Drew up with you because he didn't want Drew hurt."

"Me! I would never hurt him. Terra, he's the one. I promise. You know how it is for big women like me. Some of us have tons of sex appeal and get men right and left. I wasn't like that. I didn't have my first boyfriend until I was twenty-two.

"Of course when I started modeling, there was some interest, but I got hurt because they were only after my money. I've only got a few more years in this business, Terra. As our culture becomes more accepting of big, beautiful women, the modeling companies are going to go young. Just like they did with the superslim models. I'd love to retire and know I have love too."

"I hear you, Margaret. I'm so sorry. You know what you're doing. You don't need my advice."

"I do need your help, though."

"Anything."

"Remember you said that."

Suddenly suspicious, Terra pulled away from her friend. "Why? What's up?"

"Drew and I want to go on a double date. With you and Mike."

"No."

"Terra, Drew can't drive."

"You drive."

"My license has expired."

"Get a driver. You're a famous model. Rent a limousine."

Margaret gasped in shock, her brown eyes wide. "Terra, the frugal gourmet of money, the woman who can feed a village on one package of elbow macaroni and a tomato? What are you saying?"

"Margaret, you know I would give you blood from my veins. But not a double date. Not that. Please don't ask me to do that."

"Drew and I have planned our future, and this double date is part of it. Need I remind you of all the times I've hidden you from your family members? Trekked to Brunswick so you could push an envelope of cash into your mother's mailbox and then turned around and driven right back to Atlanta? Friends do friends favors. Pleeeease?"

She hated to see Margaret beg, because every word she said was true. "Is Mike behind this? He asked me out when he was drunk but I didn't pay him any mind."

"He's not. He knows nothing about this. I promise."

"What if he won't go?"

"Get serious. He'll go."

How could she say no? "Okay. Fine. One date. When?"

"Drew has to leave Thursday morning. So Wednesday night seven o'clock."

"Fine. Can I go now or are you going to tell me how to dress?"

"Something dressy. But not black tie."

"Great." She stepped over Margaret's family of ceramic pets and opened the door. "I'm doing this only because we're great friends. But you can't make me enjoy myself."

"Anything you say. Thanks, Terra. I love you."

"Yeah, right," she murmured as she shut the door.

"I heard that."

Terra walked to her apartment and wondered if she could develop a disease by Wednesday, because if she had to face Mike Crawford, she'd surely die.

Eleven

Walking into the lobby of the Traceler Building for the first time in weeks had an unsettling effect on Mike. He carried his gym bag out of defiance, his black-soled gym shoes an insult to the shiny marble floors.

Butch, the shoe-shine man who worked in an alcove inside the door, looked up. "Hey, Mr. Crawford. Where you been lately?"

"Getting some much-needed rest."

"Don't rest too much now." His two packs of cigarettes a day made his voice sound like sandpaper against wood.

"What's too much rest going to do to me?"

"It'll kill you. Look at all the retired men. They go home on Friday and keel over on Monday. It's a sad thang." Shaking his head, he kept shining the shoes of the man in the chair.

Mike patted him on the back. "I'll keep that in mind."

He took the elevator up to the tenth floor and stuck his head inside the suite door.

Hilary's head popped up. "Where have you been?" she hissed. "Julian left that message hours ago. The judge is clamoring for you. His arraignment is tomorrow, but he wants to see you today. "What do you have on?"

His khaki roll-leg utility pants were so comfortable he hadn't wanted to change. He also wanted to drive home the point that he wasn't back to work yet.

"I bought some new clothes. Is anyone with Julian?"

She stood, a look of trepidation on her face. "No, but are you sure you want to go in there like that? One of your suits came back from the cleaners. It's in your closet. I have one of your shirts right here." She handed him a boxed, starched white shirt and a tie. Mike smiled at his second mother.

"You're priceless, but no thanks. I'm not staying." He whispered as he walked by her, "Remind me to give you a good raise."

The older woman smiled, and the crow's-feet around her eyes buckled. "You'd better come back to do it. Go on in."

Mike entered Julian's office as he had a thousand times before and for the first time absorbed his brother's power. His authority. His responsibility. Decorated by April with heavy dark furniture and long thin statues, Julian's office had bright-colored wallpaper that offset the seriousness of the surroundings. Julian wanted their clients to feel there was some hope no matter how dismal their circumstances.

His ideology worked. Their business had grown tenfold from the days of the one-room office in a walk-up. These were the good years they'd dreamed about since the beginning. Business was great, and in large part it was because of Julian's tenacity.

Mike sat after his brother waved him over. He murmured into the phone and nodded. Comfortable, Mike tried hard not to look at the open files on Julian's desk.

"Tracey, I have to go. Just do what your mother says. Maybe she won't keep you grounded all weekend if you clean up your room and wash the car. You used it and got it dirty. What can I say, honey? You messed up." He nodded again. "Mean? I'm not being mean. Clean the room and the car, sweetheart. See you when I get home. Love—"

He cradled the phone. "She hung up. Teenagers. I swear if I ever hung up on Mom, Dad would have killed me."

"Minimum he would have broken off the hand you used to hang up the phone and slapped you with it. I can't believe he's retiring."

"He'll be missed, that's for sure. How's your vacation?" he said, minus the attitude from his last visit.

"Getting better. You swamped?" Mike asked, feeling the first tingles of guilt. He suddenly knew why he hadn't wanted to come near the office. So much of who he'd become was due to his relationship with April, including being an attorney. The past few weeks he'd begun to let go of what he thought they had.

"Not as bad as I thought. We'd talked about giving the other lawyers Shaquita and John more responsibility. It's worked. Shaquita has stepped up. So has John for that matter." Julian stood and stretched. "You up to speed about Rathborne?"

"No, give me the details."

"Apparently, Rathborne presided over a case of extortion and racketeering against a man named Qwan Lee. He sentenced him to two-to-five. Then he started seeing Lee's wife. I don't know all the details, but it doesn't look good. Rathborne knew she was married, because he'd sentenced her husband. In her complaint, she claims he forced her to have sexual relations with him in exchange for a lighter sentence for her husband. Any way you look at it, he's guilty."

Rathborne had always been a jerk. Now Mike added slimy to the list. "Why should we take it then?"

Julian shoved his hands into his pockets. "He's asking for us. You in particular. I went to see him but he wants to talk to you."

Confused, Mike stared up at his brother. "That man gives me hell every time I'm in his courtroom. I don't want to defend him. I don't care what he has to say. I'm not doing it."

"That's what I said." Julian searched his desk and pulled out a sheet of paper. "Here." Mike opened the trifold paper as Julian continued to talk. "We've been unofficially ordered by Dad to appear as counsel at Rathborne's arraignment Wednesday morning."

"He's got to be joking." Mike stared at the order in disbelief.

"What is he thinking? Rathborne's put me in jail at least six times since 1994. He can rot."

"My sentiments exactly, but that's the order. How are we going to handle it? Will you go see him?"

Mike couldn't believe his ears. The talk with Tracey must have thrown Julian for a loop. His brother was *asking* him instead of giving him a directive.

"What's going on? I leave for three weeks and I come back to have to *defend* a judge who hates me and now you're *asking* me what I'm going to do? Something ain't right. This is a setup," he said, half joking.

"You're not being set up. This is straight up for real." Julian's manner confused Mike. But his brother also looked intensely truthful. At the moment.

He decided to take the bait. For the moment. "Okay, I'll go see him. But that's it. No guarantees."

"When?"

"Right now. I don't want to deal with this another day."

Julian breathed a sigh of relief. "Good. Uh, while I like your new 'street' look, you might get more respect if you put on a tie. And shaved."

Mike stroked his beard as he stood. It was filling in nicely. "Now, that's what I've been expecting. You to put me in my place. Don't worry, I won't embarrass the Crawford name, but the beard stays."

"Fine. One more thing."

At the door, Mike turned. "Yeah?"

Julian's expression was guarded. "How's your pretty landlady?"

"She's fine." He kept it noncommittal. *I almost kissed her but I froze.* "I'll let you know what happens with Rathborne."

"You do that."

Inside his office, Mike checked his briefcase and came upon the furniture catalog. Quickly starring the items he wanted, he changed his clothes, then walked out and dropped the book on Hilary's desk. "Order the starred items for me."

"Consider it done. Shall I have them sent to your home office?"

He winked and nodded. "'Bye."

"Later, homey," she said and cracked up. Mike chuckled until the elevator door closed.

Interview room B was empty save for the dark butcher-block table and two chairs. The police station had recently undergone renovations, the color of the dingy gray walls changing to sky blue. New tile covered the floor, and brighter lights beamed from the ceiling. But none of that mattered.

The people and the crimes they committed were still heinous and for many, this was one of the last stops on the road to a life behind bars.

Mike waited for Judge Rathborne to be escorted in, battling indifference and curiosity. He opened the arrest jacket and reviewed the information. Keith Rathborne, born July 12, 1940. Height five-foot-nine, weight 220 pounds.

The charges against him were rape, assault and abuse of judicial power. Mike closed his eyes and sighed. Rathborne was in hot water and unless the judge was holding a gem of a piece of evidence, the fight would be an uphill battle.

The door was pushed open, and Mike stood, closing the jacket as he rose.

Handcuffed and in standard inmate issue stood the meanest judge on the circuit. "I can't say that it's a pleasure to see you," Rathborne said snidely.

"Neither can I. Sit down."

Rathborne stood tall against the order. "Who do you think you're ordering around?"

"You, Mr. Rathborne. An inmate of the state of Georgia. Today I am your judge and jury, and if you want a chance to see the outside world as a free man, you'll sit down now."

When the judge remained standing, Mike gathered his briefcase and legal pad. "I don't need you," he said. "You can't say the same." He raised his hand to knock on the door.

"I need you."

"Say it again."

Defiance seemed to weigh down his tongue, but Rathborne finally said, "I need you."

Mike sat and watched as the judge fumbled his chair away from the table and dropped into it.

"Why am I here?"

"I need legal counsel."

Mike waved away the words. He didn't need rhetoric; he wanted truth.

"I don't like you."

The words sank in. "The feeling is mutual. Why am I here?"

"You come into my courtroom with your five-hundred-dollar suits and your larger-than-life ego and you fight for your dime-store clients like they're members of your family. Some of them still have the smear of what they've stolen on their fingertips."

"The law says everyone can have their day in court."

"It's the fight I like. Believe it or not." Humor entered Rathborne's eyes. "I admire you. I need you to fight for me. Do you think I don't know what the legal community thinks of me? I'm hated. Feared. Up until yesterday, I thrived on that hate and fear. Today that hate and fear can keep me incarcerated for the rest of my life. You're my best shot at freedom because no matter what you think of me, you'll give me the best defense possible. That's all I can hope for now. I don't know any other lawyer in the city I can say the same about."

The judge was right about one thing. Prosecutors, defense attorneys and the clients they represented hated him. Rathborne possessed few redeeming qualities, but something kept Mike from rapping on the door and walking out of the man's life forever.

"Tell me what happened."

"I fell in love with a woman named Meesook Lee. She was the wife—"

"Isn't she still married?"

Rathborne nodded reluctantly. *"Is* the wife of a man I sent to prison for five years."

"When did you start seeing Mrs. Lee?"

"About six months after her husband went to jail. About a year ago."

"Who contacted whom first and where did the contact occur?"

"She contacted me first. She wrote to me at the courthouse regarding the ill treatment her husband was receiving in jail. I wrote back stating there was nothing I could do to help her; she would have to take her concerns to the warden."

"Then what?"

"She called and asked if I could have lunch with her."

"What did you say?"

His voice remained calm. "I said yes."

Silence fell between them, each knowing that his abuse of power and judicial misconduct had just forced his career into early retirement. Whether it would be as a free man or not, Mike could only guess. The Bar Association would have more to say on that matter.

Mike placed an *X* by the answer and circled it. "Then what happened?"

"We went to lunch a few times, and we realized we were attracted to each other. More than an attraction. I hesitate to say it was love . . ."

"Was it?"

The judge's gaze fell upon the legal pad. "Yes. I fell in love with her."

"How did she feel toward you?"

"I thought the feeling was mutual."

Mike nodded, taking in the man's sullen demeanor. He'd

never seen him like this. Rathborne was heartbroken. The whole thing was disconcerting.

"When did things change?"

"About two months ago, she came to me and told me that her husband was having more difficulty in jail and that he needed to be moved to another facility. I told her I had no jurisdiction over prisons and she'd have to contact the warden. That didn't satisfy her. She wanted my involvement immediately. I pulled some strings, called in some major markers and he was moved. After that things went back to normal and I asked her to marry me."

"What did she say?"

"No. Never gave an explanation either. I knew she was married, but I thought our relationship surpassed that farce. Obtaining a divorce would be easy, I told her, but she still refused."

"Tell me why she would consider your sexual encounters with her rape."

"She's claiming that our sex wasn't consensual, and I forced her."

Mike looked the judge dead in the eye. "Did you?"

Rathborne banged the table with his hands. "No, never."

They reviewed the remaining charges, and several things didn't add up. "Did you know she was treated at a local hospital for bruises and other minor trauma the night of one of your liaisons?"

"I never knew that."

"You never got rough with her? Not even in foreplay?"

"No."

"I saw the medical report and according to the assistant district attorney, they can match your teeth to the marks on her breast."

Defeated, the judge's head hung low. "If you're going to stand as my judge and jury, why did you come?"

"My father ordered me here." Mike looked at the sorrowful man and felt nothing. He rose from the table as he had a dozen times in the past and signaled the guard. The man across from him didn't look up with hopeful eyes. Instead they were wary, infused with defeat.

"Will you take my case?"

Mike looked at the broken man. "I don't know," he said and left the room.

Twelve

In his home office late Tuesday night, Mike sat in his favorite chair listening to the late great Grover Washington Jr. and sipping rum and Coke. Starting his morning with a visit to Rathborne had dimmed the joy of an otherwise bright day.

But it wasn't the judge that had compelled Mike to his chair in front of the open patio door, watching the stars glitter in the sky. It was Terra. His thoughts had been consumed by her. How she'd looked up at him with eager eyes when she showed him the desk and paint choices. How she'd said "we" each time she referred to them shopping for blinds or drapes.

Her suggestion of the desk and shelves was perfect, and after court this morning, he'd followed up on the order and found it'd be just days until delivery. Hillary had obviously bargained and got a great deal because two extra pieces were included in the original price. Now he'd have the complete suit. That pleased him. For so long he'd been unhappy and had measured his happiness with how well he provided for those around him.

Now he was alone. Had been alone for nearly a year and was just now coming to terms with one glaringly final fact: There was nothing wrong with him.

He liked himself and he deserved to be happy. In or out of a relationship, he deserved all the best that life offered, and there was no reason to deny himself because of a failed relationship. His interest in Terra was genuine. He'd known that for a while.

Falling out of love with one woman and in love with another was risky business, to say the least. With Terra, these were the first stages. Thinking about her all the time, wanting to hear her voice, see her eyes. To feel her skin, which reminded him of rose petals.

It could all go downhill, he knew. But he couldn't walk away either. Just as he couldn't walk away from the judge.

During his life he'd rarely backed away from a challenge. The judge represented one type, because win or lose, Mike was on familiar ground.

But Terra was different. Falling in love with her was like being on the first civilian shuttle to the moon. No one knew what would happen.

Mike felt a surge of energy flow through him that had nothing to do with the one-hundred-proof Jamaican rum. In his mind, he was at the launchpad and the countdown had begun. Wherever he landed, he hoped Terra would be at his side.

In the mirror Wednesday night, Mike smoothed a small brush over his beard. The new look wasn't bad. In the beginning, he'd expected to look like a poor imitation of Grizzly Adams and to grow tired of the facial hair and cut it off. But the beard matured his face without making him look old.

Giving himself one last look, he headed toward the living room and started the CD player. He straightened the couch and tossed the unread newspaper in the garbage.

Drew rushed up front. "Are they here yet?"

Nervous, Mike snapped, "For the last time, no. I don't know why you told them to meet us up here. We should be picking them up." He stopped tapping his foot and eased the volume down on the stereo.

Undaunted by his cousin's surliness, Drew straightened his

shirt and adjusted his pants cuff over his boots. "Margaret wanted to see how I was living."

He reigned in his temper at the insult. "You're living fine. Didn't you tell her?"

"Man, you know how women are. I hear them."

Mike didn't have time to panic because as soon as the bell rang, Drew wrenched open the door. He was in Margaret's arms, kissing her as if there were no tomorrow.

"Come on in." Mike guided Terra around the occupied path.

"Margaret," Terra said pointedly. "I'm going inside."

Her friend waved a manicured hand at her then draped it around Drew's neck.

Inside, the CD changed to Will Downing, and Mike wished he'd paid more attention to what Drew had been loading a while ago. The romantic music was provoking thoughts he was trying to control.

"I see you got your stereo working again."

"Someone sabotaged it. You wouldn't know anything about that, would you?"

"Not a clue." Before her mouth finished the lie, her eyes gave it away.

They stood just inside the door with Terra nervously rubbing her hands together.

"You're not afraid to be alone with me, are you?"

"No, I'm not." Even as she said the words, she kept her eyes diverted and fidgeted with her long dangling earrings. He didn't want her to be nervous or shy around him. He wanted her in his arms like she'd been two days ago. If only he could turn back the clock, he wouldn't hesitate.

She looked absolutely stunning in a red summer skirt and light gray sleeveless blouse that tied in the back. Tall in red sandals, Terra was nearly eye-to-eye with him.

His hands itched to touch her so he shoved them in his pockets. She finally moved to study the paintings he'd recently hung on the walls, many originals by local artist Kwesi.

When she finally settled on the couch he said, "Wine?"

"Thank you." Her gaze followed him to the kitchen, and he felt a satisfying feeling thread through his bones.

"How long do you think they'll be?" she said.

"As long as it takes for us to drink this wine. I don't have time to fool with Drew and Margaret all night long."

Terra smiled her thanks. "They're head over heels. It's hard to believe. Margaret isn't impetuous so I have to believe it's real."

"I don't know much about head over heels, but they make it look good." Terra's sudden peacefulness calmed him. Mike sipped his wine and sat on the arm of the chair. "Why did you agree to come tonight?"

"Margaret asked me to."

Her answer made him smile. "Oh, you were just doing your friend a favor. You didn't want to come?"

"Yes, I'm doing her a favor." She hesitated then added, "We're friends, you and I, I hope."

"Friends." The term could be used loosely and with different meanings. Looking at her right now, "friends" was the furthest thing from his mind. But working his way past this stage would be his goal. "Yes, we're friends." He took her glass and deposited them both in the sink. "Let's go, friend. We're going to party."

A night of laughing at Uptown Comedy Club and dancing at Club 112 was more fun than Terra bargained for. She was having a good time. Even though it was eleven, she wasn't tired. In fact, she didn't want the evening to end so soon. Mike wheeled his father's long blue Lincoln Continental while Drew and Margaret didn't come up for air in the back.

They couldn't keep their hands off each other. Terra tried to concentrate on the music on the radio but all the lip-smacking and moans of affection had her wishing it were she instead of her best friend in the throes of passion. "Where to next?" she asked.

"It's a surprise."

"Mmm." She sounded disappointed. "I hope I don't fall asleep before I can experience your last surprise."

"Now I'm boring you?" He rolled the window down a few inches, and warm air bathed her face. "That'll wake you up."

She leaned her head back against the headrest, yawned and closed her eyes. "I don't think it's working. I'm getting sleepy."

"You know what happens to the first person who goes to sleep. The other person gets to do whatever they want to her."

Terra watched his hands, the muscles that corded his arms, and thought of the sheer ability she believed them capable of. Her body thrummed in appreciation. "I'd better stay awake then."

He turned onto a side street and followed a two-lane stretch of bumpy road. It was dark except for his headlights, and creatures seemed to come forth to examine the artificial light. Gold eyes appeared out of the brush, and she hoped the tiny animals would stay put. They traveled the road for several miles, then turned onto another short road and through a guarded entrance.

Finally he stopped the car. Terra looked around. "Where are we?"

"The lake." Bright moonlight cast a glow off the surface of the water sending up a misty shadow. "We're going down there. Drew?"

Neither answered and Mike and Terra turned to look. Drew and Margaret were wrapped in each other's arms fast asleep.

"They're missing a fabulous moon." Terra's face was so close to Mike's, she could breathe hard and kiss him. She'd fought the urge all night long. He'd been attentive and gentlemanly. But his acceptance of her "friends only" relationship had backfired.

Drew and Margaret had insisted on sitting next to each other during dinner, leaving her and Mike to do the same. The Japanese restaurant had been crowded and as they sank low onto the mats, Terra had practically rolled into Mike's lap.

From that moment on, she watched his every move. His every gesture had been noticed, the sound of his voice recorded in her memory bank. She knew when he was serious and when he was joking.

His laughter tickled her funny bone and made her laugh too. He knew how to treat a woman. How his wife ever let him get away, she would never understand, and if she didn't have a thing against marriage, he'd be a strong possibility. Marrying someone meant marrying the rest of his family. Terra's family wouldn't rest until they made everyone around her miserable. She looked up when she heard him speak.

"Come on," he said softly. "We'll get a head start."

"Is it safe to leave them?"

Mike shook his head. "Woman, why are you worrying about these two, who have obviously found something neither of us have?" He touched the cleft in her chin. "You need to be concerned about what's going to happen to you." He unbuckled her seatbelt and came around and opened her door. "Come on. You've trusted me all night. Don't stop now."

Terra took his hand and slid from the car. She shivered from the breeze that rolled off the lake, and the anticipation of the unknown kept her unsteady. Her shoes tapped softly against the wooden planks.

"Drew," Mike said and received a mumbled reply, "Terra and I are going up to the *Vivian II* and if you're not up in ten minutes, I'm coming out for you."

Mike and Terra headed up to the boat, and Drew and Margaret watched the couple fade from sight. Drew kissed Margaret's chin, knowing he was the luckiest man alive. "Do you think they believed we were asleep?"

"I know so. Terra would never have left me here if she didn't believe in you."

His voice dropped. "I wouldn't either."

Drew's mouth covered Margaret's in a slow, sensual kiss. She tasted like a sweet nectar, and he loved every inch of her. His lips savored her neck as he positioned himself to sample her ample breasts.

"Do you think he'll finally kiss her?"

Drew inhaled and came up for air, fighting to control the urge to take her right there in the backseat of his uncle's car. "I hope so. I think she can heal his hurt."

Margaret put her hands on Drew's face and turned it toward hers. "You've healed my hurt. I love you."

"I love you, too."

Their lips met in a deep kiss of longing and love. Minutes later, Drew pulled Margaret from the car. "Come on, before I can't stop myself."

They walked along the pier. "What do you think is going on in there?"

The lights inside the houseboat blazed, but Mike and Terra were nowhere to be found. Drew and Margaret boarded the boat and headed for the top. They settled on deck chairs and stared at the night sky.

"I hope my cousin sees what a great person Terra is, just like I see it in you."

Margaret had wanted to ask the question all night long, but didn't know how or when. For the first time in her life she was tongue-tied.

"Drew, will you—"

"Margaret, will you—"

"Marry me," they said in unison.

"Yes," they said again, together.

Drew pulled Margaret to her feet. "Well, all right then," he said appreciatively.

"You're not scared to marry me after what you went through in your first marriage?"

"I'd be a fool to say no, but let's make a pact. Let's always talk and resolve any differences, no matter what. Agreed?"

"I do." They embraced and Margaret knew Drew was her soul mate. "You want to go tell them?"

They hadn't heard or seen a sign of the couple. Maybe they'd made a breakthrough. "Let's give them a little longer." Margaret's arms came up and draped around his neck. He ducked for a kiss. This was where he wanted to be forever.

* * *

The boat was beautiful, made by skilled craftsmen. It slept twelve comfortably and screamed of wealth.

"Who lives here?"

"Nobody. My brother Nick and his wife, Jade, just bought a place."

Settled in the living room, Terra wouldn't admit it, but Mike's family fascinated her. They were tight in ways she never experienced. She hadn't heard from her mother since she'd sent the money. No word of thanks or even acknowledgment of receipt.

As hard as Terra tried not to let her family hurt her, her heart was ripped to shreds again.

Mike settled beside her and in one smooth movement, gathered her in his arms. This was what she wanted in her life. An anchor. Someone who needed her as much as she needed him.

Tears welled in her eyes.

"Why are you crying?" he asked softly.

His kindness healed her wounded heart, and she took a deep restorative breath.

"I'm not crying."

"So, big, round beautiful glassy eyes are normal for you."

A spontaneous chuckle bubbled out. How could she share her envy of his family without sounding pathetic? No, she told herself. The dice had been rolled in her life, and if she wanted to change the outcome, she had to remain in control of her emotions and especially her tongue.

Terra let blissful silence encapsulate them. Waves smacked the boat in gentle laps, feeding the peace with a touch of sound.

Instead of answering Mike, Terra snuggled down in the confines of his arms, relishing the security his world created.

Oh, how she could get used to this. Secretly she let herself believe until Mike tapped her chin.

Terra took his hand between hers and brought his arm around her waist.

"Where are you going?" he prodded gently. "I want to go with you."

"What do you see when you look at me?"

"A woman."

"That's all?"

"Women are the backbone of the world. They carry our families, teach love and faith. I have a lot of respect for women."

"What happened, then, between you and your wife?"

He was quiet for a moment. "That's fair. We stopped giving each other chances to fail. Both of us wanted to win."

Terra squeezed his hand. "If you had to do it all over, would you?"

Mike nodded slowly as if searching for the right words. "I would, but you can't change the past."

Red lights blinked in the night sky as airplanes headed to Hartsfield. "I'm glad you'd try to fix it if you could."

"That's part of the past."

"I'd like to tell you something." She turned to face him. "I want to kiss you, but I want very little complications in my life. Without letting you, you'd become a big one for me."

She didn't add that he was the kind of guy that could make a girl forget. Forget her dreams, her goals, her desires. She'd follow him to the ends of the earth and who knows? Maybe she'd meet her personal goals. Maybe not.

Mike was the type of person she'd do that for. But for once, she was putting herself first and would see her dreams come true.

"Do you like being lonely?" he asked.

"I'm not lonely. I just like to be alone. There's a difference."

"I've never been turned down so smoothly." His eyes lit with humor.

"You don't make it easy."

"I don't want to."

He helped her to her feet, and they started out the door and walked on the deck leading to the pier. Drew and Margaret were about one hundred feet ahead of them, hugging as they walked.

"They look adorable together," Terra said softly.

"You're changing the subject again. One of these days."

They climbed in and Mike started the car. The words threatened wicked retributions. She decided not to touch them.

Terra leaned back against the seat, securely buckled, and felt as if she were back on the boat.

"Guess what," Margaret practically shouted. Mike retraced the road leading to the pier and headed to the main highway.

"We're getting married," Drew supplied. Terra shared an apprehensive look with Mike. *Married?*

"Mike, would you be my best man?"

He didn't answer right away, instead focusing on traffic. "If that's what you want."

"I do."

Stars glowed in Margaret's eyes. Terra figured a heart-to-heart was due, but for now she accepted her friend's announcement. All the heat that Mike had awakened in her was extinguished. Cold fear gripped her as a sneaky feeling crept in that she was next.

Marriage was for people who believed in fantasies. She believed in facts. If she did well in the class at school, she would get a good enough grade to be a top candidate for the Vanderbilt job. Other than that, nothing else mattered.

"Terra," Margaret called, excited. "You know I want you as my maid of honor and that silly vow you made to never be in a wedding is going to come to an end with mine. I think you'd look beautiful in pink."

Terra closed her eyes and prayed to get home quickly.

Thirteen

The bailiff's voice resounded throughout the courtroom as he gave the case number. "The state of Georgia versus Keith Randolph Rathborne. All parties please rise."

The clerk of the court read the charges.

Judge Janet Jones looked over the rim of her glasses at Rathborne. She tried to look neutral, but Mike could tell this case had already come at a price for the woman, who had her sights on a Supreme Court appointment.

Prosecuting a fellow judge wasn't something any officer of the court took pleasure in. Any actions Judge Jones took would weigh heavily on her future.

Just as Judge Jones would make sure the judge was treated with the utmost fairness, she'd granted the attorneys the same level of respect. But given the circumstances—Mike was black, Judge Jones was black and so was Rathborne—there would be innuendo and she would dispel it at the expense of everything else, making the case that much harder to win.

"How do you plead?" she demanded.

"Not guilty."

The prosecutor, Assistant District Attorney Mary Beth Pearsoy, spoke up. "Your Honor, we ask that the defendant be remanded into custody. He threatened the arresting officer and resisted arrest."

"With all due respect, Your Honor," Mike interrupted. "Judge Rathborne didn't know the officers who were placing him under arrest. Given the fact that several judges have received death threats and Judge Amos is still hospitalized from an attack from an unknown assailant, my client was merely protecting himself from what he believed was imminent danger. He believed those officers were impostors, otherwise he would have turned himself in to the court."

"What he believed is insignificant. His actions speak for themselves," Mary Beth countered.

"Judge Jones, Judge Rathborne has served the legal community well for forty years in various capacities and has had many opportunities to leave Georgia, especially within the last six months, but has chosen not to. His ties to the community are solid and if necessary, we can produce a long list of his peers who will vouch for his service as well as provide character references."

If necessary, Mike would list Judge Jones's name first. She didn't give any sign of softening. She held up her hand. "Counselor, save it for the summation. What is your offer?"

"Fifty thousand dollars."

Mary Beth jumped in, holding up Rathborne's tax statement and the warrant to accompany it. "With disposable income in the neighborhood of a half million dollars, there's a flight risk. One million dollars."

The judge considered a moment. "Bail is set for five hundred thousand dollars, cash or bond. I'll see both sides in chambers in ten minutes. This court is recessed for thirty minutes." She banged the gavel and left the bench.

Rathborne was livid. "Is that the best you could do? Five hundred thousand dollars?" Incredulity stretched the skin on the judge's face until he looked like an overblown balloon.

Mike turned away from his client to reign in his increasing temper. Mary Beth waved and pointed to the hall. He gave her the sign to wait outside. Maybe they could cut a deal and a trial wouldn't be necessary.

Anger abated, he looked his difficult client in the eye. "You were lucky to get bail. Do you have five hundred thousand dollars?"

"Worried about your fee?" Rathborne snapped.

"I'll get mine." With a final click, Mike closed his briefcase, his retainer fee already deposited in the corporate account. That had been first. If Rathborne had stiffed him, he'd have been standing up here by himself. A patchy rim of gray hair had begun to grow along the border of Rathborne's scalp, aging him ten years. Without his judicial robe holding him up, Rathborne could have been any man from the street. On the bench, he'd forgotten the feelings of the common man. Now they were coming back to him a thousand times.

"What does Pearsoy want? You meeting her later? Got something going on with the A.D.A.?" Officers of the court helped Rathborne stand and secured him in handcuffs.

"Let me worry about what she wants. Have you got the money?"

"I've got it. It's tied up so it'll take me a couple of days to liquidate some assets."

"I assume you have someone to deal with this for you."

Rathborne's beady eyes met his. "No. That's what I'm paying you for. Come see me in two hours. I'll give you all the details then."

Fury and frustration streaked through Mike. He wasn't Rathborne's personal valet. Nor would he let the man treat him as such. Mike got so close in Rathborne's face, he could smell Rathborne's stale breath.

"Let's be clear about our relationship. I'm the attorney who's trying to save your behind from rotting in jail. That's it. I'm not your flunky or your watchdog. Someone in my office will be in contact with you later this morning. Give them the name of your accountant and your bail will be arranged. But if you pull a stunt like that again, questioning *my* ethics, you'll be finding other counsel. Got it?"

Rathborne's eyes narrowed and his jowls expanded. "Got it."

The guards led him away and Mike took a moment to compose himself then met Mary Beth in the hallway. As they walked, he worked the kinks out of his neck.

"I'm surprised to see you as counsel for Rathborne."

"Why? You guys know you're on a witch hunt?"

"Be serious. I know he hates you." When he didn't speak, she regarded him from the corner of her eye. "We'll do you a favor and plead him out."

Mary Beth never did anyone favors. This case had gotten more bizarre with each turn.

"Give me your best."

"Five-to-seven on the assault and rape charge. He goes to counseling and he's up for parole in three."

They stood outside the judge's chambers, and Mike didn't bother to mask his disbelief. "You want my client to serve three years in jail for having rough sex? I'll take my chances with the jury."

She put her hand on his arm. "Take the deal. The judicial misconduct goes away and in three years your client has his life back."

"Mary Beth, you're asking my client to go to jail for having sex. Okay, we know he shouldn't have messed around with the woman. But what about her?"

The tip of Mary Beth's shoe stopped tapping against the eagle emblazoned on the floor and her eyes widened as she gazed at him. "Are you blaming the victim?"

"I'm not sure Meesook Lee is a victim."

"Prove it."

He gave her one last look. "I don't have to."

They entered Judge Jones's chamber and took seats at her desk.

Reed-thin with cocoa-brown skin, Judge Jones sat with her hands resting on top of the desk. She leaned into them and spoke crisply as the poised court reporter recorded their words. "I do not want my courtroom turned into a media circus. I'm barring all cameras from the courtroom."

"What about a lawsuit?"

"Not my problem yet. Let somebody sue and get a court order. Then I'll let them in. First things first. I will not stand for grandstanding and I will not tolerate any sign of stalling or incompetence. There is no latitude. This case is by the book." She shook her head and addressed Mike directly.

"What I personally think of Keith doesn't matter, but I won't have a member of the court treated disrespectfully. Whatever he's done in the past, put it behind you. We have a case to try and I expect everyone to do their jobs. I've cleared my calendar. I want this case out of my courtroom as expeditiously as possible. We're starting two weeks from today."

"We don't have enough time to complete our investigation, Judge Jones," Mary Beth said.

The judge regarded the prosecutor over her clasped hands. "Really?" She bit the word off at the tip of her tongue. "Then you shouldn't have pushed for an arrest warrant, Ms. Pearsoy. Two weeks from today. Not a day later."

"Your Honor, please note my objection." Mary Beth looked troubled.

"So noted. Have a good day."

Mike reviewed the data sent over by the investigators regarding Meesook Lee and waited for something to click. He waited minutes, which turned into an hour. Still nothing. From where he sat, the prosecutor had an airtight case, no matter about Mary Beth's whimperings. A headache formed from pushing himself too hard, and he stacked the folder in a crate and headed toward his bedroom to change into basketball shorts and a T-shirt.

A soft basketball sat nestled in the hall closet among Rollerblades, a baseball mitt and an ancient bat that had seen better days. Giving the ball a test bounce, Mike set out on foot to find a gas station with a pump. Three miles away at the station, he inflated the ball and wondered where he could find a good

pickup game. His apartment had a decent court that attracted
men and women of all ages, so he headed back, dribbling the
ball as he went. No easy task on the uneven sidewalk, he had
to keep stopping to retrieve the ball from where it'd roll once
he bounced it.

The Rathborne case was a difficult one, and Julian had
agreed they needed their own investigators to dig up information on the Lees. Then perhaps Mike could get a better handle
on their connection to Rathborne.

Mike dodged the elbow of an old man in a tattered coat and
could hear him muttering about sidewalks being for the civi-
lized, but Mike ignored him and kept running.

At the basketball court a young man about twenty asked for
a quick game of one-on-one.

Mike felt obliged to show him a thing or two. Two games
and forty minutes later, he was quickly coming to the conclu-
sion that this young man was going to beat the pants off him.
Mike arched, forced a three pointer and watched it air-ball out
of bounds.

That was when he noticed Terra and several ladies watching
the game from the corner of the yard.

They couldn't have been there too long, but while he'd been
busy gasping for air, the younger guy named Rocky had been
smearing him all over the court for the sake of the women.

Mike lost, shook hands with his opponent, gathered his ball
and turned to greet Terra and her friends, but they were gone.

So much for that. He headed toward the front of the building
and collapsed on the stairs.

Leaning into a cool breeze, he rested on his elbows, and
when he opened his eyes, Terra was standing over him. Mike
jumped to his feet. "Where'd you come from?"

"The back of the building."

She stood on the top step with a thin, gray skirt nearly touching her ankles, but he could still see the strappy sandals and
her toe ring. Her blouse was white and sleeveless, perfect for
summer. She looked cool and collected and unruffled by his

scruffy appearance. Terra had the uncanny knack of catching him at less than his best. He made a mental note to change that.

"Do you need a towel?" she asked.

"I guess I do."

Mike grabbed the ball, followed her to her apartment and stood at the doorway separating the kitchen and the living room.

Again her place was immaculate. Fresh flowers he now associated with her bloomed in glass vases and the softly spinning fan made him feel lazy.

"Thanks," he said.

She walked to the refrigerator and came back with a bottle of cold water and handed it to him.

"You trying to tell me something?"

"Drink," she said and giggled.

Mike gratefully took a long pull from the bottle. "Did you have a good time last night?" he asked.

"I did."

"Will you go sailing with me again?"

Terra raised her hands. "I don't know—"

"It's a great experience. I promise," he said, pushing just a little.

"I always wanted to go out on a boat and see the sea."

"That's a beginning. Say you'll try again with me."

She tilted her head, smiling. "I'll try again." He felt a change as subtle as leaves turning from summer to fall. It felt good.

"You left early this morning," she said.

"I had an early court appearance."

"You in trouble or somebody else?"

He threw his head back and laughed. "You're a regular Mrs. Chris Rock. I'm not in trouble, for your information."

"I'm sure you'll get him off," Terra said.

"How can you be so sure?"

"I feel lucky."

"Can I rub your lucky charm?" At her surprised look, they

both burst out laughing. "I didn't mean that the way it sounded."

"What did you mean?"

If he weren't so sweaty, he'd take her in his arms and show her. "I'll show you next time." He took another swallow of water, his body sufficiently cooled on the top layer. Beneath the surface, he remained fired up.

"So what's your day like?"

"I've got to study for a test. That's it." A smile came easily to her lips. Lips he intended to claim soon.

"Do you have time to start setting up my computers?"

"You have more than one?"

"Well, once I saw your operation, I realized I didn't have to get rid of my old system just to accommodate the new one."

"I can work on it for about an hour. Then I have plans."

"Going to get your hair done?" he asked casually, jealous and nosy at the same time.

She touched the short strands of black hair. "I just got it done."

He looked down at her hands. "Nails need doing?"

She giggled again. "No. I'm sure you want to freshen up before I come up."

"Right." The buzzer to her door rang, and she slid past him to answer it. She leaned forward on one foot, the other dangling in the air.

A quick flash of Terra and him and his mouth on her ankle caused him to inhale deeply and plan his escape. His body was overreacting at the wrong time.

"Who is it?"

"Jack. Open the door, Terra."

Her demeanor changed immediately. Her forehead furrowed and her hand quivered. She turned to Mike. "Uh, could you stay a minute? It's nothing, really. It's my brother. I just don't want to be alone with him."

The admission caught him off guard. "Sure. It's not a problem."

The buzzer rang insistently.

"Go in the bedroom." As an afterthought, she handed him a small beaded bag with a long strap. "Here, take my purse."

Mike took the bag but held on to her hand until she looked at him. Everything was out of order now. Even with her soft music on, Terra no longer fit the picture. "Why are you letting him rattle you? Just tell him to go away."

"I can't. My family already hates me. . . ." She shook her head as if the reason didn't matter. How wrong she was. "It doesn't matter," she said. "Please just be here. For me."

There wasn't an ocean he wouldn't have crossed for her right at that moment. "I'll be listening."

She nodded and cupped her waist with her arm. She pressed the buzzer, and they could feel the vibrations throughout the walls as the downstairs door banged open. From the room, Mike could hear the brother enter and begin to roam around.

"What's shakin', Terra? You got a surprise for me?"

"No, Jack. I don't have anything for you. Why are you here?"

"Why are you trying to rush me? Ain't you got no manners? You can't offer your brother a drink?"

"That was my last bottled water."

"Don't matter. I'll have the rest of this one." The room was silent for a moment. "You want the rest?"

"No," she said evenly. "What brings you to Atlanta?"

"You do. I hear you posted my bail, sis. Thanks. A brother really appreciates the favor. Now I need another."

"Jack, I'm all out of money. I work for a living, you know."

His voice turned menacing. "What you trying to say? You can work and the rest of us reg-lar folk can't?"

"I didn't say that."

"You saying you too good to help out your family members? I think you need someone to knock you off that high horse of yours."

"You touch me, you'll be sorry, Jack."

The terror in her voice brought Mike from her room. "Get out."

Jack spun toward him in surprise. He'd had Terra backed into a corner by the front door. Her arms were raised in defense and her eyes were scared. That was all Mike needed.

He walked toward the scruffy man he'd mistaken on the street as a down-on-his-luck older man and took him by the arm. Jack put up a slight struggle but when Mike got a grip on the back of his neck, he stopped.

"This your man? We're family, Terra. He don't have no business butting in."

"She's my business. The gravy train is over, buddy. If I ever hear, see or smell you around here again, you'll wish you hadn't woken up this morning."

Jack didn't answer and Mike applied more pressure. He finally yelped, "I hear you. Now let me go."

"Terra, your brother is ready to go. Get the door, sweetheart, look at him and say good-bye to Jack."

Terra opened the door. She met Jack's burnt gaze. "Goodbye, Jack."

"Later," he said when the pressure on the back of his neck made his eyes bulge.

Mike was back a few minutes later to find the towel he used and a fresh bottle of water waiting on the counter. No Terra in sight.

He checked her bedroom and still didn't find her, so he knocked on the bathroom door.

"Mike, can I meet you upstairs in a few minutes?"

"You don't have to be ashamed or embarrassed about Jack. You didn't make him the way he is." He sat on the floor outside the door. "What if I said every family has a Jack?"

"I'd say my family must have made God very angry because we have nine in various stages of Jack's condition. Can you beat that, counselor?"

"I'm afraid not. Let me tell you something, Terra. You can't judge a person based on the tree they fall from, otherwise it's probably a good thing I can't have children."

He held his breath, praying she didn't pick up on the *can't*.

Her laughter was soft, a sweet melody of sadness. "You're an attorney. Your brother is an attorney. You're probably made of excellent stock, Crawford."

He banged once. "Will you open this godforsaken door? I don't talk well through wood."

Slowly the door opened and Terra lowered herself beside him.

"I don't want to have a pity party."

"I'm not trying to join one. You have value, not because of where you come from but because of who you are."

"I know," she agreed with a level of self-assurance that relieved him. He didn't deal well with people who indulged in self-pity. It appeared to him that Terra's shyness had been a veil she'd used to cloak herself from forces she perceived to be bigger than she. Since he'd met her she'd expressed caring, patience and understanding to a total stranger. Him. He suspected she'd offer assistance to anyone in need and not bat an eye.

It was time she understood her intrinsic value. Saying so was one thing, but he wanted to find a way to help her see herself as others did.

Wanting to was one thing, but going about it was another.

He stood and gave her a hand up. "I need a shower and to change. Give me twenty minutes?"

"Sure."

Upstairs, Mike showered and dressed in record time. Though early to be thinking about dinner, he searched his fully stocked freezer for just the right foods. Terra needed to loosen up, and he knew just how to make her.

First, he'd start with the messiest foods and work from there.

Satisfied with his selections of lobster tails, chicken wings and pasta with tomato sauce, he started the water to boiling and went to break open the computer boxes that had arrived after he'd gotten in from court.

The buzzer rang and he jogged to the door and answered.

Terra's eyes were almost milky white from Visine or some other type of eye-whitening product. She wore a brave face, but on the fringes of her eyes were the ravages of her humiliation. Someone like her couldn't be told that her family's problems didn't matter, only time would close that geyser of shame.

"It's me."

"Come in, me. You fine?"

"Yes. Are you?"

"Good since you're here." Mike decided to act as if it were a regular day and he hadn't used force to evict her brother from her apartment. "The computer arrived this afternoon, but the desk won't be here until this weekend."

She struggled to sound casual. "I saw you on TV today. You were talking about a case involving a judge."

"So I made the news?" he said, rather grimly. That's the last thing he needed. Media attention. That would only draw more scrutiny to Rathborne. Right now they didn't need any attention from the press.

"You looked then like you look now."

"How do I look now?"

"Stern."

Mike tried to smile. "And now."

She laughed. "Scary."

The tension between them lessened, and he invited her in and guided her toward the kitchen. "Since I'm working this case, I need access to the company server. Plus, I need my e-mail up and running."

"Where do you want it set up?"

Good question, he thought scrambling. "Right here on the counter. I can sit here, get my work done and keep an eye on the pots."

He walked into the kitchen and poured the rest of the wine

from the night before into glasses and excused himself to get busy scheduling painters and the electrician.

Calm down, he thought, pacing the near empty room. Terra's apprehension touched him. He wanted her comfort. He wanted her smile. If she was comfortable thinking he encountered a junkie every day of the week, then so be it. She had nothing to be ashamed of.

When he came from the office, he found her rummaging through a bunch of boxes he'd dragged from the office to the living room.

"I need to load Windows before I do anything else. Do you have it back there somewhere?"

"Not in the office. It should be in one of these boxes. Here." He started passing her software boxes, one after the other.

"Hold on," she laughed. "I only have two hands."

"They're pretty hands," he said and took pleasure in her blush. "Pretty hands still have to work fast."

At last he unearthed the software. "Here it is. Anything else?" He stood and they were both still, holding the box. She moved out of reach right when he moved to touch her.

"No, this is exactly what I need."

Mike picked up the remote and aimed. "TV or stereo?" Will Downing was still loaded, he recalled, and prayed she'd say stereo.

"TV," she said. Local newscasters opened with the trial of the judge and mentioned Mike's name. Terra looked up at him. "That's you." They watched together.

Channel Five showed footage of Mike leaving the courthouse that morning. File photos of Judge Rathborne flipped onto the screen while the announcer quoted his high conviction rate.

Two talking-head attorneys discussed the charges and gave a low rating to the judge for acquittal. In fact, the one attorney advised the judge to pack his toothbrush. He'd be in jail for a long time.

Mike blinked slowly and shook his head. This case was going to be an uphill battle all the way.

Returning to the kitchen, he started the frozen lobster tails. "Is your case as bad as they say?" Terra asked.

"I hope not. I hate losing."

"Yeah, me too."

His brows shot up in surprise. "What do you play?"

"Why so surprised?" She shot back, software in hand, skirt billowing around her feminine legs.

"I guess I figured you for a bookworm. You play tennis?"

"Like Denise Nichols in *Let's Do It Again.*"

"Richard Pryor, Bill Cosby," he said with recognition. "I remember that flick. That bad?"

"I never said tennis was my sport."

"Basketball?"

"Not better than you," she teased, getting situated on the couch.

"I'll have you know I had that kid by five points until you women showed up. Then he got cocky."

"And beat the shorts off you."

The image of his shorts off in her presence made him leer. He stirred the lobster tails. "Let's keep my shorts out of this discussion. Baseball?"

"Ding ding. That's correct."

"As you've heard, my client isn't a great guy, yet I still want him to win. I'm not convinced that he's guilty, but even still, it shouldn't matter."

Terra inserted one CD after another, loading the software. "If it were me, I'd bunt."

"Bunt?"

"Why go for the home run when all you need is one run at a time?"

"Bunt?" he said, liking the idea. He'd have to take the case apart and attack it a small section at a time. There were holes. He just didn't know how many and how big.

"I'm not a lawyer, but that's what I'd do."

Windows was loading and the pot of lobster tails was boiling. He'd started the water for spaghetti and his coup de grâce was fried chicken wings with lots of barbecue sauce.

He came and stood by her. "You may not be a lawyer, but you sure know how to load software."

Terra laughed and Mike took her in his arms. She smelled of powder and although he'd smelled it a thousand times before, he got turned on. "What are you doing, Mike?"

He tried to look innocent. "Holding you. Wanting to kiss you."

"Didn't we cover this ground already?"

"We never actually got to the kissing part."

"I don't have a problem kissing."

"That's good news."

"It's the latter I can't handle."

The phone started to ring. "Let's handle the latter later."

"A dangerous proposition. Are you going to get the phone?"

He nuzzled her chin with his lips. "I'm not trying to kiss the person on the phone. I'm trying to kiss you."

Mike's mouth got close to Terra's, and she leaned back, her lips just out of reach.

"Timing is everything."

He had the grace to look boyish and desirable at the same time. "This isn't it?"

"No."

"Damn."

"Get the phone."

He yanked it off the hook. "Mike Crawford." He listened for a moment then pinched the bridge of his nose. "Julian, you can't tell me that later? I'm busy. Terra's here. Nick and Eric are there with you? Great. You guys are a regular mobile family reunion. I will not put her on speakerphone. No." He sighed heavily. "Terra, do you want to speak to my brothers?" Into the phone he said, "She said no. She's busy."

"I did not say that," she whispered, with this cute dimpled smile on her face.

Mike put her on speaker.

"Hi, Terra," they chimed in a rugged harmony.

"Hello. How are you?"

"Fine. Just checking on Mike to see if he's being a good boy. Is he being good?"

Mike turned from the stove. "Hang up, Terra. You don't have to talk to those perverts. Hang up. They won't be offended."

"He's being very good. Thanks for asking."

He came over and nuzzled her neck, whispering in her ear, "I don't want to be good."

"Your brothers . . ."

"Yeah, we're still here."

"No, you're not." Mike disconnected the phone.

"You hung up."

"I'm busy." He dipped his head, tasting her mouth for the first time. The kiss lasted a full five seconds. He knew because firecrackers exploded in his head five times. "More," he said, bracing his hands beside her.

"I can't."

He breathed, drawing his finger down her cheek to the collar of her shirt. "Terra, you're killing me. When it happens, oh, what a time it will be." He snapped the lip of her blouse, which lapped at her dark skin, and kept her captive in his arms.

Whenever she'd move to her left, he'd stroke her side with his right hand. When she'd move right, he'd stroke her with his left. But he didn't try to kiss her again. The next time, she'd ask for it. He'd make sure of it.

"Who's going to eat all that food?" she asked.

"You and I."

Regret filled her eyes. "I can't stay for dinner. I have a meeting this evening, and we usually eat dinner at the restaurant. I'm sorry to say this, but I've got to go."

His spirits plummeted. "You're not leaving me. You just got here."

Her soft brown eyes had dimmed and the joy was erased by sadness. "Thank you for dealing with Jack. He wasn't always like that."

"Don't make excuses for him."

"I try not to."

"Is that why they hate you?"

She jerked back as if he'd slapped her. "I've got to go."

"You're beautiful and smart and you're out of Brunswick. They resent you because of it."

She moved close and touched his cheek. "I see why you're such a good attorney. See you later."

Mike stood there, pots boiling, food cooking. Reaching Terra would take a better plan than he'd devised.

He had to have another party.

Fourteen

Terra crossed the intersecting street and strolled down the familiar block. Kay Street was always quiet just after dusk. Families had retreated inside to bathe boys who'd played in the creek that flowed behind the Allowell house and girls who'd made mud pies to feed the boys.

The neighborhood housed a perfect mixture of families and single people. A couple breezed past speed-walking and huffed, "Hello," making her smile with shame at her lack of interest in exercising.

She'd been blessed with a high metabolism, making exercise, when she did participate, fun rather than a chore.

As she climbed the curb of the third block of Kay Street, she wondered if tranquillity would follow her if she succeeded at being chosen for the Vanderbilt job.

She was certainly happy at the moment. A large part of that had to do with the secret thrill she got every time she was in Mike Crawford's presence. Mike possessed qualities she wished she'd been born with. He was strong. He showed no fear where Jack was concerned.

How many times had she wanted to stand face-to-face with Jack and tell him where he could go? She'd tried, but he knew her natural inclination was to avoid conflict. Sometimes it was just easier to give in.

Jack was the reason Tim had divorced her. And, she admitted to herself on this quiet stretch of street, because of her own lack of strength. She'd done everything to win her family's love, including give them money and a place to stay when one or another had hit bottom and claimed this time they'd straighten up.

Terra had wanted to believe but Tim had seen the light clearly. Their marriage had suffered from the strain, but it wasn't until the VCR and television had disappeared, and money had been drained from their bank account that she accepted the reality that her family was taking advantage and she was letting them. There was a title for people like her. She was an enabler.

But the realization came too late.

Tim gave Jack their last ten-dollar bill, kissed her on the cheek and told her it was over. That had been five years ago. Today she was older and wiser and working on getting stronger.

Mike aided her along that goal each time she was with him.

Her steps quickened in an effort to leave the desolate thoughts behind, but with each step, thumping music grew louder.

Inside her building, bass vibrations ricocheted off the hallway doors, coming from above. She thought of Mike first, then put the thought aside. Surely after a five-hundred-dollar fine and their personal progress, he'd given up his party ways.

Terra dropped her books in her apartment, grabbed her clipboard and squared her shoulders. Somebody was breaking the rules, and she was going to bring them back into compliance.

Even as she thought the words, her feet didn't want to obey. It was as if she had one foot stuck in her new life of property manager and boss and the other locked in the past as a scared woman who had never learned to assert herself.

Gathering her courage from the ravages of her own failed confrontations, she rounded the steps heading toward the fourth floor. Mike Crawford was at it again, and she was going to put an end to this once and for all.

Terra walked in the open door and felt her mouth drop.

Julianna and Chris were standing by the balcony discussing something hot and heavy.

ReAnn and Rusty from 1320, and Samir and her boyfriend Asaad from the second floor were learning the electric slide from her other neighbors Kira and Pete.

There were people from around the neighborhood she knew by name and many more by face, but she was stunned. Even the power-walking couple who'd passed her and didn't even live in her building were there!

Mike emerged from his office and greeted his guests as if they were old friends.

Terra beelined for him and kept a smile on her face as she looked up. "What are you doing?"

"Throwing an end-of-the-year holiday bash. A combination of Christmas and New Year's Eve."

"In September?" At a loss for words, she looked around. Icicle Christmas lights had been strung around the windows and snow sprayed on the glass balcony doors, creating an indoor winter wonderland. Some of the ladies from the block were in the kitchen drinking eggnog and eating Christmas cookies while the men sat in front of a silent television watching a game featuring the Bulls with Mike Jordan. The stereo blasted Christmas music and several young couples rapped with the group. Although this gathering was orderly, it was still a party. And Terra had an issue with that. All gatherings, no matter if tenants were involved or not, were supposed to be approved by all the tenants. And *she* surely hadn't approved any such thing.

Terra threw out her hand. "This whole thing is illegal."

"Don't worry," he said in a confidential tone. "That tape came with my *Sports Illustrated* subscription."

"I don't mean the tape and you know it. I mean this," she waved her arms. "Whole thing."

He looked around seemingly pleased. "How so?"

"Did you not read the . . ." She pointed near his chest. "The thing I put— You know very well what I'm talking about."

"I read it. In fact, I saved it. Shall we review it together?"

Her body grew hot. "No," she whispered.

He moved closer, not touching her physically but enfolding her with his desire. "Come on. You can yell at me all you want in the back room."

Suddenly very hot, she sidestepped unsuccessfully. If she went to his room, he might—she might— She didn't want to finish the thought. "I'm not going with you. Here." She handed him the warning slip and the sheet listing his fine.

He read it with an interested expression on his face, then proceeded to tear it up.

"What are you doing?"

"I'm in complete compliance."

"You are not."

"I am. Don't believe me?"

She shook her head. He went to the stereo and lowered the volume. "Everybody having a good time? You were all invited to this approved party, right?"

A clamoring of "yeah's" rang throughout the room. "Play something we can dance to," ReAnn said and Terra turned, her hand slipping from her waist in shock.

ReAnn and Rusty, her husband, had been Mike's biggest complainers about his first party. Now they were eating his crab cakes and sweet-and-sour meatballs and drinking his beer as if he were chef Emeril.

ReAnn, who'd just had hip-replacement surgery two months ago, and Rusty, who'd already suffered two heart attacks, started a conga line and their excitement caught the attention of the ladies in the kitchen. Pretty soon, Terra stood with Mike at the center of the snaking, happy revelers.

In her sixties, ReAnn goosed Terra, making her jump and Mike threw his head back and laughed. "Lighten up," he said, looking absolutely adorable in his red holiday sweater. She wanted to kiss him as much as she wanted to kick him.

She threw up her hands. "Fine. Fine. If everyone is happy,

then the building manager shouldn't have anything to complain about. Good night."

Tugged at the waist, ReAnn grabbed Mike and Rusty commandeered Terra, forcing them to dance. The CD skipped and instead of taking it off and ending the crazy circle, Rusty and ReAnn prompted everyone to do a stilted, dance-freeze step that left a lot to be desired but filled the room with spontaneous laughter.

Terra caught herself giggling and thrusting out a hip with each skip. When in Rome. . . .

Eventually, she got close to the front door and edged into position to make her escape but Mike snagged her hand just as Nat King Cole started to sing.

"I only have one wish for Christmas," Mike said.

Terra didn't want to smile, but the event was bizarre and kind of cute. She couldn't help but be flattered. He'd done all this for her. He'd even placed a two-foot tree on the counter and decorated it with tiny ornaments. "What is it?"

"To be an unwrapped gift under your tree."

She looked up at him as he captured her waist and started to move in slow beats to the music. It was almost as if they weren't moving. Under his power, they got closer and closer. Soon their chests were touching. Thighs. Legs.

His hand rested on the small of her back and his broad arm held her steady. Sadly, she thought, this is absolutely the best nonsexual experience I've had in a long time. But being with Mike made her feel sexy and wanted. She was aware of her hands roaming his back and rested them on his shoulders.

Terra struggled to find one thread of backbone. "That's a pretty pathetic line, if you ask me."

"It worked, didn't it?"

They moved around other swaying couples.

"Your parties are such hits," she said. "Why practice law?"

The laughter bubbled up his chest and hers. "You're cute, you know that?"

"Thanks."

Their bodies followed a natural rhythm when Boyz II Men began to sing "Let It Snow." "You don't say much," he observed.

"It's not a problem for me."

"Don't you ever want to speak your mind?" he teased. "Let your thoughts flow freely? Have somebody tell you to shut up?"

"No," she protested. Her arms slipped down.

He guided them up to his shoulders and kept his hands braced on her arms. Every couple in the room was paired off, dancing, sharing intimate thoughts and smiles of promise. Love was in the air, and Terra felt as if an infected bug had bitten her.

She closed her eyes and swayed with a man who equally incensed and challenged her. He stimulated her womanliness and made her feel alive, ready to flaunt her femininity.

The fact that she wanted him to do more than hold her close shook her from the fantasy wonderland he'd created. Positive she couldn't match what he wanted in a woman, she started to pull away.

"Where do you think you're going?"

"I need to study."

"Study for what?"

Terra took a deep breath of his cologne and exhaled softly. "Interpersonal communications."

"You're doing fine right now. You're getting personal with me nicely." He brushed his lips across her ear. She shivered. He hugged her closer. "You get an A."

Desire pulled at her spine and she leaned into him more.

"Can I ask you something?" he said.

"What?" Her voice didn't sound like her own. To her ears, it sounded like it belonged to a woman ready to give herself to a man.

"Did I tell you that drawl makes me have sexy thoughts?"

"No," she said, slightly breathless. "I don't believe you ever did."

"Well, it does."

"Should I apologize?"

"Not at all."

"Good." Her resistance started to fade, replaced by clouds of hope. Being in his arms was intoxicating and safe. Would allowing him access change the course of her life? And if so, for how long?

As he kept them pressed together, she made mental calculations. He was just the right size, height. But even as she felt the blush of the impending kiss creep through her blood, she had to wonder how good it would be.

Would she fall in love after this kiss or would it take another? Too much pressure, she warned herself. If it didn't happen that way, she'd be crushed. Maybe it would be better to count her losses and leave without ever knowing. Or maybe she needed to hear it again.

"You're beautiful," he whispered, his lips to her ear. Her legs grew weak.

She looked up into his eyes, and they smiled. "You're just saying that."

His eyes traveled over her face. "I don't ever say what I don't mean."

Terra closed her eyes and sank into Mariah Carey's voice as she sang "Miss You Most at Christmastime." When she opened them, they had danced into a dark corner near his office.

"What if I can't get enough?" he said, passing his hands down her cheek, through her hair, over her back. There was nothing weak about this man, even as he spoke with such need.

She looked away. They were traveling on the same track of railroad and if someone didn't give, there'd surely be a collision. "I don't know how to answer that."

Time to push him away, her conscience warned her, but her lips were parted for one reason and one reason only. She wanted Mike to kiss her.

The music stopped and someone flipped on a video.

A large clock flashed the ticking seconds of a New Year gone by.

"I hope you're with your beloved," the announcer said. "Be happy all the year through. Ten, nine, eight, seven, six, five . . ."

Mike touched the cleft in her chin and nudged up. She looked into his eyes for the briefest second before his mouth closed over hers as the peach dropped on Georgia.

He kissed her thoroughly, deeply, until she didn't know if it was day or night. Raining or shining. Friday or any other day of the week.

Everyone flowed around them, singing. But she was in a dark corner, falling in love with a man she could do little with in her future. "For the moment" burned her brain, and she reached up and circled his neck with her arms and pulled him closer, opening her mouth to him.

Mike's tongue probed with expert precision, stoking her desire. Through his lips she derived his passion and it equaled her long-ignored need to be fulfilled. His mouth sought her neck, a highly erogenous zone for Terra, and she gasped his name.

They were backed into a dark corner, and when his thumbs grazed her breasts, Terra knew from the arrows of pleasure that shot through her that making love to Mike was imminent.

"The party's over here," Mike whispered in Terra's ear, his tongue drawing a sensual path of promises.

"Mike," Julianna's Chris said with enough force to break them apart. Terra inhaled fully for the first time since his lips touched hers.

"Yeah?"

"Party's over. Everyone's clearing out."

Terra kept her eyes on Mike. They flamed with smoldering desire. "Thanks for coming." Mike shook Chris's hand.

Julianna hugged Terra. "Being in love looks good on you."

"Thank you," she whispered as she waved to the departing couple.

Mike kept hold of her hand until the door closed behind them. Kenny G's Christmas CD started serenading and infusing their lust with passionate music.

Terra wanted fulfillment, but knew it'd be a few more days before she and Mike could consummate their passion.

Mike's hands worked methodically, untying the strings to her top. Every few seconds, his gray eyes would gaze at her and there she could see how a master looked when perfecting a work of art.

With his hands, he pushed aside the top, exposing her brown satin bra.

Terra held his hands even as he backed up toward the sofa. "Mike, I can't."

"Why?" he said, his hands nudging her down on the sofa. The touch of his lips to her chest seared her skin, and she shivered. With expert fingers he popped her strap, and she felt the tip of her nipple touch his lower lip.

"Have mercy." He groaned and drew his tongue across her breast again.

"Bad time of the month." She sighed as sparkles of pleasure soared through her. She watched with a shy smile as her words finally sank in.

His eyes were his most expressive quality. They reflected regret and longing. With his gaze fixed on hers, he devoured her breasts, sucking in her sugar-brown flesh, closing his eyes in his expression of pleasure. The way he laved them with hunger and wanting had her kicking her feet in helpless abandon. He could have her any day of the week. She knew that and from the moves of his mouth and hands, he knew it too.

"I have to go," she said, not moving away from him.

"Stay with me tonight," he demanded, finally releasing her swollen nipple and burying his face in her cleavage. He kissed her and she nearly darted off the sofa. If she didn't move now, she wouldn't be moving except to give him release from his primal prison.

She cupped his face between her hands. "I would but I really do have to study. Walk me home?"

Mike studied her for a long moment, his hands playing a slow sonata with her breasts. He finally looked down at her exposed skin, and with an inner strength only he possessed, began to slowly tie the strings to her top. He walked her to her door. "There will be another time."

Terra raised on her toes and kissed Mike with a passion that surprised even her. "Definitely another time."

Fifteen

Paint fumes clung to the early-morning air as Mike surveyed the painter's work. A deep, rich red covered the walls of his office and enclosed the spacious room. "Nice. No lines."

"I'm a professional, Mike. It'll be dry in a day, but I'd give it another day to set. By midweek, you can hang your pictures. Will there be anything else?"

Juan Velázquez discreetly folded the bill between his fingers and placed it on the counter.

Heading toward the counter by the kitchen, Mike felt a deep devotion to the man who'd been one of his first clients. He'd met Juan, a member of a Latino gang, nine years ago, across a table in an interrogation room, where he was being charged with murder.

In his intensely quiet way, Juan had challenged Mike to believe in his innocence, forcing Mike to view him as a person instead of just a member of a gang. The trial had lasted two weeks and in the end Juan was a free man.

Juan had vowed to be there any time Mike needed him. Today was one of those days. Once Mike had placed the last-minute phone call, Juan responded, taking care of everything.

Time had mellowed the soft-spoken Mexican giant who stood six feet tall, bulky in build. He was a family man now and owned a thriving painting business. Gentle brown eyes looked at Mike, assessing him. "Yo. What's on your mind, man?"

Mike slipped the bill off the counter and fingered it. "Just thinking about everything a man thinks about on a quiet Monday morning."

"Women problems, eh?" Juan chose a can from the soft drinks Mike had placed in a small ice-filled chest. He drank deeply and wiped his mouth with a paint-splattered hand. "Talk to me."

Considering how much he should divulge, he shrugged, choosing to keep it light. "What do you know about women, anyway? You've got three daughters under nine."

"That's the reason you should be asking me. I'm an expert. Don't forget Ana, she gave me hell when I was trying to get with her. I live with four women." Juan spoke a few words in Spanish then crossed himself. "So what's the problem? This senorita is not taking to the Crawford charm?"

The truth was sometimes a painful pill to swallow. Right now it was wedged in his throat. "She keeps on running. I take a step forward and she retreats two."

Juan waved his hand, his expression confident. "That's an easy one, man. Find out what she's running from and deal with it. What's the problem? Job? Family? Friends?"

Mike let the words sink in. "It's her family."

"You can't slay her dragons. She'll have to put that to rest herself." He tossed the soda can away and turned to gather his supplies. "You want to mail the check to the office?"

Grabbing his checkbook, Mike scrawled the amount and his signature. What Juan said made so much sense, it was elementary. He saw his friend out and hurried back to his apartment. The office looked great. Terra would be pleased.

He picked up the phone and dialed, choosing his words carefully when her voice mail clicked on.

"Terra, it's Mike. I've been trying to reach you for a couple of days. Give me a call at my home number. The painters are finished, and I hoped you could give me some advice as to where to set up the computers and the shelves." He hesitated a few seconds then said, "'Bye."

Hearing her voice made him want to tell her how much he enjoyed holding her, feeling caution slip away, leaving just a man and woman to face their true feelings. He wanted to feel the sweet abandon of her mouth pressed against his and the way she moved while in the throes of their kiss. Terra was pure erotica. And she had no idea.

He found the idea of her abandonment so appealing he looked forward to the next opportunity to experience it. Their breath mingling . . . the taste of her mouth and the other secrets her body held.

In the kitchen, he slapped meat on bread and bit into the dry sandwich. The party had been a success; he'd gotten her up there. She'd had fun. He'd kissed her. And, boy, had she kissed him back. He grinned and chased the sandwich with ice-cold soda.

Confident they ultimately wanted the same thing, he settled down to work and hammered out additional points for the Rathborne case, realizing that the A.D.A. didn't have a strong enough case against the judge for rape.

That charge would be the first he'd have dismissed. The investigators had gathered some interesting information on Meesook Lee. This wasn't the first time she'd had someone charged with rape—while married. That tidbit was a stick of dynamite or a diamond, depending on which side of the table you were on.

Feeling better about the case, he began to draft questions for his cross-examination.

Several hours passed as Mike made headway on *Rathborne* v. *Lee* then worked on the case against Blount and Blount. Working from home had its advantages. There was no secretary to disturb him, no phone calls and no last-minute office politics to manage. After about four hours, he slowly let his brain resurface from the legal jargon that was part of his culture and focused on his surroundings.

The early afternoon sun beat down on him, and he got up and switched on the air conditioner. He hadn't thought of Terra in the last few hours but was suddenly hit with a revelation that required deep thought.

What if eventually Terra wanted nothing to do with him because of her family's past legal troubles? Terra was proud of her accomplishments and her goals. She *had* to feel some discomfort with his being a lawyer and her family members having run-ins with the law.

As he recalled, he'd taken immense pleasure in throwing Jack out. But nobody wanted their relatives treated that way. Especially not a twin.

She seemed fine now, but he made a mental note to be prepared should the subject arise.

The eraser head of his pencil bounced off the table where he tapped it. Hopefully she'd come up before she had to go to class later tonight. But for now, he had to find a reason to keep her once she came to his apartment.

A brilliant idea struck him, and he grabbed a screwdriver and pliers from the toolbox and headed for his computers.

Terra placed the call she'd been wanting to make since Saturday morning. Now two days later, Mike's phone had already rung twice, each ring heightening her sense of anticipation and dread.

Being in his arms made her want to shuck her responsibility and her clothes, and give herself to him.

They'd only shared a kiss, a touch, but she'd enjoyed them. Immensely.

"Hello." His voice sent heat spreading to her middle.

"Hi, it's me. Terra O'Shaughssey." Goofy, she thought, rolling her eyes.

"Hi, Terra O'Shaughssey. It's Mike Crawford. How are you?"

"Fine. Wet." *Yikes.* "From the water hose."

His laughter turned her insides to mush. "You've been pruning flowers?"

"Yes."

"I bet they're as beautiful as someone I know."

"Who?" Childishly she hoped he'd say her name.

He chuckled low and sexy. In her imagination she conjured up an image of a seductive smile that was probably twisting his mouth. She couldn't help it, but she'd give the ring off her toe to see his smile right then. "You're playing a dangerous game, Ms. O'Shaughssey."

"I would never . . . play with you." Heat crept up her thighs and chest, and landed in her cheeks.

"Maybe all you need is a little convincing." A pregnant pause filled the void. "Another time."

"Well," she said, feeling disappointed.

"Where were we? Oh, yes. I was telling you how beautiful you are and you were flirting with me in that shy, unobtrusive way of yours." Then in a high voice, he said, "Oh, you mean me?" He giggled, his falsetto voice cracking. "Say it again, Mike."

Terra giggled, too, as her body responded to his masculinity. Fluid pooled in the valley between her legs.

In a normal voice he said, "Do you want to hear it again? Don't say no."

"Okay."

"You're as beautiful as any flower in your garden."

If she could have leaped for joy, she would be doing cartwheels all around the room. "That's nice. Thank you."

"You're welcome," he said, sounding just as comfortable. As if making her hot over the phone was an everyday occurrence. "My computers are waiting. Any chance you can come finish them today?"

She pulled her arm tighter over her middle as if to quell the rising anticipation of seeing him. "I can come up in the morning after you've gone to court."

"I don't have to be in court until tomorrow afternoon. How about today?"

"Today?"

"Right now." Desire rose in her belly.

"Right now?"

He chuckled in her ear. "Is there an echo on the phone?"

"Do you really need me?" Her heartbeat stopped.

His own breathing sounded labored across the phone lines.

"I'll let you answer that for yourself. Let yourself in. I'll be in the back."

Mike rose from his seat and headed for his bathroom. He needed to be in the farthest corner of the apartment, or else he'd jump her bones the minute he saw her and ask questions later.

As a distraction, he straightened the already neat room and threw clean laundry in the hamper. Dragging freshly laundered jeans by the leg, he tossed the denim onto the counter and knocked the romance novel into the black marble sink.

He adjusted the business card he used as a page finder and flipped to the page and immediately fell into the story.

Florence carried herself with the grace of a dancer. She was beautiful. Short with a round and high butt, just enough for his large hands. Pretty by today's standards of beauty, she was more beautiful than any woman he thought would ever want to be with him. As far as she knew, he didn't have a college education or letters following his name like her. As far as she knew his education had been taught at the school of life: prison. She didn't know about his bachelor's degree in criminal justice or his degree in law. Lying had been his only steady habit since going undercover for the Ghetto Boy Gang. Sometimes in the wee hours, when the smell of his clothes told her where he'd been and she'd accuse him of lying about what he'd been up to, when he could see how deep the hurt ran in her dark brown eyes, he'd want to confess it all. Instead, he'd hang his head and beg for another chance, stealing tears that shouldn't have been shed for him. This assignment had taught him one truth about himself: He was a selfish man. He took the undercover assignment in GB, the Ghetto Boy Gang, two years ago and was selfish to get involved with Florence six months ago knowing he was living a lie. Selfish to have the knowledge that he might die doing his job and she'd never know the truth about him and who he really was. Bruce remembered words his mother used to say, "Don't write a check your behind can't cash." Mama had been right about one thing. He was a hardhead because he'd done just that. It had been almost too easy. Letting her fall in love with him had been the ultimate selfish act. Selfish because he loved her back and couldn't do one damn thing about it. Tomorrow the export of guns from Canada was coming and if everything went according to plan, within a matter of days he could shed his street life and give her what she'd been asking for: the truth and a real commitment. Tonight he planned on seducing her again. The last time had been sweet. This time would be sweeter.

Mike closed the book as if it were on fire and headed toward the living room with a great deal of determination.

Sixteen

Terra usually found comfort in the mindless task of loading software, but for reasons she didn't want to explore, she was having a hard time today.

Mike sat across from her in the living room reading the romance novel she'd lent to him. Every once in a while he'd grimace or chuckle, but when he moaned, she wanted to know what had sparked such a reaction. He was driving her crazy.

"What's going on?" she asked, striving to sound casual.

He looked up from the page. "I'm near the end and this is a very romantic love scene. But he could learn a thing or two."

Terra recalled the scene he was referring to and thought that it was highly erotic. And thorough. Every time she read the book, tingles of longing reminded her how long it had been since her last partner. "How so?" She hoped she sounded casual, because if she wasn't careful, Mike would know what turned her on.

"For instance, he's this undercover cop in the hood and she's a dentist, right? He's supposed to be real 'street,' but if he's going to make love to her and make a good impression, why doesn't he take her to a nice hotel instead of this place?"

He sneered and shook his head. "Especially since he can't take her back to his real home. Why keep her in a shack in the worst part of town? That's not romantic. She wants him out of the life. He should at least show her he's making the effort and is willing to blend into her world."

"But wouldn't she be suspicious if he all of a sudden changed? If he takes her to an upscale place and has a credit card in a different name, she's going to wonder who he really is."

"But she's resisting him because of what he represents. He needs to show her he knows something else." Mike spoke as if he were trying a case before a jury.

Impressed by the depth at which he viewed the fictional romance, Terra defended the couple. "He'll blow his cover if he takes her out of the hood. One of her nurses already suspects he's the cop who killed her brother two years ago."

"Don't tell me the story; I'm almost done. I want to read how it ends."

He was kidding with her. Any minute he was going to throw the book on the floor and denounce romance novels and the people who wrote them. She watched him through narrowed eyes. He was sitting on the sofa, feet elevated by a leather ottoman, his eyes focused on the book. *Surely he's not enjoying it.*

What kind of man was he? Did real men read romances?

"How's it going?" he asked.

Terra jumped, startled. "Good. Great. So you like the book?"

He glanced up, gray eyes smiling. "Yeah."

She turned away her squinty eyes and directed her attention to the computer. After all, that was why she was there. After several minutes of frustrated tapping, she pressed all ten fingers on the keys and was rewarded with a series of angry beeps.

"Problem?" he asked casually.

"Something has happened to your drivers. I'll have to reload everything, including the WIN files. I'm going to need the start-up disk. I don't get it. The computer seemed fine the other day."

"How long will that take?"

Terra had the most beautiful eyes Mike had ever seen.

Everything was mirrored in them. Even her confusion. She brushed her hair out of her eyes. "A day or two." His heart sank. "I don't know," she shrugged, stared at the screen and tapped on the keys again. "Maybe more. Something funky is going on here."

He came and stood over her. "What's the matter?"

Her delicate hand extended toward the screen. "See there? I'm only getting a blinking cursor up in the corner. No directory. Nothing. The AUTOEXEC file is corrupted."

From his vantage point, he could see her lips partially. If only she'd turn just a bit. "Maybe some of the chips are bad. This PC has all my files on it."

"You didn't back up your files?"

"I usually do, but the new ones, no. I didn't have time before I left," he said. "I really need this to work."

She looked up, and he wanted to swoop down and claim her mouth. "I should be able to figure everything out. Give me some time."

She sat in his high-back leather office chair, and he turned it away from the makeshift desk until she faced him. One thing he loved was toys, and this chair was one of his favorites. It tilted, lifted, lowered and swiveled as well as offered a stimulating massage. Right now he tilted it back until Terra's feet cleared the floor and he had her almost where he wanted her.

She didn't look at him. Her mouth was set in a straight line and she'd folded her hands in her lap. He could hear the birds outside, the whir of the fan overhead, the increased beating of his heart. But it all faded into the periphery when words fell from her mouth as soft as the beginning patter of rain.

"Are you going to kiss me?"

He straddled her legs. "Yes, I am."

His mouth touched hers in a tender meeting. She didn't move another muscle, but her breathing quickened.

Turned on, Mike slid his tongue along her lips, and she involuntarily opened to him and sighed. He kissed her again with more insistence. When he felt the tip of her tongue touch his, he let go of the chair and pulled her to her feet.

With her snugly fit against his body, he felt himself growing. He wanted her to express the churning passion in her eyes and the ill-concealed quiver of her body. There was a lot of unspent desire below the surface, and he wanted to be the one to unleash it.

They stood against each other, his arms enfolding her. Black lashes rested against her cheeks and for the first time he noticed a chocolate-colored freckle on her cheek an inch from her nose.

He nipped at the beauty mark, causing her to rest her head on his chest. Manly pride swelled within him. Terra was his.

Her hands touched the outside of his thighs.

He clenched tight as she ran them lightly over his jeans, and around to his butt. He almost didn't feel her touch, but the gentleness ignited a fiery path for her to follow as her hands grazed his rear. When she squeezed lightly, it was he who inhaled sharply.

His eyes were locked on her face, and he was waiting for her to look at him, but she kept her lashes lowered and continued the exploration. Slowly they spanned the breadth of his muscular back and the depth of the center above his spine.

She moved up to his neck and with her hands familiarized herself with the cords and muscles.

Mike was sure he'd lose control if she didn't kiss him soon. But she surprised him with those same gentle hands when she cupped his face and brought it close to her lips. "Please kiss me," she whispered.

Their mouths met like the clash of cymbals. Teeth and tongue met and danced a wild coupling as his thumbs caressed the columns of her neck. He moved his mouth and body against hers in a way that demonstrated what he wanted to do yet held back from.

When he lowered himself onto the couch with her on top, he held tight knowing she would protest.

His mouth silenced her for a moment but she pushed against his chest with the heel of her hand and he released her mouth. Kiss-swollen lips puckered down at him.

"Don't like the view?" he asked as he licked her collarbone and felt her shudder.

Her breasts pressed into his chest as she lowered herself and he claimed her mouth again. Silky smooth black strands of hair fell across her forehead, and he smoothed them away.

Under his palm, he could feel her vibrant heartbeat.

"I've never been on top."

Mike chuckled deep in his chest. "You don't know what you're missing."

"I shouldn't be fooling around with you. I have work to do."

His large hands pressed against her bottom just in case she tried to get away. "This is work." His manhood pulsed in agreement. "Hard work."

Her expressive eyes rose in acknowledgment. "But I can't get a grade on this."

"Let's change that." Their mouths entangled in a slow tango. He captured her lower lip between his teeth, and she whimpered and ground her hips into his. She tore away and buried her head against his neck.

"You got an A," he said, his voice raspy, his hands freeing her collarbone of the pink blouse that covered it. Kisses served as unspoken words as he rained them over her skin, skin that was soft as a newly budded rose petal. He couldn't get enough of her, and he told her so in whispered words and soft sweet kisses against her cheeks and eyes.

He nudged her chin up until she looked at him.

Terra tried to duck away, afraid he'd see the desire in her eyes. Feelings she'd no longer felt possible raged through her blood, igniting a fire so large she was afraid it would consume her. In Mike's eyes, she could see what he wanted and it wasn't just sex. He wanted all of her. Her desire, her heart, yes, her climax, but her soul, too. She couldn't sacrifice that for one afternoon of delight.

She pushed back, trying to separate herself from the man who'd broken years of barriers and threatened her future dreams. But he held on. Following her up, holding her against him, whispering that everything was going to be all right.

"I'm not letting you go that easily." They held each other and rocked slowly. "What's on your mind, Terra?"

Her cheek rested against his shoulder, and she wished she didn't have to move, but he wanted an answer and she could tell by the way he held her, he meant it when he said he wasn't going to let her go.

"I have dreams," she said, letting him in the crack of the door. "I can't sacrifice them for anyone. Remember when I told you you make me feel loose? I feel like a bird whose broken wing has been fixed and is ready to fly."

"You don't want to fly alone," he said with matter-of-fact authority. "Not the way you held and kissed me. I'm not a threat to you." He gathered her closer to him, making her rest her head against his shoulder. "Tell me how you feel right now."

Her heartbeat thundered. "Cherished. Special."

"Safe?"

Her breath hitched. What would that admission cost her? If she was willing to walk away, then it would cost her nothing. "Yes, safe."

He pulled her back suddenly, and her eyes snapped open. "Then what are you afraid of?"

She turned away and he shook her until their gazes met. "I'm afraid of you. I can't rely on anyone but myself."

He let her go and she went to stand by the balcony door. The long, gray skirt she'd chosen with care that morning tickled her ankles and the pink blouse was now wrinkled and gaping in the front.

With her back to him she righted her clothing and tried to straighten her thoughts as well. "You are a nice man."

"Don't say it." He moved behind her and soon was at her side. "Don't give me the brush-off because you're trying to erect barriers to protect yourself from your own emotions. I want to know what's on your mind. In your heart."

"You're newly divorced."

"But I didn't die with the marriage. I'm a man. Flesh and blood and I'm still here. And the woman who's captured my attention is here too. Don't toss that away."

"I don't want to." Rivulets of anticipation climbed her spine. "Let it be what it is."

She bit her thumbnail and chills ran up her arms.

"How?" She wanted to hear from the man who made her feel so special.

He didn't say a word but he spread his hands across her back. Warmth crawled across her skin like an infectious virus. Soon she was trembling from his heat. Convinced, she said, "I'd better get back to work."

"Work? Is that all that's on your mind?"

Her gaze traveled the length of him. "I think of lots of things. So, if you don't mind, work is most important now. I have class tonight."

He took her hands and brushed them with his.

"Why are you so worried about your class? Every time you talk about it you tense up."

He knew more about her than she'd realized. "I have to pass an oral exam to qualify and endure a two-hour interview to be considered for the job."

He nodded, continuing to sway. "And that's got you worried?"

"A little." He pressed his arms into her back and she confessed. "A lot."

He tugged and felt the soft skin of her palm heat his arms as they gently traveled up to his elbows.

Her words said one thing but her actions said another.

"I'll help you study."

She shook her head and smiled. "Help me? I have to do this myself."

"We can practice together. I can come down and go over your lesson with you in preparation for the interview."

With the exception of Margaret, no one close to her had ever offered to help her while expecting nothing in return. Except her grandfather. Except Tim.

"What do you want from me?"

"Your computer expertise before I throw this PC in the trash."

"I can fix it," she said calmly.

"And I can help you. Is there more?"

"Yes, there is," she said.

"You're so good with defining things. What do you think it is?"

Was he mocking her as her family had done so often when they didn't like what she was saying? Or did he really care to know her thoughts? She studied him for one long moment. His eyes didn't harbor the anger or jealousy that she felt every time she went home. Mike wasn't a member of her family. She had to remember that. For the moment she was safe. Waves of relief swept over her and for the second time that day she lifted her arms and held him close.

"We're two people who share a mutual interest in each other."

He smirked, his mouth turning down. "That's very clinical."

The length of him was still pressed between them. She squirmed but was locked in his strong embrace.

"I'm not going to get rid of it if you keep that up. Be still."

She relaxed, and to their own music, they moved. Nothing fast, just the inner rhythm of two people falling in love. The idea scared her, presenting too many possibilities, so she pushed it away, letting nothing intrude on their groove. The pulsing rod beat between them reminding her of his wants. Her core was ready for him; with each involuntary beat of his need, she felt a response in kind.

Soon, her body would answer.

He slowed their dance. "Look at me."

She let her head fall back. Gracious, he was handsome and the beard only enhanced his good looks.

"I don't know the common terms or the best way to say this, but . . ."

His hesitation caused her to want to pull back, but he held onto her tight and close. "What is it?"

"Will you be my girlfriend?"

Laughter rose from her belly, and she couldn't stifle the giggles. She laughed with her head thrown back, then covered her mouth with one hand.

"What's so funny? If this is the latest way to say no, it stinks."

"It's not that. You just sounded so official." She imitated him. "Will you be my girlfriend? Will you be my secretary?"

He frowned. "Will you be my secretary? Where did that come from?" They both laughed and she hugged him back. "I guess it does sound funny, but my heart was in the right place."

She wanted to touch his cheek, but she settled for stroking his back. Why would she consider such a thing? Because he made her feel whole. Even if it didn't last, she wanted to be wanted. After all she'd been putting him through, he still wanted her. "I know it was. Yes, I think I'd like to."

The next thing she knew she was being twirled in the air. "Mike! Put me down."

"As my official girlfriend, you have to get accustomed to public displays of affection.

"Really? Is this like a job?"

His eyebrows wiggled. "We'll make up the rules as we go along."

Terra groaned. "Rules?"

He kissed her knuckles and they rocked from side to side. "We'll take it slow. I have one more thing to ask you."

"We've been going together for fifteen seconds, and you've got something else? What is it?"

"My family is throwing a retirement party for my father on Saturday. Will you be my guest?"

A curiosity to see the other Crawfords in action sprang to life. Why not? She hadn't been to a good party in a while. Save Mike's illegal shindigs. "I trust it's not going to be here?"

"A smarty, that's what I've got. No. You don't have to worry. So?"

She felt as if she were a clown with that large smile on her face. "I'd love to go."

A thundering knock shook the front door. Terra jumped while Mike held her hand.

"Terra! It's Samir. My toilet is flooding. Come quick."

He kissed her affectionately. "Your work is never done."

"I left a note on the door that I'd be here. I hope my job won't be a problem for you," she said soberly.

"Terra, go take care of it. It's not a problem."

Seventeen

Rathborne was calm today. Court had been in session for just a few hours, and the prosecutors had firmly established that Meesook Lee and Rathborne had a relationship. Mike had expected that.

The prosecutors called eyewitnesses to confirm dinner meetings at restaurants, dates at the Fox Theater for concerts and showings at the High Museum.

As hard as Mary Beth worked to establish that a relationship existed, Mike worked just as hard to prove that in all their public sightings, nothing was amiss. They never argued, appeared angry or fought. Quite the contrary, they seemed smitten with each other. Before Mary Beth could object, one of her witnesses testified that Rathborne and Meesook had admitted they were in love.

The testimony went on for hours but at the end of the day, Mike was happy with how the evidence had unfolded. But he wasn't planning the victory ceremony yet.

Mary Beth was known for surprises. And he worked diligently to have his own surprise for her as well.

Tired from the rigorous day in court, Mike planned his evening with care. He was going to go home, eat a quiet meal and prepare for tomorrow. And see Terra.

He parked right in front of the building just after dusk and cut off his headlights.

The street was lit by high streetlights and the glow from

indoor televisions. Crickets and frogs stirred the air with noise and a gusty wind blew leaves and branches along the street. Rain was on the way. He sat in his car and let his body relax. His muscles ached from lack of exercise, and he immediately envisioned Terra riding her bike.

Since they were boyfriend and girlfriend, maybe they could go riding together. He smiled at the term and leaned his head back against the headrest. It felt good to just sit.

A tap on the window caught his attention, and he cracked open his eye and looked at the visitor.

Terra looked in at him, her eyes bashful but concerned. "Are you all right?"

Covered to her thighs in a blue granny-type sweater, with her arms crossed to keep it together, Terra stood like a beacon of light against the dark, windy sky.

"I'm fine, beautiful. What are you doing out here?"

"I—I was looking out the window."

She stopped speaking and looked at him with curious eyes. "And?"

"I saw you sitting here."

He grinned. "And?"

Color rose in her cheeks and she sighed. "That's all. I saw you sitting here, and I wondered if you were all right." He gathered his briefcase in his hand and opened the driver-side door. She stepped back and kept her eyes averted. "I'm all right. How are you?"

She walked by his side and stepped inside the door as he held it. "I'm fine."

They were inside the door of her apartment, in Terra's special world of fresh flowers and whale music on the CD player.

"Liar."

A modest smile parted her lips. "I'm not lying."

"I should tell you something before you proceed with that lie, Ms. O'Shaughssey, I'm the best lie detector in Georgia. I can sniff a lie at fifty paces."

He took her in his arms and kissed her soundly. She tasted

sweeter than he remembered, sealing the memory in his brain for the times to come.

Her mouth had kept his pace, and danced with his as he pulled her close and took more from her. Even as he backed off to leave himself room on the speeding train he traveled on, he could feel her following him, pressing herself into him, wanting more.

"We'd better stop before this goes too far," she warned as her arms circled his neck and her nipples bore holes into his chest.

"Don't take advantage of me like this," he teased, holding her firmly against her waist. "We have to stop now."

She giggled and met his gaze. "You're crazy. Are you hungry?"

Mike couldn't keep the shock from his voice; he was sure it was reflected on his face. "You cook?"

"How else would I eat?"

He and April ordered out or went out almost every night of their marriage. He'd grown accustomed to eating in restaurants and having strangers wait on him. He'd cooked to impress Terra, but it wasn't his forte. "I guess I didn't think about that."

She backed away and walked toward the kitchen. "You've cooked for me. You don't cook for yourself?"

"Sure, sometimes. I eat out a lot. What's for dinner?" He clapped his hands and rubbed them together.

A worn, blue pot holder mitt hung from her hand. "You don't have to put on a good face for me. I don't eat out a lot because I live on a budget. I don't want to make you uncomfortable by changing your customs."

"I'm not uncomfortable. I'm just used to things being different. I'm glad you cooked for us."

Apprehensive, she shot him a sideways look. "You are?"

"This is a wonderful surprise. I'll set the table and you check on the food. We eat; then we study. What did you say we were having again?"

"Grilled rat stew."

Mike froze and Terra smiled. "Gotcha."

The textbooks had been put away an hour ago, along with the legal briefs for the case Mike had been working on. She hadn't done well on the practice interviews but after they'd been at it for three hours, Mike decided she'd had enough for one day. Terra breathed a sigh of relief.

She sat next to him on the sofa in her living room, full and comfortable. They'd opted for a night without television, neither wanting a movie to wreck the flow of their contentment.

There were so many things she wanted to ask him about his life, his family and his marriage, but she didn't know where to begin.

At her grandfather's knee she learned that you can't chart a path if you don't know the road you've traveled and she wanted to know everything about Mike Crawford.

Early in the evening Mike had loosened his tie and rolled up his shirtsleeves. His shirt was white and crisp, even after having suffered through a full day's wear and his navy pants cooled the brightness of the starched white cotton. No jewelry adorned his hands except for an expensive gold watch that marked the twelve o'clock hour with a large, sparkling diamond.

"Did you always want to be an attorney?"

He laughed and drew her legs onto his lap. His hands caressed the length from her ankle to her knee. "Believe it or not, I was the class clown. I used to get in trouble for imitating the kids and instigating problems."

"You, an instigator, I couldn't imagine."

He chuckled at her softly delivered sarcasm. "I used to put frogs in the teachers' desk."

Terra chuckled and languished in the feel of his hands on her legs. "What was the worst prank you ever pulled?"

It was his turn to chuckle. "Well, my parents were at their

wits' end over my being so disobedient so they sent me to a small Catholic school so the sisters could straighten me out. I hated that place. Nobody wanted to have fun, plus the girls were sectioned off from the boys.

"Anyway, Sister Mary Perpetual was my chemistry teacher and she had a thing for administering punishment with thickly taped rulers. She wouldn't just hit you. She'd raise her hand above her head and bring that thing crashing down on your hand again and again."

"That's cruel." She leaned forward, captivated by his easy manner and his lack of self-consciousness.

"After the first time, I swore I would hitch a ride in a cattle car going anywhere before I let her hit me again. Anyway one day, somebody had been smoking in the boys' bathroom and she was gunning for me. She accused me straight out and when I denied it, she pulled out her ruler and said she was going to punish the sin out of me. When she finished, I couldn't sit down for a week and I vowed to get her back."

"What did you do?"

"My uncle lived up in Conyers, Georgia, and he'd told us about this house that had been condemned for having been built over a snake pit."

Terra shivered and held herself to keep her skin from crawling. "Oh, goodness. You didn't go in there and get a snake, did you?"

"I did. It wasn't as dilapidated as people had said and there weren't snakes swinging from the chandeliers, but I found a small black snake, threw it in a pillowcase and got out of there.

"Early Monday I arrived at school and went to her class. She had this yellow canary named Peter, and she allowed it to fly all over the classroom. It was over by the window sitting on the sill when I got there.

"I tossed the closed pillowcase on her chair and took off. About an hour later we heard this bloodcurdling scream and everyone ran for her class. It seemed the snake was able to get out of the bag and into Peter's cage. When Peter flew back into the cage, the snake ate him.

"Sister Perpetual retired from teaching that same day. And I thought I was finally free until I got home and my father was waiting for me."

"How did he know you did it?"

"The pillowcase was from a set my parents had had since they'd gotten married. My father tanned my hide and when he was done, I pleaded not to return to that school. He agreed but sentenced me to six months of hard labor at my Uncle Jed's construction crew moving rocks.

"The work was so backbreaking, I decided I was probably better with my mouth than my hands. I started reading the law journals that came for my father and even accompanied him to court several times. I got hooked on law at the age of fifteen."

"Are you still as passionate about it?"

"Even more so."

"Did you ever work as a prosecutor?" she said quietly.

"For a short time up in Marietta."

"You don't sound as if you liked it."

"I didn't."

"Why?"

"Because sometimes the system just didn't work. I'd rather sit on the side of the table where I can control who I represent rather than have to deal with whatever comes my way."

She struggled before she asked her next question. "I-is there such a thing as rehabilitation?"

He shrugged and looked at her closely. "Yes. The person has to want it to work more than they want to do something harmful." He drew in a deep breath. "It's hard to know who will and won't be saved, but I try damned hard to find those who want to save themselves."

She nodded and studied her hands. His hands continued their exploration from her calf to her ankles. She was completely relaxed.

"You'd make a good lawyer," Mike said.

Apprehensive, she gave him a skeptical look. "What makes you say that?"

"Anybody who can memorize the five major points of resolving conflict and cite credible arguments to support their views would make a good attorney."

"I'm too nervous. How am I going to get through this interview? I'm too shy to get in front of a roomful of people and try to convince them of anything."

"I know better than that. I heard you cleared my apartment in less than a minute."

"That was different."

"Then why be a property manager?"

"Because I like what I do. I'm good at this. I'd be good at that other job if I didn't have to endure a two-hour interview. What could they possible want to know for two hours?"

"Terra." He said her name in a way that made her want to hear it from his mouth forever. "You have the skills, the qualities and the presence to do this job well. Stop worrying that somebody is waiting to drop a bomb on you. Once you get this job, you're set. I'll tell you what." He gently placed her feet on the floor and reached toward the coffee table. "You need a diversion."

"Like what?"

"A good romance." Quickly he picked up the romance novel she'd been reading and started to read aloud. His voice was full and expressive, giving life to the words on the page. She leaned her head back and closed her eyes, letting the people come to life and make the gestures he described.

In the story, Mike had to decide if his company would purchase Sylvia's family's restaurant and drive them out of business. He loved her. He'd admitted as much to his father but had been given an ultimatum: Do the right thing for the sake of his family or lose his career.

Sylvia had seen the buyout coming for months, but her family hadn't wanted to face the fact that the business would close without an infusion of capital. She tried to put her feelings for Mike aside, but her love for him warred with her loyalty to her family.

The thin pages of the paperback rustled as Mike closed the book. He kept a finger wedged inside to keep his place. "What do you think she should do?"

"She should follow her heart."

"Is that what you would do?"

"No, and that's the reason why I want her to."

Terra sank into the couch and closed her eyes as Mike finished the story. Michael compromised with his family and didn't close down her family's business but bought it out with Sylvia's blessings. Sylvia was made V.P. in the new company and they planned to work together to build an empire in the soul-food restaurant business.

At the very end, they got together and planned their family and future.

Mike seemed pensive as he placed the novel on the table and took their wineglasses to the kitchen. His mood surprised her because she, too, was feeling down, but Terra tried to close in on the source of her abrupt mood swing. She would never have children. Born with a birth defect, she'd always been sterile. That didn't stop her from loving children and offering a nurturing heart to her nieces and nephews, but she knew she'd never be a mother. Tim had been all right with that, wanting to adopt or become foster parents. But her life had changed since she and Tim split up.

Now she knew she could give back to the world without having to contribute children to it also. She'd accepted that long ago, so she didn't understand why her mood had taken such a turn, but then she realized.

Just like Sylvia, she could marry a man named Mike and spend the rest of her life with him. What if he wanted children? His own flesh and blood, his own offspring to continue his name? Sure, they were just dating, but at their ages, wouldn't getting married and starting a family be something they might consider down the line? He came back into the living room, dimmed the lights and was about to sit down when she said, "Why did you get divorced?"

His eyes widened, then a shuttered look encompassed them. "If I tell all my secrets in one day, we won't have anything to talk about next week." He offered her a hand up and kept it until they were standing at the front door. "Are we studying tomorrow?" he asked.

"You don't have to. I could try to arrange for another study group."

"Or you could let me help you. I enjoyed it."

Desperation filled her. She grabbed him and hugged him close. Her lips sought his in a kiss that spoke her emotions. She wanted love and happiness and wanted him to have it too. Over and over she laved him with her tongue, touching and experiencing him raw and unfettered.

Her hands traveled the length of his back, and she pressed her body into his. Her breasts ached and deep in the valley between her legs, she contracted with want. It was time, but she didn't know if he would take her.

His day had been long and if she had her way, it wouldn't end soon.

Terra forced herself to break the intense coupling but stayed in his arms. He rubbed her back, holding her as if he never wanted to let go. "It's going to be all right," he said again and again, his voice leaden with somberness. "I don't want to let you go." In his eyes raged a storm. She wanted to be close to him, wanted to feel that as alone as she felt, there was another in the universe who shared those same emotions.

"I can't give you all of me," she said, her hand tracing his beard, his lips, his mouth. Their gazes met.

"Give me what you can."

The CD ended and they embraced. "Come with me." She took him by the hand and led him to her room.

Eighteen

Terra hadn't meant to be so bold with Mike but his need met hers and with each touch, blinded her with desire. His mouth on her shoulder made her tingle and shake, and her hands pushed at his clothing. The starched white shirt landed on the floor in a heap of discarded, unnecessary adornments.

He tasted her face with his tongue, his teeth grazing her chin as he moved downward to the nipples that stood out at proud attention.

How wonderful it felt to be in his arms as he suckled and savored the richness of her flesh and sent her quickly soaring high toward the stratosphere.

"You're beautiful," she murmured, breaking into the cacophony of pleasured moans and pleasing grunts. When his mouth covered her other breast, she let out a long moan of pure satisfaction. Nothing could feel better.

Her head lolled as he stroked the tips with his tongue and slid his hand into the nest between her legs.

Terra parted for him, her hands pressing into his back to hurry him into filling her. He touched slickness, and his eyes flew open and met hers, a mixture of wonder and gratitude.

"It's been a long time," she said, when he found the warm cave and pressed his finger into it. Involuntarily she rose to meet each thrust, aware of his hot member twitching on her thigh.

"For me, too. I won't last long," he said, when she pressed a sealed condom into his palm.

Terra felt shameless as she lay open and eager for him as he rolled the condom over his shaft.

"Doesn't matter. Make love to me." She twined her legs around his back and arched until her rear was off the bed.

Mike plunged into her, thrilled at such a warm, wet welcome. He held himself still for seconds, savoring the heat of her center, the arousing brush of her nipples against his chest and the tickle on his back from her nails.

He pressed his mouth into hers, wanting all the pleasure she could give and more. He started moving inside her, pushing in and out, taking his pleasure and giving it back. She lay beneath him watching his face, her hands bunching the new growth of chest hair between her fingers before they came to rest on his shoulders.

She loved this man, she knew, and would love him forever. That tremendous emotion drove her to want him even more and her body tightened. Her hands on his back, her chest to his, the very essence of her body around his manhood. "Thank you," she whispered. "More."

Terra urged him deeper and his control snapped. One fine thread at a time. "Terra," he growled.

"I'm coming, too," she said, and he would swear from the heels of her feet to the tips of her hair that she convulsed.

His name on her lips sent him spiraling over.

He rocked her back and forth, thankful, grateful they'd met and shared the ultimate gift. As her limp legs wound around his waist and his body crushed her into the mattress, he shifted, separating her body from his with a soft pull.

She groaned and he looked down quickly. Her eyes were closed, her face void of expression. Her mouth was still and if he didn't know better he'd have thought her asleep.

But her fingers drew back and forth against his back as he pulled her close to him. Chest to chest, thigh to thigh, manhood to womanhood.

Suddenly she raised and rubbed her cheek against the coarse hair on his. "That was wonderful."

If he'd been named king of a small country, he wouldn't have felt more proud. "I do my best."

"Can we do it again?" Slowly her eyes opened and pure hunger stared back at him.

He engulfed her in a large hug. "You flatter me," he said, his voice rough with emotion. Mentally, he was a step away from telling her he loved her but held back. This wasn't the time, with them so rife with emotion. Sex was emotional all by itself. He wouldn't confuse what he felt now with anything else. When he told her of his love, he'd be one-hundred-percent sure and she would believe him.

Lying on her side, she cupped his face.

"Are you sleepy?"

"No."

"Hungry?"

"Yes." She sat up and reached for a robe at the end of the bed.

He reached out and snaked her hand with his. "Where are you going?"

"To get you something to eat."

Mike removed the belt from around her waist. Her black beauty called to him.

"I've got all I need right here." The silk slipped from her feminine shoulders and pooled at her feet.

"What are you waiting for?"

"Not a thing." This time when they made love he maintained control until he was sure she was satisfied; then he allowed himself to climax.

Terra lay flat on her stomach, her breath coming in ragged puffs. He leaned on one propped-up hand and stroked the column between her shoulder blades with the other.

Streetlights stole darkness from the room and highlighted diagonal lines across Terra's body. The light showcased her eyes, mouth, breasts, navel and the perfectly shaped mound of hair between her legs.

Time had crept by until the wee hours were upon them. Neither slept, both knowing there would be a price to pay tomorrow. Neither cared.

Terra moved her legs and groaned. "I'm so sore."

"Come on," he said and helped her from the bed.

Inside the shower, he programmed a warm temperature and brought Terra closer. Their hands linked and warm water cascaded down her back. Even in the fluffy pink shower cap, nothing could diminish her beauty. She leaned her face against his shoulder and rested her cheek there. "Mmm, better," she whispered. "You sure know how to take care of a woman." She gasped and covered her mouth, her eyes wide. "I didn't mean to imply anything."

"I know you didn't. Be still." The cloths he'd found on the basin were folded into nice tubes, and he chose one and hurried back to her. Absorbing the warm water in the cloth, he caressed her body, taking extra care at the sensitive spots.

He wanted to fill his mouth with her, but she'd had enough for one night. He shut off the water, and he bundled her into a fluffy towel and walked her back to bed. Naked save for the light streaking in, she sat on the edge and watched him invade her space.

"Do you have pajamas in here?"

"Second drawer in the middle."

It was odd to watch him handle her things, naked and virile, so sure of himself as he held up a sturdy cotton top and bottom.

Terra pulled on the pajamas and crawled under the covers that smelled of them. Her eyes were heavy, yet she kept them open absorbing the sight of him in her space. It felt so right. She didn't know what to say.

Mike gathered his clothes and slipped into his boxers, slacks and shirt, leaving the shirt unbuttoned. He lowered himself beside her, cupped her head and brought his mouth to hers in a sweet, sensual kiss.

"I've got an early morning tomorrow."

"You're an important man."

The words stopped him and he looked deep into her eyes. "Not so important that I have to leave your bed right after I've made love to you. I have to get up at five. That's only a few hours away."

"I understand," she said, snuggling against his thigh.

"You're a nice woman. Don't make it too easy."

Her eyes widened. "What are you saying?"

"If I'm not giving you what you need, tell me."

"I'm Terra." Her eyes widened as she looked at him. "Remember that. Stay for a while."

He placed a tender kiss on her collarbone, then shed his clothes. "I will."

Nineteen

Judge Jones looked across her desk at the two attorneys, unamused at the recent turn of events.

Mary Beth Pearsoy perched on the edge of her seat, eager to throw her typical bone into the pot of boiling stew that featured Rathborne as the main ingredient.

"I want John Moxby added to my witness list," Mary Beth argued in the closed chambers. "During the course of our ongoing investigation, we discovered information that supports our theory that Rathborne and Lee had a violent relationship, thereby adding credence to the claim that he raped her."

Mike kept his leg draped across his knee, feeling anything but casual. He leaned forward to make his point. "It's too late. Tomorrow we begin to present our case. If the prosecutor had this witness under wraps and failed to get him here in a reasonable time, we won't help her case by allowing her to present him now."

"Judge Jones, this eyewitness's testimony is crucial."

"I don't care if your witness was splattered in the fight, you cannot present new testimony after you've rested your case."

The judge unzipped her robe and hung it on an austere, wooden coat tree. Part of the original furniture from the old courthouse, it stood tall and regal, just like the judge.

Mike stood and Mary Beth rose slowly.

"Your Honor, the prosecutor hasn't proven her case of rape. The physical evidence doesn't support the accusation, nor does the emergency room report or the phantom teeth marks the client claimed she had pictures of but hasn't submitted into evidence.

"This case is based loosely on circumstantial evidence and proves nothing against Judge Rathborne. I move for a dismissal."

"It's *Mr.* Rathborne and I object!"

"Ms. Pearsoy, I told you before we started that I would not tolerate stalling or incompetence. You haven't proven your case. The rape charge is dismissed."

"Your Honor." Mary Beth bunched her hands into fists. "It's important that Rathborne be charged. He *must* serve time for his crimes."

"Then do your job!" The judge huffed and stabbed the air with her finger. "Why does this sound like some kind of vendetta?"

In Mary Beth's eyes raged a storm. Mike wished he could help her, but her case was weak. He wouldn't even have to call most of his witnesses. Rathborne would never have to take the stand in his own defense.

Mary Beth rubbed her thumb and forefinger together again and again. "People like Rathborne think they're above the law. The rape charge will get him five-to-fifteen. He'll be dead before he sees the light of freedom again. This isn't a vendetta, but rather an assurance. If anybody brings Rathborne down, it'll be me. May I be dismissed?"

The judge studied the woman carefully then waved her hand.

"Maybe I should have given *you* a more stern talking to before we started. You don't need another *W* in your win/loss column. *This is not personal.* Do you understand me, Mary Beth?"

"I respectfully disagree. Am I dismissed?"

Mike's voice stopped his colleague. "Lee and Rathborne were legal adults when they began their relationship. While immoral, it's not worth the system's time. Why not dismiss the case in its entirety?"

Judge Jones sighed wearily. "We have to play this one out. We'd be perceived as protecting one of our own. Everyone do your job and let's end this."

Outside the office, Mary Beth smoked a cigarette. She pulled deeply on the filter, her cheeks caving in with the drag. Slumped in her seat, defeat hunched thirty years into her slender frame.

Mike sat beside her on a long bench. The ghosts of justice echoed in the silence, guilt and innocence vying for power in the closed building. A frazzled law clerk hurried by, and although the day was over for them, her day wouldn't be over for at least another seven hours. Law clerks averaged at least eighty hours a week.

"Be glad you're not her," he said, wanting to help Mary Beth if he could.

"I envy that anorexic, chain-smoking, gaunt-looking twig." He looked at the clerk again. Her skirt hung limply where her butt should have been.

"You need glasses. Any second now her body is going to rebel and eat itself."

Mary Beth grunted and watched smoke curl from the cigarette tip.

"What's going on, Mary Beth?"

Blue eyes he'd come to know as intelligent, competitive and, in rare casual occasions, funny, were clouded with dread.

He'd seen her lose before, just as had she witnessed his defeats, but this was different. She seemed almost desperate.

"Justice," she said, her eyes fixed on the large eagle on the floor, "isn't always fair." She growled deep in her chest like a bear, stood and held out her hand. When he took it, she pulled him to his feet. "Let's go have a drink and forget we're lawyers."

"Of course." He trudged alongside, knowing she'd share no more. Within minutes they were in the parking lot. "I want to help you," he offered.

"I know you do and do you know what stinks? You can't. Did I tell you I'm coming to your dad's retirement party?"

"I'm glad you'll be there."

She nodded firmly. "Come on. I'll buy you a drink and then head home and let my husband make mad, passionate love to me."

"Hey, I'll take you up on that."

She threw up her hands and climbed inside his truck. "I'm already spoken for." Through this tough moment, her wry sense of humor peeked through.

"Good thing I was thinking of somebody else."

She stared out the window, her body ramrod straight, her voice echoing her inner pain. "Yeah. That is very good."

The skies threatened to release an autumn shower that would break the cycle of endless heat, and Mike was glad to see the first smattering of rain.

He paused outside Terra's door, knocking, waiting. She'd been on his mind all day. In court today, a tall, brown-skinned sista with short black hair had walked in, and with her back to him, she resembled Terra.

His heart had jumped and started a fast trot of surprise at the thought that she had come to see him in action. But then she turned and he recognized one of Atlanta's newest reporters preparing to get a story.

Judge Jones's ruling to ban cameras and reporters had been overturned by a higher court, so the gallery was full of press.

Mary Beth's mood had affected him, leaving him melancholy. Tired, he craved a glass of wine, a steak and the touch of a beautiful woman. Only one came to mind.

Heading up to his apartment, Mike slowed as he walked down the hall. Terra sat outside his door, legs curled beneath her, her head in a book. He loved seeing her look so content. His body started to relax. "Hey," he said softly.

Seeing the light in her eyes brought a smile to his lips and a featherlight feeling to his chest. He'd been wanting to see her smile all day.

"Hey." She stood up and fixed an old-fashioned knit sweater around her shoulders.

He deactivated the lock and pushed open the door. Terra radiated nervous tension, and it was all he could do not to take her in his arms and force her fears aside. Peace was what he craved tonight, and he wanted to share that quietness with her.

Once inside, he tossed his keys and briefcase onto the chair and let his eyes feast on her. "How was your exam?"

"Excellent."

"Baby," he said, taking her face between his hands. "That's wonderful."

"Yes, it is." She unbuttoned his suit and wrapped her arms around his waist. Quietly she said, "I got the interview."

He leaned back, pleased. He knew how much she wanted the Vanderbilt job. She'd be good at it too. If only she believed in herself more. If only she'd been allowed to enjoy her successes and have her family share them with her. He despised what they'd done to her and wished he could change her past but knew he was powerless to.

"You'll ace the interview, I know it." He wished to see the light of joy in her eyes. He looked deeply and gathered her close.

They should be celebrating, shouting for joy, but Terra was distracted, afraid that the one thing she wanted badly, she wouldn't get.

He'd only felt this kind of hopelessness when he'd failed to make a baby with April. But he could do something about this. "When's the interview?"

"Monday morning at eight."

He whistled. *Not enough time.* "Just enough time."

"For what?" She said without the confidence he knew she needed to win the interviewers over.

"To get in some serious practice interviews."

"Oh, that." From her pocket, she pulled a computer card encased in a sleeve. "That's why I'm here. You need a new network card in order for me to get you on the Internet. I can have it installed right away and then get you loaded again."

He eased the card from her hand and tossed it on the chair alongside his keys. Taking the sweater off her shoulders, he tossed it in the vicinity of the chair. He started on her blouse. Lately he loved pink.

"That easy, huh?" he said, unable to resist her perky chin. He knew it was that easy because he'd sabotaged the one inside the computer. He'd wanted her there and she was with him now. One day he'd tell her of his deed and enjoy making it up to her.

Right now, they both needed to rest. Not think about work. Not tonight. Unfortunately, his opening arguments were first thing in the morning and no matter how disheartened Mary Beth seemed, a night with her husband might rejuvenate her fighting spirit. He'd hate to get waxed at the courthouse because he hadn't been prepared. "You hungry?" he asked, thinking wine and Terra. Forget the steak.

He nuzzled her earlobe, heat growing in his loins. Damn, he wished he had better control.

Her slim fingers caressed his cheek. "Not really? You?"

"For you."

"That's nice," she said with solemn assurance. First Mary Beth, and now Terra. Women were too serious. His hand slipped down and covered her breast and the weight of the naked globe flooded his body with memory.

"Shall we?"

Her eyes held mystery. "After you."

His fingers linked with hers, and he guided her to his bedroom.

Slowly Mike peeled each piece of clothing from Terra's warm body. Her body was an artist's masterpiece, and if it took him a lifetime to memorize every line curve and dip, all the better.

When he rid himself of his clothes, she reached for him, circling his neck with her arms, her breasts sliding up his chest as she raised to kiss him.

The simple move sent his emotions into orbit, and he pulled her close. The tangle of curls between her legs tickled his member, and he flinched in response. He wanted her, but he also wanted their lovemaking to last and be memorable.

Terra wedged her foot on the bed, urging him and he rained kisses down on her face and shoulder and neck. Her breasts were high and tipped with chocolate peaks and when his mouth covered one, she squirmed in his arms, moaning her delight. She breathed hard as she held his face to her breast and ran her hand down his back, raking up with her nails.

The sensation made him shiver with longing for her, so he laid her down and tried to talk himself into slowing down.

Their mouths met in a frantic kiss, and she guided him back to her breast and cried out, her head thrown back as she breathed his name, "Mike, Mike, Mike."

He had never heard a more beautiful sound. She urged him with her hands on his shoulders as he journeyed down, sliding his cheek across the apex of her body and biting her thigh.

Her long leg shot up, and she rocked from side to side, urging him, begging him to give her release.

His tongue touched the button first and she bucked up; then his mouth and tongue and teeth went on a journey of pleasure.

Terra's climax came quickly and when he rolled them, putting her on top, hot tears hit his shoulder. He slipped on a condom and took her with an urgency that shocked and embarrassed him. She was what he wanted, and he couldn't stop until he'd claimed every piece of her. Mike felt himself speeding toward the end and was powerless to stop. She took his face in her hands and plunged her tongue in his mouth.

He came, kissing her, raining inside her body, her tears streaking his cheeks.

Twenty

Love was a strange thing, Terra thought, as Mike slept beside her. It had a bizarre way of creeping up, rendering a sensible individual helpless and confusing them until all coherent thoughts turned to mush. Or maybe she'd banged her head one too many times when she climaxed.

The semidarkness caught her giggles and carried them to the far corners of the room. She turned to study the man who, without knowledge, was forcing her to examine her life's plan.

Her goals had always been simple: Get an education, a career and save lots of money for rainy days. There had never been any rainy-day money when she was growing up, her sister Paula's illness and the needs of the family absorbing any extra.

Sam had tried hard to give them more, but his illegal methods had caught up to him. When he got out of jail in eighteen months, he would come to her and she would help him. He'd stolen to help support the family, and it was costing him five years of his life.

Her thoughts slowly shifted to Mike. If she got the job, she'd have to move an hour north of Atlanta, far away from the inner city and his job. When he tired of the hassle of commuting in Atlanta's congested traffic, would he give her an ultimatum? The job or him? At this point in her life, the job was most important, but his status in her life was rising with each passing day.

The bigger question that hounded her was would he want

to rearrange his life yet again for a woman? Something inside her screamed no. Was success worth losing the man she'd fallen in love with?

"What's got you wide awake at this hour?"

His voice in the darkness startled her. "Just thinking. I didn't mean to wake you."

"Yeah, your brain cells were churning kind of loud." He drew his thumb down the center of her chest. "I'll have to remember to wear earplugs."

She pushed playfully at his shoulder. "Funny. Go to sleep and let me think in peace."

"What are you thinking about?"

Terra shook her head sadly. "Nothing for you to worry about."

"Terra, the contemporary Xena," he teased and kissed her lightly. "I'll tell you what." He glanced at his watch. "We both have to get up early, so we'll spend the next half-hour talking. Say whatever comes to your mind. No holding back."

"Why would I want to do that?" Irrational fear snaked through her and with the grip of a python, threatened to consume her. The relationship wasn't supposed to end this way! Maybe if she thought long enough, an answer would come to solve all their problems.

"We're a couple, Terra. You should know where I went to high school and who my friends are." Mike's words struck at the faceless demons, slaying each until she rested within the comfort of his arms. "I don't see them much, but I plan to change that. You should know that I hate apple juice and why I'll never go skiing again in my life."

"You hate apple juice," she said, allowing the fear to subside. He nestled her closer.

"I do."

"Do you like apples at all?"

He shook his head slowly. "I'm an orange man."

"Ah."

"Now tell me something."

"I've always wanted to climb to the top seats at the Georgia Dome."

He laughed, his chest bumping her arm. She reached out and trailed her fingers up his arm to his shoulder. Terra couldn't resist touching him.

"Don't tell me you're scared to go that high?"

She nodded, giggling again. "I keep thinking if I fall, I'll land in the middle of the court during a Hawks game and the Atlanta Hawk mascot will chase me off with his honker and I'd be totally humiliated." She laughed at herself.

"For such a quiet person, you have a vivid imagination. Is that the truth? Because the rule is that you have to be honest."

"Could I make up a story like that?"

"True," he said and was rewarded with a poke.

"Is that the only rule?" she asked and was rewarded with a tickle in the side that had her arching up. He claimed the tip of her breast with his teeth and her body responded with quivering recognition.

"One more rule," he groaned. "We have to make love before we go to sleep."

Suddenly the idea of talking to Mike in the dark stripped her inhibitions. Besides, he couldn't see her face and if she was going to share with him, she didn't want him looking at her.

"Deal." His chuckle sent warm awareness to her center.

"Ladies first." Mike braced his head on his hand and rested the other on her belly.

"I already don't like this." Terra covered her face. "Can't we just skip and go right to the consolation prize?"

"Baby," he said in teasing awe, before kissing her, slow and easy. "You flatter me, but not yet. I have to recover." He turned serious. "I promise I won't laugh."

The solemn vow broke the dam on her biggest fear.

The words had been building in Terra for a long time and before she changed her mind, she plunged ahead. "Mike, I can't have babies."

Somewhere in the building a toilet flushed. Water rushed through the pipes and when the water settled, there was silence.

His hand tensed on her stomach, but she didn't pull away. The streetlights fought the misty rain and offered a hazy glow. He looked into her eyes.

"Neither can I," he finally said. "That's why my wife divorced me."

"That bitch." Terra's words shocked even her.

Mike choked and laughter shot out of his mouth, surrounding her, filling her.

He hugged her tight and they rolled on the bed, laughing like they'd just heard the funniest joke. Tension and fear evaporated.

In between kisses he said, "You're wonderful, beautiful, as sexy as hell. My kind of woman."

Terra curled on her side facing him as he grew solemn. "Why can't you have children?" he asked.

"My mother suffered from migraines when she carried Jack and me. At the time, no one knew what the effect the medicine would have on unborn children. In a way we were spared. I'm lucky to have my limbs."

His mouth seared a kiss to each of her fingertips, her arms, her thighs and her feet. Distracted by his mouth, she felt her body preparing to be taken again. He moved up and she could feel his gaze on her. He whispered, "Are you sorry?"

The question seemed right coming from him, given his confession and what he must have gone through. Now she understood the party, the drinking and the silence afterward. She'd gone through identical emotions after her divorce. They'd just handled things differently.

"I'm not sorry. Not anymore. Okay. I can't have children. I'm useful to the world in other ways."

"Good for you."

He rolled to the side of the bed and sat up, his back to her. Maybe he hadn't gotten over the trauma of not being able to father children and here she was comfortable with fate. Maybe this was all *too* personal. Fearing she'd insulted him, she sat up too, drawing the sheet over her breasts.

"Mike, I'm sorry I called your ex a name. I had no right."

His head rested in his hands, elbow on his knees, he reached out and squeezed her hand. "I used to feel that way and"—he shook his head—"it wouldn't have done any good. It wasn't her fault."

"The divorce?"

"None of it. She wanted to have children badly. Eventually we allowed that to overshadow our needs as a couple. We just couldn't save it."

"I'm sure you did your best."

"I don't deserve any praise," he said, sounding almost bitter. "I didn't know how to reach her anymore."

"What would you have done if you met someone who wanted kids?"

He shrugged his wide, bare shoulders. "I told myself to not worry about it. I guess God feels I've been punished enough. He brought us together."

Terra eased by his side and put her arm around his waist and hugged hard. Rain slid off the building and gurgled down the gutters. A car swished by, and then the street fell silent. Terra looked at the clock and then at him.

"If your clock is right, we have fifteen more minutes of talking to do. Frankly, I'm a little scared."

They lay wrapped in each other's arms.

"Don't ever be scared to talk to me."

"I won't. You told me where you went to high school, but where did you go to college?"

"I got my bachelor's from Georgia and I graduated from Harvard School of Law. Once I returned, I got married and started the law firm with my brother. Got divorced. Moved from my house of ten years, had a terrible fight with some Tequila and met a beautiful woman. That's the thumbnail sketch of my life."

His lighthearted approach made it easy for her to give him

the short version of her life. "You already know all about school and where I'm from. What you don't know is that I eat ice cream in the bed, I love action-adventure movies and I love to watch football on Sundays." Her voice had softened. Nothing seemed too personal in the cocoon they'd created. The rain and the darkness isolated them in their comfortable haven. Terra glanced at him shyly. "I like hot baths and Snicker bars."

This brought a smile to his face. "Snicker bars?"

"I love them."

"What else do you love?"

Careful, a warning voice echoed in her mind. "I love being here with you." She hadn't ventured out onto this limb in years. She'd loved a man once, and now that love claimed her a second time, she wasn't sure how to react. "Are you hungry?"

"Starving," he said.

Snuggled in Mike's robe, Terra hurried ahead of him to the kitchen, the truth dividing yet binding them together. Mike unearthed chicken salad and made sandwiches, scrounged up a half bag of chips, some grapes, coleslaw that would expire in two days and two beers. Back in the bedroom, Terra took a moment to freshen up while Mike spread the feast on a towel on the bed.

She waited while he used the rest room and thought of all they'd said tonight. She felt right knowing that the catalyst that had destroyed one relationship wouldn't ever be a problem in theirs.

He came into the room, dressed in boxers and joined her in bed.

"When was the last time you talked to your mother?" Mike asked.

"A couple of months ago."

"If I don't call on Sundays, my mother sends out these vibes. I usually wait until Monday just to let her know who's boss."

"Did it ever occur to you she knows you're going to call on Monday and that she's got *you* pegged?"

"Don't ruin it for me."

He bit off the top corner of his sandwich, while she picked at hers. After he wiped his mouth, he studied her. "Can you make things better with your family?"

Sadly, Terra shook her head. "Maybe, with some of them. Most are trying to change their lives. But with Jack and my mom, this is as good as it gets. I'll call and sometimes we can talk nicely for a few minutes, then one of my sisters gets on the phone and asks for money. That always starts a fight." She shrugged her shoulders. "I've learned just to write. They can't hound a letter."

"What about Jack?"

She wiped her mouth, her forehead creasing. Dark-brown eyes met his briefly. "Jack will always be my brother. I can't help him, but I love him."

Mike understood. His eyes said so. He took the plates into the kitchen, and Terra sat on the side of the bed. She wondered if he was going to uninvite her to stay and if she should feel bad about wanting to be there.

He made it easy. When he walked into the room, he pulled her to her feet, eased the robe from her shoulders and scooted in the bed after her.

They cradled each other, two people healing from emotional wounds.

When he took her it was with such sweet intensity, hot tears of pleasure slid down her cheeks. Her name whispered in gruff adulation at the moment of his release was something she wanted to remember forever.

When Mike started to snore, she finally let herself drift off to sleep.

Twenty-one

"All rise. The Honorable Judge Jones presiding," the clerk of the court stated.

"Be seated." Judge Jones looked over at the jury box and studied the foreman. Without preamble she began. "Has the jury reached a decision?"

A middle-aged Latino male stood. "We have, Your Honor."

"Will the defendant please rise."

Mike stood and buttoned his suit coat. Rathborne rose, too, his military face stoic.

"In the case of the state of Georgia versus Keith Rathborne, how do you find on the charge of assault in the first degree?"

"Not guilty."

"Were all parties in agreement, Mr. Foreman?"

"Yes, ma'am."

"You have done your job. You are dismissed with my thanks. Court is adjourned."

Although sure he'd win, Mike still felt stunned. They'd won.

Rathborne looked at him with blank eyes. "It's over. Finally." A scuffle behind the prosecutor's seats brought Mike's attention around. The Lee family glared at Rathborne, Meesook Lee's face pinched in pain and anger. She yelled at Rathborne in Vietnamese and was led away by family members.

"She wanted it," Rathborne said, and Mike had to practice every lesson he'd learned in restraint.

Picking up his briefcase before he let it slip and hit Rathborne in the face, Mike moved to the side of the defense's table and away from the man he despised.

"I suppose you think I owe you my life."

Mike smirked. "Not at all. You don't have a life." He walked over to the prosecutor's table. Mary Beth sat with her head in her hands. She looked up at him with dry, dead eyes.

"Congrats, counselor. Forgive me for not getting up."

He kneeled close to her, catching glimpses of concern from the two attorneys who'd assisted her. "Take the rest of the day off, Mary Beth. Get some rest."

She shook her head and stood. "Can't let the bad guys see you sweat." Her eyes warmed briefly. "I'm glad it's Friday. I'll see you tomorrow night at the party."

He nodded and watched her walk on stilted legs out of the courtroom.

Rathborne had witnessed the entire exchange, but Mike didn't turn back once he started for the door.

Terra blinked at the dabble of glitter Margaret brushed over her cheekbones. The effect was glamorous if you were the glittery type. She didn't know if it suited her, but she trusted Margaret's judgment.

She wished Margaret had been with her earlier that day when she'd scoured the mall for the perfect dress. Out of habit, she cruised the sales racks. Price had been a factor in her decision and now she wished she'd broken her hundred-dollars-or-less rule, and splurged. Her bank account could have withstood a small extravagance, but she'd been thinking too prudently and now she wished she had more time to exchange the simple dress for another more expensive outfit. Of course Margaret looked like a million bucks.

Calm down, Terra told herself as they primped in Margaret's bathroom, in front of professionally lit mirrors. The lights cast an appealing glow on their outfits and makeup, making Terra feel beautiful.

Margaret gave Terra's hair one last scrunch at the top. "Honey, you look beautiful." She applied a light coating of gloss to the center of her lips. They suddenly looked pouty. Terra looked at her own cream-colored lipstick and wished she had a pout.

"You do this for a living. The rest of us plain old folk don't know anything about glitter except how annoying that one piece is when you can't get it off your face. Uh, do you think you can make my lips," she pointed, "look like yours?"

"Course I can. Stick out your bottom lip." Margaret dabbed and smoothed. "I can't wait to see Drew. It's been weeks," she said wistfully as tears welled in her eyes. "I can't stand being away from him. I miss him so much."

Terra hugged her friend, careful not to mess up their outfits. "He's back and he's on his way to see you. I bet he's upstairs right now getting dressed."

"I know he is. But—"

"What, honey," Terra asked, gazing into the mirror.

"I love him and I want to be with him. Always."

"Okay," she said, accepting Margaret's love for Drew.

"You're okay with our whirlwind love affair," Margaret said, tentatively.

"Your happiness is what matters to me."

Margaret forgot the dresses and hugged Terra tight. "I'm so glad. You're my best friend and I love you and I hope you and Mike can make it work."

Terra misted up. "Me, too."

Breaking apart, they looked at each other in the mirror and giggled. "Aw, we've got to start all over," Margaret said with a sly look.

"No way."

"Just kidding."

They made quick repairs and finished just as the doorbell rang.

Butterflies filled Terra's stomach. What would Mike think of the dress? Would he know she'd talked the saleswoman down another ten percent for the stain on the hem? She'd used one of her grandfather's old remedies and gotten it out.

This was an important night for Mike, and she was glad to be part of it.

Margaret handed her a shoulder wrap. "Come on, girl, we can't keep our men waiting."

Nervous, Mike checked his tuxedo and passed the boxed corsage from one hand to another.

"Why are you so nervous?" Drew said, beside him. They stood outside Margaret's door waiting to be let in.

"I don't know," Mike mumbled. "It's stupid. This is the first time Terra is formally meeting everyone. I just want her to have a good time."

"She will, but she'll take her vibes from you. Haven't you learned to chill?"

"Yeah." Mike smirked and took a deep breath. The door swung open.

"Margaret." Drew breathed her name and the two embraced, kissing passionately.

Mike's eyes sought out Terra and out of the shadow of the hallway, she appeared in a beautiful caramel-colored dress. The dress hugged her body, giving her a killer hourglass figure. Her hair was streaked with brown highlights and when his eyes dropped to her feet all he could do was smile when he saw her toe ring snug in the high-heeled sandals.

"Do you like?" she said tentatively.

"I love it. You look gorgeous."

She glided toward him and kissed him on the cheek. "You look gorgeous, too." He massaged the spot where her lips had touched. "Thank you."

He'd forgotten what it was like to be paid such a sincere compliment. "Shall we go?"

"I'm ready." They watched Drew and Margaret as they radiated love. They were truly right for each other.

Mike held out his arm for Terra. "Then let's go."

Outside, dusk hadn't fallen yet so children were still playing. Many of the neighborhood kids huddled around the car trying to see inside.

Terra gasped when she stepped on the porch. "Whose car is that?"

A black Mercedes limousine stretched the length of two regular-size cars in front of the building. "We couldn't all fit in my truck," Mike said as he assisted her down the steps.

A laugh of shock burst from Terra's mouth and she looked at him.

"Mike, I've never been in a limousine before." She held both his arms. "Thank you for making this night special."

"Sweetheart, it's only just begun."

The two couples climbed inside, and the children scattered, racing the long, black luxury car up the street until it was out of sight.

Terra held the glass of champagne Mike handed her and tried to relax. How did one act in a Mercedes limousine? She crossed her legs and Mike adjusted, giving her space.

She uncrossed them and placed her right ankle over her left. He moved again.

When she moved a third time, she smiled at him and as he leaned toward her, she thought he was going to whisper in her ear. Instead, he kissed her deeply, lovingly, tenderly.

When she opened her eyes, he was smiling. "Be still."

She laughed softly. "Okay."

"Drink your champagne."

"Okay." She took a sip and then another.

"Make love to me later tonight."

"Okay," she whispered, just as softly as he. She wrapped her arms around his neck and tasted his mouth again. What an excellent kisser. She sighed. "I don't feel nervous at all."

Drew and Margaret burst out laughing.

"What happened while I was at sea?" Drew asked. "Did a revolution take place?"

Terra felt lighter since she'd nearly finished the flute of champagne. "Yes, a revolution has happened."

Margaret gazed at her with quizzical eyes. "What was it?"

Terra and Mike gazed at each other smiling. "You never know what happens when you tell the truth, reveal a few se-crets—"

"Call people names," Mike added.

"Shh," Terra told him, a thread of guilt still niggling at her. "I said I was sorry."

"You called somebody a name?" Margaret stared at them, wide-eyed and disbelieving.

"Let's not talk about it," Terra rushed in. "It's over."

Caught in the midst of late rush-hour traffic, there was nothing they could do to escape Margaret's curious train of thought.

"Must have been bad for you to say something."

Drew tapped Margaret on her shoulder and when she turned, kissed her soundly. "Hush, woman. You're ruining Terra's high."

They all laughed and Terra relaxed again. Mike poured himself a glass of champagne and attempted to give her more, but she moved her glass. "No more. I won't be able to stay awake."

"Just enough for a toast."

"Okay," she conceded.

Everyone raised their glass. "To Pop. May his retirement be filled with fun and pleasure, and to the two couples in this car, may they find joy in each other's company. *Salute.*"

"*Salute,*" everyone chimed to Mike's toast.

Terra sat back, astonished at the Mike Crawford before her. He was so different from the man who barely had furniture in his apartment and had thrown a bawdy, illegal party in her building. This Mike was charismatic and stylish as well as *fine* in his tuxedo.

The car wound through streets she'd never traveled and pulled up to the gate of an estate enclosed by high white walls.

"Where are we?"

Everyone looked at her like she were crazy.

Mike said softly, "The governor's mansion."

Twenty-two

Terra tried not to look shocked as they stepped into the grand foyer of the governor's mansion, but she couldn't help herself. A magnificent crystal chandelier dripped sparkles of light from the ceiling as the four were escorted in and assisted with their wraps.

Drew and Margaret disappeared into the thick crowd already gathering in the ballroom, leaving Mike and Terra alone. He held her silver evening bag while she fixed his bow tie.

"You look handsome tonight." The magic of the evening connected them. "Thank you for asking me to come with you."

"*I'm* honored you're here." They shifted away from the butlers assisting couples with their coats and stood beside the wall and an antique table and chair. Being here with him was almost unreal. "Just relax and have a good time. I'm part of the tribute, but as soon as I finish, I'll be back with you, okay?"

She smiled. "Sure."

They approached the ballroom and Terra recognized dignitaries, politicians, local and nationally known ministers, and celebrities all mixing and mingling.

Just who was Mike's father that he'd receive such a royal send-off? She didn't have time to wonder because her attention was dragged to his brother Julian. He was the tallest and oldest of the Crawford brothers, she recalled, and Mike's partner. Accompanied by a beautiful woman who stood regal and proud in an African dress and head wrap, Julian shot a curious glance her way.

Mike performed the introductions. "Julian, you've met Terra. Keisha, this is Terra. My girlfriend."

Terra gazed at Mike, wondering why he finished the introduction by announcing her title as if it were part of her name.

She extended her hand to Julian then Keisha. "I'm Terra O'Shaughssey. No additional title necessary."

Keisha smiled big and bright and one of her eyebrows arched delicately. "Pleasure to meet you. Michael should have gotten us together sooner. I like you."

Terra laughed. She didn't know if it was from the champagne or because she'd passed inspection. "I'm sure we'll meet again. The pleasure is all mine."

Keisha and her husband shared knowing smiles.

Terra felt herself becoming tentative and shy under their gazes. Why were they looking at her?

She hooked Mike's arm and applied a little pressure. He turned slightly. "Do I have lipstick on my teeth? Why are they smiling like that at me?"

"Because you're beautiful. They didn't know what I'd bring in here after the party incident."

Understanding dawned on her. "So it's you and not me?"

He laughed. "Right. Let's meet the rest of the family. Where is everybody else?" he asked Julian.

He gestured toward the door and urged them ahead.

The crowd was thick with the who's who of important people, and Terra tried to quell her excitement each time she saw someone she recognized.

Several feet away she saw Margaret, with Drew attached to her side, as Margaret chatted with supermodel Naomi. She hoped they were having a good time and knew she and Margaret would have a marathon sister-girl talk soon. This party warranted it.

Mike pulled up short when an imposing bald man stepped in their path.

"Rathborne," she heard Mike say. "What are you doing here?"

"I see your manners have reverted. I was invited by your father, and since this is my first night of true freedom, I decided to let someone else pick up the tab."

Mike tensed and increased the pressure on Terra's hand.

"I misjudged you." Rathborne stared Mike down. "You're not a half-bad attorney."

"Your version of praise still sounds like an insult. Excuse me."

Terra didn't like Rathborne any more than Mike did. There was something slimy and deceitful about him. When he extended his hand toward her, she didn't move to take it. "Oh, well. There are more fish in the sea. Good evening."

Julian spoke over Terra's shoulder. "Don't let him get to you. We're done with him. The case is over."

Mike looked worried. "I hope so."

Terra and Mike moved on, slowing only when she saw Bishop Desmond Tutu. "You know that's Bishop Tutu," she whispered in Mike's ear.

He slowed and let Julian and Keisha pass. "We'll meet you up there," he said to them then turned to her. "I've met him several times. He's the keynote speaker."

"Wow. Just who is your father? I don't mean it that way, but he must be pretty distinguished to have so many important people at his retirement party."

Mike pulled her closer until she was pressed against his side. "See how important you are?"

"I'm hardly important next to these people."

"You mean more to me than they do. That makes you more important. There's Eric and Nick. Come on. I'll introduce you to their wives, then we can head up. This way."

Trailing Mike through the throng of people, Terra was too busy memorizing the notables and nearly plowed into the dainty woman who stood next to Mike's brother Eric. "I'm sorry," she said and stopped short, shocked. "Do you know who you are?"

Songbird Lauren Michaels smiled and held out her hand. "I think so. I believe I know you, too. Terra, nice to finally you."

"Me?" Terra said, her mouth still open. Lauren kissed Mike gently on the lips. "You're terrible. You should have told her. It's not fair to drop someone into the Crawford midst without a forewarning. Terra, believe me, I know how you feel. I'll have to tell you sometime how I met this crazy group."

Eric, Lauren's husband, kissed Terra on the cheek. "Welcome. Are you having a good time yet?"

Terra was at a loss for words. Lauren was only the most famous singer to come out of Atlanta in years.

Her hit song "Silken Love" stayed at the top of the charts for weeks, not to mention that it had gone platinum one week after it hit the streets. Although Terra's taste ran toward soothing nature sounds, she owned Lauren's CD and had probably worn out "Silken Love." It was hard to believe she was married to Mike's brother.

"I don't know if I'm having a good time," Terra replied to Eric. "It's almost like I'm dreaming." Lauren looked elegant in a long flowing silver dress that hugged her small form. "I can't believe you're a Crawford."

Lauren burst out laughing. "Honey, you don't know the half of it."

Mike, who'd been taking in the scene with a pleased smile on his face, took over the remainder of the introductions. "This is Jade Houston-Crawford and my brother Nick."

"A pleasure," Terra said, admiring Jade's version of formality. Instead of a dress and uncomfortable heels, Jade wore beautiful satin pants and a simple top, with low-heeled sparkling black sandals on her feet. Not that she needed heels; she was nearly six feet tall. The diamond on *her* toe ring winked and her toes glistened with bright-red polish. Terra instantly liked her.

"The pleasure's all mine." Jade's face lit up when Nick,

dressed in full military uniform, his shoulders weighted with medals and shiny bars, caressed her cheek.

The move seemed uncommon for the giant, but love was love.

Terra felt a tingle of recognition when she looked at Jade but discounted it.

"I feel like we've met before," Jade said.

Terra nodded. "I do, too. Do you work at Emory University?"

She shook her head, her eyes squinting as she concentrated. "That's not it. It'll come to me," she said, her voice husky but pleasant.

Nick took over the remainder of the introductions.

"You've met Edwin, and this beautiful lady is his wife, Ann. Finally, Justin and his wife. I don't know where she disappeared to, but you'll meet her later."

"It's only fair to tell you now," added Nick, "that Justin is the ambassador to Equador and Edwin is a dentist. This family is notorious for springing surprises on people."

"Amen," Lauren and Jade chimed in chorus.

"Thank you, Nick," Terra said, her voice growing smaller. "May I ask a question?"

Nick leaned closer to hear her voice above the crowd. "Go ahead."

"Is your father Vernon Jordan?"

"No," he said matter-of-factly, his eyes alight with humor. "But Vernon is on the program. I'll make sure you get a personal introduction. You'll meet our father right now. Shall we?" he said to the crowd of his siblings and their spouses. On his command everyone moved toward the door.

Mike held Terra's hand, but she could feel her fingers growing cold. Mike was an important man in Atlanta, his family roots strong and thriving in Atlanta society. His sister-in-law was just as famous as Lauryn Hill or Janet Jackson and one brother was a decorated war hero, while another was an ambassador, of all things. Her head swooned with the enormity of his family's importance.

She wanted to meet his father and mother, but her heart had begun to race. Were they aides to the president of the United States of America? Nothing was impossible. She was at the governor's mansion for goodness' sake.

They were led down a winding hallway with pictures of past governors framed against the walls. Terra tried to remain cool but found it hard in such auspicious company.

After a discreet tap by Nick, men in white coats with white-gloved hands opened the heavy wooden double doors. They filed in, coupled up and quiet.

Terra dried her perspiring palm on her dress as soon as she saw the current mayor of Atlanta, two former mayors and the governor.

The only person she didn't recognize was the tall brown-skinned woman, but at first glance she realized that she'd have known her anywhere. Terra came face-to-face with Mike's mom.

"Please forgive Julian. He's in the office taking a private phone call from the president."

Naturally, Terra thought.

"He shall be out momentarily."

The governor pulled Nick into a private conversation, and the remainder of the family broke rank and started to chat softly. The regal woman, who looked as if she meant business, came toward her.

"Mom, this is Terra O'Shaughssey. Terra, this is my mother, Vivian Crawford."

Terra gave Mike a grateful look for not introducing her as his girlfriend and extended her hand. "How do you do?"

"I do just fine, young lady. How are you this evening?"

"Fine thank you, ma'am."

Vivian Crawford's eyes wrinkled at the corners like Mike's when he smiled, and she looked at her with what Terra thought was approval. Gray eyes beamed back at her. *So this is where they come from.*

"I haven't met anyone with manners in a long time, Terra. It's a refreshing change. I hear you go to Emory?"

"Yes, I do. I'm just about finished with my course work and will be out very soon."

"Excellent. I taught there for nearly twenty years. I retired this past June. I'm glad to hear you're almost finished."

Terra studied Vivian's face until recognition hit. "You spoke to the League of Women when I first entered Emory. Your speech on the role of black women in the next millennium inspired me to study business."

Vivian clapped her hands as if she'd been given a wonderful surprise. "Thank you. People rarely listen to me," she joked.

"That's not true," Mike broke in. "You listen to her or you listen to my father." He kissed his mother's cheek. "You look wonderful as usual."

"How would you know? You haven't come to see me or called." She turned to Terra. "He always calls on Mondays, but this week he's trying to throw off my schedule by calling on Sunday. He never was the slick one. Honey, before I forget, Drew asked me to pass this on to you two." She handed him a note and turned toward the others.

"I'm going to hurry your father along," Vivian said. "We don't want to be late."

Mike and Terra moved aside, and he rubbed her arms. "Are you okay?"

"If being overwhelmed is okay, then I am."

"I wasn't trying to keep anything from you. My family can be very—well as you've said, overwhelming."

"They're a nice bunch, Mike." He gazed deeply into her eyes. "Really, I like them all."

"Give me a kiss."

She wanted to so badly, but apprehension got the best of her. "The mayors are here. And the governor."

"Well, if you insist on kissing them too—Bill," he said, pretending to call the current mayor of Atlanta.

"Stop it." She pecked his lips. "There."

"Chintzy, but it'll do for now." He looked at the folded sheet in his hands. "Shall we see what this is?"

"Of course." Terra read the note as Mike did. Margaret and Drew had already left the party to fly to Vegas to elope.

"I guess this means you don't have to be the maid of honor."

"And you the best man." She sighed, wishing she'd been able to wish her friend well. "I hope they're happy."

"Me, too." His arm slid around her waist just as the door opened and a tall, striking man appeared in the arching doorway.

Distinguished with gray hair and deep brown eyes, he looked at the people assembled and gave each a silent greeting.

Terra felt a flash of heat when he looked at her and then instantly went cold.

Julian Crawford Sr. walked into the room with his wife by his side and although Terra didn't hear the greeting, she knew he was talking and everyone was moving forward to give him praise.

Everyone except her.

Mike looked at her curiously. "What's the matter?"

Fear as strong as quicksand pulled at her and she suddenly felt claustrophobic around all these people.

"Who do we have here?" Julian Crawford Sr. said, his eyes kind, his smile generous.

Terra stared into his eyes, knowing she would lose her composure if she didn't find a seat and soon.

"Terra." Mike's voice penetrated the vacuum her mind had created. "This is my father and the man of the evening, Julian Crawford. Dad, Terra."

She felt her hand moving and a smile creasing her lips. Pleasantries were exchanged, and she didn't even faint when he kissed her on the cheek and welcomed her to his retirement party.

"We are a bit overpowering," his father said as if guessing her shock. How wrong he was.

Vivian shushed the crowd and directed everyone's attention to the event planner. The brusque woman gave instructions and reviewed the program, advising in a strong but respectful voice for no one, even the dignitaries assembled, to exceed their time limit.

Everyone filed out of the door and headed back to the packed ballroom.

"I need a ladies' room," she told Mike, thankful no one else seemed to have picked up on her discomfort. But he had. He immediately directed her toward a hall and a series of doors. Security noticed them and headed forward, greeting Mike with a firm handshake and allowing them to enter the private area. The easy way Mike commanded attention, the strength of his family, their unassuming power and their importance to people in the world dismayed her.

"I'll be fine," she said. "I'm right behind you."

"Are you sure? What's wrong?" Concern painted his eyes deep gray and if he were anybody else, she would have blabbed the awful truth.

"Nothing," she managed. "Go ahead with your family."

"I'll wait outside."

"No," she said firmly. "I'll join you in a few minutes."

When he looked at her she could see the confusion in his eyes and a tinge of hurt.

She didn't know how to tell him that her family knew his intimately—her family members had encountered his under unappealing circumstances.

Inside the bathroom lounge, she sank into a chair and held her face with her hands. How could she have not recognized Jade Houston right away?

Probably because the last time she'd seen her was about five years ago and she'd been standing behind the business end of a Glock semiautomatic weapon, which had been pointed at her brother Sam's head. The family hadn't known he'd jumped bail until Jade had shown up. What surprised Terra more was that she hadn't recognized Julian Crawford Sr. right away.

In a federal court a year ago he'd sentenced Sam to five-to-fifteen years for burglary.

The door opened and closed. "I see you remembered."

Terra held up her head. Jade Houston-Crawford stood before her. "Yes, Jade, I do. You arrested my brother."

Twenty-three

Mike headed up the long hallway looking for a distraction. He hadn't wanted to leave Terra, but she'd insisted. Something had happened, and it had to do with his father. For the life of him, he couldn't make the connection, but he would and they'd fix it. He'd been afraid this would happen. Afraid that Terra would be intimidated by what she perceived as the life he lived. He'd straighten out the problem, he vowed. Terra had become too important to walk away from.

Above anything else, he loved his family and whatever Terra was upset about had to be a misunderstanding. He hurried past the door leading to the ballroom and stopped when he heard familiar voices. Keith Rathborne and Mary Beth Pearsoy were embroiled in a heated argument.

His father and brother Julian, along with a security agent, walked up behind him as he stood at the cracked door.

He held up his hand to quiet them, and they all listened.

"You raped her just like you raped me and my roommate Samantha Carson. Admit it, Judge Rathborne."

"What would an admission do but upset you more?"

"Say it," Mary Beth said, her voice sounding tight. "Admit it to me and I'll be satisfied. You can't be tried again."

"If you feel our encounter was rape, why didn't you press charges? Or your roommate for that matter." Rathborne sounded smug and Mike felt his anger escalating.

"I can't speak for Sam, but I wanted to graduate law school.

You held my future over my head and told me I would never be an attorney. I had sex with you but I didn't want to. Never in a million years would I ever do anything so sordid."

"It wasn't that bad, was it, Mary Beth? You seemed to enjoy it."

"In your dreams." Mary Beth's voice rose. "I have had one victory. You will never be a judge again. Your career is over. So why don't you just admit it, you raped Meesook Lee and Samantha Carson."

Mike started to open the door, but his father stopped him.

Rathborne laughed loud and hearty. "Why not? You can't touch me. I raped Meesook Lee and Samantha Carson. Feel better?"

"You're slime." Mary Beth said. "But this time I've got you."

"I agree." Judge Julian Crawford walked into the room followed by his sons and security. The governor, Mary Beth's husband and additional security emerged from another door at the back of the room.

Rathborne was surrounded. "I was just humoring her," he laughed with false cheer. His bald head shone with the sweat of fear. "I was just repeating what she said. This is entrapment."

"Your ego trapped you," Ben, Mary Beth's husband, said. "You're going where you belong."

The governor had words with the guards, who placed the man in handcuffs.

"You're my attorney," Rathborne screamed at Mike, his face livid. "Do something."

"Our association ended when the verdict was read."

Mary Beth opened her evening bag, withdrew a dollar and handed it to Mike. He took great pleasure in announcing, "I'm her attorney now."

The officers read Rathborne his rights and escorted him from the room.

Mike embraced Mary Beth, who shivered in the moderate warmth. His father stood beside them and patted her back.

"I'm so sorry this happened to you. Had I known—"

"You couldn't have known," she told him, composing herself. "My ex-roommate is planning to press charges." She gave them a serious look. "So am I."

"He won't get away," Julian Sr. said gravely. "Are you going to be all right?"

"Yes." She shook the governor's hand. "Thank you. I appreciate your help."

"No problem, Mary Beth. I hate that we had to find out everything under these circumstances, but we've ferreted out the enemy in our midst. We'll talk again next week when things calm down. Now if you're all right, let's get this celebration underway."

Mary Beth embraced her husband and everyone moved away to give them privacy. She possessed remarkable strength given what she'd been through. "Down the road a bit, we might consider asking her to come aboard," Mike said.

"I was thinking just that," Julian said, a smile on his face.

They were outside the grand dining room when Mike turned to his father. "Why did you order me to defend him?"

His father sighed as he turned. "Years ago, before we married, your mother had a thing going with Keith."

"You've got to be kidding," Julian Jr. said, astonished.

"No way," Mike added.

"Yes, and I stole her heart and he never forgave me. For years we seemed to vie for the same jobs and for one reason or another I was chosen more often than not. Keith always accused me of taking from him and when he got arrested he wanted me to prove to him I had nothing to do with it."

"So you offered me as the sacrificial lamb."

"I knew you knew how to handle yourself. He guessed that I might sabotage him, but not you."

"He's a sick man."

"Indeed." Julian Sr. patted Mike on the shoulder. "You did your job and he got caught anyway. There is justice for all."

"What are you grinning at?" Mike asked his brother.

"I'm glad *you're* still aboard."

"Where else would I be?"

A feeling of solidarity flowed through him, and he felt one with his family. The feeling had eluded him for so long that he hadn't realized it was gone until just then. Everything was falling into place. He and Terra were in love, and his family was all together. He chuckled and nodded his head, searching for Terra in the crowd of seated guests.

Julian joined Keisha and their children at the table and Mike searched the others, but still didn't see Terra. The last place he'd left her was in the ladies' room and he turned, but nearly ran into Nick.

"You seen Terra?"

"No. You seen Jade?"

"Not a glimpse of her."

"Jade went to get Terra from the ladies' room about fifteen minutes ago."

Nick gave Keisha a curious look, then glanced at Mike. "Terra doesn't have any outstanding warrants, does she?"

"That's really funny," he said drolly, and they both started for the door.

Terra didn't hold any animosity in her heart for Jade, just sorrow for herself. Mike's family was so upstanding. Two lawyers, a dentist, a doctor, an ambassador, a Marine Corps officer, a father for a judge, retired professor for a mother and a famous singer—all in one family.

Jade came and sat beside her. "Quite a crew, wouldn't you say?"

"At the very least." Terra studied her glittery fingernails. The manicure had set her back twenty dollars, and she'd had to think long and hard before deciding to splurge. "I suppose they're wealthy, too."

"Stinking."

A burst of shocked laughter flew from her mouth. "Oh, brother. How do I get out of this one?"

"Why do you want to leave? Mike's a good guy. You two make a wonderful couple."

"Speaking of. I don't mean to be offensive, but you and Nick seem so . . . unlikely."

Jade grinned and fanned her bangs with her fingertips. "We are. That's why I love him so much. He loves me despite the loony family I have. You think you've got it bad. I've got a pervert for a stepbrother, and my mother is working on her tenth husband. Two of her exes live with her, and get this, with her new beau, she wants to have another baby."

Terra gave her a look of disbelief. "You don't have to lie to make me feel better."

"If I'm lying may warts grow on my nose."

She studied Jade's face intently. "You're telling the truth. Oh, my gracious." She started to laugh, the thought of ten husbands so absurd, she couldn't believe it.

Jade laughed, too, and sat back. Terra dried her eyes with the heel of her hand. "It's not funny," she said finally. "I've got nine ex-convicts for siblings. Have mercy, it's not funny. I would be mortified if any of them had to appear again before Judge Crawford."

Jade gave her a winning grin. "They won't. He's retiring."

Terra chuckled but shook her head. "There's always the possibility and the likelihood that someone is going to do something to get in trouble and try to use Mike or someone in his family."

She stopped talking because Jade nodded her head in understanding. "I know how you feel. My mother flirts with Nick constantly. If he weren't such a good man, she might be successful in seducing him. Honey, we've all got skeletons we want to nail in the closet and cement the door shut on, but we can't pick our relatives. We can only tolerate and love the ones we have."

Three sharp raps against the door startled Terra but not Jade. "That's my man and probably yours, too. Let me ask you something." They rose and stood facing each other. "Do you love him?"

Terra nodded. "With every corner of my heart."

A slow but kind smile spread across Jade's face and Terra realized what the admission meant. This family was so tight, word would spread faster than hot butter on popcorn. There would probably be feelings against her because of his ten-year relationship with April. But that wouldn't stop her from loving Mike.

"Well, then." Approval gleamed in Jade's eyes. "Let life happen and don't worry about those pesky family details."

"Jade," came the strong, commanding voice of Nick Crawford.

Terra's eyes widened. "He doesn't scare you?"

Jade looped her arms around Terra's and whispered. "Baby, it's him that's scared of me. Coming, sweetheart."

They walked through the sitting room and stopped at the door. "Love him for all he's worth. You two deserve it."

Terra reached out and hugged Jade. "Thank you."

Jade kissed her cheek in a sisterly fashion. "You're welcome."

Outside in the hallway, Mike stood staring up at a painting of the first governor's mansion. He turned when he heard the door and met her gaze. "What's going on?"

Nick and Jade stood off to the side talking quietly.

Terra pursed her lips, knowing she couldn't stop the love that radiated from her eyes. "Everything is wonderful." She kissed him full on the lips and looped her arm through his. "I know I sound like a broken record, but I'm very happy you asked me to come tonight."

He didn't move or kiss her back. "You are?"

She stopped trying to move his immovable form and gazed up at him. "I am."

"You're not mad I didn't tell you about my family or where we were going or anything?"

Terra smiled at his disbelief. "Nope."

Nick said softly, "Lauren's getting ready to sing 'The Lord's Prayer.' If you don't want to miss it, you'd better get a move on." He and Jade stalked forward, their strides matching. *What an adorable couple.*

"Ooh, I'd like to hear that." Terra started forward, only to be jerked back. "Mike?"

"What happened in there?"

The sweet-smelling aroma of the fresh magnolias on the table wafted around them. "I had a revelation, that's all."

"And what would that have been?" Terra wasn't surprised when he took her in his arms.

Suddenly shy, she didn't want to get her feelings hurt. "I'll tell you later. At home. In bed. Like you promised," she whispered in his ear.

She could feel him coming to life between them. "Terra," he groaned. "Don't mention bed. I'll be uncomfortable for the rest of the night. Tell me now."

"No," she whispered. "Come on. It's not every day I get to see Lauren Michaels perform."

His beard grazed her cheek, sending tendrils of longing to the epicenter of her body. "Tell me now or we're going to do something in the governor's mansion nobody is supposed to do but the governor and his wife."

As Terra stood in Mike's arms gazing at the picture of the first governor's mansion, she imagined them as an old couple in the meadow beside the house, laughing and loving each other. Her feelings grew stronger as she pictured them together.

She mustered up her courage and said, "I love you."

Her heart hammered five times real hard against her ribs. "You don't have to feel the same way or anything. I just really do. It doesn't have to change our relationship—"

His mouth descended upon hers, warm and wonderful. Taking and giving, loving her without words. Where her spirit had plunged right after she'd uttered the fateful words, it soared now, breathing life into the sweetest kiss of all time. What she felt for Mike was endless love, something that wouldn't end on a whim or break under the pain of a thoughtless act or word.

If he didn't feel the same right now, that was okay. Her love would last until he was ready.

His large hand caressed her cheek as they shared a final touch before parting. Through the silence came the melodious tone of Lauren's voice raised in song.

Terra gathered his hand in hers and smiled up at him. "Shall we?"

He looked toward the end of the hall, then back at her.

"Tonight. After we leave here. You and I are going to talk about us." He gathered her to him in a hug so tight, she thought their bodies would become one if he didn't stop. He kissed her hard, then let her go. His eyes glowed. "Tonight."

"Tonight," she echoed.

Then matching her steps to his, they hurried to the dining room so as not to miss the remainder of the song.

Twenty-four

Bishop Tutu was a gregarious and enlightening speaker. His charm and wit embraced the audience and had them standing in a rousing ovation when he ended his speech.

The governor was equally interesting as he shared anecdotes and stories about his dealings over the years with Julian Sr.

The mayor of Atlanta and previous mayors all praised the older Julian, expending on the philanthropic work he performed on behalf of the city, and each vowed they had a job waiting for him in the private sector.

Colleagues and friends, family and even foes sang the praises of the man of the hour, and Mike wanted to pay closer attention. A part of his brain registered his family members surrounding him on all sides, and his mother and grandmother sitting beside his father, smiling, proud of his accomplishments.

They were especially proud when Congressman John Lewis of Georgia read the letter of commendation presented to Julian Sr. from the President of the United States.

Mike understood that this was his father's day, a day he would never have again and therefore one to be cherished. Mike would remember it for those reasons. But he had another reason to remember this day that would never leave him.

His thoughts kept shifting to the gentle words the lady in his life delivered more eloquently and with greater passion than the dignified aristocrats around him. Terra loved him.

His mind was blown. How could he have found love so completely, so quickly? Terra sat next to him with her delicate hands folded on the table, a sparkling bracelet around her wrist that caught the light each time she clapped.

He concentrated on the words she'd said and tried to separate his love for her into logical parts.

He loved her shyness, the way she turned to him whenever she needed protection from the world. She had a way of speaking as if her words were for his ears only. He loved the way she spoke, the way her Southern accent made words sound light as a breeze in spring. He loved her devotion and desire to overcome a past she hadn't created but didn't let stand in the way of her dreams.

He loved her free spirit, her whale music, her sexy toe ring and red nail polish and the fresh flowers he associated with the goodness in her. He loved her because in spite of the fact that she couldn't have children, she knew her worth and that she had something valuable to offer the world. He loved the way she looked in the morning, like a woman at peace with herself, and he loved the way she looked at night, though weary, a smile lighting her face as if she'd found the perfect treasure. He loved her because she loved him, faults and flaws and all.

A while ago while looking at the picture of the first governor's mansion, he saw himself and Terra as on old couple sitting on the grass with people of various ages walking in the meadow. He and Terra were holding hands, their eyes glowing with the light of love.

The image gripped his heart and seared his brain and wouldn't let him go. It was his family. Terra included.

He loved her. He was certain of it. They would spend their lives together, forever. And tonight, he'd ask her to be his wife.

Mike focused on his father and mother, and his mother caught his gaze. She communicated her love for him with a warm look and a tender smile and when her eyes shifted to

Terra and back to him, she pointed to her heart and crossed her fingers.

Mike was overwhelmed. His mother knew. He winked and crossed his fingers too.

Suddenly sound returned to his ears and the applause elevated to deafening decibels as his father rose and expressed his gratitude.

Julian Sr. was a tall, husky man. When he spoke nobody moved. His manner was assured as he gripped the sides of the podium and let his strong voice carry through the microphone.

"I've often heard young athletes, you know, these young men fresh out of high school, get million dollar baseball and basketball contracts say, 'I'm the luckiest man alive.' I look at my TV and I shake my head thinking, Boy, you ain't got nothin' on me."

The older men in the crowd nodded in agreement.

"I've heard older men say they're lucky when they've hit the lottery. I've heard ex-cons express their claim of luck when they're freed from jail for a crime they didn't commit.

"I've even heard people say it when they've beaten the death angel. I still say, 'No, you aren't lucky. You just haven't done what God wants you to do, so you got to go back.' That isn't lucky.

"I contend that in some way or another these men aren't lucky and may never know what luck is. Not by their own fault or plan, or by design or dream. They could do everything right and I still say I've got them beat.

"So I declare on this day, September 25, 2000, that I am the luckiest man alive." He turned to the governor. "And since you've chosen to honor me on this day, at your home, I feel I can take this one liberty." The crowd laughed and the governor waved his hand granting him the honor.

"Why am I luckier than these other men? Because I've humbly lived each day of my life for the good of mankind. At the age of seven, I worked at my father's side farming land in

Savannah, Georgia, while learning to read in a one-room schoolhouse. When I was the age of ten, my father died and I became the man of my mother's house, and I herded cattle and raised chicken to keep food on the table. At seventeen, I entered the Marine Corps and for the next twenty years served my country.

"When I became a man at twenty-one, I returned to Georgia and married my sweetheart, then fought for the United States of America in the Korean War. Fresh out of Korea five years later, we had our first son and five more soon followed.

"In the midst of making babies, I finished law school and my wife finished her graduate degree. Together, our family has fed the hungry in Angola, Africa, and right here in Macon, Georgia. Our boys know the meaning of hunger, pain, death, humility and Savior. I have six sons. Six boys who honor their father and mother and who serve this world each in a professional capacity. Six men I'm proud to say are my sons. Julian, Michael." He gestured and they stood. "Justin, Edwin, Nicholas, Eric." Applause thundered around them.

Mike watched his father with adoring eyes. They sat.

"I looked at these men when they were boys and knew I had to help make this world a better place for them and everyone else. I became a judge to mete out fair justice for all. I've been married forty-four years, raised my family, served my country and loved my Lord. In my lifetime, I've seen the signs of change, and I'd like to think I had something to do with that.

"I'd like to think a young woman or young man who appeared before me changed their mind and their life based upon a word or a gesture.

"I know without me, change will continue and this world will become better still for all the grandchildren of the world and I've enjoyed the ride. I have lived a lifetime in sixty-five years. I've been blessed each and every one of those days. If

I never see another sunrise, I contend I am still the luckiest man alive."

Julian Crawford Sr. stepped back from the podium and took his seat.

Thunderous applause shook the room as each person present honored him in a heartfelt and emotional ovation. Mike wiped a tear from his eye. He loved his father and if he was lucky, he'd become half the man his father was.

After minutes of applause, the crowd settled for the final words and a prayer by Bishop Tutu, then began to disperse.

People filed out the door, and Mike assumed his place in the receiving line his family had formed beside his father, mother and grandmother.

Mike kept an eye on the crowd and when it thinned, signaled Terra with a wink that the night was almost over and their night would soon begin. She stood, gathering her wrap and her bag. She and Lauren had been engaged in a heavy discussion, interrupted every once in a while by one of Lauren's eager fans.

Eric stood beside Mike. "You copied my beard."

Mike smiled at the woman in front of him and shook her hand. "I did not. I grew mine out of a sense of rebellion of the status quo of corporate America."

Eric sneered. "Lawyers."

A ripple of eager greetings started at the beginning of the line as Terra approached. Mike caught her hand and tugged her between him and Eric.

She leaned toward him, speaking into his ear. "Your father was absolutely wonderful and so deserving of this nice party."

Mike heard Terra but at the same moment, he heard another familiar voice. Chills ran up his spine, and a tingle of discomfort started in his feet and stopped in his chest. Each of his family members turned to look at him as his ex-wife approached. She stopped in front of him and tilted her head to one side.

"Are you a sight for sore eyes. I love the beard. Hi, Michael. I'm back."

Then April stood on tiptoe and planted a kiss on his stunned lips.

Twenty-five

Terra wondered if the sound of a breaking heart rivaled the crashing of a hundred panes of glass. Mike's wife stood with her lips pressed to his as if superglue melded them together. To his credit, Mike seemed surprised. All he did was gurgle in his throat and look like a deer caught in the headlights of an oncoming freight train.

His hand gripped Terra's as if her hand were the joystick that controlled his heartbeat. As best she could, she loosened his fingers and slid her hand from his and was about to turn when she felt a presence at her side.

Lauren, bless her heart, injected herself beside Eric, who was also frozen in place and gave Terra's hand a comforting squeeze.

"Michael, introduce your guest."

His gaze ricocheted to Terra and he blinked once slowly. "April, this is—"

Terra looked at the woman whose stare was curious and wary. April Crawford was a big, beautiful woman. Hershey-chocolate brown, she had luminous dark eyes and long curly hair. She was dressed elegantly in an off-white suit and had long French manicured nails that caressed Mike's cheek when she kissed him. To Terra, she looked like Star Jones.

When April looked at Terra, dawning lit her eyes. She measured Terra from the shoes on her feet to the glitter around her eyes.

"I'm Terra O'Shaughssey. How do you do?"

"Fine, thank you."

Silence stretched into thin, embarrassingly long seconds, until Mike found his voice. "How are you?"

"I'm fine," she said kindly. "I came to pay my respects to your father. His speech was inspiring." Her smile was gentle as she met Terra's gaze again. "I didn't plan to make anyone uncomfortable. I'll leave."

Terra stepped forward. "No. You're a member of this family. Mike, if you would arrange transportation for me, I'll leave."

"Terra." His voice sounded foreign in her ears. "You don't have to—"

"I know." Terra reached for Eric's hand. "It was a pleasure to see you again." She kept her smile friendly and shook each member of his family's hand until she was finally at the door standing before his father.

"You are a woman of tremendous strength and confidence. I admire you."

Touched by his words, her smile was genuine. "It is I who is in awe. God bless you. Good night." With Mike at her side, she exited the ballroom and walked out the front door of the governor's mansion. The line of limousines had thinned, leaving only a snake of white luxury cars.

Mike stared down into her face as if waiting for a revelation. The car eased forward, and he opened the door before the driver could alight. "Can I come see you when I get home?"

She climbed in and looked into his eyes. They were clouded with memories, pain and love. But how could she be sure the love was for her? He'd never professed anything.

"Why don't we end our evening here and see each other at the beginning of a new day?"

"All right." He moved to kiss her, but she raised her hand and caressed his bearded cheek. "Don't kiss me with her lipstick on your lips."

His eyes shut and when they opened, were filled with an

unspoken apology. "Don't be angry. I had no idea she was coming."

"I'm not mad at you. Go to your family." Mike stepped back as the driver shut the door.

Terra slid across the long black seat alone and waited for the limousine to pull away.

The dress was the first to go. The shoes followed and then the underwear. All of her bargains lay at her feet.

She stood naked in her bathroom, shivering from the cool night air, then slid into the tub and smoothed cleansing cream on her face.

Earlier tonight when she and Margaret had been primping, she'd imagined her evening ending so differently. Her thoughts had flowed toward a romp in bed and a proclamation of love.

Not a face-to-face meeting with the woman who'd known Mike intimately for ten years.

April Crawford had everything she didn't. She had history. A life with Mike and his family. She *belonged*. Being accepted into such a tight clan was a dream, a fantasy Terra had conjured up because being with Mike made her believe in the fantastic.

She didn't want to give up, but as she dressed for bed and the minutes ticked into hours, and then dawn broke the night sky, she didn't hold out hope that her Prince Charming was going to find his way home.

His old house looked exactly the same as the day he'd left.

Plants that didn't require watering were still in the foyer with the same shiny glow that announced their artificial status. Everything had remained the same. Except he felt different.

Mike followed April in and took a seat on the stool by the bar.

She kicked off her shoes, prepared two martinis and delivered the drinks before sitting on the couch. "How's life?"

He tasted the drink and put it down. Heavy on the Vermouth: just the way he liked them. "Good."

"You seem peaceful. I guess the split didn't hurt you as much—"

"Don't say that. It hurt. More than I thought I could stand. We had a life together. History. A future. When you left, I wasn't ready to give up on us."

April's smile was sad. "I wasn't either. I was hurting, Michael. I wanted a child so bad, I couldn't see anything else."

"I know."

Her gaze shifted to him. "I don't think you understand."

"I do. You wanted a child more than you wanted our marriage or me. I tried to give you everything else: trinkets, trips, toys and all the trappings successful people have. There was only one thing I couldn't give you. And you walked away based on that one fault."

Her voice broke. "I'm sorry. I didn't mean to hurt you. I was hurting so bad."

He sat beside the woman who'd watched him grow into himself and felt only compassion. "I know you were. I hurt for you. I'm sorry, too, that I couldn't make our situation better, but life goes on."

She slid her hand into his and squeezed. "You never did carry a grudge long. I'm going to ask you to forgive me one more time."

"For what?"

"For making the biggest mistake of my life. I'd like for us to give our marriage another try."

Mike tried to count the times he'd wanted to hear her say those words, but couldn't come up with a sum that would equal his prayers. So much time had passed. Time he'd mourned the loss of their marriage and his companion. Time had healed the wound of his broken heart and in the midst of it all, he'd found love again.

April had occupied an important part of his life, time he

would never forget, but he couldn't go back. He wouldn't go back, and he wondered why she'd want to.

"What's changed so drastically since I last saw you, what, ten months ago?"

"I've lost weight," she smiled, teasing.

"You look great," he said softly.

"Thank you." She grew serious again. "I've had time to think and learn more about myself. Back in the spring, I went to China because I'd learned some doctors over there had been very successful in helping couples who were having difficulty get pregnant."

Disbelief in the words had his skin crawling. April pushed on. "I know you said you wouldn't try anything else, but this procedure is ninety-eight percent effective."

"You still don't get it."

"I do. Our relationship dissolved because we couldn't have a baby, not because we didn't love each other anymore."

"Is that what you think?"

She gave him a confused look. "Of course."

"Our relationship dissolved because we couldn't have a baby?" He said the words forcefully. "We're divorced because I wasn't willing to try anymore and you wouldn't give up on the idea that a baby was the only thing that could complete our family. We *were* a family. You and I."

"Michael, we can still be a family. This method is nearly foolproof. We can live here in *our* house. Pick up where we left off. Don't you feel sad whenever you see your brothers' children running around? Don't you yearn for a child of your own?"

He set the glass on the table and stood. "No. I don't yearn for something I can't have. I see those children and I'm proud to be an uncle. Yes, if it were possible for me to create the perfect life on a canvas, I would probably paint in children." The image of he and Terra in the meadow bloomed in his thoughts. "But my life is complete." He looked at her. "I don't have any regrets."

She placed her glass on the table and stood too. "You've found somebody else." After a moment of silence she said, "She's beautiful."

"Terra doesn't have anything to do with my decision. I can't and never could give you what you want. You're entitled to have the life you desire. I just can't be part of it."

He walked out the door and stepped onto the stoop, surprised to see the rising sun and hear the birds chirping.

April followed and when he looked at her, he felt her sorrow. Her face was pinched with emotion, and she held on to the door as his foot hit the first step. "What happens when she wants what she can't have?"

Mike leaned his head back, shoving his hand into the pocket of his rumpled tuxedo pants. He looked at her from the corner of his eye. The wind carried his words. "She won't. She's just like me."

April smiled, a gentle sadness surrounding her. "Come," she said and held out her arms.

He stepped back up, and for what he knew would be the last time, he hugged April Crawford, and said good-bye.

Twenty-six

By early Sunday evening, Terra had cleaned out her dresser drawers, purged old files from the file cabinet and washed down the kitchen cabinets before starting in on the rest of the apartment. Once spotless, she completed the monthly paperwork for the building and e-mailed it to Dr. Clinnell and Betty in administration.

She flopped onto the couch and in that one unoccupied moment, thought of Mike. All day she'd managed to keep hot tears at bay, but they flooded her eyes and streaked her face.

Stubbornly she wiped her face and grabbed her gardening tools. She would not cry over him.

Mike's silence announced his decision and her feeling like an idiot because he hadn't chosen her was foolish.

Grabbing the hoe, rake and apron, she tacked a note on the door giving her whereabouts and headed to the roof and her ten-by-six-foot plant box. Weeds had sprung up since her last visit, and she took out her frustration on the noxious plants, giving herself something to whack at.

"If I didn't know you better, I'd think you were dangerous."

Jack stood in the doorway, staring at her.

He looked the same, filthy from head to foot. She wiped perspiration on the shoulder of her T-shirt and met his beady-eyed gaze with one of unwavering strength.

"What brings you by, Jack? You're not here for a friendly visit, so let's get to the point. Is it money you want?"

He licked dried, chapped lips. "What's with you? You act like somebody clipped the head off all your roses or something. They're just a bunch of damn flowers. You don't have to look so tired and disgusted."

"If I look tired it's because I *am* tired, Jack. I'm tired of people using me and taking my love for granted. I'm tired of looking at my older brother waste away from drugs and making everyone in the family believe they're at fault for his disease." She moved closer. "I'm tired of seeing my twin slowly kill himself. So now that you know what's wrong with me, what's wrong with you?"

He looked puzzled and confused. This discussion was way more than he bargained for. "I just came by to borrow twenty dollars. If you ain't got it say so, but I don't need a lecture."

"I *ain't* got it, now go."

She turned back to the weeds and started chopping. "Terra," he said right behind her, his voice scratchy.

She turned around the spade raised. "What?" she shouted. "I don't have twenty dollars today or any other day. You don't scare me, Jack. Now leave before you regret coming into this building."

He took a startled step back and kept backing up until his back bumped the door. "You're crazy." He fumbled for the knob and finally wrenched it open.

"You keep believing that and don't come back."

"I won't," he yelled, taking the stairs two at a time. "Watch and see."

"Whatever," she yelled, liberation cleansing the fear and responsibility from her.

The spade was raised in her fist and when it glinted off the sun, she dropped it. "Oh, gracious. What have I become?"

She sat down, resting her elbows on her knees, and folded her hands. She wasn't violent. Never had been and never would be, but Jack didn't need to know that. Heat from the sun smoothed the edges off her temper and she cooled down.

If she could hold on to that fire, maybe tomorrow the interview would go well. Thoughts of tomorrow made her think of Mike and she knew all her effort to not think about him had been for nothing. She wanted to talk to him, if only to say good-bye. Nixing the idea as unhealthy, she gathered her tools and headed to the apartment. Seeing him would only delay the inevitable.

Inside the cool haven she called home, Terra examined her surroundings and fixed her thoughts on the many days after tomorrow. If she got the job, her life was going to change. She'd be moving up in the world.

No, she wouldn't have a famous sister-in-law and distinguished relatives who were ambassadors and dentists and doctors and Marine Corps officers. Who needed that? she thought, tears working their way up again.

She wiped them away and put on soothing nature sounds and celebrated her quiet afternoon tears with a glass of wine and a Snickers bar.

Her feet were propped up on the edge of the table, and she let the tears come. Instead of trying to stop them, she needed to get them out, because tomorrow was a new day.

A busy signal filled his ear and Mike ended the call in frustration. He hadn't been able to reach Terra and that worried him. She didn't know he was in a marathon settling session with his client and the Blount and Blount attorneys. They called the last-minute meeting and he had no other choice but to respond.

Julian hurried from conference room A, where their client issued demands, and was on his way to room B to negotiate when he poked his head in Mike's office.

"Did you order dinner?"

"Any sign of a fast settlement?" Mike shot back.

"Progress is slow." Julian dropped into the chair opposite Mike's desk. He noticed the telephone headset draping his brother's neck. "Talked to Terra yet?"

"I can't seem to reach her."

Julian stood. "Forget food. If they're hungry, they'll work faster. Let's go before they ruin what's left of the evening."

Early Monday morning, Terra took the bus into the heart of downtown and got off several blocks ahead of her stop to walk and think of what she'd say. The meeting wasn't supposed to take place until nine o'clock, but she was an hour early.

In the lobby of the Colony Square Building, businessmen and -women streamed by, oblivious to her. Hello, I'm over here, she wanted to say but didn't.

Even if her personal life was falling apart, she could get this job if she focused.

She muttered the five ways to resolve conflict and earned a curious stare from a man passing by. Thank you, she silently acknowledged. I'm not invisible. Folding her hands around the warm cup, she finally let herself think of Mike. He hadn't contacted her since she saw him Saturday night and that hurt more than wondering if his feelings for her were wrong.

They'd shared some good times and whatever it was that connected them, they had obviously made a misconnection. Perhaps they weren't mean to be.

She headed toward the elevator and hit the button for her floor. She might not have control over her relationship, but she could control her performance in the interview. This job was her future and just as she'd fought for independence with Jack, she would, if necessary, from this relationship.

She rode the elevator up in silence and stepped out on her floor. "Ms. O'Shaughssey," the receptionist said. "You can go right in."

Fear gripped Terra's heart. "I still have a half hour."

"We had a cancellation. Would you like to freshen up before you go inside?"

Standing taller, Terra drew her shoulders back and lifted her head higher. "No. I'd like to go ahead now."

"Good answer," she said and led the way to the double doors. "Good luck."

Terra smiled and her step seemed lighter. She entered the door and faced the interviewers.

"Good morning, I'm Terra O'Shaughssey."

"Hello, please take a seat."

The doors closed behind her, and Terra stared into her future.

Three hours later, Terra was home, her interview suit in the back of her closet and jogging shorts covering her lower half. The desire was strong to expend her excess energy, and she figured a run was the only cure.

She was bending to lace up her sneaker when a knock sounded at the door. She looked into the peephole and received a shock of awareness. Mike stood on the other side.

Her body reacted first, with her heart racing, her palms sweating and her stomach tightening. How should she react to him? What did he want? To explain? Was he going to break her heart?

"Terra?"

She leaned her head against the door. "Yes."

"Can I come in?"

Why, she wanted to know before she let him in. Instead of asking, she opened the door.

His eyes roamed over her. "Going out?"

"For a run."

"Can I come in?"

Terra looked at the man she was in love with and wondered if he could read the pain in her body, her face. "I just have a minute."

He shut the door quietly. "How did your interview go?"

"Fine. They offered me the job."

"Terra," he said with affection in his voice. "That's incredible. When does it start?"

"I'll be here for another month or so until they bring someone in to manage this place, then I'll be moving on."

He smiled. "Congratulations. We'll have to go out and celebrate your promotion."

As friends? she wondered. "Sure, whenever you get some free time. No problem."

She wasn't sure how to act, like his girlfriend or his landlady. Silence enveloped them.

"May I sit down?"

"Please." She sat on the seat across from him. Hard as she tried not to look at him, she couldn't resist. He was still handsome and a wonderful sight for her eyes. Mike was one of the good guys, and that's why she loved him.

"Why are you here?"

"I feel like I owe you an explanation. I tried to call you yesterday, but your line was busy."

The question hung in the air like a bloated balloon. "I took the phone off the hook," she finally supplied.

He perused the room. "Did you cut all your flowers down?"

A small sad smile curved her lips. "I don't want to talk about flowers. I want to know what happened with your ex-wife."

"I don't love her. You need to know that first before we go anywhere else with this talk. I don't love her anymore. I love you."

Her heart skipped a beat. "What happened?"

He got up and paced. "I knew at the governor's mansion that I loved you. I was looking at this picture—"

"The one outside the ladies' room?" she said, experiencing a flood of nostalgia and love.

"That's the one."

She spoke softly. "I had a feeling, too. There was a meadow, people who loved us—"

He nodded. "Right. That was our future."

Terra shook her head, staring into his eyes. "Incredible."

She held herself tight, wanting to know all his thoughts. "What happened after that?"

"I loved April for a long time before I met you. We were married for ten years and got divorced because we couldn't resolve our differences. She and I talked, and she understands I have another life now."

"How do you feel?"

He came and sat beside her on the sofa. "It means I want us to be together. I want us to be that couple in the meadow. I want that endless love for the rest of our lives."

Her breath hitched. "I love you, too, but, Mike, I have a crazy family." She laughed without humor. "Your sister-in-law arrested my brother," she said softly. "I knew I recognized Jade, but it never occurred to me that I'd ever see her again. This is a nightmare. Your father sentenced my brother to five years in prison."

Mike grimaced. "He did?"

"Yes, he did. Judge Crawford was doing his upstanding job and my family was doing what they do best." She folded her hands in her lap. "I don't think I could stand for my family and yours to cross paths. For goodness' sake, your family is friends with the governor."

"Sweetheart, we can't pick our relatives. Don't not love me because your family might get into trouble. Terra, I'll never treat you bad. I'll never leave you. I promise."

The words filled her body with such a spirit of joy, Terra almost couldn't contain her emotions. Her first instinct was to hold on to the man she loved.

She reached for Mike and embraced him tight. "I do love you. I'm scared."

"You deserve love. Give me a chance."

"I have to move out of Atlanta. Your office is in Decatur. The commute is so long—" He pressed gentle kisses to her face and neck. "You have responsibilities. You're important," she said, exasperated with herself for trying to push him away when he was all she wanted.

"Don't find reasons for me not to love you. I want to marry you."

"Oh, God. Yes." She kissed him with the passion that swelled her heart.

"Say you love me, Terra." He clasped her face between his hands and smoldering gray eyes looked deeply into hers. What she saw was a lifetime of love together.

"I love you. Forever."

Dear Readers,

Thank you for supporting me throughout my career. Many of you have followed the Crawford family from *Silken Love* and *Keeping Secrets* and asked for Michael Crawford's story. I sincerely hope you enjoyed it.

Thank you for the letters, e-mails, thoughts and prayers. They are much appreciated.

If you haven't read my other works, please ask your bookseller or order online, *Now or Never, Silken Love, Silver Bells, Keeping Secrets, Commitments and Wine and Roses.*

Continue to e-mail me at Carmengreen1@aol.com or visit my Web site at www.authorcarmengreen.com and I will answer each and every one of you.

Peace and blessings,
Carmen

The impact that Dolly has made on the field of popular music was felt strongly in 1978, the year when Dolly captured three Broadcast Music Incorporated country awards, proof positive that she hadn't lost her country fans while crossing over into mainstream music. The American Guild of Variety Artists named Dolly Parton Best Female Country Performer of the Year, and she won the top honor in the music business, her first Grammy Award, for Best Female Country Vocalist Performance on a single, thanks to "Here You Come Again."

But, more important than any of these, 1978 was the year when Dolly was handed what she had always prayed for; in October, at the Country Music Association's twelfth annual presentation telecast from Nashville, Dolly Parton was voted not merely Best *Female* Entertainer, but Entertainer of the Year, the single highest award that the CMA can bestow. Dolly's cup was overflowing with self-righteous happiness; she could ask for no better confirmation that her hotly disputed career moves had been wise decisions.

Dolly
HERE I COME AGAIN

PaperJacks LTD.

TORONTO   NEW YORK

AN ORIGINAL

PaperJacks

DOLLY
HERE I COME AGAIN

PaperJacks LTD.

330 STEELCASE RD. E., MARKHAM, ONT. L3R 2M1
210 FIFTH AVE., NEW YORK, N.Y. 10010

First edition published November 1987

CAN ISBN 0-7701-0826-1
US ISBN 0-7701-0751-6
Copyright © 1987 by Leonore Fleischer
Printed in the USA

TABLE OF CONTENTS

Prologue
RAGS TO RHINESTONES

Chapter 1
MAKE A JOYFUL NOISE UNTO THE LORD

Chapter 2
SINGING FOR MONEY

Chapter 3
NASHVILLE AND CARL

Chapter 4
HELLO, DOLLY. HELLO, PORTER.

Chapter 5
GOOD-BYE, DOLLY. GOOD-BYE, PORTER.

Chapter 6
DOLLY CROSSES OVER

Chapter 7
DOLLY GOES HOLLYWOOD

Chapter 8
HAVING IT ALL

Chapter 9
WORKING NINE TO FIVE

Chapter 10
DOLLY ON A ROLL

Chapter 11
THE WORST LITTLE WHOREHOUSE IN TEXAS

Chapter 12
DOLLY, HOW COULD YOU?

Chapter 13
HOORAY FOR DOLLYWOOD!

Epilogue
HERE I COME AGAIN

To the unsinkable Dolly, who has a big brain under that big yellow wig, and a big heart inside that big chest, this book is respectfully dedicated.

—Leonore Fleischer,
New York City, 1987

"If I could get their attention long enough, I felt they would see beneath the boobs and find the heart, and that they would see beneath the wig and find the brains. I think one big part of whatever appeal I possess is the fact that I look totally one way and that I am totally another. I look artificial, but I'm not."

—Dolly Parton, in a 1981 interview with *Los Angeles Times* writer Robert Hilburn

Dolly
HERE I COME AGAIN

Prologue

Rags to Rhinestones

So what do you think? Are they
as big as you thought they were
going to be?

—Dolly Parton

Seen from the audience, even in her 5-inch
heels and her towering blond wig, Dolly Parton
looks small, almost fragile, which is strange when
one considers (as everybody does) her interna-
tionally famous physical endowments, possibly
the most talked-about, written-about, joked-about
pair of flotation devices since Jane Russell's.
There's at least one major difference between Dolly
Parton and Jane Russell, though. Jane's boobs were
an integral part of her smoldering sexuality. Her

1

cleavage in *The Outlaw* was the promise of more, much more, to come. Dolly's boobs are . . . cheerful. Rather than sexy, they are a country-style exaggeration of good-natured abundance, a gift from a jolly deity poking fun.

Dolly herself makes jokes about her voluptuous figure. One of her favorites is, "The reason my feet are so tiny is that things don't grow in the shade." Often, she'll kid her audience. "Ah see you out there with your binoculars, and Ah know jes' what you're lookin' at. But what you didn't realize is that you didn't need your binoculars."

These days she's very thin, having recently lost fifty pounds; her backside is tiny, her waistline measures Scarlett O'Hara's size, 18 inches, but her breasts are still . . . Dolly's breasts. "When I try to do pushups, they never leave the floor," she quips, with a playful wink at her fans. She has always refused to reveal her bust measurement, but swears it's nowhere near the 45 inches that the press has estimated, pointing out that she's only 5 feet tall and has a small frame.

And here's a paradox: On the one hand, Dolly Parton dresses to show off those celebrated mammaries; on the other, she is constantly complaining, in person and in print, that people don't look beneath the breasts to find her heart.

But then Dolly herself is something of a paradox, this curvaceous woman with the sweet, dimpled face and breathy voice of a little girl, this God-loving country woman dressed like a city siren, powdered and painted, bespangled, besequined, bewigged, this 5-foot woman who is a creative songwriter, a great performer, the person listed in *The Guinness Book of World Records* as the highest-paid female entertainer in the world, a shrewd business entrepreneur who not only owns her own music publishing and film production companies, but her very own theme park!

Dolly Parton has taken a unique composite of country shrewdness, innocence, full-figured sensuality, and backwoods gospel-singing fervor and built it into a public persona that reaches across the footlights and takes the listener by the hand. "Howdy," she seems to say with every song. "Come set a spell." On the screen she sparkles with personality; her image comes across fresh and clean, despite the outlandishly vulgar clothing, clanking jewelry, and often preposterous trademark wigs. Even when she played a madam in *The Best Little Whorehouse in Texas*, she exuded a breath of mountain air and a healthy freshness.

Having traveled the long road from a backwoods dirt farm in the foothills of the Great Smoky Mountains to become one of the superstars of the entertainment world, Dolly earns millions of dollars and gives money away with a free and generous hand. As much as she is paid, she's worth more, because every bone in her little body is making that effort to please the people who flock to see her, to see them go away smiling.

Her small hands, covered in gold and diamond rings, strike chords on the guitar, and that famous voice swells out through the microphone to capture the audience with its sweet vibrato. On one finger, a ring revolves to catch the light. Made of diamonds to Dolly's own design, the ring features twin butterflies, one behind the other, that pivot

3

and spin when her hands move, catching the light like a precious pinwheel. Dolly loves butterflies; she has taken the butterfly as kind of a personal symbol and wears the representation of one at all times. Their beauty and freedom, the bright colors of their wings, are a mirror of her own personality. Besides, she can't resist anything bright and sparkling.

When Dolly Parton began to sing professionally, she was paid $20 a week, which wasn't bad money for a ten-year-old. Today she is forty-one, and ABC-TV has just signed her to a record $40,000,000 contract for a new series of variety spectaculars, and the network has committed to thirteen shows. When she plays Las Vegas, she commands close to $500,000 a week. In her career, she's won three Grammy Awards; among her more than 60 albums are five gold and three platinum; she's had 22 number-one hit singles. Dolly has gathered up into her small hands, with their long red nails, every award a performer can win, including being voted Entertainer of the Year by the Country Music Association. She's won many awards two or three times. *People* magazine once wrote that Dolly Parton "ought to be declared a national treasure."

Her crossover from country to the pop charts was one of the few successful such transitions in the music business. Dolly went from the cover of *Country Music* to the cover of *Rolling Stone* without a backward glance. More than once, she's graced the cover of *People*. She moved from the top of the country charts to the top of the pop charts without losing her down-home flavor or her down-home fans. Her legion of worshippers just grew larger.

For all her wigs and spangles, her elaborate dresses, false eyelashes, 3-inch blood-red acrylic fingernails, vulgar jewelry, and a Mae West figure, this is no floozy, no bimbo, no dumb blonde. She is the author of more than 3,000 songs. She is the witty, intelligent, down-to-earth woman whom the feminist magazine *Ms.* selected as one of its 1986 Women of the Year, for "creating popular songs about real women," and for "bringing jobs and understanding to the mountain people of Tennessee." Once again, the paradox.

What makes up the Dolly Parton magic? What drives her to work so hard, even in the face of illness and exhaustion? In a world where talent often goes unrewarded, how did Dolly rise to the very top of the heap? She didn't claw her way there; she didn't cheat her way there. She worked harder and longer than most others would have done without becoming discouraged. She did it on her own, with determination, grit, cheerful optimism, and, above all, deep faith in the Lord. Where others despair, Dolly Parton dreams; where others curse, Dolly Parton prays.

But as she traveled that long, exhausting road, what tolls did she have to pay? To gain what she has, what was she forced to surrender? What did she lose along the way? Nobody's life, no matter how privileged or sheltered, is free of pain. Nobody makes it to the top of the heap without changing, without sacrificing something too secret and too precious to name. What are Dolly Parton's secrets?

5

Chapter One

Make a Joyful Noise Unto the Lord

I was born with a happy nature and a happy heart. I was born with the gift of understanding people and loving them and I've never been unhappy. I've always seen the light at the end of the tunnel.

—Dolly Parton

When you think of Tennessee, you think of music. Just the mention of the name brings to mind Beale Street, Memphis, home of the blues, of W. C. Handy and the moanin' low of rich black voices. When you say "Tennessee" you say Elvis Presley the King, and Graceland, the 15,000-square-foot palace where he once reigned supreme and still does, even in death. When you think of

Tennessee, Nashville comes immediately to mind—
the "Grand Ole Opry" and the entertainment and
recording empire built by country music pickers
and singers. And, when you think of Tennessee,
you have to think of Dolly Parton.

The sovereign state of Tennessee in all its natural glory was once the property of the Cherokee
Indians. Its very name comes from the Cherokee
name *Tanasi*. Even today, one can still see traces
of the Cherokee Indian beauty in the faces of
some Tennesseans—the straight, black glossy hair,
the high cheekbones and dark slanting eyes, often
combined with the fairer features of the Irish,
Scottish, and English farmers and settlers who
came in the 1700s to fight the French and the
Indians and take possession of the land.

Eastern Tennessee, near the North Carolina
border, is a world of forests and mountains, of
rivers and national parks and wildlife preserves.
When spring arrives at the foothills of the Great
Smoky Mountains, the wild dogwood trees come
into flower, as though millions of fragile white
butterflies had settled on their branches for just
a little while. Long rows of budding forsythia
bushes are heavy with golden flowers echoing
the color of the sun. Azaleas and massive rho-
dodendrons, which thrive in the acid soil beneath the tall evergreens, burst into a dazzling
display of flowering, setting the hollows of the
hills and the fertile reddish bottomland ablaze
with crimson and purple. The pink-and-white
blossoms of the mountain laurel blanket the
hillsides, casting delicate shadows like lace over
the harsh outcroppings of granite. Hickory trees

and elms, slender poplars and sturdy oaks, fragrant pine and cedar dig their roots in deep and hold the land, spreading canopies of their leaves over the hollows and the ridges.

In springtime, Sevier County in eastern Tennessee appears lush with promise. Along the Little Pigeon River the daffodils and wild wood hyacinth come early into their bloom. But the soil of the remote hillsides in the backwoods country is often thin and rocky, and it can be mighty hard to scratch a decent living out of it.

It was into this magnificent contradiction—earth's beauty masking the hard work, hard times, and doing without—that a baby girl was born on a snowy morning, January 19, 1946, just on the cusp between Capricorn and Aquarius. She drew her first breath and hollered her first musical holler in a Locust Ridge, Sevier County, backwoods two-room cabin.

Her daddy and mama were Robert Lee and Avie Lee Parton. They named the baby Dolly Rebecca; she was the first of the Parton children to inherit her father's light coloring.

"Daddy's people are fair and blond and blue-eyed," Dolly was to tell the world in later years. "My mama's people have a lot of Indian blood, so they're dark, with high cheekbones and real dark hair. I have Mama's features, Mama's smile, and her dimples, but I got my daddy's nose. I also got my pride and determination from Daddy, but I got my mama's personality."

Lee Parton had no cash to pay Dr. Robert F. Thomas, who delivered his daughter, so they paid

9

him in kind—some cornmeal ground from corn Lee had grown himself. "That's what I cost," a smiling Dolly would proudly tell reporters after she became famous, "a sack o' cornmeal."

Dolly Parton came into this world just at the end of the hot war and the beginning of the Cold War, at the very dawning of the postwar atomic age, only five months after American bombings leveled Hiroshima and Nagasaki, thus bringing the war to a hideous end and introducing the human race to the annihilistic powers of the atom bomb.

Sevier County is not far from Oak Ridge, Tennessee, where American scientists and engineers had labored to bring to birth the era of nuclear technology. Yet, ironically, the backwoods mountain country of Tennessee would move very slowly into the modern age, just as it had remained virtually untouched by the war, with the exception of the young mountain men who had died or been maimed in the fighting.

In other parts of the South, women had moved from the farms into the cities to take on men's work when menfolk had put on uniforms and gone off to serve their country. It was one of the great American societal shifts of the twentieth century, the population change from rural to urban, and women entering the workplace in force, never to leave it again. They would never again be kept down on the farm once they'd seen a paycheck.

But in the hills where Dolly was born, on the virtual back porch of the house where the atom bomb was built, life was still very much the same as it had been before the war. Menfolk sowed and harvested the crops, and did the heaviest chores; women raised the babies and did practically everything else that needed doing on a farm. There were no electrical appliances in the Parton household, at least until the girls grew up enough to help their mother cook, clean, and look after the little ones. Sons and daughters were the only labor-saving devices mountain families had.

Dolly was the fourth Parton child, fourth in a dirt-poor but fiercely independent family that would number twelve children, eleven of whom lived to grow up. When their oldest, Willadeene, was born about a year after her parents' wedding, Avie Lee was but sixteen. When Dolly Rebecca came kicking and hollering into the world—although her family says she was born singing— her mother was only twenty-two. It's hard to get more country than that—a rural mountain cabin in the South, poor dirt farmers, kids coming year after year, and parents not much older than other folks' brothers and sisters.

"Mama grew up with us kids," Dolly would joke to the world years later. "There was always one on her and one in her." And it was true. First came Willadeene, then David and Denver; next, Dolly Rebecca, the last Parton baby to be born at home. After her, Avie Lee always went to a clinic or to the hospital, and there she gave birth to Bobby, Stella, Cassie, Randy, and Larry. Because Avie Lee suffered a life-threatening attack of spinal meningitis when she was carrying Larry, the baby lived for only nine hours after he was born.

But the family never forgot him. "We were twelve kids," they always say, which still includes Larry.

Floyd and Frieda, the twins, were next in line, and after the twins came Rachel, the youngest. All the children shared a mixed Dutch, Irish, and Cherokee heritage that is truly melting-pot America.

Avie Lee Owens, with her Indian cheekbones and silky raven hair, was fifteen years old on the day Robert Lee Parton, called Lee, first set eyes on her and fell in love. He was seventeen, with reddish-blond coloring inherited from his ancestors in the British Isles. He saw her in church; she was the preacher's daughter, and he made his mind up there and then to marry that pretty Avie Lee. Even by mountain people's standards they were very young to marry, but they were a determined pair, and two days later they were man and wife. That was almost fifty years ago, and they are still like bride and groom today, still deeply in love.

Life in those days was a struggle; although Lee Parton was an unlettered man who could neither read nor write, he was "the smartest man I've ever known," as Dolly praised him. Hard-working, independent, and proud, he rose before dawn every morning to pull a meager existence out of the ground. When crops failed, or when the harvest was in, he would hire himself out as a construction worker, carpenter, or day laborer to support his rapidly growing family. In the early years of their marriage, Lee made and sold moonshine whiskey out of corn mash; it was an illegal activity, because moonshine carried no revenue tax stamps, but it was hardly an uncommon practice in the hills. When Avie Lee, the preacher's daughter, disapproved, her husband gave up moonshining to please her.

But, hard as the couple worked, the kids kept coming and Avie Lee was often ill. The spinal meningitis she had when carrying Larry nearly killed her; her fever was so high that she had to be packed in ice. The doctor gave her up for lost, telling the stricken family that, even if Mama lived, she would be a cripple for life. But, just like a miracle, the following morning there was Avie Lee, sitting up in bed and smiling. Nevertheless, the illness took its toll on her strength and left her deaf in one ear.

In between the childbirths there were miscarriages that further sapped Avie Lee's energies. In her song "In the Good Ole Days When Times Were Bad," Dolly would later immortalize those difficult days. No amount of money could buy those years from her, she would write, and no amount of money could pay her to go back and live them over again.

"In a big country family," Dolly would tell interviewer Cliff Jahr years later, "you're just brought up by the hair of her head. You do what you got to. I—believe it or not—was a tomboy. I could climb a tree or wrestle or run as fast as any brother. We faced starvation, but Mama and Daddy taught values you don't learn in schoolrooms—God, nature, how to care for other people and for the land, how to trust people and when not to. In a way, I'm still that little stringy-headed girl who ran around barefoot, sores on her legs, fever blisters, no clothes, who dreamed of being someone special someday."

The kids slept three or four, sometimes more, in crude beds, with no sheets, only stitched-together rags. "As soon as I'd go to bed," Dolly remembers, "the kids would wet on me. That was the only warm thing we knew in the wintertime. That was our most pleasure—to get peed on. If you could just not fan the cover. If you kept the air out from under the cover, the pee didn't get so cold."

In winter, the Parton kids would bundle up in clothing before going to bed, and huddle together for warmth.

Since there wasn't a hope of indoor plumbing in the cabin, and the outdoor plumbing consisted of little more than a one-holer, a tiny shack hiding a hole cut in a board over a limepit, well-worn by generations of backsides, with cut-up donated newspapers for toilet paper, how did the Parton family bathe? It was a question that Lawrence Grobel would ask Dolly in his famous *Playboy* interview in 1978.

"We made our own soap," replied Dolly, "and in the summertime, we'd go to the river. That was like a big bath. And we'd all go in swimming and wash each other's hair. Soap was just flowin' down the river and we were so dirty we left a ring around the Little Pigeon River."

And in the winter? "I had to take a bath every night, 'cause the kids peed on me every night. We just had a pan of water and we'd wash down as far as possible, and we'd wash up as far as possible. Then, when somebody'd clear the room, we'd wash *possible.*"

Yet, even if the Partons had none of the "luxuries" that to most Americans are necessities—running water, flush toilets, decent clothes for school—even if there wasn't an extra penny to buy the things children dream about when they see pictures in someone else's old magazines or in the Sears Roebuck "wish book," even when crops were poor and there was only one hog a year to butcher for two grownups and eleven children and the kids went to bed fed only on starches with no meat, they never went hungry for affection.

"We got no money, but we're rich in love," wrote Dolly later in "Poor Folks Town." She took this saying from her mother; it was a favorite of hers. "We're rich people because we know we got love and we got each other," Dolly's mama always said. Love there was aplenty, along with Avie Lee's famous Stone Soup.

When crops failed and there were only a few vegetables in the house—potatoes, onions, maybe a few greens and tomatoes—Avie Lee Parton would send her children out to find the biggest, smoothest stones they could find. Then she would choose the best stone to add to the pot.

"Mama made such a big ole fuss about pickin' out the right one," remembers Dolly. "She'd laugh and say, 'Oh, there's magic in *this* one. I kin feel it.' "

In that way, Avie Lee passed her love, her sense of imagination and wonder, along to her children. It was a gift no amount of money could buy. "Some people may think we were real poor, but I can't see it that way," says Avie Lee Owens Parton. "We were just ordinary Americans, and I was always real proud of what we had."

Because their mother was ill so much of the time, worn out with childbearing and fevers, the older children looked after the young ones. Willadeene, Dolly, and Stella each had a "baby" of her own to look after; Dolly's was to have been Larry, but he died a few hours after birth.

"Oh, that really hurt me deep, 'cause I was at that age where I took things so hard." Dolly was only ten when Larry died—"ten years old, just tryin' to grow up and be a child at the same time." The whole family mourned the baby for a long time.

The Partons moved around a lot in search of more room, better farmland, and a more comfortable life. When Dolly was three, they moved to a tar-paper shack on a farm of several hundred acres between Locust Ridge and Webb Mountain, in the Great Smokies. There they stayed for five years, while Dolly's daddy grew a small cash crop of tobacco and food to feed his growing family, taking out the most the stony earth would allow. This was Dolly Parton's "Tennessee Mountain Home," the subject of one of her most popular country songs. A picture of the shack is on the cover of the *Tennessee Mountain Home* album, her first concept album, and possibly the first concept album in country music history. Naturally, the price of the shack itself has skyrocketed because Dolly Parton has made it so famous.

In Dollywood, the 400-acre, $6,000,000 theme

park tucked into the Great Smoky Mountains just outside Pigeon Forge that she opened in 1986, Dolly has reproduced that Webb Mountain shack, complete in every detail right down to the brass spittoon, the old foot-pedal sewing machine (the original shack had no electricity), and the sepia photograph of Lee's daddy, Luther Parton.

But actually growing up there, running barefoot, keeping the kerosene lantern burning all night so the rats wouldn't run over the bed where she was sleeping—to this day the grownup Dolly still sleeps with a light on—was often a lot less picturesque than the custom-built amusement park replica would indicate. Not to mention that, ironically, the replica most have cost a fortune to build—possibly a hundred times more than the original, and the same amount of money that was spent on the replica Dollywood cabin would have made the *real* Parton family cabin comfortable while the kids were growing up. But that's America.

"We had nothin'," Dolly told *New York Times* writer Chris Chase, "so far as material things. If you had a nice sweater or a lipstick, in our mind you had to be rich. We were so small all at once, and my daddy didn't have money to buy things." She went on to enumerate the things that entranced her as a child—flowers, birds, butterflies, junk jewelry, anything that was brightly colored or caught the light.

"When my daddy used to plow the fields, and the sun would shine down, that quartz stuff would glisten, and I was sure we had struck diamonds. I used to pick up all kinds of glass and shiny rock. I just loved the beauty of the things, the sparkle."

Dolly is still attracted to sparkle and bright colors. She once furnished her Nashville mansion with valuable antiques, as many wealthy people in the South do. "You know, everybody in Nashville collects antiques. And when we first got our house, I bought a bunch of old stuff, too. I didn't like it, it was just too drab. I like things a little more gaudy."

So Dolly got rid of all that costly antique furniture, preferring more "cheerful" and colorful brand-new pieces.

If they didn't have much in the way of material wealth, the ever-increasing Parton family had one of God's greatest gifts—the gift of music. Both sides of the family, the Owenses and the Partons, were musical, and just about all the children inherited at least some talent for it, even if none of them was to prove quite as gifted as Dolly.

"My mama's people were all of 'em singers and musicians, even songwriters. My daddy's kinfolk were musical, too. But mostly they sang at home or in the church; nobody ever thought of venturin' out of the hills and the hollers. But I was always full of dreams and plans, and I was the one had the grit to do it," states Dolly.

Grandpa Jake Owens, the hellfire reverend, wrote hundred of songs and hymns, some of which, such as "Singing His Praises," were recorded by Kitty Wells, then the acknowledged Queen of Country Music, who was most famous for "It Wasn't God Who Made Honky Tonk Angels." Years later, Dolly would record her granddaddy's song "Book of Life." Avie Lee composed songs, too, and knew many folk ballads that she would sing to her children in the family "singalongs."

Even before she could talk, Dolly could hum little tunes and she was always on key. At the age of eighteen months, she was hearing little melodies in her head and humming them, unaware that they were original. Soon, she was putting simple lyrics of her own devising to the melodies. Dolly began writing complete songs by the time she was five, earlier than she learned to read and write.

"I had this little doll, and it was only made out of a corncob, and Daddy made a little wig for her out of corn silk, you know, with the tassel? I called the doll Little Tiny Tassel-Top, and I made up a little song about her. I was five years old."

It was at that age that Dolly first realized the songs she hummed were her own, because it was then that she went to her mother and asked her, "Mama, will you write this song down for me?" And she sang "Little Tiny Tassel-Top" for Avie Lee.

To this day Dolly Parton can't read a note of music. When she writes a song, she sings it into a tape recorder and then sends it out to a professional service to have the music transcribed onto music paper. But even back then music flowed naturally from the little girl with the rosy cheeks, the bright blue eyes, and the deep dimples. Her grandfather, the Reverend Jake Owens, said that "Dolly started singin' as soon as she quit cryin'."

"I used to make up songs and my mama would write 'em down for me," says Dolly. She said I was makin' up songs *before* I was five, but by the

19

time I reached that age I used to beg her to write 'em down so she could read 'em back to me. When I was about seven years old, I started playin' the git-tar. It's all I've ever known."

Actually, Dolly's "git-tar" was little more than "a busted-up ol' mandolin" that was fitted out with two guitar strings. Primitive and limited as it was, to Dolly it was a genuine musical instrument and she wrote many songs with only its few chords.

"Music was a freedom," Dolly told Toby Thompson of *The Village Voice* in 1976. "My mama's people all picked some musical instruments and sung. Most of my daddy's people did." Her heritage of song came from gospel music, from the Church of God assembly, Avie Lee's father's little backwoods church, where everyone would gather together to "make a joyful noise unto the Lord."

"I been makin' a joyful noise ever since." Dolly laughs. The Parton kids' granddaddy, the Reverend Jake Owens, is the hero of Dolly's song entitled "Daddy Was an Old-Time Preacher Man," and he preached a hellfire-and-brimstone sermon. In Dolly's words, "He preached hell so hot you could feel the heat." Before and after the scripture readings and the sermon, the congregation would sing. The faithful would bring their country instruments—fiddles, tambourines, guitars, banjos, mandolins—into the church to give God praise with their picking. And they sang the simple but powerful strains of gospel hymns and old-time spirituals, which has been perhaps the strongest musical influence on Dolly Parton to this day. From the age of six, Dolly would sing

her heart out in that old country church, sing the
hymn tunes she loved, first with her sisters and
her granddaddy, and later solo, her sweet child-
ish soprano soaring to the wooden rafters of the
little church.

The Church of God was a very free church.
Aside from the scripture reading and the sermon,
there was no structured service for the worshippers. "If anybody wanted to get up and sing or
shout out an emotion," says Dolly, "they would
do it. There was freedom there, so I came to
know what freedom is, so I could know God and
come to know freedom within myself." She would
always associate this freedom with making music.

"I think that the soul feeling I get in my voice
started with my church-singing days. The same
feeling and sincerity leak over into anything I
sing now."

Thanks in part to Avie Lee's deep religious faith,
the family sang church hymns at home, too, accompanied by Lee Parton's banjo and guitar. But
there were also "play-party" folk songs like "Old
Joe Clark" and variations on the old Elizabethan
ballads brought from the mother country, usually
mournful songs of young men and women dying
of blighted love. It was a rich, if mixed, legacy of
music. Soon, Dolly was singing solo again, at
home as well as in church. The child, nicknamed
"Blossom" by the family ("That's gonna be the
title of my autobiography, Blossom," vows Dolly),
sang constantly, at work and at play, either hymns
or the songs she had made up herself, songs
about her life with her family on the farm, about

sick children dying and going to Jesus, and other facets of her own experience.

Although after she had achieved success Dolly could joke about her family's poverty, her growing-up years were not an easy time for any of the Partons. "Sure we had plumbin' where I grew up. Out back! You heard o' four rooms and a bath. Our house had four rooms and a *path*! Out on Locust Ridge, the way you could tell a rich family from a poor family is that the rich family had a two-holer, and the poor family had a one-holer. We had runnin' water—that is, when one of us ran to get some. Whenever company came, Mama would say, 'Run out an' sweep the yard.' With all them children runnin' around, we didn't have no grass left out front, just a plain dirt yard, but Mama always wanted it kept nice. We'd sweep it out slick as a mole."

In the backyard, the Partons kept their vegetable garden, a pumpkin patch; they also raised some potatoes, corn, beans, turnips, greens, and other vegetables for their scanty table.

"We canned a lot. Never had much meat, mostly beans and taters. Plus biscuits and gravy. We were never really hungry, except for variety. I still love biscuits and gravy."

You can take the girl out of the country, but you can't take the country out of the girl. "When we was kids on Locust Ridge," Dolly would tell *People* magazine in a 1986 cover story, "we would always drink out of a tin can. And I still do. It seems to keep things colder. Even at my beautiful homes, I'm always drinking out of a tin can, which drives my secretary nuts. I'm saving coffee cans to drink out of and she's throwing them out and it makes me so mad. I still like to pee off the porch every now and then. There's nothing like peeing on those snobs in Beverly Hills." Dolly Parton's honest earthiness puts the Beverly Hillbillies in the shade!

The true mark of the artist is the ability to take the sad things of life and transform them into art; even more so, to take a catastrophe befalling one and weave it magically into something that can reach out and touch *millions*. Dolly Parton does this time and time again, using the raw material of her own childhood, a childhood of poverty, affection, and early dreams, but nowhere does she do it more artistically or touchingly than in one of her most beloved songs, her tribute to Avie Lee Parton's goodness and loving heart, "Coat of Many Colors." This is the song of which Dolly says, "This means more to me than any song I wrote."

The never-forgotten episode behind the song goes back to the time when Dolly was ten years old, and owned no new clothing to wear to school, only patched-up and shabby hand-me-downs. Until Dolly was nine, the Parton children attended a one-room country school, where shabbiness was universal, and nobody made fun of anybody else. But the little schoolhouse burned down, and Dolly and her brothers and sisters were forced to transfer in the middle of the term to a different school, new and modern, where the children all had unpatched and unshabby clothing to wear. The Parton children were immediately set apart, not only because of their hand-me-down clothing, but

23

because they brought their lunches to school in paper sacks since they were unable to afford school cafeteria food.

Dolly's song says, "I didn't have a coat and it was way down in the fall." Wanting to give her daughter something new to wear to school, and mindful of Dolly's favorite Bible story about Joseph's coat of many colors, Avie Lee stitched together a coat of bright-colored corduroy scraps out of "a box of rags that someone gave us" for her little girl.

It's a story that Dolly would tell often. "Mama worked hard for weeks makin' that coat out of whatever material she could find, because she wanted me to look real nice. They were takin' our picture at school for the first time. She'd tell me how Joseph had a coat of many colors just like the one she was sewin' for me. When I put it on, I was so proud of it; I thought it was just beautiful! I thought I looked exactly like Joseph in the Bible! But when I got to school, all the other kids laughed at me and pointed their fingers.

"Rag Top! they hollered. 'Hey, you, Rag Top!' And they grabbed at my coat and pulled it until the buttons started poppin'.

"I kep' tellin' them, 'No! This is a coat of many colors, just like Joseph had in the Bible.' But they just made mock and went on yellin', 'It's just a buncha stitched-together rags!' "

Dolly didn't have a shirt or anything on under the coat, and her young breasts were just beginning to bud. The tugging at her buttons was the ultimate humiliation, and when the camera clicked for the class picture in the schoolhouse,

Dolly Parton's anguished face was captured on film, stained with tears. The episode haunts her to this day.

"I was just so ashamed I wanted to die! It was years before I could even talk to anyone about what happened."

But she fought the taunting children like a tiger. "It was one of those times when you fight to survive. Even with all the shame I felt, them kids couldn't make me not be proud of my coat of many colors."

When Dolly came home from school crying, her mother gathered her up in her arms and tried to console her. "They can only see with their eyes," she told her daughter. "But you can see with your heart."

Possibly because of painful experiences like the one with Joseph's coat, the things that always attracted Dolly as a child and to this day were luxuries the family could never afford. Somehow the little five-year-old girl took the notion that if she could write enough songs and sell them, she would have the money to buy all the pretty things she wanted, but even given those long-ago fantasies of stardom and great wealth, nobody could have foreseen just how true those dreams would come. Not even Dolly herself could have dreamed that one day she'd become the highest-paid female entertainer in the world.

There was another, even more important impetus behind Dolly's dreams other than mere pretty luxuries. She wanted to become rich so she could give her parents an easy life. Seeing her mother ill so often, and the family unable to afford doc-

tors or decent medical care; watching her father
bend his back and work until his hands cracked
open and bled; seeing him injured and limping as
the result of a construction accident—these tore
at the young girl's tender sensibilities. If she were
rich, Mama and Daddy could live comfortably
and well, having all the luxuries they could never
before afford. Dolly vowed that someday she would
provide handsomely for her parents, and she has
fulfilled that promise many times over. As soon
as she had earned enough money, she bought her
mama and daddy the comfortable home she always dreamed they would have. In fact, they live
in a mansion high on a hill ("It's just like a Hall-
mark card," says Dolly), even though they still do
their shopping at the local grocery store.

When she and her husband, Carl, built their
23-room dream house outside Nashville, Dolly
had a special mobile home set up nearby to house
her parents when they came to visit and to give
them some privacy.

But that was far into the future. When Dolly
was little, not only her dreams but her make-do's
took the place of reality. Like most little girls,
Dolly was fascinated by women's makeup, but
the Partons were too poor to afford even a lipstick. "A lipstick looked like a million dollars to
me," Dolly says, laughing. Avie Lee was a lenient,
forgiving mother who was growing up alongside
her children and who allowed them certain lee-
way in their activities, because she was sensitive
to how her children, especially the girls, felt.

But Robert Lee Parton was a strict father who
didn't hold with girls painting their faces. He

never hesitated to back up his disapproval with "a whippin', but the whippin' was worth it for a few days with a red mouth." Even so, the Parton sisters often "made do," experimenting with whatever homegrown ingredients they could lay their hands on—flour for face powder, burned matches to get the carbon to darken their eyebrows, mercurochrome or merthiolate to color their lips instead of the lipstick they couldn't afford. The good thing about merthiolate was that it took a long time to wear off, so Dolly had "lipstick" on for a week or more. The medicine might have stung, but Dolly never minded. "Daddy could never rub *that* off.

"I knew I wanted to be a singer from the time when I was seven or eight and learned my first chord on the guitar. I also wanted to be a star—the biggest in the world. I wanted pretty clothes and attention and to live in a big house and buy things for Mama and Daddy. Of course, I didn't have better sense in those days.

"But as I got older, I didn't lose track of my dreams. I just thought, *Well, why can't I do all that?* The secret was to take one step at a time. And that's what I've done." Although Dolly is modest about the direct, simple way she went about obtaining her heart's desire, there is little doubt that the secret of her success lies in her spunk, her country grit, and her down-to-earth courage.

At a very early age, the precocious Dolly made up her mind that someday she'd leave the harsh and painful realities of poverty on Locust Ridge and travel the 200 miles to Nashville. There she

would become a country singing star like Patsy
Cline or Kitty Wells, and her dreams would all
come true. Dolly never doubted those dreams.
Her mother was her chief supporter, her biggest
fan, and truest believer, her most constant source
of encouragement. "Mama never let us lose our
hopes."

Meanwhile, all Dolly could do was pick out a
couple of thin chords on her old mandolin with
its two bass guitar strings, write song after song,
and sleep five and six in a bed with her brothers
and sisters.

But there was something more than melody in
Dolly's soul. There exists in the mountain chains
of the Appalachians and the Great Smokies a
centuries-old bardic tradition from the British Isles,
passed down from generation to generation through
song, story, and "play-party" games, which gives
the simple country speech of the isolated people
a lyrical overlay. Dolly's song lyrics exhibit this
oral poetic tradition; they are rich in simile and
metaphor, always evocative of real life; they are
pictures painted with words.

All Dolly's songs were autobiographical; they
dealt with the themes she knew best: growing up
barefoot; a passel of brothers and sisters; the
strength and pride of her parents; her deep religious feelings and faith in Jesus; the death of a
child or of a beloved relative or friend in the
Korean War; the love between mother and babies;
the respect she had for her father and her grandfather—meaningful subjects that expressed true
and recognizable emotions. To strike a chord

in the heart of the listener, a song must be pulled from the very heart of the writer and singer.

When Dolly Parton was eight years old, on a momentous and joyful day, her mother's brother, Uncle Robert Owens, who believed in Dolly from the start, gave her a real guitar of her own, a little Martin. It was then, for the first time, that she learned to play full chords on a complete set of strings. It was to be the first definite step up on Dolly's stairway to the stars. Once she had her Martin, her "real" guitar, nothing could stop her.

Her childhood fantasies of fame and fortune took on an even straighter direction: 200 miles west, to Nashville, the Mecca of country music, and, especially, the "Grand Ole Opry." Until you had been invited to sing on the "Opry," you weren't anybody to be reckoned with. But once you had, you could be on your way to being a star, to a recording contract on a country and western label and to concert appearances and road shows. And who knew? One might get even luckier, and be awarded that prize valued above all others—to be chosen as an "Opry" regular. Dolly knew that there was a place called Nashville, where she could go to become a star. But it seemed to her to be a million miles away. Even so, day by day, Nashville increasingly became the bright, beckoning focus of little Dolly Parton's driving ambitions.

Chapter Two

Singing for Money

I always knew I was somebody.
I dreamed big dreams and I got
out early.

—Dolly Parton

But even the most talented and precocious child doesn't run until she learns to walk, and Nashville wasn't just sitting there waiting for Dolly Rebecca Parton, amateur, no matter how gifted her friends and family believed she was. So Dolly began singing in public.

She was already singing in church on Sundays, so it seemed almost natural that she would sing in school on Mondays. Not her own songs, though, but hymns, a kind of continuation of the

Church of God, because the one-room school-house in Mountain View held chapel services every Monday morning. Either they had never heard of the Constitutional separation of Church and State, or they didn't much care, and what federal agency was going to come down salty on a little backwoods schoolhouse with not more than 15 students in all the grades put together?

Singing hymns in public led Dolly to singing old folk songs and ballads, as Dolly's confidence in herself and her powers grew. It was still a tiny world that surrounded her—family, church, and school probably didn't come to 100 different people all told—but Dolly's philosophy was always, "You gotta start somewhere, even if it's small. Anything's better than sitting still." So she sang for that 100, and dreamed of singing for thousands, even millions.

Good attendance at school wasn't easy for the mountain children of east Tennessee in the 1950s. In Dolly's day there weren't paved roads or scheduled school buses painted bright yellow. Boys and girls had to walk miles to school, some of the way over rocky and treacherous back roads, which never got plowed out in the winter.

"There weren't many people who lived way back in the holler where we did. We walked a long, long way to school. It was only a one-room schoolhouse that had no more than 10 or 15 kids in the whole school and one teacher. We sat in rows by grades. Maybe there was one or two kids in the first grade, might be two or three in the second, one in the third, and so on. Teacher'd sit with us grades one at a time, while the other grades read

31

their books or did their exercises in their note-books till she could get to them."

Sometimes Dolly would arrive at the little schoolhouse with freezing feet; warm boots were a rich kid's luxury. She'd have to thaw out her blue feet in front of the wood-burning stove before she could begin her studies.

Often, too, the children of farmer folk would have to miss days, even weeks, of school when the crops had to be seeded, or dug out and stored. Survival took priority over education. "In the mountains, schoolin' is just not that important," recalls Dolly. "My daddy didn't 'specially want me to go to school, and my mama, she didn't care."

Nevertheless, Dolly was determined to get an education and be the first Parton youngster to graduate from high school. Even though she was more motivated by music than by arithmetic and spelling, she was bright enough to make up the schoolwork she missed on her absentee days.

It was around this same time that the Partons moved once again, to a farm in Caton's Chapel, about 40 or 50 acres, and there they would remain until Dolly graduated from high school in 1964. Caton's Chapel wasn't even a dot on the map of Tennessee; it was little more than a name and a cluster of cabins not far from the church.

When Dolly was eight, she attended a music show at the Pines Theater in Sevierville with her mother and some of her brothers and sisters. It took all the courage the small girl had to ask the man in charge if she could go up on the stage and sing, but Dolly was never short on courage. The audience loved her, and it was her first real taste of applause. She had sung before on a TV show in Knoxville, but that had been with her class from school; this was just Dolly alone. If she needed any extra assurance that singing in front of an audience was what she was born to do, the sound of clapping and cheering gave her that reinforcement.

Like many mountain families whose cabins had no electricity, the Partons owned a battery radio, which, Dolly said, "would whistle in and out. I remember us pourin' water on that ground wire to try an' pick up 'The Lone Ranger.' " Not that the family could always afford new batteries, but whenever the batteries were working, they listened to "Grand Ole Opry."

More than just a radio program, "Grand Ole Opry" is a Saturday night institution all over the Southland. It had started out over radio station WSM as a program called "WSM Barn Dance" on November 28, 1925, and it hasn't missed a performance since, the longest-running continuous radio program in America. Its combination of earthy, hee-haw hillbilly humor and the best singers and songs in country and western music had made the "Opry" so popular that by the time Dolly was born, hundreds of people would get up extra early every Saturday morning just to line up outside the broadcast studio at the old Ryman Auditorium in the heart of downtown Nashville, hoping to get a precious ticket to see the stars in person.

And big stars they were—the biggest. At first, the "Opry" featured mostly fiddlers and banjos in bands, the Fruit Jar Drinkers, Dr. Humphrey

Bate and the Possum Hunters, the Gully Jumpers, and other bands like them. But soon, individual stars would begin to emerge, and by the time the Parton family was crowded around the old battery portable, country music legends were appearing on the "Opry."

There were hillbilly comics like beloved Sara Ophelia Colley, known as Minnie Pearl, with her funny hats and her trademark "How-*dee!*"; the team of Lonzo and Oscar; Jerry Clower; singers and songwriters such as the immortal Hank Williams and his sad songs; the King of Country Music, Roy Acuff, and his band, the Smoky Mountain Boys; Maybelle Carter and her daughters; Bill Monroe; Ernest Tubb and his steel guitar; Red Foley; Chet Atkins; Eddy Arnold; Hank Snow; a very young Johnny Cash; Patsy Cline; Jean Shepard; Kitty Wells—the list goes on and on. These were the important men and women who had influenced the very way country music was expected to sound. Most of them were songwriters as well as performers.

Back then, tickets to the "Grand Ole Opry" didn't cost big bucks, but times have changed. Today, the "Opry" is on television as well as radio, it broadcasts from its own new concrete-steel-and-glass 4,400-seat Opry House, and a good seat costs $10. Nashville has become "Music City, U.S.A.," with its other attractions, the Country Music Hall of Fame, and its theme park, Opryland. On a good weekend, perhaps 20,000 tourists will pass through Nashville, buying tickets and snapping their flashbulbs.

But the biggest attraction is "Grand Ole Opry";

the show is still the same magnet drawing aspiring country singers as it was when Dolly was a girl. The "Opry" is the country equivalent of an actor's goal of Broadway or Hollywood, or the old vaudevillian's dream of playing the palace; it's the big time, now as then.

The first genius behind the "Opry" was founder, manager, announcer, and master of ceremonies Judge George D. Hay, a father figure to his many performers. In his later years, he set down in writing the philosophy of the "Grand Ole Opry," a formula still adhered to. Reading his words, one comes to understand what made the program so very successful for so very long.

"Our show is presented for the rural and industrial workers throughout the states. Above all, we try to keep it 'homey.' Home folks do the work of the world; they win the wars and raise the families. Many of our geniuses come from simple folk who adhere to the fundamental principles of honesty included in the Ten Commandments. The 'Grand Ole Opry' expresses those qualities which come from these good people."

Although Judge Hay wasn't aware of it when he wrote those words, he was describing Dolly Parton's genius to a "T."

But if the "Opry" is the biggest country music show on the air, it's not by any means the only one. When Dolly was growing up, there were famous radio programs such as "Louisiana Hayride" out of Shreveport, "Big D Jamboree" from— where else?— Dallas, "National Barn Dance," broadcast from Chicago, and many others. Just about every city in the South has its own mini-version of a big-time country music show, heard locally and featuring local talent. Patsy Cline got her start on a local show, "Jimmy Dean's Town and Country Jamboree." So did many others; it would be wrong to underestimate the value of these 5,000-watt "Hoedowns" and "Hayrides" in giving some of the superstars of today that first, vital push that would get their careers into gear.

The only radio station of any importance close to Sevierville was WIVK in Knoxville, Tennessee, about 40 miles away. Thanks to WIVK and a very energetic man named Cas Walker, little Dolly Parton would receive a push early in life.

Cas Walker was by all accounts a dynamo; he was just about everywhere one looked in Knoxville, running a successful chain of supermarkets or running for mayor or a seat on the town council—it was all the same to him. Politics and business had made him something of a local celebrity; he was not only elected three times mayor of Knoxville, but was the only mayor in the city's history to be recalled in a special election and kicked out of office.

Where Cas really shone was in his first love, country music. Not only did he pick a little and sing a little himself, but he sponsored country music programs on radio and TV, in addition to live performances in theaters. Those who knew him then say Walker was a colorful personality, and he would be of major importance in furthering Dolly's career. He would be her first talent scout, and the first impresario to pay her to sing.

It was Cas Walker who had brought that country music show to the Pines Theater in Sevierville,

Cas Walker who had sponsored the TV program on which Dolly's class had appeared. His most important and successful contribution to the furtherance of country music was an early-morning TV show, "The Farm and Home Hour," broadcast over WIVK every morning at 5:30, with a kind of reprise live radio show around noon, and another TV program in the evening. It was the most natural thing in the world for eight-year-old Dolly to go and sing on Cas Walker's shows.

Forty miles is a long way for a little girl to travel to sing at 5:30 in the morning; to do so, she had to get up at 4 A.M. But Dolly was no ordinary little girl. Her uncle, Bill Owens, himself an ambitious musician and a staunch supporter of Dolly's, the man who gave Dolly her little Martin guitar, would drive her down from Sevierville, and drive her back in time for school.

"I heard her singin' many times," says Uncle Bill, describing Dolly's first real audition for Cas. "And, man, even then she was mighty good. She sang when she was washin' the dishes, or puttin' the little ones to bed. The thought came to me that she oughta be singin' on Cas Walker's programs, so I drove her on down there. This particular show was comin' from a downstairs studio. When Dolly started singin,' why, announcers from upstairs and the other people from all over the building came in to listen to her. She made a big hit, and Cas Walker hired her on the spot."

Dolly sang on the Walker radio shows from time to time from the age of eight to the age of ten. Then she took another step up on the ladder of success.

Cas Walker asked Dolly Parton to be a regular on his show, and he offered her a salary of $20 a week! To a ten-year-old, it was a fortune. And in 1956, it was no small amount.

Nineteen fifty-six was the epicenter of the Eisenhower years. America was in the grip of atomic fever; people building and stocking bomb shelters in their backyards, determined to be dug in safely when the Russian atom bomb exploded over Topeka. But, even with the Cold War, the Hungarian uprising, Sputnik, the Berlin Wall, and all the truly terrifying global events, America was enjoying a postwar boom time, plus all the technological miracles that Americans had been promised and had been waiting for all during the long grim war. Americans went on a buying spree, and, with wartime price controls lifted, costs kept rising and inflation set in.

Music was changing, too, moving away from the bland and saccharine melodies of crew-cut harmonic groups toward bouncier singers like Peggy Lee and Doris Day, toward rhythm and blues and toward something new called rock 'n' roll. Nineteen fifty-six was the year of Elvis Presley, of "Love Me Tender," "Hound Dog," and "Heartbreak Hotel." Among ten-year-old Dolly's personal favorite singers were Brenda Lee and Connie Francis.

In 1956, a country music songwriter, Ivory Joe Hunter, had two hits that each sold over 1,000,000 records, "My Wish Came True," and "I Need You So," which Elvis, Pat Boone, and Sonny James recorded. And a twenty-four-year-old singer named Johnny Cash was creating a sensation on

38

"Grand Ole Opry" with a song called "I Walk the Line." For the first time, urban America was becoming aware of Nashville, Tennessee.

So there was Dolly Parton at the tender age of ten, singing on the radio just like a professional. She worked hard for that $20; Cas Walker got his money's worth and more. When school was in session, her appearances were, naturally, scheduled around her classroom attendance, but she usually managed the early show, and sometimes even the midday one. On weekends and school holidays, she did every broadcast; and on Wednesday nights, when Cas Walker had a live TV show, she would stay late and sing on that, too. When her Uncle Bill didn't drive her back and forth, her Aunt Estelle Watson, who lived in Knoxville, did. Her family had a powerful faith in Dolly, whose energy and persistence impressed them as much as her talent.

During the summer months, Dolly stayed on in Knoxville with her Aunt Estelle and sang on Cas Walker's shows three times a day, three days a week. Once, when she was away in Knoxville, her precious Martin guitar was loaned out, and the borrower was careless. "That hurt me real bad," Dolly said. "It had its side busted out and the neck got broke off. I reckon some kids had jumped up and down on it or somethin', never did find out what had happened. So I put it away and said that when I got enough money together, first thing I'd do I'd get my git-tar fixed. Took me a while, though.

"They said they'd pay me twenty dollars a week to start with. My aunt in Knoxville said she would

39

take me up to the radio stations and the TV shows if Mama and Daddy would let me stay, and she did. And I sang country music, some songs I wrote. I was singin' by myself and playin' the guitar. But I guess it was because I was a little kid they were sayin' that the audience liked it, because I wasn't really that good."

If she wasn't "that good," she was getting better fast. Music was now the central obsession of Dolly's life. Not only was she singing on the radio and on TV, she was making a round of local personal appearances in church halls, school auditoriums, Kiwanis clubs, and anywhere a country music show was performed. And she was cutting tapes, at night, in the studios at WIVK.

Dolly and her uncles Bill and Louis Owens would drive down from Sevierville to record demonstration tapes of the songs they had written to send to Nashville. The studio engineers donated their time, the studio musicians would back up their arrangements, and Dolly's sisters would sing the harmony. The main targets of all this energy and labor were the Nashville music publishers, record companies, and, of course, "Grand Ole Opry." "I never stopped writin' songs or sendin' off tapes," Dolly remembers.

When Dolly was thirteen, she actually made it on the "Opry," although her appearance on the show was strictly a fluke. For one thing, the "Opry" was a union shop, which meant that no performer not in the musicians' union could play the show. When they told Dolly she had to be "in the union," she had no idea what the word meant.

40

"I kind of had the idea that it might be a costume, or maybe a room to practice in," says Dolly.

For another thing, the "Opry" had a rule that nobody under the age of eighteen could play the show. Even though Dolly's burgeoning and abundant figure could easily be mistaken for an eighteen-year-old's, she was five years under age. It was faith and determination alone, plus persistent nagging, that finally got her on the program.

But none of that was in Dolly's mind when she made the trip. Her Uncle Bill borrowed a car, and the two of them drove to Nashville; their goal, to get Dolly on the stage of the Ryman Auditorium and let the world hear her sing.

"First time I was on the 'Opry,' I went with the intentions of bein' on. Nobody ever told me that you couldn't do anything you wanted to do. I just always thought, *Well, all you gotta do is just go there, and if you sing good enough, you can be on the 'Grand Ole Opry.'* Gettin' up the nerve was the hardest part, but we were already blessed with more nerve than sense anyway."

Once backstage at the "Opry," Bill and Dolly buttonholed everybody about getting Dolly onstage to sing. At first they had no luck at all. Dolly was too young, they said, and besides, her name wasn't on the list. But Dolly persisted; she wasn't one to give up easily, especially after coming 200 miles.

Finally, she got a break. She had approached a country music star named Jimmy C. Newman, who was scheduled to go on next, imploring him to help her. The way things went on the "Opry" was that every performer came on and did two numbers back to back. So impressed was he by her determination and her pretty face that he gave up one of his own spots on the show, turning it over to Dolly. He told Johnny Cash to announce Dolly Parton's name before his.

Suddenly, a long-held dream came true. All at once, Dolly found herself in front of a microphone and a huge, dedicated country music audience on the most important show of them all. She sang a George Jones song, "If You Want to Be My Baby," and "just tore the house down. I had to sing it over and over and over. I thought I was a star. That was the first time for me."

Maybe Dolly didn't suspect it then, and maybe she did, but it would be the first of many times that Dolly would be tearing the house down on the "Opry."

After that, Dolly and Bill would from time to time drive the 200 miles back and forth to the song publishers, record companies, and concert promoters of Music City, making the rounds, knocking on doors, looking for the big breakthrough, with no success.

"My Uncle Bill had him an old car with the sides all busted in," Dolly told her biographer, Alanna Nash. "We'd save up enough money to go back and forth to Nashville, tryin' to get somethin' goin' for us. Uncle Bill said I was goin' to be a star, and I was fool enough to believe him. So we'd take out every time we'd get a chance. We'd sleep in the car and clean up in fillin' stations."

In 1959, when Dolly was thirteen, her Uncle Robert was in the service, stationed in Lake Charles, Louisiana. Lake Charles is the home of Goldband Records, a small studio that recorded a number of major country and western artists at the beginning of their careers while they were still unknowns, including Freddy Fender, Mickey Gilley, and Larry Williams. Dolly packed up her repaired Martin, got on a bus, and went down to Lake Charles to cut her first record.

For Goldband she recorded two sides: One was a lively teen number called "Puppy Love," which she wrote herself and which she sang in Brenda Lee style; the other, a sad song about a girl gone astray, "Girl Left Alone," she had written with her Uncle Bill Owens. Not quite five feet tall, Dolly was so short that she had to sit on a high stool to reach the microphone. The record was released and went nowhere, but it was one more piece of valuable experience for Dolly's growing collection.

By the time she was thirteen years old, Dolly had reached her full growth—in more ways than one. Having attained her full height of 5 feet, she continued growing in other directions. Her hips grew round, full, and womanly, and that amazing bosom, Dolly's most outstanding physical attribute, had reached its full size. No more little-girl calico dresses for Dolly Parton. Always concerned with her appearance, she graduated to skintight clothes.

She bought her jeans small, and shrunk them down even smaller, until they hugged her little round behind so tightly she could barely sit down. She teased her hair into the latest styles, experimenting with hair coloring to lighten it, and with other cosmetic products to give it body. But its appearance never quite met with her approval.

Thanks to her appearances on television, Dolly had already become proficient in the art of makeup, and now she wore it almost every day, layering it on thickly. At this time she began to experiment with wigs, covering her own shoulder-length, very fine brown hair with masses of artificial golden curls. The Dolly Parton image was beginning to emerge, like the butterflies she loves, and with which she so identifies that she has chosen them as her personal symbol.

Now she became popular with boys, but for the wrong reasons, as she herself has recalled a little sadly.

"When I was thirteen I looked like I was twenty-five. A lotta stories went around about me, but they was a lotta lies. It was because I had these big boobs and this big behind, and this little tiny waist. I got to lookin' real mature, and from then on I tried to make the most of my looks and to improve them, and that meant I wore my clothes tight, and I mean *skintight!* I wore makeup and flirted a lot with boys. Sometimes I was embarrassed by my figure, but mostly I accepted what God gave me. I was popular in high school, but not in the right way. But I reckon it didn't bother me a lot, 'cause music was on my mind a lot more than boys."

Even so, Dolly found time to flirt and tell dirty jokes, aware that some of the other students were snickering about her behind her back. Some were even convinced that she'd filled her bras with tissue in order to give the *appearance* of a big chest. But if the hair and eyelashes were false, at least her chest was quite real, a gift from Mother Nature.

"A lot of people take me wrong," she told reporter Jerry Bailey, "because I look like the type of person that might be tryin' to show off, because I wear gaudy clothes. I guess it's because when I was little I never really had anythin' at all, and when I would see somebody dressed up real fancy, that would just impress me no end. I just thought that one of these days I was going' to wear fancy clothes and hairdos and makeup and shiny jewelry. It's just part of my personality."

At fourteen, Dolly entered high school, a different kind of world from the one-room schoolhouse and the supportive comfort of family and friends. Sevier County High School was a much wider arena than Dolly had grown up accustomed to; boys and girls from the small city of Sevierville mingled somewhat uncomfortably with kids from the mountains. But even among the country kids Dolly Parton stood out like a bandaged thumb.

High school is a crucial passage in life. Even as boys and girls take those first tentative steps on their way to independence, trying to find out who they are and of what they are capable, conformity is prized. And remember that we are in the year 1960, before "doing your own thing" became the thing to conform to.

At fourteen, Dolly, with her woman's figure and the gaudiness of her appearance, was very different from the ponytailed bobby-soxers in poodle skirts. Boys would snicker with embarrassed delight and girls would sniff indignantly at the sight of those majestic breasts that defied concealment. Dolly found herself with virtually no friends, although she did have a claque of fans among the teen-agers who were mountain kids like herself, and who followed her appearances on local radio and TV. The city kids weren't impressed.

Another thing that caused a rift between Dolly Parton and her schoolmates was her certainty that she would someday be a star. Hadn't she already cut a record? Hadn't she appeared on the "Grand Ole Opry"? Wasn't she still singing on Cas Walker's TV and radio shows? By the time she graduated from Sevier County High, her salary would be $60 a week. She was a professional entertainer; the others were just high school kids. She couldn't get excited about the teen-aged dating and the kind of clothes that turned them on; they couldn't share her dreams and ambitions. Also, to the more citified boys and girls, she was the worst kind of hick, the professional hillbilly who was making money at it. And, though they would rather have died than admit it, they must have been a little jealous of her.

Even though she persevered, determined to become the first Parton to earn a high school diploma, Dolly hated school. The confinement of it, its rigid schedule, stifled that butterfly soul of hers that yearned to fly free. Besides the promise of a diploma, the main thing that kept Dolly inside school walls was the fact that things were worse at home than they were at school. Her mother was always ill, and there was the constant squabbling among the Parton siblings, and the wailing of babies cutting teeth.

Intelligent though she was, Dolly wasn't a good student, and the main thing that got her by was her grade in "band," 98. The 98 pulled up the rest of her average. She also did well in home economics, thanks to good teaching at home, and she became a member of the Future Homemakers of America, which was something like the female equivalent of the Junior Chamber of Commerce.

Even though she chafed under the discipline of high school, while other students laughed at her behind her back, Dolly shrugged and pretended not to care. Music was the center of her life. During the years when girls are pursuing boys and boys are pursuing their daddies' cars, Dolly was pursuing her career.

As for her outrageous appearance, Dolly just smiles when asked about it. "I like to be gaudy. It makes me different. When I first started singin', I decided I would dress in gaudy, outrageous clothes because it fit my outgoin' personality. It was also like a dream come true. I always wanted to be glittery and stand out. Why should I hide the parts of me that are extreme? I just try to make the extreme more extreme. Life, you know, can be kinda borin', so I like to spice things up a little."

It wasn't until she began playing snare drums in the high school marching band that Dolly made a few friends and became more popular. The band was important to her, and still is. After she achieved stardom, Dolly played a number of benefit concerts in Sevierville, turning over the proceeds to the Sevier County High School band to buy equipment, instruments, and uniforms. She also established a scholarship fund at the school in 1970. Now the same boys and girls who didn't talk to her in the old high school days are the men and women who proclaim Dolly Parton Day in Sevierville.

When she was fourteen years old, Tree International Publishing of Nashville signed her to a songwriter's contract, and at the age of fifteen she cut her second single, "It May Not Kill Me but It's Sure Gonna Hurt," released on the Mercury label. It was a song she and her Uncle Bill wrote, "but it never did nothin'," as Dolly told Toby Thompson in his *Village Voice* interview more than fifteen years later. "I came back home after that, decidin' I wasn't gonna do nothin' else till after I graduated."

The fact that she *did* in fact graduate from high school is amazing when one considers that she spent more time writing songs than term papers, and more time singing than learning. But graduate she did, the first in the Parton family to earn a high school diploma, " 'cause I wanted to say I did it."

She was graduated on a Friday in June 1964. As part of the ceremony, there was a baccalaureate at the First Baptist Church in Sevierville, when each graduating senior stood up and announced what goal he or she was going to work toward.

Dolly didn't falter when her turn came around. She told the audience what she had always told everybody who would listen—she was going to Nashville to become a singer and a songwriter. Only this time it wasn't only a dream. The bus fare was in her purse, and when a ripple of derisive laughter passed through the audience, Dolly just lifted her stubborn little round chin and her eyes threw out sparks. She knew better.

Later, she drove over to WIVK for her last appearance on local TV, and announced on the air that she was "goin' to Nashville to be a country music singer and songwriter, and I ain't comin' back until I make it!"

Early the next morning, Saturday, an eighteen-year-old Dolly Parton, dressed in a modest brown dress with long sleeves and a high collar, her hair in a bouffant flip, was on a Greyhound bus heading for Nashville. She took with her a cheap cardboard suitcase, tied up with string so it wouldn't burst open, and crammed with just about everything she owned in the world. She also carried along her Martin guitar, a folder full of songs she wrote herself, the love and the fears of her anxious parents, and her dirty laundry. She had left town in such a hurry that she hadn't had time to wash her clothes.

But Dolly Rebecca Parton didn't care; she was anxious to get started on fulfilling her destiny. Laundry could wait; Nashville couldn't.

Chapter Three

Nashville and Carl

I never had a doubt I would
make it, because refusing to think
I *couldn't* make it is the reason
I *could.*

—Dolly Parton

Believe it or not, that sack of dirty laundry was
to turn out to be a godsend; it would be the cause
of yet another major change in Dolly's life. But
let's back up a little.

Every year, high school graduates from small
towns, villages, and hamlets all over America
come to the big city with stars in their eyes and
no money in their pockets. Whether they land in
New York or Los Angeles or Nashville makes no

difference—it's all the same. The same ambitions, the same dreams, the same new feeling of freedom and independence, the same sweet taste of being on one's own at last. The same fears and doubts, the same struggles, the same longing for friends and family back home. They work, they go hungry, they meet rejection, their hearts break again and again; they see their bright dreams first tarnish, then fade. Most of those kids go back home again and marry the girl or boy next door, go into daddy's hardware business, or raise a couple of kids. One in perhaps 10,000 becomes a star.

But that one person in 10,000 has what it takes, and it takes a lot more than talent alone. It takes determination to make it no matter what life throws at you—aching feet or an aching, hungry belly or an aching heart. It takes the ability to roll with the punches, to face rejection by looking it straight on and saying, "Whatever you may say, I *know* I'm good, and I'm going to *prove it*." It takes what Dolly Parton was born with.

A few weeks before Dolly graduated from Sevier County High, her Uncle Bill had moved to Nashville with his wife, Cathy, and baby son, and had rented a place with room in it for Dolly. Bill was playing in his own band, backing up Carl and Pearl Butler, and he was out of town a lot, and Cathy was holding down a job as a waitress, so they really needed Dolly as a live-in baby-sitter for her baby cousin. Besides, Bill and Dolly were a singing-and-songwriting team, and her uncle was certain that Dolly and he were going to open

the doors to success as a team. It was only because Dolly was going to be staying with near
kinfolk that her parents reluctantly allowed her
to leave home, especially to go to the big city.

"I felt that Dolly was too young to be turned
loose alone in a city the size of Nashville," said
her mother.

But Dolly saw Nashville as her only possible
future, and her Uncle Bill, who was ambitious for
himself as well as for her, agreed. Bill had made
contacts in the music world, and he had confidence in his own talents and Dolly's. Whether
they would make it as singers or songwriters was
as yet unknown, but make it they would, of that
they were equally certain. Besides, even Dolly
had a slim contact in Music City; she was still
under contract to Tree Publishing, even if the
Mercury record they had arranged for her hadn't
been a hit or anything like a hit.

This was the summer of 1964, and the times
they were a-changing. A President of the United
States had been brutally assassinated, shocking
the world and traumatizing a generation. Lyndon
Johnson was in the White House, touring Appala-
chia and declaring war on poverty, while an un-
declared war was beginning to escalate in a
faraway place called Vietnam. More than 100
American lives had been lost to date. A group of
Liverpool moptops called the Beatles were revo-
lutionizing music, and other groups like the Rolling Stones were imitating them with almost as
much success. This was also to be, although nobody knew it, a civil rights summer, when the

bodies of three missing civil rights workers would be dug up from a shallow grave in Mississippi. The South would be a-changing, too.

But Dolly's head was filled with lyrics and melodies, not global and political changes. She was eighteen years old, and all filled out—more than all filled out. Men's heads turned when this tiny pretty thing with the sparkling smile, the tiny waist, and the big boobs came sashaying down the street. She had stars in her eyes and a suitcase bursting with her songs. Dolly Parton was in Nashville at last, ready and eager to begin a new life. Stardom, here she came!

With the rise of "Grand Ole Opry" to predominance in country music, the heart of the business became Nashville. Not only did many of the star performers on the show buy or build luxurious homes and ranches in and around the city, but management, record companies, music publishers, studio personnel, sidemen, backup singers, show promoters, and just about everyone else connected with the business had moved there, making it "Music City, U.S.A." The streets around the Ryman Auditorium were choked with bars, honky-tonks, and cheap hotels. Some of them, like Tootsie's Orchid Lounge, were favorite after-work watering holes of the country music greats; others did a thriving business in the overflow of the not-so-great. Downtown Nashville possessed a sleazy, neon-bright ambience that was alien to everything Dolly Parton knew growing up. Even so, she fell in love with the city on sight, declaring "I'm home."

Remember that sack of dirty laundry? The first thing Dolly had to do when she arrived on the Owenses' doorstep in South Nashville was get that dirty laundry clean so she would have something to wear. Off she went to the Wishy-Washy Laundromat near her uncle's home. The owners ought to put up a bronze plaque there—if, in fact, the laundromat is still in business—to commemorate the fact that, on the first day she was in Nashville, within hours of her arrival Dolly Rebecca Parton met the man who was to be her future husband.

Dolly put her clothes into the machine, dropped in the coins, and started the wash cycle. But she was never a girl to sit still and wait. Outside, Nashville was beckoning; it was a bright day in early summer, and she was in a strange town. So she bought a Royal Crown Cola from the dispenser and, bottle in hand, went out to have a look at the town, or at least that part of Nashville that was close to the laundromat. What she was doing was walking around the block, sipping her soda, and enjoying the sight of new places.

"We met at the Wishy-Washy, and it's been wishy-washy ever since," joked Dolly for the thousandth time, on the "Oprah Winfrey Show" in April 1987, when she and Carl Dean had been married for 21 years. For theirs has been an enduring marriage. You can call it unique, since they are rarely in the same house at the same time, but their relationship began in the most traditional way—boy sees girl, boy picks up girl, girl marries boy.

On that fateful day in June 1964, Carl Dean was at the impressionable age of twenty-one, and how his eyes must have popped out of his head at the sight of those dimples, those round, rosy cheeks, and bright eyes, not to mention those . . . other attributes of Dolly's sensational figure. More than likely, Carl wasn't even thinking about the possibility of a brain under that fluffy yellow hair (by now Dolly had dyed her brown hair a whitish-blond, but she still had it covered with wigs; in those days the wigs were beehives and Jackie Kennedy bouffants), so it must have come as a pleasant surprise to discover that this pretty girl from the country could think, too.

A native of Nashville and an asphalt paving contractor, Carl Dean was about to go into the army, and was enjoying the time he had left by "cruising." Although today the word carries a heavy sexual overtone, in 1964 it was a relatively innocent pastime. Boys would drive around in their cars looking for pretty girls, and try to persuade them to go for a ride. Naturally, they hoped they'd get lucky, but most of the time it turned out to be nothing more than an afternoon's or evening's flirtation, with maybe a hamburger and a soda thrown in.

When Carl saw Dolly, he did what any red-blooded American boy would do—he leaned on his horn to get her attention and waved at her like crazy. Dolly, naïve and country-friendly, waved back.

"I got me a big RC Cola," recalls Dolly, "and when my clothes were washin' in the laundromat, I went out walkin' to see what I could see of Nashville. I was jes' walkin' down the street and along came this really handsome boy in a white Chevrolet. An' he was flirtin' with me. In the country, you speak to everybody, and me bein' from the country, I didn't want him to think I was stuck-up or nothin', so I waved back. Didn't mean nothin' special by it; I was just bein' friendly. Well, maybe in the back of my mind somewhere I was noticin' how cute and handsome he was, but mostly I was just bein' friendly."

The next thing either of them knew, he'd pulled his late-model white Chevy over to the curb and got out to walk alongside Dolly. Soon, they were deep in conversation. He asked her where she was from, and Dolly, certain that he would never know where Sevierville was, told him she was from Knoxville.

Explaining that her clothes were at this minute spinning in a machine at the Wishy-Washy, and that she was just taking a little stroll to see some of Nashville before the rinse cycle was over, Dolly flashed her dimples, and Carl Dean was lost.

Naturally, Carl wanted to take Dolly riding in his car and show her all the Nashville sights. Just as naturally, Dolly was tempted by this tall, good-looking young man (Carl is her favorite type—tall and thin and dark-haired, the perfect contrast to her little fluffy blond self), but her mama had raised her right. One did not go riding with strangers, no matter how cute, so Dolly said a definite "no." Carl got out of the car and walked her back to the Wishy-Washy, the two of them talking away, especially Dolly. Even on her first day in Nashville, Dolly was homesick for her mountains and her family, and she found this handsome stranger easy to talk to.

Up until then, Dolly hadn't dated much. It wasn't that boys didn't want to take her out—how could they help wanting to, with that face and that figure and that merry disposition and giggly laugh? It wasn't that Dolly didn't want to; she was perfectly normal, with natural development and urges. But Dolly had always been too busy with her music to pay much attention to boys. She didn't have weekends or school holidays free, and she would often have to break a date with a boy because she had been hired to sing somewhere.

But Carl was different from the high school boys and the band members or studio musicians she knew and with whom she occasionally went out. There was a mature, quiet strength about him that must have reminded Dolly of Robert Lee Parton. Very often, girls who have grown up with strong fathers choose strong men as husbands; they have come to rely upon and need that masculine strength. More importantly, they recognize that strength when they encounter it.

There was something else about Carl that kindled a spark in Dolly. Whenever she told boys about her dreams of stardom, of making it to the top as a country music star, it had somehow turned them off. Sometimes it would make them laugh, but usually the thought of Dolly Parton as tomorrow's star provoked resentment. Masculine and feminine roles were rigidly defined in those days, and it was the man who brought home the bacon, the woman who cooked it up in the pan, served it, then washed the dishes, swept the kitchen, and put the babies to bed. Anything about a girl's hopes and plans for a career was very threatening to a boy.

Of course, Dolly had gone out with some band musicians by the time she was eighteen—pickers and singers from the radio station and guys she had met on her gigs. They were more understanding of Dolly's ambitions for a career in music, but there was a jealous tinge in that understanding, as though she were a rival for the one and only opening for stardom. Or maybe it was her obvious talent they resented.

Carl was different from all of them. When Dolly told him, as she did, right away, about her ambitions and about the suitcase crammed with songs, he was instantly supportive. There wasn't a jealous bone in his body, and he didn't feel threatened by the thought of Dolly's career. He responded to Dolly's self-assurance. Because of his maturity and his own self-assurance as a man and as a person, he took her exactly as she was—songs, guitar, ambitions, and all. Although Dolly wasn't aware of it at the time, this was exactly what she had been looking for in a guy of her own.

Perhaps the most important quality about Carl was that he wasn't a part of the music business. He had his own life to live, his own living to pursue—his father owned an asphalt-paving business—and music was a field that Dolly could have all to herself. Which is the way she always liked it.

So there they were, side by side at the Wishy-Washy, stuffing Dolly's laundry into the dryer and getting acquainted. By now Carl was really interested in this bright-eyed hillbilly girl with the big dreams, and he could see that he had made an impression on her, too. He continued to press her to go out with him, and Dolly continued to evade him, even though saying no went against her innermost wishes. But she really didn't know this boy at all, and her mother and father would be horrified and furious if they knew she had let a strange boy pick her up on the street so easily.

In the end, Carl Dean went back to his Chevy, but not before he had made a date with Dolly to call on her the next day at her uncle's house, the only right and proper way for a mountain girl to begin seeing a boy.

And that's how the love story of Dolly and Carl began. He came over to the apartment the following day, about two in the afternoon, and "We sat on the steps. Actually, it was the fire escape. The next day he came back, and the next day he came back, until I got to know him pretty well. When my aunt, who was working at Shoney's, got her first day off, we had our first date. We talked for about five days before I went out with him."

Carl would come and visit her at Uncle Bill's South Nashville apartment, but she'd never let him inside the door, because Bill was playing gigs and Cathy was away working. Instead, the two of them would sit on the fire escape, hold hands, and talk about their "somedays." And if a kiss or two was exchanged, well, surely it was nobody's business but theirs.

On their first real date, Carl took her home to meet his parents, and that made it official. They were going together. Dolly was ecstatic, and her letters home were filled with *Carl this* and *Carl that* and *Carl says* and *Carl does.*

But even falling in love with Carl didn't stand in the way of Dolly's ambitions. She had come to Nashville to be a star, and she began to work at it as soon as she unpacked her suitcases.

A letter she wrote home very soon after she left Sevier County is filled with a girlish blend of enthusiastic optimism, love, nostalgia, loneliness, and the thrill of independence. She called herself "a little lonesome and a whole lot homesick," but assured her mama and daddy that she had arrived safely and was settling into her new, strange life. Dolly was afraid they would be worrying themselves sick over her back home, and, while things were still striking her as very different from the mountains, she was getting used to the new ways, and had no intention of going back.

Dolly hadn't realized quite how much she loved her parents "and all them noisy kids" until she had cut the cord and broken away. There had been tears shed at the parting, shed on both sides, and Dolly had continued to cry almost all the way to Nashville. More than once, she had wanted to turn around and go back. But her dream lay ahead of her, not behind.

Everybody who knew Dolly knew how badly she had always wanted to go to Nashville and be a singer and songwriter. Dolly had great faith in herself. She knew that if she tried long enough and hard enough, and let nothing discourage her—no amount of rejection, no amount of sheer hard work—she would succeed at last. "Someday I'll make it," was always in her thoughts.

Meanwhile, although she was always short of money, she kept up a brave front, assuring her parents that everything was fine and that she did not need any cash, because she had landed a job singing on an early-morning television program, *The Eddie Hill Show*. She also had a few nibbles from other performers, who might record a couple of her songs. Dolly assured her parents that she was not going hungry, when in truth, often she was; she was always broke. And, knowing what worried them nearly as much as her starving to death, she did renew her promises to be a good girl and not to get into trouble or yield to the temptations of the big city.

But it was a long way from a singing gig on a local television program to real success. Dolly and Bill kept making the rounds of Music Row, knocking on doors that never seemed to open to them. On Music Row were the offices of the major producers and promoters, and such publishing companies as Window Music, Mercury Studios, Combine Music, MGM Records, and Columbia and Capitol Records.

Naturally, Dolly wrote an autobiographical song

about those lean and hungry, frustrating Nashville years, "Down on Music Row."

After Dolly became a star, Willadeene, Dolly's oldest sister, published a book about her entitled *In the Shadow of a Song*. She describes those early days of struggle:

She and Uncle Bill traveled to shows all over Tennessee and to the surrounding states in his old car. Many times Dolly came from shows wrapped in a quilt because her car had no heater and cold air poured in through the holes that had rusted through the floorboard. They always packed sandwiches and a Thermos of coffee and fruit jars filled with tea, because they couldn't afford to buy anything at a restaurant. Dolly would have to shift her position in the seat each time a bump in the road brought a new spring through the upholstery.

The next two years were to be among the hardest of Dolly's life. Although she sold a few of her songs to other artists, they weren't hits, and she couldn't seem to get her career off the ground. Carl, with whom she was in love, went into the U.S. Army, and their courtship was interrupted just when his presence was most necessary to her. She missed her home, and the warmth, love, and approval with which she had always been surrounded. Things just weren't working out the way she had hoped and even expected. It didn't seem as though Nashville had been just sitting and waiting for Dolly Parton to show up.

She stayed with the Owenses for about 6 months,

but after Bill Owens went on the road she moved out and got an apartment of her own, a small, inexpensive place with no telephone and an empty refrigerator. She couldn't afford even a used car to get her to her gigs or make the rounds.

Dolly, who loves to eat and who has fought a weight problem since she turned thirty, was facing a bare cupboard and going hungry for the first time in her life. Many times she has told the story of eating relish and mustard on . . . nothing. That's all there was, and "to this day, I still can't eat a bite of relish." Her weight dropped to 90 pounds. When she visited her family back in Sevier County, they were so horrified by how skinny she was that Dolly came back to Nashville loaded down with flour, sugar, and jars of the fruits and vegetables that Avie Lee pickled and preserved.

Dolly says the only time she ever got a decent meal in those days was when she was out on a date and her companion bought her dinner, but she wasn't doing a lot of dating with Carl in the service. So, while Carl was away, Dolly didn't do a whole lot of eating.

Much worse than hunger pangs was the loneliness she must have felt as she cried herself to sleep every night. Growing up in a two-room shack with two parents and ten brothers and sisters had surrounded Dolly not only with noise, but with comfort and company. She had never had a bed to herself, but that was all right, too.

Now, not only was Dolly alone, without the support of her close-knit family to lean on, but the man she loved was in the service, and they weren't in a position to marry. Long, lonely days and nights for a girl who had never been away from home before.

Working part-time as a waitress, she managed to get singing gigs from time to time, and continued writing songs, alone and with her Uncle Bill. At first, every record company executive in Nashville shook his head no. Then, Fred Foster of Monument Records heard her material and liked it. Soon after Dolly arrived in Nashville, she had left Tree and gone on to sign with Monument Records as a recording artist, but the company didn't really understand how to utilize her.

Dolly's voice is special; it has been described by John Rockwell, a music critic for *The New York Times*, as a soprano that "can shift from eerily accurate girlishness to a weepy little vibrato to a high, hard nasality . . . and she phrases and ornaments like the great artist she is."

Dolly herself says her voice was "so strange, and still is." Monument wanted Dolly to sing a rocking kind of pop that was sweeping the nation, and she says, with typical kindness, "Monument Records was doing what it thought was best at the time. They didn't think I could possibly sell any country because they thought I sounded like a twelve-year-old girl. It wasn't commercial enough for them. They didn't think I could sell any hard-message song or sad story, sing about an unfaithful lover or a cheatin' husband or a busted-up marriage, because nobody would believe it. I guess they thought my voice was so weird that country people wouldn't go for it." Dolly often describes herself as "an acquired taste. You either get used to my singing or you never like it at all."

Dolly wanted to sing country, and only country. Monument wanted rockabilly, an uneasy marriage blend of twangy country and bouncy pop. Meanwhile, she and Bill Owens were under contract to write songs for Monument's publishing company, Combine. Her advance draw was $50 a week against royalties, barely enough to put some food into that empty refrigerator, especially when Dolly was sending money home to the family.

Even though Dolly was frustrated about not being allowed to record her own kind of music— "When you ride the fence you just kind of sit there; I wasn't writing much or choosing any of my own material, and I have to do both to be happy"—she was gaining valuable experience. She was starting to learn how to dress and move like a professional performer, not an amateur, although she still had a long way to go in shaping her image. She was becoming aware of her vocal limitations and how to get around them. And she was getting more used to big-city ways and the ins and outs of the record business.

Nineteen sixty-six was a watershed year for Dolly Parton. Carl Dean came back home from the army and asked Dolly to be his wife. This required serious thought on Dolly's part. She loved Carl; of that she had no doubt, but she loved music, too, and she had no intention of merely settling down into a Nashville kitchen and tying on an apron.

Dolly approached the offer of marriage the same way she approaches everything in life—with straightforward, dead-on honesty. If Carl could accept her as a wife exactly the way she was, a woman with a dream to fulfill, a woman determined to let nothing stop her from success as a writer and entertainer, then she would marry him. But she needed to be free, to be herself, to do what she set out to do, and if that kind of woman stuck in Carl's craw . . . well, maybe he should find himself another, more traditional kind of wife.

Carl wanted Dolly. "If that's what will make you happy, that's what it's gonna be," he told her. On May 30, 1966, Memorial Day, just a few days before Dolly's twentieth birthday and two years after they had met, they were married in Ringold, Georgia, and have been married ever since.

They were married in a church, in the presence of Avie Lee Parton, the only member of the family to drive all that way to attend. After the ceremony, the three of them were driving back and had almost reached Nashville when Dolly's mother suddenly discovered that she'd left her pocketbook back in the church. She had put it down on a bench when she snapped the newlyweds' photograph, and had completely forgotten it! That was how they spent most of the hours of the wedding night, driving with Dolly's mother back and forth between Georgia and Tennessee in quest of a handbag.

"I think the Lord intended for me to marry Carl," says Dolly to this day. "I think we were always destined to be together. I just can't imagine being married to anyone else."

The marriage is unique in a number of ways. The more public Dolly became, the more private Carl became. Never did he interfere in her career or attempt to manage her affairs. Instead, he stuck to his own livelihood, asphalt paving, becoming extremely successful at it. They spend most of their time apart, often living in separate houses (Dolly collects residences the way other women collect earrings), and Carl never permits himself to be photographed with his famous wife. He doesn't want to be known as "Mr. Parton," although Dolly takes pride in being known as "Mrs. Carl Dean."

Carl Dean is so private a man that there was a joke going around the Nashville music business that he doesn't actually exist, that he's only a figment of Dolly Parton's imagination. Even today, Dolly still occasionally gets hit with that myth by some enterprising reporter, and always giggles when she hears it.

But Carl and the marriage have been a great stabilizer for Dolly. It has given her a measure of creative freedom that is rare for a woman in a marriage. It has left her free to write songs and make records and films. Her energies are focused elsewhere, on her career, not on her marriage, exactly as she warned Carl before she married him.

"Whenever I'm making a movie or cutting a record, or spending a lot of time on the road, we make up for it when I'm at home. I really think it's been good for the two of us to be away from each other a lot of the time. I'm not sure that this makes any sense, but sometimes you can be closer because you're apart. You're just so happy to see each other and be together, and you don't have time to pick at each other's faults or fight. Carl and I have never had a fight. There's never been any time for one."

Also in 1966, lightning struck. Dolly and Uncle Bill had written a song together, "Put It Off Until Tomorrow," and Bill Owens had taken the demo tape, with Dolly singing, to one of the most important record producers in Nashville, Owen Bradley, who was then with Decca Records. Owens wanted a Decca artist, country star Bill Phillips, to record it.

Bradley listened to the demo and agreed. He liked the song, but he also liked the girl singer, and he made it a stipulation in buying the song that Dolly sing the harmony on Phillips's record. Some versions of the story say it was Phillips himself who heard the song and took it to Bradley, insisting that the girl singer work with him on it. Another version insists Dolly made the recording of "Put It Off Until Tomorrow" with Phillips "by accident."

The last version goes this way: Phillips didn't have the melody down pat, so Dolly sang along with him at rehearsals, to keep the tune straight in his mind. The two of them sounded so good together that when the cut was made, Dolly stayed at the microphone. She was paid as a backup singer, but because of her contractual ties to Monument Records, she couldn't get credit on the label. Even without billing, Dolly was eager to oblige.

The record went into the Top Ten on the country charts, with the song winning a BMI (Broadcast Music Incorporated) Award, Dolly's first, but certainly not her last. Ten years later, at the age of twenty-seven, she would be the holder of 14 BMI awards, as well as many other honors.

People were soon wondering who was the sweet female voice harmonizing on the song. They read the record label in vain, looking for the name that wasn't there. It was a mystery that was to be solved on the air, as the disc jockeys, fielding inquiring telephone calls, informed their audiences of the identity of the "li'l gal singer, Dolly Parton."

Dolly had proved to Monument that she was right—that she *could* sing country, and that audiences would buy it and her. Taking its cue, Monument swung into action, and in 1967 Dolly had a record of her own, a country record, in the stores and on the air. The ironically titled "Dumb Blonde" wasn't even a song she'd written herself —it was by Curly Putnam—but she gave it her all (" 'Cause this dumb blonde ain't nobody's fool"), and it became a hit. Before the age of twenty-one, Dolly Parton had attained her first hit record.

"Dumb Blonde" was followed up by a bouncy, sassy little number, "Something Fishy," a song Dolly had written. In it, she sings about her man's unfaithfulness during "fishing trips," that ages-old excuse. It, too, became an instant hit, and the name and talents of Dolly Parton began to be noticed in Nashville. A deliriously happy Dolly wrote a joyful letter to the folks back home to tell them that her "Dumb Blonde" had risen into the Top Ten nationwide, and that she had gone into the studio to cut an album called *Hello, I'm Dolly*,

which would feature the single "Dumb Blonde."
She promised to send them one when it came out
in a month's time.

But that wasn't all the news she had to report.
Dolly had recorded a song she had written herself, "Something Fishy." She called it "real good."

Dolly Parton was working very hard now, out
on the road playing gigs here and there for small
money, and writing new songs, always composing. She was hoping for success with "Something
Fishy," so that she could get another album out
of it. Other singers were picking up on her material. Hank Williams, Jr., had recorded "I'm in No
Condition," and Kitty Wells, the Queen of Country Music, had decided to record "More Love
Than Sense." Another Owens/Parton tune, "Fuel
to the Flame," had gotten as high as number 7 on
the national country music charts.

Finally! Dolly Rebecca was on her way. Other
artists were starting to record her material, and
she was cutting hit records of her own. She was
earning a reputation as a songwriter of great promise. The name Dolly Parton was becoming familiar to people of influence in Music City, U.S.A.
She had established with Monument the crucial
fact that she *could* record country music, and
that the public *would* buy her records. The dreaded
rockabilly had become a thing of the past.

Very soon she was to team up with the man
who, of all the people in the world, would give the
biggest boost to Dolly's career. Dolly was about to
make that quantum leap over the chasm between
success and stardom. The hand held out to her

across the gap was Porter Wagoner's. Nashville, which had once seemed a million miles away to the young Dolly, and which she declared to be her new home, was about to become her personal property.

Chapter Four

Hello, Dolly. Hello, Porter.

I learned a lot from Porter. He inspired me and I inspired him.

—Dolly Parton

If in 1967 Roy Acuff was the acknowledged King of Country Music, then Porter Wayne Wagoner was surely its Crown Prince. What Roy was to radio, Porter was to syndicated television. A star for twenty-five years, a regular on the "Grand Ole Opry" since 1957, he'd had his own nationally viewed TV program since 1960, "The Porter Wagoner Show." He also took this show on the road, playing numerous concert dates.

Tall, thin, and ruggedly handsome, a long drink of country water with a crooked nose and a prominent lower lip, his yellow hair piled high in a pompadour and slicked down with pomade, Wagoner could have been the original model for the Rhinestone Cowboy. Dressed up, he was a sight to behold.

Porter togged himself out in outlandish, exaggerated western suits of the type made by Nudie of Hollywood, fringed and fancy-stitched all over and decorated with bright-colored stones and sequins. A typical Wagoner Wagon Master suit would feature covered Conestoga wagons (a play on his name) and tall cactus plants, all picked out in "jewels." He also sported one with rhinestoned wagon wheels on the shoulders and the sleeves, with a rhinestoned neck scarf to match, and cowboy boots, frequently colored red.

Despite his flamboyant attire, Porter's singing style was down-home and simple, usually accompanied by a steel guitar and a fiddle. He was an accomplished picker. His repertoire of songs was traditional, sacramental, or pure country; he ignored rockabilly and pop, and he leaned heavily on sentimental recitations and favorite songs, on the old-time-religion hymns his audiences loved, and on his country-boy humor. It was this combination of show-biz and good ole boy that had made him a star.

And Porter Wagoner *was* a star, no lie. He had the big audiences, the gold records, the Grammys, and the bookings to prove it.

Norma Jean Beasler, known professionally as Miss Norma Jean, was a bright, peppy blonde. She was the female singer with the Wagon Masters male quartet on Porter Wagoner's syndicated TV show since its inception seven years earlier. She was very popular with Porter's audiences. But now, Norma Jean was quitting to get married and move to Oklahoma, leaving Porter looking for a female singer to replace her. Dolly Parton was one of the girls he thought of.

Porter's background wasn't so different from Dolly's. He, too, had been born dirt-poor, raised on a hillside farm near West Plains, Missouri. Unlike Dolly, who had sloughed her way through high school to earn her diploma, Porter hadn't made it through grammar school. He had had to drop out before seventh grade, in order to get a job and help support the family after his father fell ill.

But being uneducated didn't make Wagoner ignorant; on the contrary, he was as smart as they came, and in 1967 he was on the top of the country heap, with an audience numbering more than 45,000,000 viewers, and with more than 100 television stations carrying "The Porter Wagoner Show," some in prime time. In 1966 he won the Country Song Roundup People's Poll Award for the favorite country television program. Among the many songs he made famous, and which made him famous, were "Satisfied Mind" and "George Leroy Chickasaw."

The show featured an extremely popular hillbilly comic, Speck Rhodes, who milked a lot of laughs out of having no front teeth; a quartet called the Wagon Masters, who dressed in watered-down and not nearly so flashy versions of Porter's famous outfits; fiddler Mack Ma Gaha; and

Buck Trent on steel guitar. And the obligatory female singer, dressed in a frilly country-style long dress of gingham or calico, with nipped-in waist and full skirts over crinolines.

In addition to his TV success, Porter had signed with RCA Victor in 1950, and had been a recording star since 1955, with hits in the Top Ten and even the Top Five on numerous occasions. Even before he teamed up with Dolly, he had won two Grammy Awards, both for religious recordings, *Grand Old Gospel* and *More Grand Old Gospel*. Porter's recorded hit singles included "The Green, Green Grass of Home," "Ole Slewfoot," "The Cold, Hard Facts of Life," "Julie," and many others. He was a top moneymaker, booked for concert appearances more than a year in advance, and somebody who knew how to invest one dollar and see it grow into one hundred.

The success of "The Porter Wagoner Show" in the 1960s and 1970s was the inspiration for the launching of a number of similar country music television programs, such as "Midwestern Hayride" out of Cincinnati, "The Wilburn Brothers Show," which started Loretta Lynn on her way to superstardom, the "Los Angeles County Barn Dance," an important show from California, and a program out of Nashville called "Good Ole Nashville Music," which utilized the talents of a number of "Grand Ole Opry" stars. Country and western was truly entering into a Golden Age; its popularity was not confined to the Southern states alone. Country music was as popular in California and the Midwest as it was in Nashville, Tennessee.

Porter had gotten his start much like Dolly— singing on an early-morning local radio program before he was out of his teens. Radio led eventually to "The Ozark Jubilee" on television out of Springfield, Missouri. That was thanks to Red Foley, Wagoner's mentor, who put the show together and selected Porter as a featured artist.

In 1960, the Chattanooga Medicine Company was set to sponsor a half-hour country music television show, but the star performer they were looking for also had to be the pitchman for their products, which included laxatives, deep-heat rubs, a weight-gain compound, and other such down-home self-medications with wonderfully evocative names like Black Draught and the Wine of Cardui. The firm's calendars were considered so "artistic" that they were found on walls all over the rustic Southland. What Chattanooga Medicine was auditioning for, in addition to musical talent, was sincerity and credibility. All of these qualities they found in Porter Wagoner, whose delivery on the commercials was so good, it made tens of thousands want to run right out and buy the products.

As soon as he got his own contracts from the Chattanooga Medicine Company, Porter signed up Norma Jean, who had been a fellow performer on Red Foley's "Ozark Jubilee." A country star in her own right, Norma Jean was heavily in the running for the unofficial title Queen of Country Music, a title held by Kitty Wells until Patsy Cline took it away from her.

But Patsy had died in 1963, at thirty-one tragically young, in the crash of a private plane that had also taken the lives of "Grand Ole Opry" stars "Hawkshaw" Hawkins and "Cowboy" Copas, The Hillbilly Waltz King. Since then the title had been up for grabs, and Norma Jean's name was frequently mentioned as a worthy successor to Patsy. She was a familiar face and voice; therefore, she became an immediate favorite with the audience of "The Porter Wagoner Show." Add to this her success on records, first with Columbia and later with RCA, and she would be a difficult talent to replace. She had been with the show for seven highly visible and flourishing years.

Now, in 1967, Porter Wagoner found himself suddenly without a girl singer. He began auditions immediately, looking at and listening to established performers as well as hopeful newcomers. What he was seeking was that indefinable something—that combination of looks, talent, and personality that would create a chemistry for the show. He kept coming up empty, and then he thought of Dolly.

Although Porter and Dolly had never met, there had been contact of a kind between them. When Dolly was pounding the pavement trying to sell her songs, she had submitted several to Wagoner, for Norma Jean. Although Wagoner had rejected the songs as wrong for his girl singer, he was impressed by the obvious talent that went into writing them. And now, with two hit single records back to back, Dolly Parton was enjoying a certain celebrity in Nashville. Her songwriting talent convinced Porter, who was no mean songwriter himself, that not only could she sing, but that she might be able to supply new material for the program. So Porter Wagoner picked up the phone.

"I had never seen Porter Wagoner in person," Dolly told Jerry Bailey in her first cover story in *Country Music* magazine, back in 1973. "We were big fans of his back home and watched his show on television. I had met a lot of people, but no stars. He called me one day and told me who he was, and I just couldn't believe it."

By this time Dolly Parton could afford a telephone, and even an automobile. But her success was still so brand-new that it kept surprising her. When she heard Porter Wagoner's voice on *her* phone, Dolly's first thought, she says, was that he was calling to get some songs for Norma Jean. She had heard through the music grapevine that Norma Jean was high on one of the songs Dolly had sent her. Porter set up an appointment, and Dolly went to keep it, carrying her guitar.

Dolly Parton claims to believe it was her songs that Porter was about to audition, never dreaming it was herself. Yet, it was hardly a secret that Porter Wagoner was looking for a girl singer to replace Norma Jean; he had been auditioning singers for some time then, and it was likely that Dolly Parton's name had come up for the job. If she didn't *think* he was planning to try her out, she certainly must have *dreamed* it.

Dolly impressed Porter at once. He thought she was beautiful to look at and that she sang quite well. But what really won him over, he's said many times, was her warmth and her sincerity. "She had the type of genuine, likable personality that I could sell to people on television and in person." Notice the operative word "sell" rather than "present." Porter Wagoner always kept a sharp eye on the monetary value of things.

"Dolly came to my office, but she didn't really know what we were going to talk about," Porter told interviewer Jerry Bailey. "She brought her guitar. And she sang a song for me, a song about everything being beautiful. She had written it. And this song told me so much about her. I knew if a person could sit down and write a song like that, they'd have to have a real soul inside 'em."

When Porter pitched her his offer, to come and be Miss Dolly, the girl singer with "The Porter Wagoner Show," Dolly was first flabbergasted, then, when she had managed to catch her breath, delighted. It would be a giant step up for her, exposure to the 45,000,000 viewers of "The Porter Wagoner Show." She jumped at it, accepting with joy.

Thus started a seven-year relationship that was Dolly's first real big break, the phone call that led her to stardom. From this collaboration would come fame, honors, and a series of smash-hit RCA albums.

But first, Dolly Parton had to make good on the show. It was far from easy, and it didn't come overnight. Filling in for Norma Jean was one of the hardest obstacles Dolly would ever be called on to overcome. Although the money was much more than she had earned before in her life, Dolly found the going rough. Norma Jean had had her own loyal following for seven years, not to mention that Dolly's voice was very different from hers.

Whenever the show played the road, as it often did, Dolly would come out onstage to be introduced and, when she stepped to the microphone, instead of applause, she would hear shouts of "Where's Norma Jean?" and "We want Norma Jean!" It was painful (she described it later as "torture") and all Dolly could do was to grit her teeth and go on singing her heart out, trying her best to win them over, even though more than once she came offstage crying. It was almost a year before audiences began to forget Norma Jean and accept this curvaceous little blonde with the girlish soprano in her place. As Dolly herself says, her beginning months with "The Porter Wagoner Show" were "stepping into big, big shoes."

In the seven years of Dolly's collaboration with Porter—1967–1974—they spent far more time together than Dolly spent with her husband, Carl, a fact of which the press was to make many a mention. But Porter and Dolly were both workaholics, and their rigid schedule kept them as close as chain-gang prisoners linked at the ankles.

For two to three weeks out of every month, they were touring to play dates in Wagoner's elaborately luxurious custom bus. When they weren't picking and singing in local auditoriums, theaters, and concert halls, they were taping "The Porter Wagoner Show," writing and rehearsing songs, or cutting records in the studio.

In 1967, when Dolly joined Porter, society was in ferment; America had committed half a million troops to Vietnam, and antiwar demonstrations were escalating; it was the year of the first Human Be-In in San Francisco, the Summer of

Love and the Monterey Pop Festival, the musical watershed year of *Sergeant Pepper's Lonely Hearts Club Band*; it was the autumn of the March on the Pentagon. Yet, on "The Porter Wagoner Show," business went on as usual, with blond Miss Dolly, for better or worse, replacing blond Miss Norma Jean.

Dolly's salary was $300 a night, which equaled $60,000 a year. This was big money in those days, and even bigger money for a girl from Tennessee whose family didn't even own a two-holer. Dolly really earned her money, because Porter Wagoner was on the road so much, and the show gave so many performances, both live and on TV. Porter was booked for at least 100 live gigs a year, and a great deal of time on the road was spent traveling between engagements. But work was the stuff of life to Dolly Parton—she breathed it, ate it, drank it, and asked for second helpings.

Shortly after she joined Porter's show, Dolly's contract with Monument Records and Combine Publishing expired. It was the right time now for two giant steps. First, she formed Owepar Publishing (for Owens and Parton) with her Uncle Bill Owens, to publish and hold the copyrights for their songs. And she moved over to RCA, Porter's label, where she stayed for the next 20 years. How she did it is a classic Parton story, many times reprinted, but always good for one more telling.

Porter took a demonstration tape of Dolly to RCA, to country star Chet Atkins, who headed up the Nashville studio. Atkins listened to the demo, but shook his head. "Porter, I'm sorry, but that girl just can't sing," he told Wagoner. "I don't think she'd sell a single record, because she just can't sing!"

Porter Wagoner wasn't fazed. "Tell ya what," he replied. "S'pose you take out of my royalties every penny she loses RCA, because I believe she *can* sing, and I'm gonna prove it!"

On the strength of Porter's influence alone, RCA signed Dolly, and the rest is history. Not only didn't she lose money, leaving Wagoner's royalties intact, but her first single for RCA, "Just Because I'm a Woman," went to number one on the country charts, selling 150,000 copies. Today, she sells more records for RCA than does rock star David Bowie. Dolly also took on a new manager, Don Warden, who had been managing Porter Wagoner for years.

But what really launched Dolly's career skyward was the series of duet albums she made with Porter, including *Just Between You and Me; Always, Always; Porter Wayne and Dolly Rebecca; Once More; The Right Combination/ Burning the Midnight Oil; Together Always* (an ironic title, given the future); *The Best of Porter Wagoner and Dolly Parton; Say Forever You'll Be Mine; Porter 'N' Dolly; Love and Music; We Found It; Two of a Kind;* and *Just the Two of Us.* Thirteen hit albums in seven years—a remarkable achievement. But all of that was still to come. First, the duo itself had to come into being.

Early in their association, while she was still trying to persuade audiences that she was a fit replacement to walk in Norma Jean's big, big shoes, Porter and Dolly had begun rehearsing songs together, singing duets on the bus going between live engagements. It's been said that he did this to get her over her anxieties and unhappiness; following Norma Jean in front of live, hostile audiences was agony on young Dolly's nerves, and the pressure on both of them was excruciating.

It's also been said that the duets were strictly a commercial idea from the first. But whatever it was, altruism or shrewd business sense, it worked. The harmonic blend of their voices—hers so girlishly sweet and his so masculine, the purity and simplicity of their individual singing styles melting and merging together to form an overwhelming unified sound—was a winning combination from the start. It's as though they had been born to sing duets.

A man and a woman singing country music together was not new. Johnny Cash and his wife, June Carter, were a highly successful duo. Other singing teams included Buck Owens and Susan Raye, Jim Ed Brown and Helen Cornelius, Johnnie and Joni Mosby, Waylon Jennings and Jessi Colter, and Don Gibson and Dottie West. Later, Loretta Lynn and Conway Twitty, George Jones and Tammy Wynette, and other famous duos would cut many hit albums. But Porter had never sung duets with Norma Jean; he'd always been a solo performer. This was as new for him as it was for Dolly, but whatever it was, it worked. Clicking from the very beginning, they hightailed it into the recording studio.

In October 1967, just months after Dolly had joined "The Porter Wagoner Show," they recorded their first duet. The song was Tom Paxton's "The

Last Thing on My Mind," a single. Its success was almost instantaneous, as the record made it into the Top Ten by December. It was followed up at the beginning of 1968 by "Holdin' onto Nothin'." Other smash hits soon came, one after another: "We'll Get Ahead Someday," "Just Someone I Used to Know," "The Pain of Loving You," "Daddy Was an Old-Time Preacher Man" (the song Dolly had written in honor of her grandpa, Jake Owens), "Run That By Me One More Time," "If Teardrops Were Pennies and Heartaches Were Gold," and many others.

Their duo album, *Just Between You and Me*, was on the country charts for a long time in 1968, and in 1969 Dolly and Porter collaborated on a popular album, *Just the Two of Us*, and two big hit singles, "Always Always" and "Your Love."

In 1968, the Country Music Association chose Porter and Dolly as the Vocal Group of the Year, and in 1970 and 1971, Dolly Parton and Porter Wagoner were voted the CMA's Vocal Duo of the Year. In 1969, one of Dolly's most precious and long-held dreams became a reality—after many appearances there, she was asked to be a regular on "Grand Ole Opry." Fame had caught up with her at last, even if she had achieved it as the prettier half of a singing duo rather than as her solo self.

"I'd always wanted that glamorous way of life. I wanted to be in the lights and the glitter and have beautiful clothes and jewels and fat hairdos," says Dolly. Now she had it. But was it going to be enough?

Also in 1969, Dolly Parton wrote the song that

has become a country classic, the song that means more to her than any other, "Coat of Many Colors." It was one of the songs she composed on the Porter Wagoner tour bus, and it became the biggest hit she had written thus far. Of the autobiographical nature of her songs, she has said, "You can clean the hurt out of your own self, and you can also help other people who hurt the same way but maybe can't express it."

Dolly Parton had a number-one single in 1970, "Mule Skinner Blues," and RCA issued a retrospective album, *The Best of Dolly Parton*, which was only moderately successful, but which was to turn gold years later, after her crossover into popular music.

In April 1970, Dolly went back home to Sevierville, but this time she carried no cardboard suitcase filled with dreams and dirty laundry. This time it was to celebrate Dolly Parton Day and receive the keys to the city. She established the Dolly Parton Scholarship Foundation for her old high school, Sevier County High, to aid needy students in obtaining a college education. Dolly was photographed admiring a bronze commemorative plaque with her image on it.

It was a glorious day for Dolly Rebecca Parton, the hometown girl receiving the honors of which she had always dreamed. How proud her parents and brothers and sisters must have been, as speaker after speaker stood up to sing Dolly's praises. The general manager of "Grand Ole Opry," Bud Wendell, was one of the laudatory speakers; another was good old Cas Walker, who had given Dolly Parton her start over station WIVK.

More than 2,500 people turned out for Dolly; in a town the size of Sevierville, that was a mob scene. After a parade that traveled two miles from the town center to the high school, they crowded into the auditorium to watch Dolly record a live LP for RCA. A special bus had brought the band and the engineers down from Nashville. Porter Wagoner made a surprise appearance.

During the presentation ceremonies, BMI gifted her with a set of silver cups. She was a hometown hero; how it must have thrilled her when she looked back on her virtually friendless high school days. The very people who had laughed at her ambitions and her dreams of stardom were now cheering her, and telling one another, "Dolly and me, we was *this* close in high school!"

She went back again to Sevierville in 1971 to play a benefit concert for the high school, as she has done many times since, and there Dolly received a gold disc from BMI for "Just Because I'm a Woman."

In 1971, honors were heaped on Dolly Parton, both as singer and as songwriter. She won two BMI awards, one for "Joshua" and the other for "Daddy Was an Old-Time Preacher Man," the song inspired by her grandfather, the Reverend Jake Owens. *Billboard* named Dolly as the Best Female Songwriter, and she was in the top five in the category of Best Female Vocalist in all the trade papers. She was only twenty-five years old.

Obviously, the combination of Porter and Dolly was working well for both of them. Porter gave Dolly the exposure she needed in TV and to live audiences, and taught her a lot about the music business, information the intelligent girl sopped up and stored away. Dolly gave Porter beautiful songs, her sweet soprano blended with his deep voice, and a new lease on his professional life as part of a team. "Because of my songs, Porter makes money," she was to say later. "Because of Porter, I make money."

They looked very natural together, Porter tall and thin, Dolly short, round, and dimpled, both of them blond, and decked out in sparkly finery. Many of their fans assumed they were man and wife. The press assumed they were lovers, especially when Porter began lavishing gifts on Dolly, including diamond jewelry and a Cadillac. "I have diamond rings for all of my fingers, and all of 'em except for my wedding ring are presents from Porter Wagoner," bragged Dolly.

Were they lovers? Porter and Dolly have denied it, but their constant proximity on the road and in the rehearsal studio, their involvement with their music, the many hours spent in each other's company—with all these taken together, it would have been stranger if they hadn't been.

Still, Dolly insists, "Everybody always thought there was somethin' goin' on between Porter and me, but there wasn't, not sex, anyway. He wasn't my lover or my sugar daddy. A man and woman don't necessarily have to have sex to have a love relationship goin', and I'm not ashamed to say I loved Porter Wagoner. There was a great love and respect between us, and it was a unique relationship, one of a kind. But if we was goin' to bed together, my husband would have been the first to know, 'cause you can't hide a thing like that. I would never hurt Carl that way. Besides, Carl always knows he's the one I love."

A few years after Owepar Publishing was founded, Uncle Bill sold his interest to Dolly. One Christmas during their seven-year association, Dolly either gave to Porter Wagoner (or sold; there is more than one version of the story) a half interest in Owepar, which held the copyrights to the songs she had written with her Uncle Bill Owens and by herself. By now, Uncle Bill seemed to be very much out of the picture, although another of Dolly's uncles, Louis Owens, was at the helm of Owepar.

But, whether gift or sale, Porter and Dolly were now partners in a profitable venture, owning jointly an extensive catalog of songs, including Porter's as well as Dolly's, and a hit list that included "Jolene," "Coat of Many Colors," "Joshua," "Daddy Was an Old-Time Preacher Man," "The Last One to Touch Me," "The Right Combination," "Katy Did," "Burning the Midnight Oil," and many others.

That co-ownership was to prove disastrous to Dolly after she broke with Porter Wagoner. It would lead to bitter recriminations and a multi-million-dollar lawsuit.

Meanwhile, Porter was smoothing out the rougher edges of Dolly's image, grooming her and teaching her a great deal about how to dress for the stage, and how to project her personality to an audience. The first thing he did was to get her out of those frilly dresses and country calicos and glamorize her image to match his own. This was show business, and country music audiences enjoyed the glitzy glamour of tinsel and glitter.

Dolly's appearance kept improving, and her wigs and flashy sequined and jeweled clothing became a female echo of Porter Wagoner's. She even wore tightly fitted custom-made trousers suits with jeweled patterns down the legs, just like Porter's. But where Porter's personal logo was always the wagon or the wagon wheel to match the name of Wagoner, Dolly's became the butterfly, which she had by now adopted as her own symbol, and always wore, often in the form of diamond jewelry given to her by Wagoner. Porter once estimated that during the years of their relationship, he gave Dolly five diamond rings, a diamond necklace, and two Cadillacs. Dolly's little hands were covered by so many rings from Porter that one could barely see the wedding ring from Carl Dean.

Diamonds may be a girl's best friend, but much more important to Dolly was her career as a songwriter. She was writing furiously, song after song spilling out of her thoughts and onto the strings of her guitar. The Porter Wagoner era was the time in which Dolly's creativity reached its zenith—"Coat of Many Colors," "Joshua," which became a number-one chart-topper for her, "I'll Never Stop Loving You." The hits just kept coming, tumbling over one another as though they had waited years to be released from inside Dolly. In 1972, Dolly wrote "Washday Blues" and "Touch Your Woman"; in 1973, "Travelin' Man"; between 1973 and 1974, the great "Jolene." She and Porter collaborated on "Please Don't Stop Loving Me" in the same year, and in 1974, Dolly composed her trademark classic, "Love Is Like a Butterfly." Nineteen seventy-five saw "We Used To" and "The Seeker." Nineteen seventy-six brought forth "Hey, Lucky Lady," "All I Can Do," and, as a duet with Porter, "Forever Is Longer Than Always." There seemed to be no stemming the creative tide; Dolly was pouring the deepest part of herself into her songs.

The relationship between them inspired them both, because Porter Wagoner, who had abandoned his songwriting for almost two decades, began composing again, too.

"She's as creative as anyone I've ever met, including Hank Williams," said Wagoner of Dolly Parton. He spent a lot of time and energy producing her albums. "To me, a record is like a monument," he told Toby Thompson of *The Village Voice*. "Important that it's done right. Dolly's voice is a hard voice to capture on record—very piercing, gives the equipment a fit. . . . I cain't hardly place Dolly in any vocal tradition. She's very unique. I've never known anyone in my twenty-two years with RCA like Dolly at all. I cain't fix our duets in any sort of tradition, either. Our harmony is so close it's almost like blood kin. Brother and sister, you know, can harmonize better than a great tenor and a great lead singer gettin' together. . . . Dolly and I sound nearly like brother and sister."

Hit albums followed one right after the other, most of them showing up on the country music charts, including: 1969—*Blue Ridge Mountain Bow*; 1970—*Best of Dolly Parton, Fairest of them*

All, Real Live; 1971—*Coat of Many Colors, Golden Streets of Glory, Joshua;* 1972—*Touch Your Woman, My Favorite Songwriter, Porter Wagoner,* and the duet album with Porter, *The Right Combination/Burning the Midnight Oil;* 1973—*Bubbling Over.*

But there was trouble in paradise.

In 1974, Dolly was no longer the wide-eyed naïve little girl that she had been in 1967. She knew that for every dollar she was earning, Porter Wagoner was earning at least ten. She was twenty-eight years old, and as famous as she had become, she was not yet the star she intended to be. She was *half* a star, half of "Porter and Dolly." Also, Wagoner was going around saying that he had made Dolly Parton a star, that he had created her, and those words chafed.

"He *helped* me become a star, but he didn't *make* me a star!"

But it was Porter's show, and Porter was pulling the strings. Porter handled the business end of things, and made most of the decisions for the two of them. Dolly began to feel like a marionette. Wasn't it *her* songs that were making their duet records such huge hits? Wasn't her talent at least equal to his, and (she thought secretly) even greater? Wasn't she standing poised just at the beginning of her career, while he, much older, was beginning to wind down? Who was riding on whose coattails? And, bottom line, wasn't Dolly Parton's ego every bit as large and every bit as demanding of satisfaction as Porter Wagoner's?

Even in the recording studio, Dolly and Porter weren't seeing eye to eye anymore. As Dolly told her biographer, Alanna Reed, "When he was producing me, I got some of my ideas across and the big part of my ideas were written in the songs, the arrangement ideas and all. But there was so much I wanted to do, and he heard it so differently that we just couldn't agree on so many things. It just took away the joy of me recordin' the song at all. Because then it wasn't what I'd created it to be. It had taken on somebody else's personality. That's hard to explain to people who aren't writers, but without Porter, at least I can write the songs and get them down the way I hear them."

Dolly began to feel choked, locked into a relationship of business and image that restricted her and held her back. She wanted to be Dolly Parton, free to fly, not the soprano side of Porter Wagoner, held to earth. She wanted something that would be entirely her own, with all the fame that could come with solo stardom. In short, she wanted to run her own show.

Money was no small consideration. "Why should I make hundreds *and* thousands, when I can make hundreds *of* thousands?" she demanded, with some justice.

In a clash of wills and temperaments, they began to fight. Porter and Dolly had similar personalities; each was as stubborn as the other, each as set in his own ways. The bloom was off the rose; the magic had gone out of the partnership. Dolly Parton became determined to go it on her own. Porter, it goes without saying, didn't want her to quit the show. He refused his permission, but she went ahead and did it anyway.

For her, it was a natural progression, up and out, leaving Porter Wagoner behind. It was like a spacecraft jettisoning booster rockets when they are no longer necessary, when they keep the craft earthbound, not allowing it to soar free into outer space. Dolly Parton had done it before, and she would do it again. Many great stars behave in this way, always putting their careers above their relationships, and Dolly Parton has never made a secret of it, not even when she married Carl Dean. Career to Dolly—her music and the free expression of it—would always come first in her life.

Porter Wagoner had given her a lot, but now he had nothing left to give. Dolly had learned everything she needed to learn from Porter. She had charmed his audiences and held them in the palm of her small hand. But now she'd outgrown him, and it was time to go on to the next phase of her life, to try her wings . . . solo.

Chapter Five

Good-bye, Dolly. Good-bye, Porter.

We were good for each other in a lot of ways and just a disaster for each other in a lot of ways. I'll always love him, in my own way. You have to follow your own dreams.

—Dolly Parton

It wasn't a new story by any means; it didn't happen to Dolly Parton alone. A young girl, standing on tiptoes at the beginning of her professional life, needing all the help she can get. A successful man, much older, much wiser, a mentor. A relationship, professional and personal, benefiting both, profitable to both. He teaches her everything he knows, and she proves a willing pupil. But then it goes on for too long. The man is

94

satisfied, but the girl grows into a woman. She discovers she has no identity of her own, but is merely half a team. She longs for that identity, longs to be herself, to be recognized for her own attainments, her own talents. She is certain that by herself she can surpass everything they have accomplished together. She dreams dreams, and she longs to put "legs on them." She struggles to break free and fly like an eagle into the clear blue morning, but the man doesn't want to let her go. Why should he? For him, everything is just fine the way it is. It leads to quarrels, it leads to bitterness, it leads to recriminations, and, eventually, to hatred. The woman gets her way, but the process is not unlike open-heart surgery without anesthesia.

"Porter knew I was plannin' to leave, and he didn't like it one single bit. I tried explainin' things to him, hopin' we could work it out between us, but he wasn't of a mind to listen. He just wouldn't talk to me, and when I saw I wasn't gettin' through to him, I just made up my mind that I was goin' to go the best way I knew how. He wasn't ever gonna give me his permission, so I just took it and left."

Dolly Parton makes it sound so easy, but it was far from simple, cutting the personal and professional ties of seven successful years. It involved lawyers, contracts, and percentages. Porter wasn't merely her singing partner and friend. He was also, by a contract they had both signed in 1970, Dolly Parton's manager and record producer. He wasn't about to let her go without a sizable piece of the future action.

Dolly didn't walk out; she bought herself out. She agreed to a percentage of her recording royalties in perpetuity, plus a percentage of her net income for the five years following the split. This was to compensate Porter for the loss of income he would suffer, no longer being her manager and producer.

Yet there would be other kinds of suffering; feelings were bound to be torn to shreds in the break. Breaking up is hard to do, as the song says. When Norma Jean had left his show, Porter had simply gone looking for another girl singer. If he let out any howls of anguish, it wasn't where anybody could hear. But with Dolly Parton it was different. They had been a hit duo, and maybe more. Breaking up with Dolly really hurt. Porter Wagoner would complain that Dolly Parton had used him as a stepping-stone on her way to bigger and better things. Dolly Parton would respond that Porter had gotten his money's worth in the seven years she had been his singing partner, and especially because he produced her albums.

Even after Dolly had announced that she was leaving "The Porter Wagoner Show," even while they were squabbling in private, the two were still singing in public as though nothing had happened. When they concertized in the Civic Auditorium in Oxnard, California, Bob Kirsch of *Billboard* wrote: "Dolly Parton is surely destined for superstardom in the country field, with a beautiful voice and a great writing talent. She has had her share of number-one records, but her material is becoming more consistently excellent and her hits are coming with more regularity. . . . Ms. Parton should have no trouble carving a permanent niche for herself in the country field, even after leaving the Wagoner show this summer. . . ."

In 1974, RCA released a number of Dolly's Porter-produced hit albums, including *Jolene* and *Love Is Like a Butterfly*. But by then, the duo was in big trouble.

Even Porter Wagoner had to admit that there had been conflicts between them, on the show and in the studio. In an interview he gave writer John Morthland, he said, "We were gonna do things my way. Because that's the kind of person I am. Dolly Parton's career up until she left me was done my way. That's the only way it could be successful operating with me, because if we had done it her way it wouldn't have worked. Had we done the songs she'd have liked to do, the way she'd have liked to do them, it just would not have worked. Because I couldn't produce them that way, first of all, I would not allow them to be done that way on my show. I signed the checks at that time, so we did things my way, and that was the way I was born and reared to do it—that if you paid a man to work for you, he worked for you; he didn't tell you what to do. If he did, that would be called an advisor. I wasn't looking for an advisor when I hired Dolly. We were using my ideas, my guidance, and my direction. That's the way it was."

For Dolly, breaking out of that stifling atmosphere, breaking away from the continual quarreling, and breaking up with Porter Wagoner were the next natural upward steps on her ever-ascending ladder to the stars. That decision had probably been in the making ever since she had reached number one on the charts as a solo artist with "Joshua" back in 1970. She was becoming a star attraction.

It wasn't her first such career move; she had left Uncle Bill Owens and Monument Records after Fred Foster had spent time and money fostering her (some $20,000 Monument spent for Dolly's voice lessons was one of the sums bandied about); she would one day leave RCA for Columbia. Success so often involves a series of opportunities taken and people left behind.

But Porter Wagoner was bitter; he has gone on record saying that he had devoted some 95 percent of his time to Dolly Parton, he had spent a fortune on shaping her and molding her, and then he didn't hear from her for a year.

Country music lovers reacted to the breakup of Dolly Parton and Porter Wagoner in the same way that rock 'n' roll fans reacted to the breakup of the Beatles—with shock, horror, and disbelief followed by outrage. The parting of the ways between Porter and Dolly was like a divorce in the family. Dolly's resignation from the show occasioned nearly as much press coverage as the resignations of Israeli Prime Minister Golda Meir, West German Chancellor Willy Brandt, and British Prime Minister Edward Heath, all of which took place in 1974. Those three were merely global leaders, while Dolly Parton and Porter Wagoner were *stars!*

Some people around Nashville were claiming that Porter and Dolly had had a lovers' quarrel, but others maintained that the split was much more about money than about love. More word had it that Porter Wagoner was: a. fit to kill; b. broken-hearted; c. jealous. Take your pick of one or all the preceding. The fact remains, and future events were to show, that Porter was very opposed to Dolly Parton's leaving "The Porter Wagoner Show," and very bitter about what he thought of as her ingratitude.

In 1978, Dolly told Lawrence Grobel in *Playboy*, "Porter has been one of the greatest and most popular country artists of all times. I can never take the credit away from Porter for givin' me a big break." But, "We just got to where we argued and quarreled about personal things. Things we had no business quarreling about. It was beginning to tarnish a really good relationship. We didn't get along very well, but no more his fault than mine. We were just a lot alike. Both ambitious. I wanted to do things my way and he wanted to do things his way."

Dolly Parton made no secret of the fact that she felt trapped with Porter Wagoner, but Porter's angrily bitter retort was, "That trap was pretty nice to her. There were no complaints at the beginning. I didn't set the trap to catch her, you know. It was set in a very humble manner of 'Would you help me get started, 'cause I'm just a little country girl from east Tennessee who's tryin' to get started in the country music business as a singer and songwriter?' But it's awful easy to convince yourself that 'I'm the only one that can do this, ain't nobody involved in this but me, and I gotta do it my way.' "

In July 1974, Dolly thought she was ready to do it "her way." When she left Wagoner's show, she was ready to become a superstar, and she couldn't accomplish it working for somebody else. It was the age of "do your own thing," and Dolly's own thing was a need to assert her own creativity and personality and musical ability. She was ready to be a whole entity, not half of one. She was also ready to earn $2,500 a night, which is what she commanded when she started down the solo road.

Nineteen seventy-four was a most important year in Dolly's songwriting career; it was the year she wrote "Jolene," her biggest chart-buster up to then, becoming the number-one country music song in the nation, and an international hit, recorded by Olivia Newton-John and Patti Smith. In the same year, Dolly also wrote "Love is Like a Butterfly," and "I Will Always Love You," which went into the Top Five.

Nineteen seventy-four was also the year she formed her own backup group, the Travelin' Family Band. Since all the Partons are musical, it seemed very natural for Dolly to keep it in the family and select her backup from among those nearest and dearest to her. Dolly spent a year touring with members of the Travelin' Family Band: brother Randy, twins Floyd and Frieda, an uncle, and a cousin named Dwight. It wasn't as good an idea as it sounded; in fact, it turned out to be more of a mistake, something of a false step in her career, but at the outset she was high on the concept of making music with her family.

Dave Hickey interviewed Dolly Parton in a cover story for *Country Music* magazine in July 1974. Dolly told Hickey, "I been getting my band together, lately. Two of my brothers are gonna be in it so we can sing family harmonies. And I'll tell you, however much work it takes to get it right, that's how much I'll do. I'll work myself to death for my music, 'specially for my show. That's what I've always wanted: to be a singing star with my own show.

"Writing and performing," she went on, "they're really my life, and I'm getting more mature about it. I don't run myself into the ground like I used to, staying up for days on the road."

"Now that I'm on my own," she told *Rolling Stone* reporter Chet Flippo, who was to follow her career adoringly, "I'm becoming more of what I really am, instead of having to be just a part of somebody else."

On August 25, 1974, in only her fourth concert appearance after leaving "The Porter Wagoner Show," Dolly was second-billed to Merle Haggard at the Anaheim Convention Center in what *Billboard* said "may well be the California country concert of the year." The trade journal noted that Dolly "was simply outstanding. Given a full hour to do her material, Miss Parton has ample chance to demonstrate all facets of her fine material. . . . Highlights were the excellent 'I Will Always Love You,' 'Jolene,' 'Coat of Many Colors,' 'Sacred Memories,' and the beautiful 'I Believe' encore. As a singer and a writer she is marvelous, and her voice must rank as one of the most distinctive and best in country. Her band is competent. . . ."

In public, Porter and Dolly were still playing kissy-face. Even though she'd left "The Porter Wagoner Show," Porter was still Dolly's record producer, on albums such as *Dolly*; *The Bargain Store*; *Best of Dolly Parton*; and *Say Forever You'll be Mine*, the last-named their duet album of 1975. Publicity releases were sent out assuring the press, who in turn assured the public, that Dolly and Porter "were still good friends." Besides, each still had a half interest in the phenomenally successful Owepar Publishing, which had become one of the giants of Music Row in Nashville.

In fact, the official version stated that it was Porter Wagoner who "coaxed" Dolly Parton into becoming a television star in her own right, with her solo TV show, "Dolly!," syndicated on 140 stations, making her, according to the trade journal *Billboard*, "the first female country star to headline such a show." The fact is, even if it wasn't Porter who "coaxed" her—and it was hard to think of Dolly Parton as needing persuasion to do her own TV show—the program was produced by Bill Graham of Show Biz, the same outfit that produced "The Porter Wagoner Show."

The show, simply called "Dolly!," was something of a mishmash. Taped at Opryland in Nashville, it featured a gigantic butterfly as the backdrop to the set designed by Rene Lagler; Dolly's theme song for the show was her hit "Love Is Like a Butterfly."

"Dolly!" had a sizable budget—between $85,000

and $100,000 a show, the largest budget for any syndicated TV show that ever came out of Nashville. During its 6-month run, the program featured such guests as K. C. and the Sunshine Band, the Fifth Dimension, and the Hues Corporation, all of whom were pop and disco favorites, not country music artists. Dolly even donned a platinum-blond Afro wig to sing and dance with the Hues Corporation. Of course, there were great country singers on the show, too, like Linda Ronstadt and Emmylou Harris, Anne Murray, Mel Tillis, Kenny Rogers, Ronnie Milsap, Tennessee Ernie Ford, and Tom T. Hall. The childlike Dolly even had Captain Kangaroo on as her guest, and poet-singer Rod McKuen. The one guest she longed for, but who continued to elude her, was Bob Dylan.

Dolly herself wasn't too crazy about the show; her favorite ones were those in which she had her entire family on, pickin' and singin', and the one where Linda, Emmylou, and Dolly sat quietly on the stage, their voices harmonizing beautifully, a little foretaste of the great *Trio* album to come ten years later.

But if Porter Wagoner seemed to be taking pleasure in Dolly's success in public, in private it was a very different state of affairs. Porter was mighty displeased with his protégé's actions, and he was still smarting at her remarks to the press about not wanting to continue being a part of somebody else, or that Porter Wagoner hadn't *made* Dolly Parton a star, but only helped her to *be* one.

Porter wasn't happy about little Dolly leaving the nest to fly on her own, maybe even to fly higher than he could. He had spent a lot of time and effort grooming her, giving her half his spotlight, and the fact that Dolly had repaid him a thousandfold wasn't enough. He still accused her of base ingratitude. He simply couldn't understand Dolly Parton's overwhelming need to go it on her own, find her own place in the sun.

Whenever Dolly was quoted in a newspaper or magazine as saying things like Porter Wagoner was one of the greatest country music stars in history, and how he gave her her big break, and how grateful she was and how she would never, ever take a lick o' credit away from him, *but* ... Porter would become righteously indignant. He felt she was already patronizing him, downgrading him by "making nice" in public, as though he were a child.

"I'd be less than truthful," Porter told *Country Style* magazine, "if I said I wasn't disappointed in the way the relationship turned out. I put a lot of energy into making her records great and my own records suffered."

The rift between Dolly and Porter was to widen; misunderstandings and anger would increase, charges and countercharges would be hurled, until finally their partnership would dissolve in mutual recriminations.

The trade journals tell the whole sad story: From *Variety*, 8/25/76: PARTON, WAGONER DISSOLVE VENTURES Nashville—The click country music team, Porter Wagoner and Dolly Parton, have officially dissolved all of joint business ventures. The pair, together since 1966 [sic], decided in 1974 to bill Parton separately from "The Porter Wagoner Show," although Wagoner still produced her records. Parton has now signed with a West Coast management agency and plans to produce her own records, relieving Don Warden as manager. The business aspects concerning the publishing of songs and a Wagoner-Parton-owned publishing firm have yet to be resolved.

From *Billboard*, 3/31/79: DOLLY PARTON HIT WITH $3 MIL SUIT. Nashville—Porter Wagoner has slapped his one-time partner and protégé Dolly Parton with a $3 million lawsuit.

Alleging breach of contract, the suit was filed Wednesday in Chancery Court for Davidson County, Tenn.

Wagoner filed the suit individually and doing business as Porter Wagoner Enterprises, and on behalf of Owepar Publishing Co. Defendants are Dolly Parton Dean (her married name), individually and as an officer and director of Owepar Publishing, and doing business as Velvet Apple Music, Song Yard Music, and Dolly Parton Enterprises.

The action seeks an accounting of all Parton's net income and record royalties to the date of judgment, 5% of her net income from June 1974 through June 1979, and 15% of her record royalties from the date the payments ceased to the date of judgment. Wagoner also wants the court to issue a declaratory judgment that Parton "is liable under contract to pay Porter Wagoner 15% of her record royalties earned from the date of judgment for so long as she receives such record royalties."

As an alternative to the above demands, Wagoner seeks $2 million for "future loss of income from Dolly Parton Dean's net income and record royalties."

From *Variety*, 3/28/79: GOOD-BYE DOLLY IS WORTH $3 MIL IN WAGONER SUIT Hollywood—Dolly Parton's former singing partner, producer, and manager, Porter Wagoner, has filed a $3,000,000 breach-of-contract suit against the singer, claiming that she has failed to make certain payments to him since their 1974 breakup.

Parton and Wagoner ended a seven-year partnership in July, 1974, after recording a series of albums together and performing as a duo on Wagoner's TV series and in concert. Wagoner also produced Parton's solo albums during that period.

According to the suit, filed in Nashville Chancery Court, Wagoner agreed to free her from a 1970 contract in exchange for a percentage of her recording royalties in perpetuity, as well as a percentage of her net income for the five years following the split. The sums were to compensate for Wagoner's loss of producer's royalties and his loss of future income as her manager.

The suit seeks 15% of her net income from June, 1974, through June, 1979, and 15% of her recording royalties forever, or a flat

$2,000,000 payment. Wagoner also seeks $1,000,000 for loss of producer's royalties during the June 1974–June 1979 period.

The suit also asks for the return of some 130 songs which were part of Parton and Wagoner's joint music publishing company, Owepar. . . .

The lawsuit was to drag on for years, growing more and more bitter, making only the lawyers rich, until it was settled out of court for an unspecified amount.

Meanwhile, from 1974 through 1975, Dolly was doing her syndicated TV show and going on the road with the Travelin' Family Band. And writing songs. In 1975, she turned out "The Seeker," "We Used To," and "The Bargain Store," all of which were produced on albums for RCA by Porter Wagoner.

But if her career as a songwriter was zooming higher than ever, her career as a soloist had taken a backward step. The Travelin' Family Band was nobody's idea of backup heaven; there was an amateurish quality about the entire show that was disappointing to Dolly's fans, who were used to the gloss and polish of "The Porter Wagoner Show."

When Dolly played the Felt Forum in New York City in September 1974, two months after the split with Wagoner, she couldn't bring in enough audience to fill the theater. Top-billed with Bobby Bare and Ronnie Milsap, she apparently didn't have, according to *Variety*, "the pop spillover needed to sell out in Gotham. The second season of country concerts at the Felt Forum got off to a good artistic start . . . but proved a box office dud. Only slightly more than half the 4,500 seats were filled for the show, which headlined Dolly Parton, who looked and sounded great, but whose set was a bit too long.''

John Rockwell of *The New York Times* was equally impressed with Dolly. In an often-quoted review of the concert, he wrote, "Country in New York got off to a rather disappointing season . . . the Felt Forum was nowhere near full. . . . But if the concert was a commercial disappointment, it was nothing like that from an artistic standpoint— at least so far as the headliner, Dolly Parton, is concerned. . . . She is an impressive artist. Her visual trademark is not far from that of Diamond Lil: a mountainous, curlicued bleached-blond wig, lots of makeup, and outfits that accentuate her quite astonishing hourglass figure.

"But Miss Parton is no artificial dumb blonde. Her thin little soprano and girlish way of talking suggest something childlike, but one quickly realizes both that it is genuine and that she is a striking talent; she really is a young woman from the Smoky Mountains of east Tennessee with a strong family sense and allegiance to the basic American rural virtues. . . .''

On the other hand, a loudly dissenting voice was heard from Nick Tosches, a music writer for *The Village Voice*, who reviewed her performance grimly: "There is a darker, more dismal side to Dolly Parton; I went to her recent show at Felt Forum, expecting at least a taste of her proven abilities. Instead I witnessed one of the shoddiest routines this side of 'Hee Haw.' Since she split from 'The Porter Wagoner Show' earlier this year, Dolly has been touring with her own band, made up mostly of relatives. Without exception, the group is third-rate. The lousy music is complemented by Dolly's feigned stupidity; she shucks and gee-whizzes and flutters her baby blues. . . . And let's not forget that painfully obligatory gospel number. . . . All the nonsense that Dolly steers clear of in her writing and recording, she dives into in her live performances. . . . Until Dolly abandons the ersatz yokelisms, her live performance will remain a mere travesty of her worth, not to mention bad. What she is capable of doing with words and sounds is 'act' enough."

Among Dolly's engagements in 1975 was the Waterloo Music Festival, a country music jamboree held in Stanhope, New Jersey, a beautifully restored town dating back to the days of the American Revolution. She wasn't even the sole headliner; Dolly and Gary Stewart, who had a new, successful album out, shared that honor. John Rockwell, the popular-music critic for *The New York Times*, reported on the concert, headlining his piece "A Beguiling Dolly Parton Sings at Jersey Festival."

Rockwell enjoyed Dolly's music, but the act with the Travelin' Family Band left him cold. He called her "a country singer and songwriter of enormous individuality and charm. She retains all of that in concert, but seems more quintessentially country than ever. . . . Her performance was pretty much like any other Parton performance: superb music mixed with canned corn. . . .

She is doing things she has done innumerable times before. The patter is often appallingly corny. . . ."

Yet, Rockwell easily perceived the great source of Dolly Parton's musical strength and artistry. "Miss Parton's songs deal mostly with her own memories. But her poetry has such a range of emotion and such a truth to it that—as always happens with the best art—the very specificity of her imagery becomes universal." *Universal imagery*—it must have been words like those, so often spoken and written about her work, that made Dolly Parton determined to broaden her horizons and reach out to larger audiences.

During 1974 and 1975, Dolly Parton was busy, but she was far from happy. Now she had the freedom to go wherever she chose, but she seemed to have chosen the wrong direction. She appeared to be "spinning her wheels," not making the progress she had expected. She wasn't satisfied with her management; her backup band, the Travelin' Family Band, hadn't worked out as she had expected; she didn't care for the quality of her TV show. "The show isn't me," she complained, and, after taping 26 shows, production stopped. She was still be be seen on occasional TV shows, such as the October 1975 network special marking the fiftieth anniversary of "Grand Ole Opry." Dolly, dressed in a bright pink tight-fitting pantsuit covered with a pattern of hearts outlined in rhinestones, appeared with the greats of country music, including Loretta Lynn and Roy Clark.

In 1975, Dolly Parton had a banner year for honors and awards. She was chosen by the Country Music Association as Female Vocalist of the Year. She was named Best Female Vocalist not only by *Billboard*, but also by *Cash Box* and *Record World*, trade publications of major importance in the music business. *Billboard* also selected Dolly as Best Female Singles Artist and Best Female Songwriter. She was beginning to amass quite an impressive collection of engraved plaques, cups, and framed citations to hang on her walls.

Yet, except for the record albums and the composing, nothing seemed to be going right. It was time for some major career moves. It was time for a whole new set of decisions that would carry Dolly Parton in an entirely new direction. It was time for what country music historians will always refer to as "Dolly Parton's crossover."

Chapter Six

Dolly Crosses Over

I'm still the same Dolly Parton.
I'm not leaving country; I'm taking
it with me.

—Dolly Parton

By 1976, although other artists had recorded Dolly's best songs—star performers as diverse in style as Linda Ronstadt, who recorded "I Will Always Love You"; Maria Muldaur, who did a version of "My Tennessee Mountain Home"; Emmylou Harris, who sang wonderfully "Coat of Many Colors"; Olivia Newton-John, who had chosen to record "Jolene"; Nancy Sinatra and Lee Hazelwood, Merle Haggard and even Patti Smith, who had also cut "Jolene"—Dolly herself still hadn't broken through with that million-copy seller, the platinum record.

Her own version of her biggest hit to date, "Jolene," had sold about 200,000 copies, which is monster sales in the country charts, but which left Dolly Parton dissatisfied. The admiration and respect of her peers and her country music fans were no longer enough; Dolly Parton's ambitions needed an even bigger pond in which to swim as an even bigger fish. She wanted to reach a lot more people and make a lot more money. "No matter how country you are, you hope for a cross-over hit," she said. "Why not? There's more money and recognition involved. Why are most of these people working, if not for that?"

Dolly Parton was beginning to make a name for herself outside the country milieu. Important journalists on the music scene, like rock 'n' roll writer Chet Flippo of *Rolling Stone*, to whom country music was still something of a sacred subject, discovered her and wrote long, rhapsodic pieces about her and her musicality. There were interviews in major media spots, not the least of which was the long story about Dolly written by Chris Chase for the Sunday magazine of the august and staid *New York Times*.

Chase, who went on to become the biographer of Rosalind Russell and Betty Ford, was captivated by the Parton sound. "Her voice is an amazement," she wrote in the *Times* Sunday magazine, after watching a country music concert at the East Burke High School outside Hickory, North Carolina, where Dolly and the Travelin' Family Band shared the bill with headliner Merle Haggard.

"She has said she sounds like a child 'with grown-up emotion,' but there's more to it than that. In 'Love Is Like a Butterfly,' Dolly's work is itself as sheer and delicate as a butterfly's wings; she skitters over the surface of the words, barely touching them, while in 'Travelin' Man' she hoots and hollers and drives and mocks. Sometimes she hits a high note and it breaks into pieces, and a little shower of crystally sounds comes down; sometimes she hits low notes soft and furry and filled with loneliness. Her voice can quiver, pure and tremulous, or it can twang flat like a banjo string; it can throb, it can lift, it takes an octave jump with foolish ease, and it is almost always true and sweet."

When the same Merle Haggard show played the Anaheim Convention Center in Orange County, California, a Mecca for country music fans, *Variety* reviewed it. The show business bible said that the Travelin' Family Band "ably backed up Parton, but was only passable on its own." But of Dolly herself, *Variety* stated, "Dolly Parton clicked with her hour's worth of material."

Good press, no matter how soothing to the ego, was not the stuff of which Dolly's dreams were made. What Dolly dreamed of was the whole ball of wax, tied up in silver ribbons. She wanted to step out of the confinement of the "country" label. Instead of Best Female Country Music Entertainer of the Year, she wanted her albums to be *numero uno* on the pop charts in addition to the country charts. She wanted to do television shows that weren't merely syndicated locally in country markets, but big prime-time hits in the big cities, too. She wanted to play Las Vegas. She wanted to make films. To do any of that, to break into the big time, she would have to change. To achieve her larger ambitions, Dolly Parton would have to take the biggest risk of her professional career, even greater than the one she took when she left Porter Wagoner to go solo.

There had been rumblings and speculation about Dolly going pop and breaking away from country as early as 1976, because her TV show, "Dolly!," included pop guests as well as country stars, and Dolly sang right along with them. Were significant changes in the offing? But, when Dolly won Best Female Vocalist of the Year for the second year running at the nationally televised 1976 Country Music Awards, she came onstage with just a simple banjo and sang a mountain ballad of her own, "Applejack," with a sound that was pure Tennessee.

A few weeks later, when she went into the studio to record "Applejack," she was backed up by such "Grand Ole Opry" stars as Minnie Pearl, Kitty Wells, Roy Acuff, Wilma Lee and Stoney Cooper, Chet Atkins, Ernest Tubb, Carl and Pearl Butler, and her own mama and daddy, a group of people she called "the best. They are my greatest inspiration."

Now was the ideal time for her to think things over and make plans. By the middle of 1976, Dolly was exhausted, worn out from going on the road with the Travelin' Family Band, and her vocal cords were beginning to trouble her. This was an ailment that would continue to plague her for years. Heavy tensions were developing in her relationship with Porter Wagoner.

The two of them were very much alike, as Dolly would be the first one to admit, both stubborn and bull-headed. "He won't accept things sometimes the way they are. I won't either, sometimes." As the tangled legalities between them grew more complicated, with Dolly wanting to buy back her song catalog from Porter, and Porter wanting his royalties from Dolly, the situation worsened. Not only did they stop speaking to each other, they stopped seeing each other.

It was obvious to Dolly that things were not working out as she had expected when she went off on her own. For one thing, the Travelin' Family Band would have to go. They simply weren't good enough, and were cramping Dolly's style. She needed an entirely different image; no more would she be Daisy Mae backed up by a bunch of Li'l Abners. Before she'd be ready to widen her horizons and tackle the much more lucrative crossover market, she would have to have more polish and some sophistication. And she needed national exposure to middle-of-the-road audiences. These were things with which the Travelin' Family Band couldn't help her; in fact, they were one of the stumbling blocks in her way.

Her health came first, though, because Dolly's throat was in serious trouble. She had nodes growing on her vocal cords; they were not painful, but did cause hoarseness and a loss of voice. Worse, the voice loss could possibly become permanent. "A node," reported Dr. Edward A. Kantor, "is a small tumefaction—like a rounded corn—on the

Just a pair of pickers — that's Carol Burnett on the banjo.

(Nancy Barr/ Globe Photos)

Dolly Parton at Opryland, free and as pretty as a butterfly.

(Nancy Barr/ Globe Photos)

Dolly Parton — Here I
Come Again!

(Nancy Barr/
Globe Photos)

Another key to another
city — Dolly conquers the
Big Apple with a free
concert at Mayor Ed Koch's
city hall.

(Zelin/Globe Photos)

Dolly Parton and Porter Wagoner — their seven-year collaboration made her a star.

(Phototeque)

Tara, Dolly's 23-room dream house outside Nashville.

(Norcia/ Globe Photos)

𝒟olly with her Grandpa Jake Owens, the hellfire reverend.

(Norcia/Globe Photos)

𝒟olly's loving husband of 21 years, the handsome Carl Dean.

(Norcia/Globe Photos)

𝒜vie Lee and Robert Lee Parton — Dolly's beloved mama and daddy.

(Norcia/Globe Photos)

Above, a very
famous trio:
Linda Ronstadt,
Dolly, Emmylou
Harris with
George Merlis.

(Globe Photos)

The movie they
should have left on
the cutting room
floor. Sylvester
Stallone and
Dolly Parton in
Rhinestone.

(Phototeque)

Dolly's "Tennessee mountain home."
(Norcia/Globe Photos)

Dolly Rebecca at home with her family in Sevier County.
Dolly is at the extreme left in the back.

(Norcia/Globe Photos)

"The most painful thing" Dolly had ever done was to make *The Best Little Whorehouse in Texas* with Burt Reynolds, *left*.

(Phototeque)

"Not one bad moment on the whole picture." Lily Tomlin, Jane Fonda, and Dolly Parton star in *Nine to Five, right*.

(Dominguez/ Globe Photos)

Two megastars — Dolly with Neil Diamond, *left,* at the party after her successful Amphitheatre opening, September 22, 1979.

(Nancy Barr/ Globe Photos)

"The Mountain Sidewinder" — a one-of-a-kind family fun machine at Dollywood.

(Globe Photos)

vocal cord, a swelling or growth. It is noncancerous, benign. But it's still something you have to check; hoarseness for more than six weeks is cancer until proven otherwise."

Dolly's doctors warned her that if she didn't give her vocal cords a long rest so that the growths would have a chance to soften and recede, the long-developing nodes might have to be removed surgically. Not only is vocal-cord surgery risky and painful, involving an operating microscope, but there are no guarantees that the nodes won't reappear or that the vocal cords won't thicken as they heal. Sometimes the vocal color is altered or even lost entirely. Dolly opted for a long rest.

The first thing she did was to cancel a large number of road engagements and concerts, 65 concerts, worth $325,000, set up for the months of June through October, and go "into seclusion." "Seclusion" meant no interviews and no public appearances. Dolly didn't even talk, but kept a pad and pencil by her side with which to communicate. Meanwhile, she was doing some heavy thinking and mulling over a lot of high-powered advice, much of it from her friend Mac Davis, who had successfully crossed over into pop-rock, and who had enjoyed his own prime-time TV variety specials.

No doubt, while she was paying attention to the practical side of things and crunching the numbers, she was at the same time praying to the Lord for guidance and for the strength to make these heavy decisions and carry them out. "I don't know what it is with me and God," she has said. "I'm just totally aware of Him. I talk to Him just

117

like I talk to you. If something's going wrong I'll talk to Him about it. In my heart He's a true friend.

"The joy of living is just doing what you really want to do," she has said many times, and by now Dolly was pretty sure of what she really wanted to do. She wanted to move in a new direction, free her creative drives to take her wherever they went, without the restrictions of strict labeling such as "country music." She wanted to be more than a country artist; she wanted to be an artist, period.

Other country stars before Dolly Parton had attempted to cross over into the pop-rock market, with limited success, like Johnny Cash. Other country stars after Dolly Parton would attempt to cross over, also with limited success, like Crystal Gayle or Tanya Tucker, Ronnie Milsap, Tammy Wynette and George Jones, Loretta Lynn and Conway Twitty.

But some had it all—Linda Ronstadt, Willie Nelson, Mac Davis, Waylon Jennings, Kenny Rogers, Kris Kristofferson—these are a few names that come to mind, singers whose records sell to pop-rock fans as well as to country fans. And there was Bob Dylan, who had crossed in the other direction, and whose sound by now was real country.

The gulf between success and failure, it seemed to Dolly, could be bridged only by effective management. Certainly, the artists who hadn't made it were as talented as those who had; it was sound professional guidance that had made the major difference. Dolly Parton needed jet fuel to rocket her to the top instead of the super-unleaded she had now. And that meant moving the base of her operations from Nashville, Tennessee, to Los Angeles, California, a move that Dolly knew would be looked on by country music fans as "The Great Betrayal." She began to shop around for new management, new representation, and new musicians.

Before Dolly made any announcement of her future change in direction, rumblings were heard as far west as Beverly Hills and as far north as New York City. It is hard to keep major career moves a secret. John Rockwell, pop music columnist and critic of The New York Times, was an ardent Dolly fan who had told his big-city readership about Dolly Parton before. Rockwell had interviewed Dolly back in August 1975, when she came with the Travelin' Family Band to play the Waterloo Music Festival in New Jersey. At that time, Rockwell wrote that ". . . there doesn't seem to be much likelihood that she will or could change her image of her music to fit a broader audience's expectations. What is more likely is that the sheer quality of the music and the irresistible charm of the person will win her a wider audience on her own terms."

Although Rockwell couldn't foresee change then, others did, especially in Nashville, and it disturbed them. "People kept tellin' me that I was goin' pop," said Dolly, "but they just plain didn't understand. Everything just got blown right out of proportion. I could hardly believe it. I was changing things that weren't right in my organization, not myself. How could I change myself?

And what would I change into, anyway? A pumpkin at midnight? Naw, I'm so totally me it would scare you to death!"

Her extensive road tour, her television appearances, and the long studio sessions recording her hits had taken their toll, working their damage on Dolly's delicate vocal cords. The node problem that dogged her so painfully was the same one experienced by other singers—Elton John, Neil Young, Fleetwood Mac's Stevie Nicks, to name only a few. Once more, Dolly Parton had to cancel concert bookings, and early in November 1976 RCA records announced to the press that Dolly Parton's doctor had ordered "a long vocal rest, at least through the end of the year." Dolly was forced to cancel at least 25 concerts, and once again to limit her talking.

Alarmed, *Times* columnist John Rockwell telephoned Dolly for an interview. The combination of her illness and the rumors about the impending crossover led to the interview, which Dolly managed to give him over the phone despite the swollen nodes on her vocal cords.

"Dolly Parton is at the brink of a radical shift of direction, one that should, if there is any justice in the pop-music heaven, make her one of the great stars of American entertainment," Rockwell wrote prophetically. ". . . Although she doesn't like to dwell on the subject, it's clear that Miss Parton believes that emotional strain may be partly the cause of her throat problems. 'Any time you make a change,' she worries, 'you gotta pay the price.'

" 'I'm grateful to Porter, I'm very proud of all the

things we've done before. But I'm just so proud of the new things. A lot of country people feel I'm leaving the country, that I'm not proud of Nashville, which is the biggest lie there is. I don't want to leave the country, but to take the country with me wherever I go. The truth is, I am country. I am Dolly Parton from the mountains, that's what I'll remain. If people outside want my music, then I'll do my best. If you ask me if I'm pop, I can only be Dolly Parton, and that's country.'

"Miss Parton peppers her conversation now," concluded Rockwell, "with phrases like 'a totally free feeling,' 'there are really no limits now,' and 'after the first of the year, when my new life begins.' "

The storm of protest that greeted her new career decisions was even louder and angrier than she had expected, louder and angrier than that raised at the breakup of Porter and Dolly. Going solo was something her fans could understand, even if it pained them, but going Hollywood? Leaving country music for slick pop with its lush arrangements or even, God forbid, rock 'n' roll or brassy disco? The country music press assailed her, and letters poured in from anguished fans everywhere, begging, pleading, cursing, and threatening.

"I'm still the same Dolly Parton," she reassured her fans. "I'm not leaving country; I'm taking it with me." She also said, "Country music is like a family that should be held together. If somebody is country-oriented and can still appeal to a rock audience, like a Waylon Jennings or a Kris Kristofferson, this is great. But it's important that the audiences know where your roots are. You can be country and pop at the same time if people know where you're really coming from."

And she proceeded with her plans, disregarding all the advice to the contrary, well meaning and not. She wanted a full, new "now" sound, one that would combine with the story-songs she wrote to bring them within the range of a much larger audience.

Chapter Seven

Dolly Goes Hollywood

Attention ain't affectin' me none.
My life is exactly the same as when
I was settin' out.

—Dolly Parton

The Los Angeles management firm of Katz Gallin Cleary was the one Dolly Parton selected to help launch her on her new career. Not only did they handle Mac Davis, but, along with other entertainers such as Anthony Newley, Florence Henderson, Paul Lynde, and Joan Rivers, Katz Gallin Cleary managed such vocal artists as Olivia Newton-John, Cher, the then very popular Tony Orlando and Dawn, Donny and Marie Osmond, Gregg Allman, Thelma Houston, and the Amaz-

ing Rhythm Aces. It was no less a coup for Katz
Gallin Cleary than for Dolly herself when they
signed the management contracts.

As she signed them, Dolly made other major
changes. She switched her booking agency from
Top Billing to Monterey Peninsula Artists, a California firm that booked such top-grossing acts as
Carole King, The Eagles, Chicago, and Cheech
and Chong. At the same time, she took on International Creative Management, the monolithic ICM.

Much more important, she went to RCA and
told them she was going to produce her next
album, *First Harvest, New Gathering*, herself. That
left Porter Wagoner, who was still producing her
albums, out of a job and icily furious. He had
only just finished producing her latest-released
album, *Bubbling Over*, and was still working on
Bargain Store, and *All I Can Do*. Not only that,
but Dolly also announced that in the future she
would be finishing the recording of *New Harvest,
First Gathering* in Los Angeles, not Nashville.

At this time, Dolly formally and completely
broke away from all her former business ventures
with Porter Wagoner. Her album, *All I Can Do*,
released in 1976, was the last album he would
produce for her. It contained some beautiful songs,
among them "When the Sun Goes Down Tomorrow," "Shattered Image," "I'm a Drifter," and a
plaintive ballad, "Falling Out of Love with Me,"
in which Dolly wrote that she had "left while
love was still alive," because she didn't want to
stay "and watch it die." Did she mean Porter
Wagoner? From that point on, Dolly would be her
own producer; at most she would co-produce.

"My work is very important to me. I take such pride in it. It's self-expression to me, really my way of being what I am. Lately I've found such happiness and new inspiration in being able to have the freedom to do what is so totally me. I'm writing more and better than ever," she declared. "It's still the same Dolly Parton, but I feel I'm ready to fly. I'm really a pretty brave little number."

The next decision Dolly Parton made when she came out of "seclusion" was that the Travelin' Family Band had to go. They simply were too cornball, too full of what Nick Tosches had called "yokelisms," too hillbilly for the new image that she and Katz Gallin Cleary were about to spring on the world. As musicians, they were barely adequate, nothing more. They had received bad or so-so reviews, had been called "merely competent," and had played to unfilled auditoriums.

Naturally, the press had a field day with this one.

"They made it sound like I had fired my family," complained Dolly, hurt, to *Playboy*'s Lawrence Grobel. "I didn't fire my family, and it hurts me for anybody to say so. I was goin' through a very rough time—poor lighting, poor sound, poor management, poor everything. I just decided I was goin' to quit for a few days, just stop everythin' and do some thinkin'. Because I won't let somethin' run me to a psychiatrist or to a doctor; I can take care of my own things; me and the Lord can talk it over."

To others, Dolly protested, "I had brothers and sisters and cousins in my band. How could I fire them?" Nevertheless, that was the end of the Travelin' Family Band, and the beginning of Gypsy

Fever, a much more professional backup—"more versatile and qualified" musicians, not necessarily from Nashville—with a big pop-rock-country sound. However much she protested she hadn't, Dolly actually *had* fired her family.

"I decided to change so I could expand my music," Dolly told interviewer Stanley Mieses in *Melody Maker*. "I just know I have a lot more music in me than I've ever known, and I just wanted to be able to say, 'Leave me alone to become whatever I want to become.' You hafta understand that it wasn't the fans who were telling me to change. I found myself ruining my voice, playing in places that didn't have good microphones, places that had no class at all, killing myself, knocking myself out night after night. And there wasn't all that much money in it, neither. You can't make a lot of money in country music unless you're a real superstar, and I knew I could make more than I was makin', a lot more."

As Dolly lined up at the starting gate, ready to make the move she would call "the smartest thing I ever done in my life," Katz Gallin Cleary set up a publicity barrage the likes of which Dolly had never seen before. They snagged for her the cover of *Rolling Stone* and the cover of *Playboy*, on which she appeared coyly dressed in a Playboy Bunny suit, revealing that awesome cleavage.

Dolly Rebecca Parton made the cover of *People* for the first, but not the last, time. Katz Gallin Cleary booked her on all the major national talk shows, those of Dinah Shore, Merv Griffin, Mike Douglas, "Hee Haw," "The Today Show," and the rest. You name the show; Dolly was cracking

126

her good-ole-girl jokes on it. Most important, Dolly made her debut on The Johnny Carson program, the "Tonight Show," the present-day equivalent of playing the Palace.

At first, there was some concern in the halls of Katz Gallin Cleary about Dolly Parton's larger-and-sparklier-than-real-life presentation, her gaudy rhinestoned clothes, tight bodices bursting with cleavage, diamonds winking from every finger, those huge preposterous wigs. Should her physical image be softened for the middle of the road? There was anxiety about how she would appear to a non-country audience. How would she go over with the savvy late-night viewer of "The Tonight Show"?

The less sophisticated country people were comfortable with spangles and glitter; they were accustomed to it; they even expected it. Many cowboy singers were flamboyant, like Porter Wagoner, who wore rhinestones and custom-made suits from Nudie of Hollywood. Female country singers were flamboyant, too, often dressing as cowgirls with heavily fringed jackets and skirts and tall, "jewel"-encrusted boots. It was an accepted look. But how would Johnny Carson and his public react? Would Dolly Parton become a national laughingstock on "The Tonight Show"?

Stubbornly, Dolly Parton was not yet ready to tone down her look for city sophisticates. She adored all her baubles, bangles, and beads, and was in no hurry to give them up. Besides, she reasoned, "First, you have to get their attention." Dolly's was an attention-getting show-biz way of dressing. Why shouldn't city folk dig it as much as country folk? She wasn't afraid of going on the

Carson show gaudily decked out in all her jeweled Christmas tree finery, because, as she said, "I work best one to one. I was a fan of Johnny Carson's and I wanted people to notice me. I didn't care if it was for the right reasons or the wrong reasons at first. I felt I had a gift as a writer. I may not be a great singer, but my voice is different. I'm secure in those areas."

Katz Gallin Cleary needn't have worried. Dolly's instincts turned out to be right as country rain; Dolly Parton's overblown way of dressing became her most recognizable trademark in the crossover, and the city slickers loved it. Just as Johnny Cash was always identifiable as The Man in Black, Dolly Parton was identified as the blonde in the wigs and the rhinestones, the gal with the huge boobs.

Dolly Parton's first appearance with Johnny Carson on "The Tonight Show" was a memorable one. It took place on January 19, 1977, Dolly's thirty-first birthday. She sang "Higher and Higher" and "Me and Little Andy," her little-girl-voice song in which an abandoned child and a puppy die and head for Heaven together, which brought tears to everybody's eyes. She told stories about her childhood, laced with her earthy humor. She made jokes about her clothing, the poverty of her Tennessee childhood, her "invisible" husband, the size of her chest, although as usual she declined to give out her measurements, inviting the public to guess.

The Parton quick wit and down-home frankness, her outlandish clothing and wonderful singing, so captured Johnny and his audience that

128

Dolly became a frequent, favorite guest. In fact, she turned up visiting on so many talk shows that one couldn't switch on the set without encountering those dimples, that Tennessee twang, and those oh-so-recognizable breasts.

A late-night sitcom, very popular with sophisticates, was Norman Lear's "Mary Hartman, Mary Hartman," starring Louise Lasser in pigtails. One of the leads, Mary Kay Place, played Mary's next-door neighbor Loretta Haggars, a country music singer and songwriter whose ambition was to be as famous as Dolly Parton, so that she could go to Nashville and buy outlandish clothing "just like Dolly's." Loretta was a thinly disguised spoof of Dolly herself, and Dolly loved it so much that when Mary Kay Place cut an actual album, *Tonite! At the Capri Lounge: Loretta Haggars*, Dolly Parton sang backup.

RCA had a new album of Dolly's, and they wanted national exposure of the new Dolly. The record company decreed: It was time to go out on the road with her new rocking sound and her rocking band of "glitter gypsies," as she called them, Gypsy Fever, a name she made up herself. "They make me proud of them and proud of myself," said Dolly of her new musicians.

But first, Dolly took a two-week hiatus from work to rest those chronically troubled vocal cords, whose nodes had once more swelled. Her doctor was now the eminent Beverly Hills throat specialist Dr. Edward Kantor, who had operated on Neil Young's nodes. Dr. Kantor ordered total rest of the troubled cords. No singing, no talking for

14 days. Then she would be ready to roll out in her custom-built $180,000 tour bus.

The bus, in which she traveled with "her family," as she called the band, is Dolly's home away from home. It sleeps 11, with a separate little bedroom for Dolly, and comes fully equipped with color TV, a full recording studio with reel-to-reel tape deck and cassette stereo, small kitchen with refrigerator, not one but two bathrooms, a CB radio, and some sizable closets to hold all her shiny costumes and wigs. When, in 1987, Oprah Winfrey asked Dolly Parton how many wigs she owned, Dolly laughed and said, "Lemme see, there are three hundred sixty-five days in a year, and I have a different wig for every day. . . ." But she usually brings no more than 30 or 40 with her for a month-long tour.

In January 1977, Dolly Parton and her backup band of eight men, Gypsy Fever, began a tour of one-night stands in small cities—Battle Creek, Peoria—as a kind of shakedown cruise to get them ready for the big time. Then, aiming at the stars, they went for the big cities—San Francisco, where they played the Boarding House and scored a monster hit with transvestites; the Roxy on Sunset in Los Angeles; the Anaheim Convention Center, where they shared the bill with Mac Davis and opened the show for him, warming up the audience with a 50-minute set by a performer "fresh from a Grammy nomination as Best Country Vocalist," as *Billboard* called Dolly.

Everywhere Dolly Parton and Gypsy Fever played, it was standing room only, with scalpers' prices for the hotly desired tickets. *Time* magazine reporter Jean Vallely, covering one of the gigs, wrote, "A Dolly Parton concert is a treat, like a hot-fudge sundae after a month of dieting."

Having reached for the stars, Dolly Parton next turned her attention to the moon. "If you can make it there, you'll make it anywhere" is sung only of New York City. The climax of the Gypsy Fever tour was New York's most famous music club, The Bottom Line in Greenwich Village. A small room, but highly selective in its choice of music acts, it is what's called in the business "a showcase." From a successful run at The Bottom Line, many performers have gone on to fill Madison Square Garden.

Dolly was booked into the club for a heavily publicized three-night gig beginning May 13, 1977. Apart from her opening number, Jackie Wilson's famous rhythm-and-blues classic, "Higher and Higher," she performed only her own music, accompanying herself at various times on her guitar, her banjo, and that sweet, sad instrument of Elizabethan ballads, the dulcimer.

Rolling Stone's Chet Flippo was among the reporters covering her opening, and he was obviously smitten, pointing out that "Anyone who writes the way she does and sounds like Linda Ronstadt and Emmylou Harris double-tracking themselves and who looks like a triple-dip Baskin-Robbins can probably do no wrong." (Parenthetically, this was hardly the first time that the Parton looks were compared with ice cream. All that pink-and-white-and-golden lusciousness has most often been called "vanilla ice cream." But Dolly herself says, "I don't want to be vanilla. I want to be Rocky Road.")

"The moment she sashayed onstage in a cloud of pink chiffon," rhapsodized Flippo, flipping, "and lit into 'Higher and Higher,' New York City was in the palm of her hand: King Kong with blond hair/wig striding unchecked through lower Manhattan. . . . About the time she started doing only her own material, Parton could have just waved a magic wand right then and there and been done with it, so utterly charmed was her [supposedly] tough New York audience. Hard-bitten Gotham critics were leaping to their feet cheering, and later, at her party atop Kong's World Trade Center, all of them told similar stories to the effect of 'I knew her when.' "

That was quite a party on the night of Dolly Parton's opening, her first engagement in New York City since the disastrous joint concert at the Felt Forum. RCA Records footed the bill for the extravagant party, held at Windows on the World, the class-A restaurant on the 107th floor of the World Trade Center, where, in 1977, every publicity party worth its salty canapés was held.

Dolly played a midnight concert at The Bottom Line. Then the "A" list of invitees was limoed downtown to Windows for a champagne breakfast around 2 A.M. Her performances were packed with celebrities the likes of Mick Jagger, Phoebe Snow, Berry Berenson, Olivia Newton-John, Robert Duvall, who would play a country music singer years later in *Tender Mercies*, Candice Bergen, song stylist Barbara Cook, "Saturday Night Live" star John Belushi, rocker Patti Smith, Bruce

Springsteen at the beginning of his own meteoric rise, and Andy Warhol, who, it was said, would go to the opening of an envelope. They showed up on opening night to cheer the country girl who was crossing over. They were among those who were ready, in Chet Flippo's words, "to crawl right up into her sequined lap and live there happily ever after." Dolly Parton had arrived, and was taking the town by storm with her music.

Her old friend and fan from *The New York Times*, John Rockwell, was also at The Bottom Line on opening night. "It was a triumph," he wrote. "The packed crowd cheered on Miss Parton supportively from the moment she swept onto the stage, and rewarded her with an idolatrous ovation at the end. ... The band was far better than her old family ensemble had sounded ... her repertory of self-parodying, sexist jokes was much tamed, very much to the good ... and her singing sounded finer than ever [she had had a shot of cortisone for her throat troubles]. Miss Parton is blessed with a remarkably individual soprano, nasal and bluegrassy at full volume, and innocently girlish at softer dynamic levels. Her sense of phrasing and pitch are impeccable. Above all, there is her radiant charm, which emerges all the more unencumbered now that she's jettisoned some of her more corny country routines."

Dolly's personal manager at Katz Gallin Cleary was Sandy Gallin. Sandy had wanted Dolly to work with a record producer when she cut her next album, *New Harvest, First Gathering,* but Dolly was determined to produce the album herself. After much discussion, the two arrived at a compromise.

"When Dolly came to me she wanted very badly to write and produce her own material," says Gallin. "She had always been under the auspices of Porter Wagoner, and I felt it was only fair she be given a chance to produce her own album. But we made an agreement that if *New Harvest, First Gathering* wasn't a sales success, or if it didn't produce a hit single, that I could pick an outside producer to do the next album."

Released in the summer of 1977, *New Harvest, First Gathering* was a qualified success when it was released. Dolly was backed up on the album by her new road band, Gypsy Fever. All but two of the songs on the album—"My Love," a reworking of the old Temptations hit "My Girl," and "Higher and Higher"—were written by Dolly, and they included "Getting in My Way" and "Light of a Clear Blue Morning," the only song on the album released as a single, and the song that *Time* magazine called a "declaration of artistic independence."

There was some rock beat and even some disco beat to be heard, but the portrait of Dolly on the album cover, wearing a faded old Levi's jacket and a workman's cap on the back of her wig, went to prove that, be it rock, pop, disco, or country, it was still the same good ole down-home Dolly Parton. Still, it was overproduced and overarranged, neither one thing nor the other.

As stated earlier, the success of the album was qualified. The single went only to number 11 on the country charts, not even into the Top Ten, and reached a dismal number 87 on the pop charts, in the Top One Hundred, but only barely.

The album itself fared somewhat better, number 1 on the country charts, and on the pop charts rising as high as number 38, the highest any album of hers had ever gone on the non-country charts. But it wasn't high enough to suit either Sandy Gallin or Dolly Parton, and she bowed to their previous agreement: Sandy would select a co-producer with professional know-how to guide Dolly's choices, her arrangements, and her work in the studio.

The new record production company was to be Charles Koppelman's The Entertainment Company, and the producer selected by Gallin was Gary Klein, a man of proven creative direction. Klein had been Mac Davis's producer on *Stop and Smell the Roses*, and he had also produced Glen Campbell's *Southern Nights*, which went to number one on the charts, and Barbra Streisand's hit album *Superman*. Dolly Parton's first single with Klein was to become her first mainstream hit.

"Here You Come Again," the upbeat song that was to become a Dolly Parton all-time classic, a song that came to be one of the four or five identified with her, was, oddly enough, not written by Dolly Parton, but by the team of Barry Mann and Cynthia Weil. Also, oddly enough, it wasn't even written *for* her, but had been recorded previously by several other artists, including B. J. Thomas. Released as a single on October 6, 1977, as the title cut for the *Here You Come Again* album, her eleventh solo LP, it went climbing up the pop charts at the same time it went to number one on the country charts.

At first, Dolly didn't want to record the song;

she objected to it as simply too slick and pop. Afraid it would offend her country audience as the wrong material, terrified that her fans would think she was selling out, she told Gallin, "I'm not going to trust you again if the country people don't like this."

But Gary Klein had faith in the song; he felt in his bones, even before the song was mixed, that it would be the breakout crossover single for Dolly Parton. Still, he listened to Dolly's creative suggestions; for example, when she requested that he add a pedal steel guitar, the quintessential country music instrument, to the arrangement, he did so.

"Here You Come Again," the first song Dolly did after she made her changes, was not exactly what she had in mind; she knew it would be a hit, but she wasn't sure it would be a good thing for her to be identified with, because it had such a smooth pop sound. "That's such a good song a monkey could have made it a hit. Well, you're looking at a million-dollar monkey," she laughingly said about it later.

Klein also took Dolly Parton one major step further into the mainstream, cutting the number of original Dolly songs on the *Here You Come Again* album to four, instead of the eight that she had written on *New Harvest, First Gathering*, which included "Applejack," the song she had backed up with so many of her "Grand Ole Opry" pals. The four included "Me and Little Andy," a song she sang in a child's voice, about the death of a child and a pet dog, that is a real tearjerker, and which Dolly still sings in concert; "Cowgirl and the Dandy"; "As Soon as I Touched Him"; and her famous "Two Doors Down."

As soon as the single was released, it was promoted heavily to pop stations. By that time, the publicity blitz set up by Katz Gallin Cleary, the guest appearances on Johnny Carson and other major television shows, the live appearances in clubs that didn't pull in country audiences, had made the pop stations and deejays very aware of the new Miss Dolly Parton, and they gave the cut heavy airplay. Dolly was on her way to the top of the pop charts, just as she had planned to be.

Even the album cover for *Here You Come Again* was designed as a cross between country and pop. Photographed by the eminent album cover camera artist Ed Caraeff in a far more glossy and glamorous way than any of her previous albums, the cover showed not one but *three* laughing, strutting Dollys against a neon background. So much for pop. But the Dollys were dressed country-Dolly style, in skintight jeans rolled up at the cuffs, and a bright red polka-dot blouse tied at the waist. Unmistakably Tennessee. At the same time, Caraeff devised the exuberant signature scrawl of her name, "Dolly," that would be used as a logo on the covers of her other albums.

The combination of Dolly Parton and Gary Klein was a winner; for the first time she had a record producer who was listening to her. For the first time it was a collaborative effort, not Porter Wagoner's "my way," and Dolly's creative instincts and musical input were heard, appreciated, and followed. Under the aegis of Gallin, Koppelman, and Klein, Dolly Parton had a potentially plati-

num album in *Here You Come Again*, and it did
go platinum in early 1980. But in late 1977, it
went soaring up the charts, one of the Top Ten in
both the pop and the country lists, and was still
on the lists through 1978 and into 1979. Her next
album with Klein, *Heartbreaker*, went gold. Not
only that, but an album she had released back in
1975, *The Best of Dolly Parton*, also went gold,
selling more than 500,000 copies, proving that
her acceptance as an entertainer, not just a *country*
entertainer, was confirmed.

To back up the album, Dolly Parton and Gypsy
Fever went on the road again, kicking off their
fall tour with a concert in Memphis, and following it the next day with a benefit performance for
the Sevier County High School, Dolly's fifth such
benefit in seven years. Proceeds from the sold-out
concert, which was held in her old high school
gymnasium, were donated for uniforms, equipment, and instruments for the high school marching band, Dolly's only happy memory from her
own Sevier High years. Sevierville, no longer
satisfied with holding a Dolly Parton Day, now
proclaimed it Dolly Parton Week.

In October, the Country Music Association held
its annual awards presentation, with gala television coverage. Dolly was very much present, although she garnered no awards, probably because
there were still bitter feelings that Dolly Parton
had deserted country, her protests to the contrary
notwithstanding. But a high point of the televised
proceedings was the hilarious dialogue between
Dolly and Minnie Pearl, proving that not only

could Dolly be funny, but that she could still be as down-home as the best of them. There they were, as different-looking as two women can be, Dolly all glamorous in her glitter, with a large jeweled flower in her wig, and Minnie in her trademark "store-bought" hat and calico dress, but sharing the same roots and the same country wisdom and folksy humor.

In December, Dolly arrived in Sacramento, California's state capital, for Dolly Parton Day. She was named Honorary First Lady of Sacramento, and was presented with the keys to the city, the twelfth time within three months that Dolly had been handed keys to a city. Her key ring must have weighed 1,000 pounds; on it were keys to the two Kansas Cities, both in Kansas and Missouri, Wichita Falls, Texas, and St. Louis, among other burgs that had likewise honored her. After a sold-out concert in the Sacramento Memorial Auditorium, Dolly flew back to Los Angeles to appear as Johnny Carson's guest on "The Tonight Show" for the third time that year. In December 1977, she was accorded an outstanding sign of recognition, being chosen as a guest on a Barbara Walters TV special. There, with a sizable block of time at her disposal, she was able to deliver a serious version of her life story along with her many famous wisecracks. There, for the first time, a large audience got to know the real Dolly Parton, the heart underneath the rhinestones and the brain underneath the wigs.

Although she didn't win any awards from the Country Music Association that year, which was most probably due to resentment about the break with Nashville, the move to Los Angeles, and the crossover, Dolly Parton finished 1977 in a state of triumph. Her financial situation had improved dramatically, from the $60,000 a year she had been making with Porter Wagoner, to the $2,500 to $3,000 a night she had been earning with the Travelin' Family Band, to $30,000 for a single engagement. She was now a successful entrepreneur, owning several companies—3 music publishing companies, lots of property, a 23-room mansion in Nashville, other homes, tax shelters by the dozens; she was even about to launch her own film-production company. But she had made much larger strides forward than money alone could measure.

Dolly Parton's crossover had been, on the whole, an immense success—how big, even she couldn't begin to suspect yet. She had held on to her faithful country fans and added millions of new ones. She had proved that she could communicate her thoughts and emotions, as expressed in her songs, to a much wider audience. As a performer, Dolly had evolved naturally, successfully crossing the line, and making "the line," in her case, an imaginary boundary. Now her records were high on both charts. Yet there was more—much more—to come. The fruits of the changes Dolly Parton had made were still to be reaped.

Chapter Eight

Having It All

I want myself to be happy. I like myself. I'm all I've got. So why can't I have the best for myself?

—Dolly Parton

The impact Dolly Parton made on the field of popular music was felt strongly in 1978, the year Dolly captured three BMI country awards, proof positive that she hadn't lost her country fans while crossing over into mainstream music. Dolly also received important recognition from her peers, the very prestigious Hitmakers Award from the Songwriters Hall of Fame.

Nineteen seventy-eight was also the year when

AGVA, the American Guild of Variety Artists, named Dolly Parton Best Female Country Performer of the Year, an honor repeated in 1979.

Nineteen seventy-eight was the year when Dolly Parton won the top honor in the music business, her first Grammy Award, for Best Female Country Vocalist performance on a single, thanks to "Here You Come Again."

But, more important than any of these, 1978 was the year when Dolly was handed what she had always prayed for; in October, at its twelfth annual presentation telecast from Nashville, Dolly Parton was voted not merely Best *Female* Entertainer, but Entertainer of the Year by the Country Music Association, the single highest award that the CMA can bestow. Dolly's cup was overflowing with self-righteous happiness; she could ask for no better confirmation that her hotly disputed career moves had been wise decisions.

It wasn't in Dolly *not* to be outrageous, even when accepting honors. She had been gaining weight steadily ("Everybody loves a fat girl," she joked), but she was still stuffing herself into skintight gowns like sausage into a casing. Only minutes before the announcement that Dolly Parton had won Entertainer of the Year, the front of her overfilled custom-made dress split right down the middle, proving that "they" *were* real and "they" *were* all hers, the two questions most frequently asked by interviewers and the public alike.

"Oh, well," said an embarrassed Dolly, grinning. "My daddy always said you shouldn't try to stuff fifty pounds o' mud into a five-pound sack." Only Daddy didn't say mud.

"It sure feels great to win when you know you've done your best," said a smiling Dolly, tightly clutching the long-awaited CMA Best Entertainer award. "It's nice to be a winning horse. If I win, I'm always glad. If I lose, well, I just try to work harder the next year."

In 1976, Dolly Parton turned thirty, a traumatic year for any woman. Instead of checking her mirror for crow's feet, Dolly did a reality check on who she was, where she was heading, and, most important, what she wanted out of her life and her career. As usual, she made up one of her "lists." While the nay-sayers protested her change of direction, Dolly had relied as usual upon her own inner strength, and had carefully selected a new "cabinet," a new set of high-powered advisors whose performance in business was well matched to her own.

It had taken her most of two years, 1976 and 1977, to set her career into motion and pick up momentum. But by the end of 1977 a whole new world had opened up to her, a world where Dolly's own assessment of her potential was realized in practical terms—money and fame. Now it was time to maximize that potential to its fullest.

Nineteen seventy-eight and 1979 were big years in Dolly's hot new career, years in which she consolidated her gains and took bold forward steps under the guidance of her new management. *Here You Come Again* was still high on all the charts; her earlier *Best of Dolly Parton* album went gold. By late summer she had two hit singles, "Heartbreaker" and "Baby I'm Burnin' " backed with "I Really Got the Feeling," followed by the *Heart-*

breaker album, which began climbing the charts. Less country than middle of the road, *Heartbreaker* featured a new, lush Dolly Parton with new, lush arrangements, plenty of horns and plenty of strings, arrangements the angry *Rolling Stone* reviewer Tom Carson said "sound like the Longines Symphonette on angel dust." Carson, furious at what he believed to be Parton's MOR sellout, called Dolly "a great American joke—a celeb windup doll."

Heartbreaker was followed by *Great Balls of Fire*, which contained the hit singles "Sweet Summer Lovin' " backed by "Great Balls of Fire" and "You're the Only One," neither song written by Dolly. Noel Coppage of *Stereo Review* sneered at the album, saying that it "seems openly to take aim at the Me Decade's sugar/junk fixation, and what it shoots are not great balls of fire, but little balls of bonbons," and sniping at Dolly herself as "a stalker of superstardom." Both albums had the mellow or brassy arrangements that assured them of popular if not critical success, and both did well at the cash registers—*Heartbreaker* went gold in early 1980. *Great Balls of Fire*, which also went gold, contained only four Dolly-written songs (she was composing less since the crossover) —"Sandy's Song," "Down," "Star of the Show," and "Do You Think That Time Stands Still?"

But if some critics turned away in disgust from the new Dolly Parton, she was crying all the way to the bank, and the tears she shed were solid gold. The public adored her. Now, thanks to the magazine covers she adorned and the TV shows she guested on, her mass-media exposure on the

Johnny Carson and Barbara Walters shows, Dolly Parton was instantly recognized, even by the non-musical public. Those wigs and those boobs—they were known everywhere. Drag queens and transvestite performers added Dolly to the catalog of drag acts; she became a great favorite, both live and in cross-dress takeoff, of female impersonators and homosexual enthusiasts. She was delighted by the fervor of her gay fans.

"I have a pretty large gay following, particularly in New York, San Francisco, and Los Angeles," she was quoted. "They're a great audience; they really know how to stir up an entertainer's energy. And I think they like me 'cause I look like fun. They get a kick out of me, especially the guys who dress up in drag. Let me tell ya, it's really somethin' to look out in the audience and see ten or twelve Dolly Partons starin' back at me."

Dolly wasn't one to sit around doing needlepoint. Spending more than a week in the Nashville dream house with Carl the dream husband made Dolly itchy and nervous. She needed to be out there performing. On tour to promote her new albums, she filled houses everywhere she went. Even Down Under in Australia, where she played two concerts in 1979, with the opening act an Australian group called Goldrush, business was SRO. Her personal manager, Sandy Gallin, accompanied Dolly on a "business tour" of Australia, which sent tongues a-waggin' all over again, but Dolly came home to Carl Dean.

In 1978 and 1979, she toured with Eddie Rabbitt

as her opener, even singing duets with him (shades of Porter Wagoner!), but it was as a single that Dolly Parton conquered New York again in the summer of 1978, when she packed the Palladium with wall-to-wall fans and celebrities for two days of concerts.

In New York Dolly did a typically Dolly thing—she gave a free concert, what she called "a people's concert." She even gave a "people's press conference," answering with great good nature the shouted questions, most of which inevitably had to do with those old chestnuts: Were those famous twin assets of hers real, and were they all hers?

"Ah guess they better be, honey," she called out. "Nobody else I know would wanna lay claim to 'em."

Outdoors, on the steps of City Hall, in the bright heat of an August noontime, dressed in a long ruffled chiffon gown with handkerchief hem, Dolly sang to a crowd of 5,000 downtown workers during their lunch hour, and she captured every heart, including Mayor Edward I. Koch's, who doted on show-biz showoff occasions like this one.

"New York," said Dolly after Mayor Koch had presented her with yet another key to yet another city (by then, her key ring must have attained the weight of a small pickup truck), "is the center of the world. I just want to personally thank the people here who have helped me on my way." Then, to wild cheering, she gave them the songs from her *Heartbreaker* album.

Dolly Parton's Palladium concert, played and sung before a crowd of 4,000, took her back to her country-music roots. She sang "Jolene," "Coat of Many Colors," "My Tennessee Mountain Home," "Applejack," "Me and Little Andy," "The Tennessee Waltz," and other down-home favorites. Then she crossed over into "Here You Come Again," "Heartbreaker," and "Two Doors Down." As Country Music magazine said, "That night at the Palladium, she could have been a flat-chested brunette in army fatigues and it would have made no difference."

Time magazine described Dolly as "looking like a purple Popsicle (dragging out that old ice-cream image one more time) in a gown designed to accentuate more curves than a good knuckle ball."

Dolly's major triumph after New York was playing the Universal Amphitheater in Los Angeles, an auditorium so large that "I never wanted to play there until I thought I could draw a big crowd." Even with the monster house entirely sold out, "It's fillin' me with tension, because I know there will be a lot of music and film people and a lot of writers and critics in the audience."

Dolly needn't have worried her pretty little platinum wig; the series of concerts—September 21–24, 1979—played brilliantly.

But Dolly couldn't stay on the road forever. Sooner or later, she had to come home to Carl.

Five years earlier, Dolly and Carl had built their dream house, from the ground up, an antebellum Southern mansion on a fenced-in hill about 5 miles outside Nashville, surrounded by 200 acres of lush farmland. In October 1973, in his interview in Country Music magazine, Dolly had told Jerry Bailey, "We're going to raise whiteface cattle when we get our own farm. We've just got about ten acres now, but we're waiting until we can get into our new house, which will be in early spring. It's out in the Brentwood area, in the farm section. Out there, there's about seventy acres, and we have another farm out near Franklin. That's where we have our cattle and pigs and everything.

"When we get our house, we're going to move the animals we want around us out there. We've got half our house done; it's a Southern plantation house. In fact, we're going to call it Willow Lake Plantation. We have a lake with a lot of willow trees planted around it.

"It's a real big house—one I always dreamed about. I don't have many rooms, but the rooms I have are real big and I have a real big living room and dining room and a long kitchen. In fact, I'm going to have two kitchens in one. One end will have the modern conveniences I really need, and the other will have an old wooden stove that really works. In the wintertime, sometimes, I'm going to use it."

The finished house was not much different from Dolly's rhapsodic description, although the "not many" rooms turned out to be 23, which translates into "many" in anybody's vocabulary. But they needed the room, because of Dolly's large family. Dolly and Carl took on the job of raising her five youngest brothers and sisters at Tara, which was what they called the six-pillared home with its deep verandas on the upper and lower stories, because it was modeled closely after Scarlett O'Hara's plantation in *Gone With the*

Wind. With no children of her own, Dolly expended her maternal energies on her kid brothers and sisters, as she would later on her many nieces and nephews.

She needed the room, too, for her "working clothes," 12 walk-in closets packed with rhinestoned and sequined outfits, a reported 3,000 of them, not to mention the many, many pairs of 5-inch-heeled shoes, and storage for a couple of hundred very expensive wigs. "You'd never believe," Dolly would quip to her Las Vegas audiences, "how danged expensive it is to look this cheap."

At one point, Dolly moved her parents, Avie Lee and Robert Lee, to a large house in Nashville to be near her, but they hated being in the city, so she bought them a farm with a large, comfortable house, near Sevierville, and they gratefully moved back home.

But Dolly doesn't let go of her kinfolk that readily. Most of her close relatives live close by Tara, and Dolly and Carl keep a mobile home at the big house to accommodate her mama and daddy when they visit. Dolly and Carl raise whiteface Hereford cattle, as well as a couple of bloodhounds and a pair of peacocks. Because, as Dolly says, her own taste runs so much to the gaudy, she called in professional decorators to embellish her home—in fact, all her homes. But there were many finishing touches in it that were Dolly's and Carl's own, such as the wooden facing for the living room fireplace, made of logs taken from the original Pigeon River cabin in which Dolly had been born. The logs were salvaged when the cabin was being torn down. The house is set well back from the road, and is fenced in for complete privacy, with tall gates in front of the long driveway.

However, in 1976 Dolly Parton had told Chris Chase of *The New York Times* that, while the house was beautiful, she didn't know "if I'm enjoyin' it or not. It just bothers my mind to feel that I have so much and that so many have so little," and, although, as Chase added, that Dolly couldn't "bring herself to put in a swimming pool ("That's one of them things like a five-hundred-dollar coat; I keep thinkin' there's something else I can do besides build a pool")," Dolly and Carl did in fact wind up with a swimming pool (and Dolly with at least a $500 coat). Not only a pool, but a hot tub, and all this in addition to the creek that runs through the property and the small picturesque private lake surrounded by willow trees that gives the estate its name of Willow Lake Plantation. As for Dolly Parton having "so much," she wanted more. And she got it.

Mr. and Mrs. Carl Dean enjoy the good life on the farm, whenever Dolly isn't in Los Angeles or New York or on the road or in the studio. They have so many visitors that "the house is like a hotel," jokes Dolly. "We got a register book and we even put up some credit card stickers on the door." But the visitors are all private—family and friends, people with whom Carl Dean feels comfortable. No business associates are allowed at Tara; Dolly keeps a place in Los Angeles for that, another in New York, and a third in Nashville.

In 1979, Dolly Parton added several new dimensions to her professional life. She opened an office in New York City, which is actually a modern art-filled, decorator-adorned apartment on the twenty-sixth floor, high above Fifth Avenue, which she shares, a few days a month, with her personal manager, Sandy Gallin. Naturally, there was gossip about the two, the same kind of gossip that surrounded Dolly and Porter Wagoner, and, just as naturally, Dolly denied it. The apartment was strictly for business, she said. Parton and Gallin were forming a new music company of their own, together with RCA Records and Gallin's partner Raymond Katz of Katz Gallin Cleary.

The name of the new company was White Diamond Records, to be distributed by RCA, and based in the Katz Gallin Cleary offices in Beverly Hills. They aimed to have a new Dolly Parton album out by the time Dolly made her first Las Vegas appearance at the Riviera Hotel.

The apartment was decorated and furnished in cool whites and neutrals by designer Barbara Rosen, and adorned with costly artworks that Gallin collects, such as two Claes Oldenburg paintings and one by Robert Rauschenberg. Dolly ignores them, although she collects paintings herself; hers are by Ben Hampton, whose Tennessee scenes remind her of Norman Rockwell. Dolly Parton may not know much about art, but she knows what she likes.

"When I see a picture I like, I buy it, whether it costs a lot or a little," she told Georgia Dullea of *The New York Times.* "But I have to be honest and tell you some of the pictures in this apartment cost a lot and I can't help thinkin', 'Good

Lord, I coulda done that in first grade. Guess that just goes to show you I ain't got no taste.' "

In October 1979, country music came to the White House. The President, Jimmy Carter, was a good ole boy from Georgia, and he proclaimed October as Country Music Month, perhaps because of a televised country music concert to be played October 2 in Washington, D.C. Carter, who went to the concert, invited country favorites Johnny Cash, June Carter, The Oak Ridge Boys, Ronnie Milsap, Bill Monroe, Tom T. Hall, the Bluegrass Boys, Glen Campbell, Dottie West, and others to lunch at the White House. President Jimmy went down the reception line shaking hands with everybody until he came to Dolly Parton.

"You're the one I've been waiting for," he said, grinning that famous toothy grin and grabbing her for a hug.

"Get a good one now." Dolly grinned back. Presidents or big-rig drivers, it was all the same to her. Dolly Parton loved them all, and they loved her back.

Also, toward the end of 1979, after holding out for years while her price increased astronomically, Dolly Parton signed a multimillion-dollar agreement to play Las Vegas, another long-held ambition of hers, no matter how often she'd denied it publicly.

"I got to the point where I could have a big deal in Vegas, but I didn't want to work Vegas until I could go there as myself with good music, until I could have the power to draw people, and also have enough power to say what kinda show I would do."

Vegas was where the big money was to be found, not to mention the boost such an engagement would give her record sales. The contract called for Dolly to play the Riviera Hotel, six weeks a year, from 1980 through 1982, and the sums involved made Dolly one of the richest female entertainers in the world. The amounts most commonly mentioned varied between $6,000,000 and $9,000,000, the highest price ever paid to a Vegas entertainer, which for an 18-week contract breaks down to $350,000 to $500,000 a week! All this for a girl who had started her singing career at $20 a week! What a way to bring a decade of change to an end!

The "holdback" Dolly Parton felt within her was gone now. "I really don't know anythin' but what comes out of my own heart. I'm happier now than ever before, bein' more my own person, goin' in new directions."

Dolly Parton had everything an Entertainer of the Year could possibly want—money, tax shelters, honors and awards, fans, a platinum album, royalties from records and songs, all of them tangible proof that she'd made the right moves and the correct career decisions; a high visibility quotient—she was so recognizable, so much larger than life. Drag shows throughout the country had added Dolly Parton segments to their lip-synch performances, and straight as well as gay Dolly Parton Lookalike contests were held somewhere in America in any week one would care to name. When shown photographs of the contestants, Dolly usually selected the male entries as better-looking and more "real" than the females!

Dolly Parton now had fame and fortune.

She owned property, houses, apartments, and stores. She was occasionally living in her dream house, the one she had always wanted, designed and built entirely to her own specifications. She had an apartment in Los Angeles, one on Fifth Avenue in New York, offices, corporations, copyrights, cars, youth, beauty, health. She had the satisfaction of knowing she was taking good care of her mama and daddy, and her sisters and brothers. She had a husband she loved and who loved her, who didn't keep her chained, but gave her instead as much freedom as she needed to fly like an eagle.

Dolly Parton had a $9,000,000 Las Vegas contract for only 18 weeks of work a year.

Dolly Parton had a platinum record and a den whose walls were filled with plaques, awards, scrolls, keys to the cities of America, silver and gold cups, and pictures of herself with the President of the United States and with Queen Elizabeth and Prince Philip.

Dolly Parton had everything—except . . .

Dolly Parton wanted to make a movie. She wanted to conquer Hollywood in the same way she had conquered Nashville and later New York and the rest of the country. Without a hit film, one really couldn't call oneself a superstar. Look at Barbra Streisand. A great voice, but it wasn't until she had a few box-office smashes behind her—most notably *Funny Girl, The Way We Were,* and *A Star is Born*—that she was admitted into the permanent pantheon of the greats. A hit picture—that's what Miss Dolly was hankering for, and it didn't even have to be a musical.

In 1978, this most recent of Dolly's dreams began to come true. Twentieth Century-Fox signed her to a 3-picture contract. Was Dolly Parton going to be the new Mae West? The new Marilyn Monroe? She had already been approached with tentative plans for vehicles about both legendary sex goddesses, and had turned both projects down flat.

"I'll just be unique," she protested. "I don't like to be compared to anyone, not Marilyn Monroe, not Mae West, either. I'm just gonna be myself, movies or no movies. I'm gonna play Dolly Parton, or at least a Dolly Parton-type character." She also denied she was planning to take acting lessons before breaking into pictures.

But what was the first picture to be? How would Dolly be handled in her film debut? Would she become a movie star overnight, or fall flat on her plump round keister? Dolly Parton was no ordinary property, and this could be no ordinary film. Dolly was thinking hard, and so were her managers, Katz Gallin Cleary. The important thing was not to push her in the water before she could swim, not to launch Dolly Parton into films before she was ready, and then see to it that it was a strong script, the proper vehicle, and a good showcase for her talents. This is not as easy to do as it sounds, and Dolly had been turning down poor or tasteless scripts with some regularity.

Meanwhile, in Los Angeles, Jane Fonda was driving down the Santa Monica Freeway, listen-

ing to a new hit song on her car stereo and thinking very, very hard. The song was "Here You
Come Again," and what Fonda was thinking about
was a film she had decided to produce herself, a
film that would be made by her own company,
IPC Films, and released by Fox, a clever feminist
message-comedy called *Nine to Five.* And she
was also thinking hard about a gutsy, busty singer
named Dolly Parton.

Chapter Nine

Working Nine to Five

I don't even understand that women's liberation stuff, don't know what it's about. I'm a lucky person. I'm liberated, free-spirited, free-minded, but it's not something I promote or push—just a natural way I've always lived.

—Dolly Parton

The first murmurs about *Nine to Five* began to be heard in the late summer of 1979; the film was tentatively scheduled to begin shooting sometime in November, but there wasn't yet a final script. The concept sounded amusing—a comedy about secretaries who get even with their chauvinist boss, and the leads, Jane Fonda, Lily Tomlin, and Dolly Parton, were a riot of a combination, enough to amuse even the most hardened moviegoer.

Here's Fonda, a serious-minded political activist (and fitness nut), and Tomlin, a serious-minded standup comic, two feminist figures teaming up with a feminine figure like fluffy Dolly to make a feminist comedy about exploited women who get their revenge.

From its concept, Jane Fonda, who had a business interest in the film, wanted Lily Tomlin and Dolly Parton to co-star; she was quoted as saying that, when she saw Dolly's photograph on an album cover, she thought to herself, *Boy, does she ever look like everybody's idea of a secretary.*

In a far more serious vein, Jane told Chet Flippo of *Rolling Stone* that, once the decision had been made to make a movie about secretaries, she knew immediately that Dolly should be in it. "I had never met her, but I was really into her music. Anyone who can write 'Coat of Many Colors' and sing it the way she does has got the stuff to do anything. This was not a woman who was a stereotype of a dumb blonde. I felt that she could probably do just about anything she wanted, that this was a very smart woman. We developed a character based on who she is and what she seems like. Did we coach her? No. Her persona is so strong, you get somebody mucking about with that and making her self-conscious, and it could be negative. Even though we're from different backgrounds and different classes, we're very very alike in many ways. Dolly's not political, but her heart, her instincts—she's on the side of the angels. Very often someone will wow you, but as you get to know them, the mystery wears off. One of the things that just flabbergasts me about Dolly is the amount of mystery she has. She's a very mysterious person."

Nine to Five wasn't the first movie Dolly Parton had been offered; but it was the first one she accepted. "I didn't say yes until I saw the script," said a savvy Dolly. "If it was only gonna be a buncha boob jokes, I wasn't interested." Even the first-draft version of the Nine to Five script intrigued her.

She had been very picky going over scripts. "I hadn't found a script I thought was good enough. I was amazed at how little talent there is among the writers of Hollywood. But Nine to Five fascinated me, and I knew instantly that I should do it. I felt it in my heart it was a career move."

"I'm anxious and excited about doing it," she told syndicated movie-biz columnist Marilyn Beck in early September 1979, "but I won't be doing it unless I can do it right—unless I feel I can do my part well. And I won't know that until I've seen the latest rewrite, and then work on it with the writers." Even in her first film, Dolly Parton was already insisting on a measure of artistic control.

"All of us [Tomlin, Fonda, and Parton] have to approve our characters, to make sure they're right for us. And the script, which has already gone through several rewrites, is just now beginning to blossom into the kind of thing that's good—well, at least comin' closer to being good."

Dolly needn't have worried. The part of Doralee Rhodes, the boss's voluptuous secretary in Nine to Five, was custom-written for her by Patricia Resnik and Colin Higgins, tailored specifically to suit her personality. Dolly wasn't 100 percent won over by it; after the film opened, she said, "The Doralee role in *Nine to Five* wasn't so great, but she was okay for Dolly's first Hollywood movie role. She could kinda sneak in as a little old fat secretary, cute and lovable and fun." She also commented, "There were places I thought I was real good, but there were also places I was real average and places where I was yuck."

Doralee, with her platinum hair and her tight clothes wrapped around her hourglass figure, is at first a figure of scorn and derision. Because her slavering boss (played brilliantly by Dabney Coleman) so obviously lusts after her, the entire office is certain that she's sleeping with him and that she's nothing but a brassy, cheap-looking bimbo. Actually, she is a hard-working, intelligent young woman, very much in love with and faithful to her husband, who cannot understand why a friendly Southern gal like herself can't make friends with the other women in the office, or why everybody treats her so coldly.

"I'd say that eighty percent of all bosses would make a pass at their secretary, given the chance," commented Dolly, speaking of her role as soon as the producers had the final script in hand. "Sure the boss would try to come on to Doralee; that's human nature. But as the movie goes on, they certainly don't play me as some dumb blonde. Doralee is an intelligent, caring person.

"The film appealed to me because it felt so right. It's a comedy, which I thought I could carry off much better than something heavier. But also, the character was always going to be pretty much the same way as I am. Doralee pretty much has my own personality, so I didn't feel I was going to be just thrown into something real difficult first time out. In the movie, I look like myself. I wear the kind of clothes I usually do wear, like sweaters and tight skirts. I like to dress pretty, and so does Doralee. I don't see her as sexy. I think she's kind of cuddly.

"I don't see myself the way that some people might. I don't think that I look particularly sexy. I had created this image that I liked. You know, the big hair and the costumes. I had been looking the same way since I was about sixteen, and I liked it, so I made it my look. I like to be outrageous, because my personality is so outgoing. And, anyhow, it's worked real well."

For Dolly, *Nine to Five* was a "blessed thing," a "real special project." She said that she "did not have one bad moment on the whole picture."

From a practical point of view, she had chosen well. Her first picture was not a film she would have to carry herself. Starring with such experienced actresses and formidable talents as Lily Tomlin (who had starred in *Nashville*, for which Tomlin had been nominated for an Oscar, and in *The Late Show*) and Jane Fonda (fresh from a personal triumph and an Oscar for *Coming Home*) took a lot of the burden off Dolly's own shoulders. If the film should go floppo and belly-up, Dolly Parton wouldn't be held totally responsible. If, on the other hand, the movie *did* make it at the box office, there was a good chance of Dolly's getting a cut of that success.

Then, too, there was always Dolly's way of looking at the positive side of things, and her optimistic nature. "I was never really afraid. Once I'd said yes to the contract and committed myself to making movies, I knew I'd find a way to make it all work out. I'm a very positive thinker, always have been. I never could find it in myself that I'd fail, and that's why I succeed." If Dolly felt any misgivings about exposing her inexperienced acting (she had never taken an acting lesson) side by side with the proven skills of Tomlin and Fonda, she kept those reservations to herself.

Even so, as something of an insurance policy, Dolly sat down and turned out the film's theme song, a bouncy little number also titled "Nine to Five," which she would sing over the opening credits. If the film bombed, she could always go back to singing. Little did she know.

That Hollywood had opened its doors to the budding actress was made evident when the Motion Picture Academy asked Dolly to be an Oscar presenter in the 1980 Academy Awards ceremonies. Dolly turned up in a skintight dress cut all the way down to "there," causing gasps of shock and delight. But this time, alas, it stayed in one piece.

Although Dolly has always denied that she is a sex symbol, others have not been so unrealistic. In the fall of 1980, Dolly Parton journeyed to Nashville to kick off a special campaign to lure tourists to the state of Tennessee. "If they won't follow Dolly Parton to Tennessee, they won't follow anyone," declared the state governor, Lamar Alexander, as Dolly's 7-foot-high image was plastered on the sides of about 30 18-wheelers carrying the slogan DOLLY DOLLY DOLLY: FOLLOW ME TO TENNESSEE. At a Nashville truck stop, Dolly sloshed champagne over the lead rig, and the campaign was launched. Did Dolly Parton see into the future some 6 years, to a time when she would be making personal millions out of Tennessee tourism?

"I'd never seen a movie being made before," admitted Dolly when Nine to Five was wrapped. "I was so silly. I thought that movies were just done as the script goes. So I memorized the whole thing, my part and everyone else's. I knew the whole movie word for word before I ever came out here [Hollywood], which I found hilarious once I saw how movies were made—out of sequence and everything. You open a door one week, and you walk into the room three weeks later.

"But then I found that I didn't have to study so hard during the making of the movie, and making movies is a lot like recording an album, because you go back and do the same things over and over again. Jane has been so helpful about camera angles and lots of technical things, and Lily has been a great inspiration to me. Lily and me, the two of us have a great communication thing going between us, and I get such a big kick out of her."

Nine to Five was certainly a comedy, but Jane Fonda also conceived of it as a film with a very

definite message—that women are frequently dis-
criminated against in the workplace, receiving
less money, less responsibility, and less recognition than their male counterparts.

"Office workers are the power force of the eight-
ies," said Fonda, who had had the idea for a
movie about secretaries for 3 years, and had been
speaking to office workers' groups as part of her
political activism. A number of the groups were
called "Nine to Five," the inspiration for the film's
title. Cleveland's Working Women, the national
association of office workers, gets a line in the
movie's credits.

"Y'know," Jane Fonda told writer Cliff Jahr,
"I'm not going to spend a whole year of my life
making a movie that doesn't raise consciousness,
and it is *unbelievable* what's happening. "One
group I spoke to in Milwaukee—the clerical workers couldn't use the elevators; they had to walk
up the back stairs. Only male executives had a
key to the front door. Women were followed to
the john, even monitored when they went to lunch.
The office structure also pits women against each
other very viciously: older women versus young,
black and brown versus white, pretty versus ugly,
thin versus fat. It's important who dresses better
than whom. The sexual tensions, the pay problems, the lack of promotion . . ." Fonda's indig-
nation would be captured by the film.

Budgeted at $10,000,000, *Nine to Five* was also
a blatant commercial for Sisterhood Is Powerful.
All the women in the film are smart and funny
and capable (with the exception of the butt-kissing
company fink who is in love with Dabney Cole-

man), while none of the men in the movie is worth what it costs to dress him. The possible exception is Dolly's handsome truck-driving husband, but he is little more than a beefcake prop.

In a large corporation run by men, where the hard work is done almost entirely by poorly rewarded women, three women work for Dabney Coleman. Fonda's role is Judy Bernly, a recently divorced, timid, and insecure housewife of forty-one, forced, for economic reasons, to take her first job in an office after years of staying at home and being supported by her husband.

Tomlin plays Violet Newstead, the super-efficient and very intelligent office manager (a lower position than it sounds) whose good ideas are always swiped by the boss and passed off as his own, and Dolly is cast as the blond, bubbly personal secretary after whom Coleman, in his role as Franklin Hart, Jr., a braggart tyrant and weenie, lusts in vain, although the liar has boasted to every man in the company that he has already enjoyed her ample charms.

The three women are leery of one another, but one evening, after a particularly trying day for all of them, they bump into one another in a bar, have a few drinks together, and Lily Tomlin and Jane Fonda discover that Doralee isn't sleeping with the boss at all, and isn't teacher's pet or the company fink, but instead stands on the side of the workers.

They wander back to Tomlin's house, where they get high on some grass she scores from her teen-age son. Giggly and stoned on pot, and becoming firm friends, the three women fantasize about getting even with Coleman. Jane Fonda's fantasy is the goriest—dressed like a Great White Hunter, she tracks him through the maze of offices as though he were a wild beast. Then she wastes him with an elephant gun. In Lily Tomlin's fantasy, she is dressed like Snow White, complete with animated Disney bluebirds twittering overhead. She poisons him with a magical potion, then shoves him out a high window.

In Dolly Parton's fantasy, she is a rootin'-tootin' cowgirl, dressed in boots, fringe, Stetson hat, with a gun. In a complete role reversal, *Doralee* is the boss, and the boss is her secretary. Now she turns the tables on Coleman, becoming overtly sexually aggressive, and subjects him to the identical sexual harassment with which he's been torturing her. "Hey, hot stuff!" she yells at him. "Grab a pad and pencil and bring your buns in here!"

Deliberately, Dolly drops the container of pencils off her desk, making her "secretary" go down on his hands and knees to find them, so that she can leer at his behind, just as he has done to sneak a peek into her cleavage. She calls him "cutie," and "sweetheart," and presents him with a necktie he doesn't want, just as he has gifted her with a scarf and forced her to accept and wear it. She ropes and ties him, like the bull that he is. Of all the fantasies in the film, Dolly's is the most lighthearted.

Naturally, the pot-smoking scene was controversial, but, as Dolly explained, "We were just three women trying it once. It's not like we do it all the time. I don't take drugs myself; I don't have to rely on anything like that, not when I've got my music, my family, and the Lord for solace."

Through a farcical series of events, the three women actually manage to kidnap Coleman and keep him locked up in an empty house, then proceed to run the company themselves, doing a bang-up job, of course. They make many changes, and all of them for the better—shared jobs, so that two women can each work part-time; a day-care center for nursery children; and, of course, raises and promotions for the underpaid, over-worked female employees. Despite all their radical moves, business improves. *Nine to Five* ends with all three of them getting promoted, making decent money, and gaining recognition.

The women improve, too. Fonda loses her timidity and gains a new feeling of self-respect and independence as she earns her own living. Tomlin's overly critical character unbends and softens as she achieves solidarity with her fellow workers and earns her long-overdue promotion. The only one who doesn't change is Doralee-Dolly, who was pretty damned perfect to begin with. But at the finish Dolly's situation in the office has been completely reversed—her value and abilities are recognized and applauded, while her bimbo reputation is exposed as a pack of lies. It was an auspicious film debut, especially for an entertainer with no previous acting experience who had been known only as a singer-songwriter.

Journalist Lawrence Grobel, who had interviewed Dolly for *Playboy*, now interviewed her for *Playgirl*, as the publicity wagons for *Nine to*

Five began to roll. "Who did you feel closer to during the filming, Jane or Lily?" he asked her.

"Actually," answered Dolly, "I felt a bit closer to Lily because I had a chance to get to know her, and Jane had so much business stuff to do. Lily and I are both with the same agency now. I spent more time talking to Lily. With Jane, we got to be close, but we really hadn't gotten together enough to totally relax and be just pals. I have such admiration for Jane. I'm not starstruck, but I know when a person's great."

There had been a lot of industry snickering in advance of the filming, as Hollywood pundits tried to imagine Dolly, Lily, and Jane working together. There were jokes about the size of their egos, about their different kinds of bodies, about their different mind-sets. Fonda's radical-style politics are a matter of public record, while, to Dolly, politics are something one never discusses. She won't tell you what they are, but you can bet dollars to greasy doughnuts that a country music gal from the South hasn't the same outlook on the state of the world as an actress who has hit the Chou En Lai trail and visited Hanoi.

"A lot of people were sayin', 'Boy, I would l-o-o-o-ve to see that,' " Dolly said laughingly to Chet Flippo. " 'There ain't no way them three bitches are gonna get along. Can you imagine three women like that?!' And you know, we had the greatest time."

Actually, the pundits were way off base. From day one there was mutual respect, mutual admiration, and a mutual-support group among the three stars on the set of *Nine to Five*. They went out of their way to be good to one another, as if to throw the rumors of potential temperament clashes back into the teeth of the rumor mongers. They drank champagne together, cooked spaghetti, and traded gossip in a sisterly love fest. Shooting the picture was like one big sleepover. The three women did everything but get out their high school yearbooks and give one another Toni home permanents, and maybe they did that, too.

It goes without saying that, during the 9 weeks of filming, Dolly Parton and Jane Fonda did not discuss politics. No doubt they didn't discuss workouts, either, since Dolly has often told her public how much she hates to exercise, and that what she really likes is to watch exercise videos like Jane Fonda's workout tapes while sitting still and stuffing her face with greasy, fattening foods.

"She's so nice. She's cotton candy," says Jane of Dolly.

"I'd always loved Lily, but I wondered about me and Jane. Jane comes across hard at times, but she's so much sweeter and softer. She's almost like a little girl," says Dolly of Jane.

But why shouldn't they have gotten along like sisters? If one puts aside their surface differences and examines their similarities, Dolly, Lily, and Jane would be seen to have many characteristics in common. All three are highly intelligent businesswomen who run their own business ventures. All three are hardworking and dedicated to that work. All three are innovative performers, each with a style very much her own. And, bottom line, all three are consummate professionals. Even

the non-actress Dolly knew instinctively from the
outset of filming how and when to give a scene her
all. Her stage sense and presence, her many years
of experience before audiences of all types, has
made her nearly as much of an actress as a singer.

Of course, there was a lot of technical information and nuances Dolly had to learn about making films. When one is larger than life on the
stage, as Dolly is, it has to be toned down for the
camera, which is subtle and catches everything.
Jane Fonda taught her a number of the professional tricks of the trade, telling Dolly how to
look, or turn, or the right way to pause.

"She was always sayin' little things like 'Don't
talk on the same voice level.' 'Don't get too excited when you've got nowhere to go.' 'Don't start
out high.' 'Make a definite look . . . don't move
your eyes around.' Things like that. She also suggested that as a part of my contracts in the future,
I might want a coach on the job with me. And she
gave me names of directors to think about. A lot
of people think she's hard because of her strong
beliefs, but I found her very sensitive. She's very
firm, very intelligent. She said to me, 'I'd like to
see you someday do something really serious and
dramatic. Not comedy, not funny.' "

Nine to Five opened in 1980 as a Christmas
release and was an immediate box-office smash.
Variety said, "The bottom line is that this picture
is a lot of fun. Fonda, Tomlin, and Parton provide
charm and distinction to their sketchy characters. . . ." In summation, the trade paper opined,
". . . will get paid handsomely for overtime at the
box office." *Variety* was right on target.

Before her first film wrapped, the announcement hit the media that Dolly's second picture would be *The Best Little Whorehouse in Texas* with Burt Reynolds. Dolly Parton had been spoiled by the "blessed thing" that was *Nine to Five*. Her next picture would be a totally different story.

Chapter Ten

Dolly on a Roll

> A star, you know, is something
> bright. Something that stands out,
> that's special. Something shining.
>
> —Dolly Parton

The success of the picture *Nine to Five* didn't take many people by surprise. The combination of Parton, Fonda, and Tomlin would make even the merely curious line up for tickets. But what knocked everybody out was the meteoric, phenomenal success of the title song. "Nine to Five," an upbeat country number delivered in Dolly Parton's unmistakable style, swept the nation, soaring up the charts with the speed of an eagle, reaching number one in both the country and the pop markets. Both the single and the album, *Nine to Five and Odd Jobs*, went platinum.

More than that, the song "Nine to Five" became a kind of anthem for working women everywhere, a theme song that expressed their frustrations with "all takin' and no givin'." "I knew that I could write a song about myself and my daddy and my brothers and my sisters and my friends and all the people who work nine to five. 'Workin' nine to five, what a way to make a livin'.'

"I've been tryin' all these years to win my musical freedom so I could introduce myself to another audience, a more universal audience," Dolly had said more than once.

With *Nine to Five*, Dolly Parton had achieved at last that true universality—not everybody grows up poor in Tennessee, but all women work, whether in an office, a factory, the home, or even on a Las Vegas stage. From the launching of the song, there was talk of a Grammy, maybe even an Oscar. When the time came, "Nine to Five" would win two Grammys—as Best Country Song, and for Dolly, as Best Female Country Vocal Performance. It won the 1981 People's Choice Award and was nominated for an Oscar, losing to "Arthur's Theme (Best That You Can Do)" from *Arthur*.

Dolly wrote "Nine to Five" on the set. The only thing that made her itchy about making movies was "hurry up and wait," those endlessly long breaks between scenes, the mindless tedium of the process in which one stands around doing nothing for hours at a time. Dolly Parton is not a nothing-doer, so she filled the idle hours on the set writing songs. She was more creative while making Nine to Five than she had been in a good long while.

"The hardest thing was the long wait between shots," she told writer Kip Kirby, "the hours you'd sit in makeup and costume and all. And I thought to myself, now I am not gonna sit around here like this. 'Cause it was the first time in my life that I've ever had to sit around and do nothin'. I can't embroider or nothin' like that, so I figured if I started writin' songs, it would change my mood. So I started writin' right on the set, and I was amazed at how easily I could do it. That's how I wrote 'Nine to Five.' "

After the film was wrapped, Dolly and Jane Fonda took a trip together down South. Jane's next project was to be a TV movie, "The Doll-maker," based on the prize-winning novel by Harriet S. Arnow; it would win a well-deserved Emmy for Fonda. Set in the Appalachian Mountains, it's the story of a mountain woman, dirt-poor, with the miraculous skill of hand-carving folk-art dolls, and Jane went south to research it, taking the mountain woman Dolly Parton with her.

"We traveled around together for a week," Dolly told Lawrence Grobel. "We just had the best time you could imagine. We totally relaxed. It was like I was a little girl having a great time in the country entertaining a city cousin. In fact, we came up with some great ideas for movies and series and stories. It was really special. It was hard to say good-bye. We became good friends."

Nine to Five was a favorite with the press and the critics, as well as the public. It became one of the smash hits of 1980–1981. The lion's share of the publicity on the picture went to Dolly Parton, who not only made an excellent film debut as Doralee, but had written the title song and a number of others on the soundtrack album.

Nine to Five and Odd Jobs was the title of the album. It was a concept album about working people, just as My Tennessee Mountain Home was a concept album about Dolly's days of struggle before her success. It included a Merle Travis classic about coal mining, "Dark as a Dungeon," a Woody Guthrie classic, "Deportee (Train Wreck at Los Gatos)," and "The House of the Rising Sun," a low-down blues about girls who are ruined in a New Orleans bordello. "Hush-a-Bye Hard Times" was written by Dolly in the bluegrass mode; another Dolly Parton original was "Working Girl."

Nine to Five wasn't the only Dolly Parton album RCA released in 1980—she'd also done Dolly Dolly Dolly and Heartbreak Express. Of Dolly Dolly Dolly, Kelly Delaney wrote in Country Music magazine that the album was "like a brand-new car—polished to a fine glaze with chrome shining brilliantly. . . . Much of the album is like mindless car radio music which fits nicely between jockey chatter, traffic reports, and the latest afternoon racing results. With few exceptions, there are no memorable music or lyrics. . . . Dolly Dolly Dolly is only so much folly folly folly."

But it was a much different story with Nine to Five and Odd Jobs. In October 1981, the title song won the BMI Robert J. Burton Award for the Country Song of the Year. It was also on BMI's published list of "Most Performed Hits" for 1981, and the listing carried a star, meaning that it had passed 1,000,000 performances. Dolly was on the program of the 1981 Academy Awards telecast, where, dressed in sequins, she sang the nominated "Nine to Five," which received an ovation, even though it didn't win.

Record reviewers fell all over themselves to praise the *Nine to Five* album. Stephen Holden, who had dismissed the Dolly Parton of *Dolly Dolly Dolly* as sounding "like a windup toy," said of *Nine to Five*, "After a string of abysmal pop records on which her kittenish treatment of fatuous material turned her into a bad joke, Dolly Parton makes an impressive comeback with *Nine to Five and Odd Jobs*." Holden concluded his review: "It's nice to have Dolly Parton back from the trash bin unscathed."

Bob Campbell of *Country Music* magazine said that *Nine to Five and Odd Jobs* "is more varied and down to earth than what we have heard from Dolly in some time, and she gives us our money's worth. But I suspect her next album will be the real killer."

It was.

Between *New Harvest, First Gathering* and *Nine to Five and Odd Jobs*, Dolly Parton had recorded a series of Gary Klein-produced albums at Hollywood's Sound Lab studios. They were popular, they were well-put-together, and featured heavy-beat, full-instrumentation arrangements. Even though they all made the charts, they showed a side of Dolly that was offensive to country purists. A number of the songs were "country-flavored," but none of them was country music as the old Dolly Parton could do country music.

Probably nobody was more aware of that problem than Dolly herself, because Parton went back to Nashville to record *Nine to Five and Odd Jobs*, her first album to be cut in Music City, U.S.A., since *New Harvest, First Gathering*. The sound she was looking for, she said, was a sound that lived in Nashville.

The "return" to Nashville was a triumph, as Dolly revealed her plans to open her own company on Music Row (as though she didn't have heavy business interests there already, with companies like Owepar Publishing). But this new venture, by means of which, Dolly announced, she would put "back into Nashville some of the things I learned since I started out," was to be a high-powered, multilevel organization that would combine management, booking, recording, and song publishing, not only for Dolly Parton herself but for other artists. She also promised to build a recording studio in Nashville, and she made a vow that her next album after *Nine to Five and Odd Jobs* would be pure country, all her own songs.

This announcement of the new company "coincided" with the Nashville premiere of *Nine to Five*, which included, in addition to all the hoopla that attends such a media event—the press conferences, the photographs of celebrities on the front pages of the local papers, and the interviews on radio and TV—a gala invitation-only screening of the motion picture, plus a big party afterward, for the top-drawer crowd of country music and record executives.

Since Dolly Parton and Porter Wagoner had finally settled their dragged-out lawsuit out of court, Dolly tried to bury the hatchet by inviting Porter to the premiere of the film. Wagoner didn't show up, and the two of them were not to get together publicly until the sixtieth anniversary of "Grand Ole Opry" in 1985, although, as part of the out-of-court settlement, there was to be another Porter and Dolly recording released, containing only their older material.

True to her word about the Nashville Sound, and *almost* keeping her promise that her next album would be pure country and all her own— two of the songs on the album were the old R&B Esther Phillips hit "Release Me," and the other, released as a single and an immediate hit, was "Single Women," written by Michael O'Donoghue of *The National Lampoon* and "Saturday Night Live" fame—on *Heartbreak Express* Dolly Parton took a backward step—back to the pre-Hollywood Dolly. As she had promised, she recorded it in Nashville, co-producing *Heartbreak Express* with Gregg Perry, her keyboardist, instead of with Gary Klein. This was to be one of her most important albums, especially significant coming directly after the watershed *Nine to Five and Odd Jobs*.

Noel Coppage, *Stereo Review*'s acerbic reviewer, who had trounced the Hollywood albums, was completely won over by the new one, composing a valentine to it headlined "Dolly Parton in Full Flower." "If you grew up, as I did," he wrote, "with the idea that singers are not like you and me, that singing voices are special, mysterious, a little foreign, capable of non-ordinary feats, this album will resonate. Dolly's extraordinary singing style is what it's really about, and there is simply more of the vocal art going on here than the ordinary person can keep track of, which means that one can listen to it again and again and keep making discoveries. You can come on home, Dolly. I reckon we're just going to have to forgive you for them disco records.''

Heartbreak Express contained a couple of Dolly's older songs—"My Blue Ridge Mountain Boy," "Do I Ever Cross Your Mind," and "Barbara on Your Mind," and some of her newer works, like "Prime of Your Love," "Heartbreak Express," and "Hollywood Potters," but the cleaner, less lush arrangements and simple vibrato singing was the old Dolly Parton. It was as though Dolly had realized what had been missing in her string of recent "windup toy" albums, which even she, in candid moments, admitted to the press that she wasn't too crazy about. *Heartbreak Express* was a concept album about feelings, most of them melancholy, about Dolly Parton's idea of the sadness of life and the heartbreak of love in pure music.

There was a running joke between Dolly and the press, in which she maintained that her husband, Carl, had never heard her music. Or, sometimes, the joke went that Carl had listened to it, but didn't care for it much, or that he told her she might amount to something "someday." With *Heartbreak Express* she admitted for the first time that her husband was a fan; he really liked this album. And so did she. It was as though a pendulum, having swung in a wide arc between country and pop, was finally coming to rest in a true and comfortable center.

One of the major entertainment events of 1981 was Dolly's opening at the Riviera in Las Vegas. The debut was delayed for a couple of days, thanks to Dolly's old devilment, a bad throat and laryngitis. For the show, the Riviera charged $45 for dinner and $35 for cocktails, making the ticket $70, which sounds like an enormous bargain, but not when you consider that, in Vegas, what you save on the meals and entertainment, you lose in the slots and on the wheel.

With Dolly Parton earning $350,000 a week (or $500,000, depending on who was doing the reporting), the inevitable joke quickly flew around town: "That's $175,000 each."

Dolly herself contributed to the wisecracks. "I gotta have a lot of money; you have no idea how expensive industrial bras are." She was quite plump by now, at least 30 pounds overweight, which on a 5-foot frame ("I'm six-four in heels" or "I'd be six-two if it didn't all get so bumped together at the top") was a considerable extra amount for her to carry ("My jeans aren't Jordache, they're lardache.")

Fat or thin or in between, there is only one Dolly Parton, and she wowed the opening night crowd. Her set was a giant fairy-tale castle, complete with drawbridge. Under the musical direction of Gregg Perry, she gave them 78 minutes of her best, including a fantastic takeoff on Elvis Presley in "All Shook Up." It took her two or three numbers before her voice loosened up, thanks to the cortisone injection, but by the time she launched into "Here You Come Again" and "Jolene," followed by "Two Doors Down" and "Coat of Many Colors," Dolly had them eating out of her diamond-ringed hands. When she gave that cynical and savvy audience the sentimental "Me and Little Andy" in that childlike voice, you could hear a tear drop. She sang and sang: "There's No Business Like Show Business," "Nine to Five," which brought down the house, "House of the Rising Sun," and more. When she finally left the stage, cheering fans brought her back for an encore, "I Will Always Love You."

What Dolly Parton accomplished in Las Vegas was what she had meant to accomplish—to bring to the high rollers her unadulterated act, her essential country self, without sellout. While it is true she doesn't use a medieval castle as a backdrop in an ordinary concert, she didn't compromise her material, nor her feelings, nor her religious beliefs.

Dolly Parton was on a roll. It seemed to her and to the world that she couldn't make a wrong step. Every decision she made had worked out well for her. She had made a hit comedy, and it had been a sweetheart filming. Jane Fonda said afterward that Dolly Parton had changed an entire movie crew for the better, and that her spirit and her goodness had made all the others come up a little to meet Dolly's standard, and that the film itself was better because of Dolly.

Dolly had a platinum single and a platinum album in *Nine to Five and Odd Jobs*. *Heartbreak*

Express was on its way to going gold. Her name was up for a couple of Grammys and an Oscar. She was writing furiously, and the songs were good. She was pleasing her critics again. Her Las Vegas opening had been a smash. She was ready to begin shooting her second picture, with the number-one box-office star, the sexy Burt Reynolds. Life was sweet, and was probably going to go on being sweet, and become even sweeter.

What a good thing Dolly Parton didn't have a crystal ball. If she had seen what was in her future, she would have been mighty unhappy!

Chapter Eleven

The Worst Little Whorehouse in Texas

> There was a lot of blood on this
> project. When it ended, it was the
> most painful thing I had ever done.
>
> —Dolly Parton

Dolly, Lily, and Jane, posing in grinning cama-
raderie, made the January 19, 1981, cover of *People*
magazine. The cover line was: "Dolly Parton: After Her Racy Debut in *9 to 5*, Burt Reynolds is
next, but, she insists, 'I'm not selling sex.' "

It took an offer of $1,500,000 and a percentage
of the gross (there is never any net profit, never)
for Dolly Parton to consider doing the R-rated
The Best Little Whorehouse in Texas, even though
her male co-star was to be the hottest property in

films and the biggest box-office draw at the moment, Burt Reynolds, whose contract was for $3,500,000 and the inevitable percentage of the gross.

The novel-turned-into-musical-play on which the film was based had been written by Texan Larry L. King, who had co-authored the book of the play and co-authored the original movie script. When the show had opened off-Broadway, the influential syndicated columnist Liz Smith, herself a Texan and devoted to all things bearing the "Texas" brand, was so taken with it that she touted it in her column day after day for months on end, contributing greatly to its success. It was a happy show, revolving around a sixty-two-year-old sheriff and a middle-aged madam, with rollicking songs and cheerful performances. Eventually it would move to Broadway, where it became an even greater hit.

The idea of playing a madam in a picture with "Whorehouse" in its title turned Dolly on, but it also turned her off. When the film was first offered to her, she shook her golden curls no.

"After all, my granddaddy, the Reverend Jake Owens, was a hellfire preacher, and I'm a very religious person," Dolly pointed out. But that was before she went to New York to see the show and had herself a foot-stompin' good time at the bawdy, raunchy hit musical.

"I could just imagine what my family, my religion, and my fans would say," Dolly told *People* magazine. But, after seeing the musical for herself, Dolly changed her mind. "The character's not trash, just caught in this situation. She's probably like I would have been had things been different.

"I said I'd do the picture if the script was rewritten to establish more of a relationship between Miss Mona and Sheriff Earl," Dolly confided to Hollywood reporter and author Bob Thomas. "It would give me a chance to write songs and sing in a picture. I didn't sing a bit in *Nine to Five*. . . . The character of Miss Mona is more like me. I get a chance to dress up the way I like, with the crazy wigs and the wild clothes, and everything juiced up. . . . I like having the freedom of speech in the movie, bein' able to talk the way I talk. I can say *damn* or *hell* if I want to.

"Before I accepted the picture I discussed it with the folks back home, and they all thought it was fine for me to go ahead." Nevertheless, as the film proceeded, Dolly softened Miss Mona's character, against the author's will, just for the folks back home. She gave her role of Miss Mona a Mary Magdalene-type of motivation.

Like all such ventures, Universal-RKO's $20,-000,000-budgeted *The Best Little Whorehouse in Texas* (it eventually would cost $26,000,000; the cost of Dolly's costumes alone shot up over $100,000) began with happy press releases, high hearts, and high hopes. Nobody at that stage could predict that the film would take so long to complete, or make so many people miserable.

The role of Miss Mona Strangely, the madam and owner of the legendary Chicken Ranch of LaGrange, Texas, The Best Little Whorehouse in Texas, seemed to be tailor-made to suit Dolly's looks and talent. The author, Larry King, thought that casting Dolly Parton was just *too* obvious. "She looks like she might run a whorehouse or work in one," he growled.

Dolly admitted publicly that she had always had a "thing" for Burt Reynolds ("I don't want to miss a chance with Burt").

Conversely, Burt leered publicly that he always had a "thing" for her, and would be glad to show her what it was. "She's sweet and pure as the driven snow mounds, and I can't wait to begin work. Dolly Parton was made to be a movie star."

Seriously, Burt had been after Dolly professionally ever since he had filmed *W. W. and the Dixie Dancekings*. He had wanted her for that film, and wanted to do a picture with her for years. A press release went out stating that Burt Reynolds had refused to do *Whorehouse* unless Dolly Parton was signed for the role of Miss Mona, at the same time that Dolly was refusing the film unless Burt Reynolds played Sheriff Earl Ed! What a happy coincidence! How believable!

As usual with a big-budget picture that depended on "bankable" names, changes had been made in the script to accommodate the stars, and they made the writer, Larry L. King, furious. Sheriff Earl Ed Dodd—played by Reynolds, of course—would no longer be sixty-two years old, but thirty-five (Burt was then forty-six). There would be love scenes between Dolly and Burt, although there had been no love scenes in the musical play. Dolly wanted to be in charge of the music, although the film was to include the original score of the musical show, written by Carol Hall.

In fact, King was so angry with the way the

project was going that he offered to punch Reynolds out, an offer that seems never to have been taken up. Also, good newspaperman that he was, Larry King kept a journal of the making of the film, and Viking Press published it as *The Whorehouse Papers*. In the book, King accused Reynolds of wanting to make *Smokey and the Bandit Go to a Whorehouse*, and charged Dolly with throwing her considerable weight around to get several of her songs added to the Carol Hill score, and for pushing for love scenes between herself and Reynolds.

"Wouldn't you feel like you was cheated if you paid five dollars for a ticket and then didn't get to see me and Burt Reynolds kissin'?" she demanded. But Dolly went on record immediately to state that nudity and graphic sex were two mammoth Parton no-no's.

"When I say love scenes, I'm talkin' about holding, hugging, kissing, and things that make sense. I could never do a nude scene. I'm not selling sex," she told *People*, which stuck the line on the cover of the magazine. "The magic of the whole thing is that I am one way and look another."

Dolly Parton had never made a secret of her fascination for whores. She has even said that the trademark way she dresses owes a lot to the prostitutes she saw as a girl.

"I always liked the look of our hookers back home. Their big hairdos and makeup made them look *more*. When people say less is more, I say *more* is more. Less is *less*. I go for more."

To Chet Flippo of *Rolling Stone*, Dolly added, "Some of my best friends have been hussies or called whores because they are usually the most honest and open people. And, even if they don't do it as a profession, I just relate to it, and I've often said that I honestly do look like a whore or a high-class prostitute, not even so much high class, with the makeup and the bleached hair and the boobs and the tight-fittin' clothes and the high heels . . . except that I'm not a whore. But if I hadn't made it in this business, who knows?'' She also said mischievously, "I make a better whore than a secretary.''

"Prostitutes,'' Dolly told Cliff Jahr in the *Ladies' Home Journal* after the picture was completed, "are some of the sweetest, most caring people I've known because they've been through *everything!* I've met them at parties, and I've talked with them. Usually, they're people with broken dreams who never had a chance in life or were sexually abused or ignored as children. A lot sell themselves to get some kind of feeling of being loved. The movie will show these women have feelings. You're gonna cry your eyes out.''

The Best Little Whorehouse in Texas was shot at Universal Studios in Los Angeles and on location, in Halletsville and Pflugerville, Texas, and soon the word was out in the press that things were not going along so merrily with the production. It was a problem picture. There was a series of changes in producers and directors. Two directors—Tommy Tune and Peter Masterson, who had directed the original New York show—were fired. The final director of the film was Colin Higgins, who had directed and co-written the script of *Nine to Five*. One set was pulled down and built over again from the ground up.

"Each time they changed," said Dolly, "I had to write new songs, forty or fifty in all." Although she fought like a tiger to defend her songs, only two of them actually made it into the finished film—a duet with Burt Reynolds, "Sneakin' Around," and an old song of hers, "I Will Always Love You," which was released as a single and which she had already adopted as her signature encore number. However, she did record the soundtrack album.

What was the core of the problem? Most of the insiders agreed that it wasn't a "what" but a "who," Burt Reynolds. Reynolds had become moody and difficult, "a nightmare" to work with, making demands, pushing people around, storming off the set. He had recently broken off with his lover, Sally Field, and it had been a long and very close relationship. Earnings on his last three pictures had been disappointing; Reynolds hadn't been achieving in the recent years the success he was accustomed to, and he was running scared.

In particular, Reynolds appeared to be afraid that the buxom, earthy Dolly, with a role she could sink her teeth into, might prove to be funnier than he, and walk off with the picture. There is nothing in the world more perilous to an established star than to have a picture stolen from him by a comparative amateur. The bigger egos are, the more fragile.

"On the movie, we've gone through so much bitterness—tensions, quarrels, hurt feelings. I threatened to quit so many times," said Dolly. "I don't ever want to work that hard again. There's this tiny voice in me that keeps saying, 'This is the last movie you'll ever make.' "

When Bob Thomas asked her why, Dolly replied, "Well, it's hard to make compromises, and that's what you gotta do in this business. I don't want to lose my values. The only way I would do another picture was if I could maintain control of the project. That way I could be sure of workin' with the people I wanted to work with. On a picture you're dealin' with so many people and bendin' so much that you lose control."

Caught between Larry L. King's bitter attacks and Burt Reynolds's sulks and temper tantrums, never knowing from day to day when she would have to work with a brand-new producer or director, Dolly Parton must have longed for the good old days when she, Lily, and Jane were giggling over herbal tea and swapping the names of designers and directors. *Nine to Five* had been "a blessed thing" and "the best experience I could have had." *The Best Little Whorehouse in Texas* caused Dolly "more problems, sorrows, and enlightenment" than she had ever known before. Making the film "was a real painful thing," she said. As an experience, it was "the worst."

"It's been kind of a bloodbath all the way through. The people who wrote it got ushered out, and so many people changed—they just weren't right for the picture, so they had to be fired. Well, it just hurt me real bad. I saw so much compromising being done, it just about killed me emotionally."

But Dolly Parton always takes the fabric of her

life—it doesn't matter if it's rosy or black—and stitches it into something artistic and beautiful. This time was no different. Something of the agony she experienced making *The Best Little Whorehouse in Texas* came out in a song on her twenty-eighth album, *Heartbreak Express.* In "Hollywood Potters" Dolly described Hollywood poetically as the "dungeon of drama, the center of sorrow, the city of schemes, the terrace of trauma, the palace of promises and the dealer of dreams."

Most interviews she gave regarding *The Best Little Whorehouse in Texas* quoted her as being understanding about Burt Reynolds's problems, no matter how they may have impacted on her personally. But there was no question but that she gave almost as good as she got; inside that blond fluff and under those curves is a core of stainless steel.

"People think of me as all smiles," she told *People,* but I can get aggravated. When I got somethin' to say, I'll say it." Some of the things that she and Reynolds said to each other "brought tears to his or my eyes." But "we agreed that we would stick together no matter what. If he left the picture, I'd leave. If I left, he'd leave. We knew it was going to be a very big movie, and that we had to stick it out."

And yet, despite the tempers and the temperaments, despite the harsh tear-inducing words, a large number of people in the press and on the set of the picture are convinced that Dolly Parton and Burt Reynolds were lovers during and for a short while after the making of *The Best Little Whorehouse in Texas.* They point to passionate kisses that continued after the cameras stopped rolling, to a trip the two of them took together; the supermarket tabloids ran screaming headlines that had the pair sneaking off to a private tête-à -tête in Burt's Florida hideaway. They also wrote that Burt had spent several nights in Las Vegas when Dolly Parton debuted there.

"Dolly Parton Agrees to Have Burt Reynolds's Baby!" screamed the headlines, ironically, for, as it would soon be known, Dolly wasn't in the physical shape to have anybody's baby.

Were those nights in Las Vegas a love tryst for Dolly Parton and Burt Reynolds? Dolly, needless to say, issued the usual denial. Admitting that she had been *tempted* ("I'm not dead yet"), she added, "We didn't have enough of that to spoil our friendship. Besides, I'm a married woman." Once more, Carl Dean was conveniently there.

But Dolly and Carl were spending more time together than usual. During the filming of *Nine to Five*, Carl had come to Los Angeles, a city he normally avoided, and stayed with Dolly in her new, rented two-bedroom Beverly Hills digs. When *The Best Little Whorehouse in Texas* finally wrapped, Dolly and Carl went off to Australia together for a short holiday. Was it to quell the rumors about Dolly and Burt? Or maybe was it to make up for the business visit to Australia that Dolly had taken in February, to look at potential real estate?

With her manager, Sandy Gallin, Dolly had gone land-shopping by helicopter, scouting beachfront property for another of her many houses. The trip occasioned many rumors of an affair between them.

It seems that every time Dolly Parton works closely with a man, "affair" is the word on everybody's lips but hers. Dolly swears her relationship with Gallin is strictly platonic; they are partners in several ventures.

"I do have a right to some secret spots," Dolly told Cliff Jahr about a month before Whorehouse opened in the summer of 1982. Dolly had had some personal problems in 1981—an "affair of the heart, not a love affair," she hinted mysteriously, refusing to name the person. There was speculation that the person was Porter Wagoner, and that the problem was the $3,000,000 legal suit he launched against her that year to recover royalties. These business problems were an emotional body blow to Dolly; she felt betrayed, and the prospect of a public lawsuit made her feel quite ill.

"It just about killed me. I cried an ocean. Then also last year my throat was bad. I was trying to write, there were lots of family problems, and this came on top of all the movie's putdowns and dragouts and misunderstandings. Suddenly, six months into the year, everything switched, cleared up, and turned into a year of enlightenment. It will happen again, I'm sure, in seven years when I'm forty-two." Actually, in seven years Dolly would be forty-three, but perhaps her memory had slipped a year.

Dolly's throat wasn't her only physical problem; far, far worse lay ahead of her. Dolly and Sandy Gallin had to cut their Australia trip short, because she was suffering severe pain. As soon as she and Gallin came back from Australia, Dolly went into a hospital in Los Angeles for what was termed "minor" gynecological surgery.

For years, Dolly Parton had been struggling with health problems connected with her menstrual cycle. Under the gun on the set of *The Best Little Whorehouse in Texas*, she had been suffering for about 6 months with terrible headaches and excruciating cramps. What she called "my woman's problem" and "my hormone imbalance" had already forced her to cancel her 1982 Las Vegas appearance, an Atlantic City engagement, and a string of other concerts, including Houston, Cleveland, and Merrillville, Indiana. Because the picture was taking so much longer to wrap than was scheduled, Dolly had put off doing anything about her worsening physical condition, and had let the problem go a little too far.

Dolly's illness, plus the anguish involved in *Whorehouse*, had caused the usually optimistic, positive-thinking Dolly Parton to suffer a most uncharacteristic depression, which accounts somewhat for the *tristesse* of the songs on *Heartbreak Express*.

It was everyone's hope that minor surgery would relieve the condition, and avoid a complete hysterectomy. Although Dolly Parton was thirty-six and had been married sixteen years without children, and although the likelihood of Dolly and Carl's having children was remote in any case, a hysterectomy is a drastic step for any woman. "I didn't want to have the complete job done. I was hopin' that a lot of it was just overwork and mental anguish. I was under a lot of stress, and out of balance."

Dolly entered St. John's Hospital in Santa Monica on Monday, February 15, 1982. Since the operation was minor (the nature of it was not disclosed, but it was most likely a dilation curettage) she was out of the hospital only a day or two later.

Her physician's post-surgery recommendation was "complete rest away from work and other strenuous chores for at least four to six weeks."

After the operation, Dolly and Carl went to Tara, where Dolly recuperated for a few months. The original plan was for Dolly to go back to work by the end of April, but she didn't recover as quickly as was expected, so she canceled her bookings for May and June, too. There was some concern that she might not be well enough for the gala premiere in July of *The Best Little Whorehouse in Texas*.

When Dolly's song "Nine to Five" won two Grammy awards—the songwriting award for Best Country Song, and the Best Female Country Performance—and was a finalist in two other categories—Best Song of the Year, and Best Album of Original Score Written for a Motion Picture or TV Special, a nomination she shared with Charles Fox—Dolly couldn't attend the ceremonies in Los Angeles.

Because she was still filming *Whorehouse*, Dolly had missed out on the ceremonies the previous October, when Broadcast Music Incorporated had given "Nine to Five" the Robert J. Burton Award for the Most Performed Song of the Year in both the country and pop categories. Dolly had to be content with sending BMI a wire saying, "I'm thrilled. Songwriting is my heart and soul."

But Dolly's attitude was, operation or no operation, recuperation be damned; she wasn't going to sit around on her duff forever. When the American Guild of Variety Artists (AGVA) presented her with two honors, the Female Country Star of the Year and the Entertainer of the Year awards at their May telecast, Dolly Parton was there wearing rhinestoned bells. AGVA had honored her twice before, in 1978 and 1979 as Country Star of the Year, but this time they gave her their highest accolade, Entertainer of the Year, and she wasn't about to miss that as she had missed the Grammys.

At the end of June 1982, Dolly announced a new deal in Nashville. She had assigned Tree International, the music publishing company that had taken her in years ago, when she was but a young hopeful, to manage her song publishing. To Tree she assigned over 900 songs, past and present, for management and administration. The deal included Dolly's own material and those of other songwriters in her stable at her companies Velvet Apple and Song Yard, including her siblings Randy, Rachel, and Frieda, songs by her Uncle Bill Owens, and around 100 Frank Dycus songs. Copyrights were not involved in the deal, and the song catalog to be managed by Tree did not include the songs still in the Combine Music catalog, songs written between 1966 and 1968.

The purpose of this deal was ostensibly to reduce Dolly's overhead by consolidating her publishing with a fully staffed company, but in fact it was another way of freeing Dolly Parton from some of her earlier family ties. Relationships with some of the kinfolk working for her had become too tangled and strained, and the new Dolly, with her new management, was oppressed by the old constraints. Also, it added to the tension she had experienced with Burt Reynolds and *The Best Little Whorehouse in Texas*.

The film opened at a televised gala premiere in Austin, Texas, in August 1982. Dolly was there, looking terrific, and apparently feeling great, although in actuality she wasn't at all well.

In its review, *Variety* said the picture "ideally teams powerhouse stars Burt Reynolds and Dolly Parton, a combo which should please mass audiences thoroughly. Film delivers on all the traditional levels of popular entertainment, so there's no reason it shouldn't prove a substantial box-office winner. . . ." As usual, *Variety* was prophetic. *The Best Little Whorehouse in Texas* went on to become the third top-grossing movie musical, grossing $87,000,000 at the box office alone, not counting foreign sales and video, and proved to be a success for everybody. Liz Smith hated it, and said so in her column. But then, Liz is a friend of Larry L. King's.

As for Dolly, she was quoted as saying, "This was a picture that got way, way out of hand. There was a lot of blood spilled just turnin' it from a Broadway show into a picture. The fightin' was real terrible. I feel real bad about how Burt and Larry King kept fightin' it out in the press. But I don't regret anythin' I ever do. If nothin' else, it's a good experience, and it teaches me a lot."

What it taught her was that, in Hollywood, if you don't have control of a project, then you're nothing but a hired hand, no matter how high your salary.

The release of *The Best Little Whorehouse in Texas* as well as the release of the soundtrack album and *Heartbreak Express*, the album on which she'd "cried an ocean," was the customary occasion for a tour. Dolly scheduled an 8-week, 35-stop tour of the U.S. and Canada. As usual, she had taken on enough play-dates to wreck the health of a younger, stronger person, but that was always Dolly's way. She was fat, unhealthy, and unhappy, and she thought that what she needed most in the world was to get out there and work. Besides, she had canceled a lot of play-dates earlier in the year, and it was time to make good on them.

"Nothing beats getting out on the stage and singing direct to my fans, the people who've been my friends all through the years, plus the new friends I've met along the way." What Dolly loves best are the plain folk who wash up the supper dishes and come to see her shows.

For her fourth concert in the series, Dolly Parton was scheduled to sing at the Ohio State Fair in Columbus. Her fee: $50,000. Suddenly, she began hemorrhaging internally. Doctors advised her strongly against going on, but Dolly wouldn't listen. She not only played and sang both a matinee and evening concert, but insisted on going forward to her next concert, the fifth of the 35, on Sunday, August 22, 1982, at the Indiana State Fair in Indianapolis. She spent a really bad night on her bus between Columbus and Indianapolis. The internal bleeding, with intestinal complications, started up again, but she didn't change her mind. These people had paid to hear her sing, and sing she would. She even counted on playing the dates after Indianapolis—the Houston, Texas, Rodeo, Merrillville, Indiana, and Cleveland, Ohio— bookings she had canceled when she entered the hospital for her earlier surgery, in February.

There was a ferocious, driving rainstorm at the Indianapolis fairgrounds, but her fans didn't seem to mind. No one left. They sat enraptured in the rain, not even noticing that they were getting soaked through to the bone. Once more, doctors warned her that to go on was foolhardy and dangerous, but she paid them no heed. Dressed in a glittery sequined gown with long fringes on the sleeves, Dolly gave them what they wanted— "Jolene," "Coat of Many Colors," her standard encore of "I Will Always Love You"—the songs with which she was most identified. Although Dolly herself was under a canopy, the pelting rain swept in to drench her, chilling her through. She was also hemorrhaging internally with abdominal bleeding, but the audience of 8,000 fans never suspected.

Because Dolly was afraid she might be forced to cut the concert short because of the weather and her physical condition, she had rescheduled her biggest numbers to go right at the beginning, so that her listeners wouldn't go away disappointed. She played the concert through to its cheering ovation, then came offstage and collapsed, doubling over in agony.

Hours later, Dolly was on a plane to New York, to undergo confidential tests at an unnamed hospital. The balance of her tour through mid-September was canceled on orders from her physicians. Carl Dean flew in from Nashville to be at her side.

A publicity spokesperson issued a statement: "She has tried to forestall surgery at all costs in the past, but now just about every doctor she talks to advises her to have it."

"I never again want to postpone my personal or professional life because of these problems," announced Dolly from her New York apartment while waiting for her doctor's verdict about whether she would have to undergo surgery, although it was evident that this time minor surgery would do little to relieve her condition. It would have to be major. "Thank the Lord that Carl and I never wanted children that bad." But, Dolly being Dolly, she also tried looking at the bright side. "It was God's way of sayin', 'Sit down and think about everything.' Before that, I had always gone full blast." Now she was praying, calling on the Lord for help and strength.

When the inevitable verdict was given—that Dolly Parton should go under the knife for a major operation—she flew to Los Angeles and had it done. Exactly what surgical procedure followed was never announced, but speculation had it that the operation had stopped just short of a complete hysterectomy.

The operation left her weak; it would take Dolly months of complete rest to recover. Between the medication and the inactivity, she gained more weight, 30 pounds more. She had endured a year of pain, bad health, tension, anger, and frustration. Not to mention that mysterious broken heart that had made Dolly "cry an ocean."

Just talking about it to *People* magazine depressed Dolly. "That was a real hard one for me—when you've always been the rock and then you turn to sand."

She told syndicated writer Jack Hurst, "I just wasn't in such a radiant mood as I have been in the past. A lot of people think I'm all sunshine and flowers. But I've had my share of sorrow. I just seem to handle it better than other people do. I refuse to waller in it."

Although Dolly Parton's health worries were behind her, other troubles were really only beginning.

Chapter Twelve

Dolly, How Could You?

I thought Stallone and I would be good together, the way I thought Burt Reynolds and I would be good together. But I didn't finish singing a song in the whole movie, and I don't think people want to see Stallone with his shirt on.

—Dolly Parton

To Dolly Parton, the road was life, heartsblood. She always thrived on performing before thousands, hearing them call out requests for their favorite songs, seeing people leaving her concerts with their spirits refreshed. Touring in her big, comfortable $180,000 tour bus with the boys made a restless Dolly happy.

In late January 1983, Dolly Parton quit the road.

The trouble began a week or so earlier, with death threats that forced her to cancel her concerts, 10 play-dates into a 31-city tour. Dolly and the band had been booked into the Executive Inn in Rivermont, just outside Owensboro, Kentucky, for 2 sold-out, $52-per-ticket appearances.

Ninety minutes before she was to go onstage, an anonymous female caller phoned the Owensboro police and told them that Dolly was in danger of being killed "by a man who hates the ground Dolly walks on." The woman went on to say the potential assassin believed that Dolly "had done him wrong." Refusing to give police the man's name, the caller stated, "I can't tell you who he is. He'll kill me and my family."

Many celebrities are targets of death threats by mentally disturbed people who believe they have a grievance, or even by stupid pranksters with nothing better to do with their time. But this was Dolly's third death threat in recent months, and the police were taking it very seriously. They were afraid she was being stalked by somebody, perhaps by an ex-con who, misunderstanding Dolly's lyrics, took her songs to be about him personally. He also seemed to be laboring under the delusion that Dolly had once been married to him.

Under the advice of the police, Dolly canceled the Executive Inn concerts, but not until 15 minutes before show time. This gave her time to get herself and her band back into the tour bus and leave the grounds secretly. Dolly left Kentucky under police escort, going from the city police to the state police, then to the Kentucky–Tennessee border, where Tennessee authorities took over. Dolly headed straight to Nashville and Carl.

"We don't take chances with Dolly," said a Parton spokesperson, who added that her Nashville manager Don Wharton had hired detectives to track down the threatener. The case was never solved.

"Dolly was real upset," said band member Don Rutledge. "She couldn't go onstage thinking someone would actually try that and maybe shoot one of us or something. It just really freaked her out."

Dolly went into seclusion, beefed up the security at her home, hired a bodyguard, and canceled the rest of her January dates—concerts in New Orleans, Fort Worth, and Beaumont, Texas. At the same time, an announcement was made to the press that Dolly Parton would lay off her band and quit the road after her London concert in March. The London concert was a biggie, because it was taped live for a 90-minute Home Box Office cable special, "Dolly Parton in Concert," which was seen in June 1983, tied in with RCA Records' cross-promotion of Dolly's new album, *Burlap and Satin*, released in late May, containing some of the numbers from Dolly's cable-TV debut.

Among the songs on the album were "Send Me the Pillow You Dream On," "Appalachian Memories," "Gamble Either Way," "I Really Don't Want to Know," and a very upbeat number, "Oo-Eee."

"She has plans for movies for five or six months," said Dolly's publicist, Katie Valk. "So there will be a long block of time with no touring. There's a possibility that she'll do two films back to back during that time." Dolly actually stayed off the road for 18 months, a record for her.

Dolly laid low for a few months, taking the time to think, write songs, read a lot of books, and go to Hawaii, a favorite place of hers, where she bought yet another home, a vacation retreat on Oahu. At the same time she bought herself a nightclub, the Blue Indigo on Oahu. She was disheartened, tired, almost suicidal, as she would later reveal to the press. She determined to choose her next projects with the greatest care. Among them for 1984 were an album, a TV Christmas special, and a tour with beloved country-crossover star Kenny Rogers. Meanwhile she prayed, asking the Lord what she should do next. The connection must have been bad, or maybe the lines got crossed, because Dolly thought that God said "Go thou and make a movie called *Rhinestone*."

Once again, as she did with *Nine to Five*, she dubbed her upcoming film "a blessed project," with much less reason, as it turned out. As a business decision, making *Rhinestone* was somewhere on a par with changing the formula for Coca-Cola.

Sylvester Stallone had never made a comedy or a musical, and there was no reason on earth to believe he could do either. But that didn't stop him. In fact, it kind of nurtured the plot, if one can use the term "plot" for so creaky and predictable a set of circumstances. The plot of *Rhinestone* was based on one of the oldest gags in the world—"I bet I can take the next person who walks by the door and, in only two weeks, I'll turn him into a star!" In this case, the "next person" was Sly Stallone, a New York cabbie, and the person making the boast (and the bet) was Dolly Parton, who was then forced to turn this lumpish piece of "dese-dem-and-dose" protoplasm, who cannot sing a note, into a country music star.

Dolly Parton had vowed never to make a picture again unless she had control, but *Rhinestone* was Sylvester Stallone's personal project for Twentieth Century-Fox. It had been originally conceived as a modest film to be based on the great song by Larry Weiss, "Rhinestone Cowboy." That was before Rocky got his mitts on it. Stallone had co-authored the screenplay with Phil Aldon Robinson, and Fox, hoping it was backing another of the Stallone blockbusters, had given Sly a huge budget. Paramount, which had dropped a bundle on the Stallone-directed turkey *Staying Alive* a couple of years later, must have snickered at Fox's naïveté. A nonviolent Sylvester Stallone sells no tickets.

So Dolly settled for musical control, and for getting Sandy Gallin and their partner, Ray Katz, in as executive producers. She was determined to keep musical control, because Stallone's brother, Frank, is a singer and a songwriter, and Dolly didn't want him muscling in.

The first thing Dolly did was perhaps a bit ill-advised. She canceled her summer tour. This was the concert tour that was to have made up for the concert tour she had canceled when she received those death threats and quit the road. The tour, which would have included the cities she had canceled out the previous year, was supposed to have started in July and run through the middle of August, 25 play-dates in 20 cities. The reason Dolly gave was that she had to prepare for *Rhinestone*. Because a film rider was part of her touring contract, the promoters had to let her cancel without penalty. Earlier cancellations had led to lawsuits on the part of the outraged bookers and promoters who had been forced to give back enormous sums for unused tickets. Was Dolly Parton burning her bridges? Would she ever concertize again? Or was she becoming reclusive, going "Hollywood"?

There was some talk that Dolly might be hurting herself in the concert markets by her repeated cancellations. But Dolly was far more interested in getting ready to compose and record the *Rhinestone* soundtrack. She also canceled some scheduled television appearances, wishing to reserve all her energies for the picture; on this film she would be musical director, writing and supervising the film's original music score and soundtrack album. According to the press, she was also consulting with Stallone on any additional material for the script. Dolly Parton was learning very rapidly how to escalate her control and her production participation.

"I am very excited and looking forward to a wonderful creative partnership with Sly," purred Dolly. "From the beginning of my career, my goal has been full involvement with, and artistic control of, the movies I make."

Sly Stallone purred back. "There is no one I feel more secure with and inspired by than the incredible Dolly Parton."

When, after her illness and a long hiatus, Dolly Parton finally began working again, she started writing and soon got up a full head of steam. Returning to Nashville in August 1983, to get back in touch with her country music roots, within 3 weeks she had written the 13 songs that were used in *Rhinestone*, plus 7 additional ones.

"Those songs just fell into my lap," she said happily. "I was feelin' just great again, just to get that old energy goin'."

Dolly told *People*, "I thought, since these are country songs, I should go to Nashville and in and around Kentucky. I went home and took my camper and my girl friend Judy Ogle, who's always with me." Dolly's best friend Judy acts as Dolly's personal assistant and has devoted her life to being with Dolly Parton.

"We'd just go out and sit on the riverbank and just park and check into these dinky little motels, which I love to do anyway. When I finished, I told those producers, 'Look, these are the songs and this is exactly what we need. Now, if anybody wants anything different, don't come to me.' "

Mindful of her family, Dolly brought in some of her kin to work on the the production. Two of her brothers—Randy and Floyd, who used to be with the Travelin' Family Band—were heard on the soundtrack and were also seen singing "Waltz

Me to Heaven" on the screen. Friends also joined in, including Speck Rhodes, the toothless comic of "The Porter Wagoner Show."

Sylvester Stallone, more body-conscious than any Miss America, lost 40 pounds before going before the cameras. Dolly, whose weight was up there in the stratosphere, was aghast. "He's so self-disciplined, I tell you, if anybody told me to lose forty pounds for a movie, I'd say, 'You can kiss my country ass.' "

Still, Sly's regimen and his diet set Dolly to thinking. She was more than 30 pounds overweight, thanks to the medications she had taken and the inactivity caused by her long illness. She had had to watch her weight since the age of twenty-eight or twenty-nine. Her diet consisted largely of fried foods and starches; she was also a junk-food junkie, and she loved to eat. Now at thirty-eight, she poked fun at her embonpoint, saying, "My fat ain't never lost me no money." Yet, inside was a thin person crying to be released.

As the picture got under way, it seemed to be jinxed from the start. The first director was Don Zimmerman, a friend of Stallone's who, up until *Rhinestone*, had only been a film editor. Less than a month into the picture, Zimmerman left. With him went three and a half weeks of shooting. The new director, brought in to replace Zimmerman, was Bob Clark, whose claim to fame was *Porky's*, a gross film, perhaps, but an even grosser grosser.

"I'd heard a lot of stories about Sylvester Stallone, that he was impossible," admitted Dolly.

"The chances of it working out were pretty remote," admitted Stallone.

But the two of them "got their shit together up front," in Dolly's words, and the filming proceeded more calmly than expected. Dolly told Sylvester Stallone right up front that she wasn't going to stand for his dumping on her with the same unbridled criticism he heaped on others, or taking out his black moods on her. "But I could hardly wait to see who he was goin' to fire or cuss out next. He was smart, though, and it was never me."

The problems were not with the stars' egos, and the problems were not with the direction. The problem lay in the fact that the film was ever made at all. A bummer with a terrible script, *Rhinestone* wound up costing Fox big bucks it didn't earn back.

Market research showed that Sylvester Stallone fans did not want to see him with Dolly Parton, and that Dolly Parton fans did not want to see her with Sylvester Stallone. A three-year-old could have predicted it. There was no chemistry between them—zilch. Stallone was too wooden and Dolly too animated; it was as though each of them was playing in a different film at the same time. Only an actor with a flair for comedy could have brought off a script as bad as *Rhinestone*'s, and Sylvester Stallone did not possess that flair. Besides which, he couldn't sing a note, even with the voluptuous coaching of Dolly Parton for two fun-filled weeks.

Dolly's third film, which opened in July 1984,

was a total disaster, a big-budget stinkeroo, a box-office bomb. Heads rolled.

Variety, that bible of show biz, lamented "Mismatched Sly and Dolly in an off-the-wall comedy." *Variety* went on to say, "Effortlessly living up to its title, *Rhinestone* is as artificial and synthetic a concoction as has ever made its way to the screen. . . . Neither Stallone nor Parton strays at all from their past personae, and major shows are actually put on by their costume designers, since the two leads seem to change their clothes every three minutes [which, considering how tight they fit, is no small achievement]. . . ."

Of all the deservedly abysmal reviews that *Rhinestone* received, Kip Kirby's in her "Nashville Scene" column in *Billboard* was among the most eloquent. Ms. Kirby's review was headlined, "Dolly, How Could You?" It read, in part, "It's baffling to try to figure an explanation for Dolly Parton's association with *Rhinestone*, a film which could set the image of country music—not to mention the South—back ten years. *Rhinestone* parodies everything connected with country, portraying its entertainers as hicks and its fans as stereotyped obnoxious boors. . . . Why would Dolly, who has personally done so much to upgrade country's image around the world, appear in a film which reinforces every miserable negative that country music has had to fight against . . . ? Dolly's presence in *Rhinestone* lends credibility to a project that is an embarrassment to many people in the country entertainment industry."

Stallone was devastated, but Dolly was a lot more philosophical. "Sly probably thinks I wrecked his career with that movie, but to me, I was the one taking the chance. I've done *two* musicals with men who can't sing—Sly and Burt Reynolds—and here I am a singer. Both were bad casting, of course, but I have only myself to blame.

"He's pretty to look at, too," said Dolly to Cliff Jahr, "and I know that when Sasha, his last wife, was getting her divorce, she said we were having an affair. Not true at all. Sly and I are just not each other's type. Both he and Burt are egomaniacs, but Sly is the perfect balance of total ego and total insecurity. I see how his mind works. If you were in love with him, he'd pick out all your weaknesses and either use them to help you or use them against you."

Dolly hasn't made a film since *Rhinestone*, but "I think I will do movies again," she says. "The people seem to like me in them, and I guess I owe it to them. But I don't have the kind of stars in my eyes anymore that could lead me to destruction. I see movie pictures as a business, and it ought to be run that way. If and when I do a picture in the future, I'm definitely gonna be involved in the producing end of things. I'll probably write the story, too. I'm gonna have a lot more control than I've had up to now, and I'm gonna use it."

For a couple of years now, Dolly Parton has been promising a film project that would reunite her with her old buddies Lily Tomlin and Jane Fonda. Not a sequel to *Nine to Five*, but an adventure comedy. But so far, a script has not come together.

Dolly Parton is never one to look behind her, only ahead. So, after the catastrophe of *Rhinestone*, she picked herself up, dusted herself off, and went on with her life. Much was happening.

For one thing, she began losing the extra weight she had picked up over the years. She started out by doing "everything"—she fasted, went on liquid protein, did the Dr. Atkins diet, all the quick-weight-loss programs that one cannot stay on forever because they are too dangerous. Then, as the pounds began to melt away, Dolly discovered the secret of her own dieting success. She began to eat again the foods she loved, anything she wanted or craved, only in tiny portions. A bite or two, not the whole thing. She ate numerous little tiny meals, and still she lost weight. "I'm in hog heaven," she crowed. She lost 10 pounds, 20, 30, until she was back to the old zaftig Dolly. But then Dolly went on, until today, to the point where she has lost a total of 50 pounds. She is 5 feet tall, and weighs 100 pounds, most of it, as she'll be the first to tell you, above the waist.

In March 1983, Monument Records and Combine Music, Dolly Parton's first record company of so many years ago, filed for bankruptcy under Chapter XI, citing $7,300,000 in debts and $8,800,000 in assets. In November 1984, an investment group consisting of LeFrak Entertainment Ltd. of New York, Lorimar Productions, and Dolly Parton filed a reorganization plan for Monument and offered to buy Fred Foster's 70 percent inter-

est in the company for $4,900,000 and Bob
Beckham's 30 percent interest for $2,100,000, a
total of $7,000,000. An additional $1,000,000 was
offered for the company's master recordings and
the Monument-Combine building, owned by Fred
Foster, on Music Row in Nashville. The eighteen-
year-old girl with the cardboard suitcase filled
with songs was now a multimillionaire superstar,
ready to buy back and reorganize the company
herself. She was identified to the Bankruptcy Court
as having a net worth "of not less than five million dollars," although of course it is a lot more
than that.

It was Dolly's intention to be actively involved
in the management of both Monument and Combine, to reactivate the company, pay off the
creditors—among whom were Roy Orbison, Kris
Kristofferson's producer David Anderle, Larry
Gatlin, Rita Coolidge, Jennie Seely, and Dolly
Parton—and make the company into a country
music giant. It had an enviable catalog—included
in the Monument archives were hits by Roy
Orbison, Larry Gatlin, Tony Joe White, and others, including Dolly Parton's "Dumb Blonde," and
a duet that Dolly had recorded in 1982 with Willie Nelson, "Everything Is Beautiful In Its Own
Way," from Nelson's *The Winning Hand* album.
Combine, the music-publishing arm of the firm,
was a treasure trove of classics and was the successful end of the business.

It's a shame the deal didn't go through; if it
had, it would have made Dolly Parton one of the
three or four biggest music-publishing outfits in

Music City, U.S.A. And Monument Records, for whom she planned to record her new material, would be on top of the heap.

In the fall of 1984, two giants of country music got together again—Dolly Parton and Kenny Rogers. In 1983, they had recorded "Islands in the Stream," for Rogers's first album on the RCA label, *Eyes That See in the Dark*, a collaboration that made the Rogers album go platinum, while the song itself went to the number-one slot on all the charts, country as well as pop, and became the most-played, most-requested song of the year, as well as the best-selling single, going platinum. It was one of the biggest hits of both their long careers.

"You pray for a song like 'Islands in the Stream' to come along," said Rogers. "The most wonderful thing about it was the chance to sing with Dolly. As soon as we'd finished recording it, I knew it was going to be an enormous hit." The song won the Song of the Year Award at the 1984 presentations of the Country Music Association, and was named BMI-Nashville's Most Performed Song of the Year. It also sold more than 2,000,000 copies of the single, and pushed the Rogers album over the platinum 1,000,000 mark.

Having tasted success together, the two superstars went on for the full meal. Actually, they had talked for years about working together on projects and even a road tour, but Dolly's ill health and the three pictures she had made had not allowed her to commit any of her time to Kenny Rogers.

215

But now, a Christmas album, *Kenny Rogers' and Dolly Parton's Once Upon a Christmas*, also went platinum faster than you could say "Kenny 'n' Dolly."

That was all they needed to inspire them. At the tail end of 1984, Kenny and Dolly launched into megabucks, what *Variety* called "a major creative combination," a one-hour TV Christmas special, "Kenny & Dolly: A Christmas to Remember," originated for them by CBS and obviously based on the success of the earlier album. The TV special, which aired December 2, 1984, featured 5 original Dolly Parton songs, as well as such standards as "White Christmas" and "Silent Night," and a group of animated elves who stole the show. It was a co-production of Dolly's company, Speckled Bird Productions, and Kenny's company, Lion Share Productions. Both the stars' personal managers—Sandy Gallin for Dolly, and Ken Kragen for Kenny—were named as producers. It goes without saying that the RCA album of the show, more than 1,000,000 copies of *Kenny Rogers' and Dolly Parton's Once Upon a Christmas*, were in the record stores during Thanksgiving week, and went platinum, predictably, without delay.

What's more, the superstar pair was going on the road together, as one of the most eagerly awaited package acts ever. It had been more than a year since Dolly's health problems had forced her to cancel and give up her last bus tour, and some two and a half years since she had managed to finish any of her tours. This equal-billing tour started off December 28 at the Oakland, California, Coliseum, and was to carry Dolly and Kenny through 42 cities until the end of March, including a big-ticket New Year's Eve gala at the Los Angeles Forum, with seats selling for $30 and $50.

One of the New York City concerts in March was played for the benefit of the African Relief Fund, as part of Kenny Rogers's ongoing commitment to the cause of world hunger.

Dolly Parton was on the road again.

Chapter Thirteen

Hooray for Dollywood!

A long time ago, I wrote down
all the things I wanted out of life
and what I had to do to get them.

—Dolly Parton

In January 1986, Dolly Parton celebrated her
fortieth birthday. For many women, forty is the
time when youth slips away from them and middle age says hello. But not Dolly. She really had
something to celebrate in 1986; the best part of
her life was just beginning. She had never felt
better; her health problems seemed to be behind
her. Determined not to be fat and forty, she had
begun a new diet regimen that was working wonderfully. Her excess weight was literally melting

off, and she would begin 1987 some 50 pounds lighter.

She was at the top of her profession; Dolly's earnings were a reported $15,000,000 a year. She had set up a multimillion-dollar entertainment empire that many a male corporate executive would envy. The corporation she owned in common with Sandy Gallin, Sandollar, had recently signed a major film production deal with Universal Pictures. The first picture under discussion, to be scripted by Dolly, would reunite her with her favorite co-stars, Lily Tomlin and Jane Fonda. The film, tentatively titled *Brass Angels*, was, as they say in Hollywood, "in development."

Dolly's legal problems seemed to be over now. The $3,000,000 suit that Porter Wagoner had brought against her, the agony of which had sapped her emotional energies for years, was settled. Her other troublesome lawsuit had been dismissed.

In December 1985, the Grammy Award-winning "Nine to Five" made the front pages again, but this time in the most destructive way. The songwriting team of Neil and Jan Goldberg had accused Dolly Parton of plagiarism, of stealing the chorus of their song "Money World" and using it for "Nine to Five." In December, the case went to trial in Santa Monica, naming, as co-defendants along with Dolly, Jane Fonda and her husband, Tom Hayden. With celebrities like Dolly and Jane on the witness stand, the case never left the headlines or the 6 o'clock news for the 12 days during which it was heard. The jury deliberated for under an hour, and on December 20, it brought in a unanimous verdict for the defendants. Dolly Parton had won.

Three days later, the Goldbergs moved for a retrial, claiming that the jury was "starstruck" by Jane Fonda and Dolly Parton, and had reached its verdict against the weight of the evidence. The couple's request for a retrial was denied after a hearing in January 1986.

"That was so degrading," winced Dolly to her chronicler, Cliff Jahr, in the June 1986 *Ladies' Home Journal*. "One of the most painful things I've ever gone through. It damaged my reputation, I think, because there'll always be some people out there who think I would stoop so low as to steal from working people. Besides, there were only five musical notes in question, and they've been used in a hundred songs. The jury was out for twenty minutes, and we won. The court awarded me attorney's fees, which is a lot of money. Then the couple who sued me tried to get a retrial, claiming I charmed the jury because I played songs on the witness stand. The retrial was denied, and then they actually started trying to get me to record some of their songs."

There was irony involved here. Years before, Dolly had said in print that it was easier for her to do her own material because she didn't have time to go looking for songs. Also, listening to other people's material might always contain the possibility "that I might unconsciously take someone's tune." She didn't know then how her words would come back to haunt her later.

Dolly had released another hit album in the spring of 1985, *Real Love*, the title song for which she recorded as a duet with Kenny Rogers. The album cover showed a very different Dolly, a face that might have been photographed through a layer of Vaseline and eight layers of gauze, a shorter, less blatantly artificial wig, pale romantic colors, a white gown ... a photograph shot *above* the chest. Who was this soft-focus apparition? Where were the gaudy sequins and the rhinestones? Nowhere to be seen. Dolly Parton was obviously classing up her image.

Dolly had just aired a second TV Christmas special—this time without Kenny Rogers—"A Smoky Mountain Christmas," which aired as the ABC Sunday Night Movie on December 14, 1985. With a flimsy plot dealing with seven orphans and one burned-out movie star (Dolly), it was a heart-wrencher starring Dolly Parton and Lee Majors, directed by Henry ("The Fonz") Winkler, and written by Dolly Parton. She also wrote six new songs for the special, including the title song, "A Smoky Mountain Christmas."

Dolly described the show as being "a combination of 'Snow White' and 'Sleeping Beauty,' " and hoped that it would become an annual TV event, and that the title song would become a Christmas classic, like "Jingle Bells." "Every songwriter dreams of writing a Christmas song that somebody's going to pick out and record."

Dolly had earned just about every honor the entertainment world could bestow, many of them more times than once. She now has a star of her own embedded in the Walk of the Stars on Hollywood Boulevard.

Creatively, Dolly is the author of some 3,000

songs, over 600 of which she has recorded. She owns enough platinum albums to start her own platinum mine.

Dolly Parton has bought or built homes in Nashville, a 6-bedroom house on Oahu, apartments and houses in Beverly Hills, Manhattan, and, recently, a large lakefront hideaway in Tennessee, this last one mostly for Carl to enjoy. By now she was making no secret of the fact that she and Carl Dean were sharing an open marriage, although she never revealed the names of her lovers. She had just about everything a woman could require to make her happy—youth, health, money, fame, the respect of her colleagues, and a great love life.

But *was* Dolly Parton completely fulfilled? Not yet.

There was a list of things she had sworn to do. There was always a list.

One was to get rid of some of the dead wood in her life. This she did periodically, and without mercy. It took a lot to make Dolly mad, but once she got mad, she was implacable. With her customary mysteriousness, the mystery that Jane Fonda had remarked upon, Dolly will not say who that dead wood was, but admits that she sat down and wrote a series of letters, severing some business and some family ties, and that took care of that.

"Y'know what I did?" she asked Cliff Jahr in his June 1986 interview in *Ladies' Home Journal*. "I got up early and went straight to a list of names I'd made. I wrote letters to four people, some family, some business, who I had let mess with my head. They're people who's had the upper hand on me for years. When I saw them comin', I'd cringe. When they called, I wasn't in.

"The letters were very blunt. They said: 'I'm not going to put up with your B.S. anymore. You have no control over me, and little control of yourself, so you should examine things very carefully.' Then I made some phone calls, too. I decided to get all the grief and worries over irresponsible people out of my life. And it worked—it really cleared the air."

The next thing on Dolly's list was Dollywood.

A decade earlier, when she was interviewed by Barbara Walters on Barbara's TV special, Dolly had confessed that she wanted to build a fantasy world somewhere in the mountains for everybody to share with her. It was an ambition Dolly Parton was to talk about wistfully over and over throughout the years when she was becoming successful. She also said, again and again, that her dream was for people to be able to see just what her part of the country was really like, how her people really lived. Too, it was an important part of Dolly's ambition to pump money back into her rural east Tennessee, bring in the tourists with their open pocketbooks, and create jobs for local people.

In 1986, Dolly Parton's threefold ambitious dream came to pass at last.

Dollywood was by no means a unique concept. In 1948, Roy Acuff opened his Dunbar Cave resort near Clarksville, Tennessee. Among the other famous country artists who have their own museums or theme parks are: Conway Twitty with

Twitty City; Barbara Mandrell and Mandrell Country; Jimmie Rodgers; Minnie Pearl; Roy Rogers, who houses a stuffed and frighteningly lifelike Trigger in his Roy Rogers Museum; Lorretta Lynn's Hurricane Mills dude ranch; Jim Reeves; Hank Williams, Jr., and his Kawliga Corners; Merle Haggard's Silverthorn fishing resort; Waylon Jennings; the House of Cash owned by Johnny Cash—the list goes on. Not to mention the most famous hillbilly Disneyland of them all, Graceland, which was Elvis Presley's home when he was alive, and a multimillion-dollar money-coiner after his death. Tourists flock there to the tune of 500,000 visitors a year.

It's not the price of admission alone that brings the gold tumbling into the coffers; it's the souvenirs, the fast foods, the rides, the price of film and the photo developing, the bumper stickers, the motel accommodations—all adding up to tourist dollars in the millions. Naturally, when Dolly Parton decided to open her own amusement park, it had to be the biggest and the best. Fighting off the leering wags who suggested she call her project Titty City, Dolly opted for Dollywood. "It just popped into my mind that it would be a good name for a park."

When Dolly made up her mind to build the biggest and best theme park of any of the country music stars, and bring business flowing into her part of Tennessee, she didn't have to start from scratch. There was an already existing historical-theme amusement park on Route 441 at Pigeon Forge, first known as Gold Rush Park, later as Silver Dollar City. Why compete? Why not simply join forces and expand? Accordingly, the Parton organization joined hands with Jack Herschend, who founded Silver Dollar City, and thus was born Dollywood (in the logo, the "W" is a butterfly with wings spread), now called "A Silver Dollar City Theme Park," which is a 400-acre spread located 30 miles south of Knoxville, in the foothills of, and gateway to, the Great Smoky Mountains, where Dolly grew up. The new park has 50 percent more acreage than Silver Dollar City had.

In July 1985, Dolly returned to Sevierville to put the plan for Dollywood in front of the city council and get its financial support. The city kicked in $600,000 and the state of Tennessee $1,600,000, to update the streets, the lighting, the sewer system, and other amenities in and around the proposed expansion. The newly cosmeticized and updated park is a $20,000,000 venture in which Dolly's and her partner's investment is said to be around $6,000,000. The park opened in a blizzard of publicity on May 3, 1986.

Dolly's personal part of the park is Daydream Ridge, which has been built to resemble rural Tennessee sometime before the turn of the century. In a craftsmen's village are to be seen local Tennessee artisans creating the homespun crafts of yesteryear: sewing quilts, carving wood, making wagons, blowing glass, and shoeing horses, all before tourists' eyes.

Dollywood offers, among other treats and the obligatory thrill rides, a rags-to-riches tour of Dolly's life, in the Dolly Parton Story Museum, which contains many of her costumes and wigs, gold records, guitars, photos, and other Parton memorabilia. There's Rivertown Junction, which has restaurants like Aunt Granny's Dixie Fixin's (her many nieces and nephews call Dolly "Aunt Granny"), and Apple Jack's cider press and mill, which serves apples in more ways than one wants to know about.

Dollywood boasts a Nine to Five and Dime Mercantile, and a gift shop that can't be passed up—The Parton Back Porch Theater, which is a copy of her old back porch, but which is now an outdoor concert stage with 700 seats. Dolly hired her sister Stella, herself something of a country music star, to stage country music concerts, along with her brother Randy and her sister Frieda, and her Uncle Bill Owens, all alumni of the Travelin' Family Band.

There is also white-water rafting on The Smoky Mountain Rampage, a miniature railroad called The Dollywood Express, and a lot more. The park offers mountain crafts, bluegrass festivals, restaurants where visitors can stuff their faces with Dolly's "favorite foods," such as apple fritters, banana pudding, funnel cakes, hickory-smoked meats, Mountain Burgers, and more.

Nobody goes away without visiting the replica of her 2-room Tennessee Mountain Home, complete down to the spittoon, and bearing a plaque in front that reads: "These mountains and my childhood home have a special place in my heart. They inspire my music and my life. I hope being here does the same for you."

"Dollywood is not about Dolly Parton," she said. "It never once crossed my mind that it was an ego trip. It's about Smoky Mountain people and their way of life. These are my people and I was in a position to do something great for them. Dollywood has provided a lot of jobs and rejuvenated a lot of pride my people have in their heritage. People in New York and Los Angeles may not know it, but Smoky Mountain National Park is one of the most visited national parks in the country [9,000,000 visitors a year]. I knew all we had to do was put Dollywood right in the middle of all that traffic, then get ourselves some publicity. I knew it would work. We had one and a half million people the first year. Now we're expanding to accommodate even more the second. I'm going to make some good money, too. I may be a country bumpkin, but I'm a *smart* country bumpkin."

Even as Dolly Parton was crossing Dollywood off her list of Things to Do Today, another item on the list, an item already ten years old, was coming into fruition.

In its March 23, 1978, issue, *Rolling Stone* ran an item headlined "Ronstadt, Parton, and Harris's Secret Project." The story said that three of the hottest women singers in the business—Linda Ronstadt, Emmylou Harris, and Dolly Parton—were recording an album together, and had sworn one another to a secrecy "worthy of the Manhattan Project [which yielded the atomic bomb]." Because the three singers were signed to different record labels, it was a difficult deal to work out, but it was agreed that Asylum, Linda Ronstadt's label, should release the album, and tentative plans were made to set up a group of charity concerts

227

when the album was completed. That was in 1978.

Dolly Parton met Linda Ronstadt at the "Grand Ole Opry" more than 12 years ago, and they became friends. In 1974, Linda and Emmylou Harris had cut a country song together, "I Can't Help It If I'm Still in Love with You," and it went to number one on the country music chart.

Nineteen seventy-four was a crossover year for Linda Ronstadt, the singer from Tucson, Arizona. That was when Linda, queen of the "L.A. country-rock set," spanned both the pop and the country charts with her classic *Heart Like a Wheel* album. Her Nashville album was *Silk Purse*, containing the beautiful ballad "Long Long Time."

From her crossover into country in 1974, Linda Ronstadt began to have one platinum award-winning album after another: *Heart Like a Wheel; Prisoner in Disguise; Hasten Down the Wind; Linda Ronstadt's Greatest Hits; Living in the U.S.A.* The list is virtually endless, like Dolly's own catalog of hits. And, just like Dolly Parton, Linda Ronstadt drew her fans from a cross-section of the record-buying population, crossing age, gender, and regional barriers.

As for Emmylou Harris, she is one of the most admired and respected country music singers; her voice is pure country. As *Country Music* magazine said about her in 1984, "With her crystalline voice, her rhapsodic beauty, her plaintive emoting, her winsome onstage shyness, her delicate wholesomeness combined with a sort of freewheeling rambunctiousness, Emmylou has inspired something almost like worship among her follow-ers.''

Dolly respected them both; they respected each other and Dolly, especially as a composer. Both Linda and Emmylou had recorded Dolly Parton songs; Emmylou Harris's version of "Coat of Many Colors" is enough to make a stone weep. So, when the three women got together for the first time in Emmylou Harris's Los Angeles home, magic began to happen.

"We just got a guitar and sang 'When I Stopped Dreaming,' " says Emmylou. "Then we sang the Christmas song 'Light of the Stable' to an acoustic guitar. And it sounded so good, I asked the other two, 'If I record "Light of the Stable," will you come and sing with me on the track?' And they both said yes. So it was natural that we sort of went on from there."

Said Dolly on "The Oprah Winfrey Show" in the spring of 1987, "The three of us became friends about twelve or thirteen years ago, and the first time we were together we were in Emmylou Har-ris's living room, and we just started to sing some of the old gospel songs and country songs, and we said, boy! This sounds good! It was the kind of harmony that usually just family can get. You know how in family if you sing there is a certain blend. We thought we sounded like sisters and we should record it. We tried it almost ten years ago, and it didn't come together then because there was so much pressure on us. The labels were telling us to do this, do that, do some rock 'n' roll, do some country. We just decided that what we had in our minds was too good to be wasted on so much frustration, so we put it on the shelf. Every time we'd get together through the years, we'd say, 'We just got to record this album.' So this past year, Linda called me and Emmylou and said, 'Let's make the time,' so we did."

They began recording on Dolly's birthday, and this time the Trio album came together as though it had always just been there, waiting to be set free into the world. Said Dolly of the album, "I know it took forever to make, but we just love it. It's real country, acoustic, and very down-home. Emmy sounds so good. And no one can sing a rock or country song like Linda."

Is it possible that an album of pure country singing by three of the most famous and most beautiful voices in country music could fail? No.

It didn't.

Is it possible that such an album as Trio wouldn't head directly for the top of the charts and stay there? No.

It did. At this writing, it is still at the top of the charts.

When the feminist Ms. magazine released its list of Women of the Year at the end of 1986, Dolly Parton's name was on it. She was honored for "creating popular songs about real women," and "for bringing jobs and understanding to the mountain people of Tennessee."

Gloria Steinem herself, one of the founding editors of Ms. and the personification of American feminism, wrote about Dolly: "She has crossed musical class lines to bring work, real life, and strong women into a world of pop usually dominated by unreal romance. She has used her business sense to bring other women and poor people along with her. And her flamboyant style has turned all the devalued symbols of womanliness to her own ends. If feminism means each of us finding our unique power, and helping other women do the same, Dolly Parton certainly has done both."

Nineteen eighty-seven was the year Dolly left RCA Records and signed with CBS Records. "It was like an old marriage," she explained. "We'd begun to take each other for granted a little bit. What I needed was a fresh start, and some real success in my recording career. With this new deal at CBS, I'm going to do one great authentic country album every year, and one pop album. No more mixin' them up and tryin' to please everybody all at the same time."

As though Dollywood, *Trio*, a new slimmer figure, a new recording contract, validation by the feminist movement, and a new lease on life weren't enough goodies for Dolly to find in her Christmas stocking, 1987 brought Dolly Parton another piece of something wonderful—a $40,000,000 contract with her production company for her own ABC-TV 60-minute variety series, "The Dolly Show," to debut in the fall of 1987.

"It's goin' to be a tough battle—there are some really great shows to beat—but we're going to come out on top," she promises. "If you think you've seen a TV variety show before, forget it— you ain't seen nothin' yet. Variety has been off too long, and I have a lot more talent than people realize."

Even though there has not been a successful variety show on television in ten years, not since the Barbara Mandrell series, the ABC network has committed to two full seasons of the specials at $1,000,000 per show. Brandon Stoddard, president of ABC's entertainment division, says, "There are few stars in the world who have the instant recognition and sheer likability of Dolly Parton, and to say we are delighted that she will be part of our weekly series lineup this fall is the understatement of the season."

Sandy Gallin, Dolly's partner, is producing the program. "She wants to utilize her talents," he said. "Dolly doesn't want to sit around waiting for the perfect movie script to come in. She feels she is a performing talent and should be in front of an audience entertaining people. What better platform to do that than a weekly variety show?"

Dolly is planning a "lot of surprises" that will make the show different from any others, and she bets it will run at least five years.

With Dolly Parton at the helm, who can doubt it? The ten-year-old hillbilly girl who stood up and sang to her first TV audience at 5:30 in the morning over WIVK in Knoxville grew up to become the forty-one-year-old woman who is one of the world's greatest entertainers, not just a superstar but a megastar. The girl who left the mountains to see the big wide world has introduced millions of people to an understanding of those mountains.

Anybody who can do that can do anything.

Epilogue

Here I Come Again

I'm Dolly Parton from the mountains, and that's what I'll remain.

—Dolly Parton

The importance of music in Dolly's life cannot be overemphasized. Music is her best friend, her deepest and longest-held love, her chosen companion. Movies and television are wonderful, but they will never take the place of Dolly Parton's music. It is her strongest commitment. Above all, she thinks of herself as a songwriter. She writes anywhere, everywhere, getting up in the middle of the night to do it, interrupting a meal in a restaurant to jot down lyrics or titles on paper napkins and matchbooks. When she is writing a song, she forgets everything else in the world.

"I'm a songwriter first, a singer and performer second. I want to be known as a great writer—now, that's a dream of mine. I would describe my writing as being simply complicated. It's got enough depth to be appreciated, and enough simplicity to be understood. Everybody wants to be successful at whatever their inner dream is. I'm not near finished with what I want to do, with what I want to accomplish yet. I want to be somebody that left behind something good and beautiful for somebody else to enjoy."

Dolly once said to Kip Kirby, "Music is my personal addiction. So much of everything I've done has only been to open more doors for the music itself. It all gets back to the fact that I am, first of all, a songwriter and a singer."

Dolly has been known to write as many as 20 songs in one day. She has "thousands more" either already down on paper or in her head.

When interviewed on "The Oprah Winfrey Show," Dolly demonstrated how she used her very long artificial nails as a musical instrument, clicking them together in rhythm. Sometimes, when she is without her guitar, and a scrap of music enters her head, she will use her fingernails to capture it before she can get somebody to write it down. She still can't read a note of music.

As for the future of her open marriage to Carl Dean, it is difficult to see it ever coming to an end. Why should it, when it allows Dolly so much freedom, and at the same time so much support? Ten years ago, Dolly said to Barbara

Walters about her husband, "He's the kind of person that if bein' apart, if I should meet somebody, I would never tell Carl. He would never know and I would never tell him. And it wouldn't hurt him. It's the same way with him. I wouldn't want to know it. As long as he loves me and as long as he's good to me and as long as we're good to each other. I don't think it happens, but I'm just sayin' I wouldn't want to pry in it.

"My husband is a very home-based type of person. He's very moral and the most unselfish person I've ever known. He's very deep and very witty. He's good for me because he's so different in nature from me. There's nobody else like him and I know in my heart that there will never be another person for me. I just know it."

She has often said, "Carl's not a jealous person and neither am I. He understands that music is so much a part of me and he understands that I couldn't be happy without my music, as much as I love him. There would be so much of me missing, I wouldn't be myself. He's the one man in my life, and I want to grow old with him. If he should die first, I'd probably never marry again. That's how deep my love for him is."

Dolly's country wit is celebrated, and it's often been turned against herself. "I'm six-foot-four in heels." "I don't look this way out of ignorance. If people think that I do, they're dumber than I am." She also has a tendency to speak of herself in the third person—"Dolly does this," or "Dolly does that." She has talked about the possibility of "Dolly changing her look."

"If I felt strongly enough about the character

was going to play, I wouldn't mind changing my look. Eventually, that will be one of my challenges, to be another personality."

It would seem that Dolly Parton has in fact recently changed her look. She is so thin now that she has an odd birdlike appearance. Her breasts, while certainly smaller than they were when she was 50 pounds heavier, are still the largest part of her body. Her waist is 17 or 18 inches around, but her chest measurement can't be less than 38 or 39 inches. She dresses far more modestly, even turning up in tailored costumes that outline her brand-new figure. Is the old gaudy, spangle-loving Dolly Parton gone for good?

There is even some trepidation among her friends (and in the supermarket tabloids) that Dolly may have gone *too* far with this weight-reduction regimen of hers. She is down to a perfect size, and weighs no more than 100 pounds, but still she continues to diet. Is she a borderline anorexic, or has she crossed that border? Or is she the victim of an eating disorder that will make her thin, then fat, then thin again, then fat once more, for the rest of her life? Dolly Parton is a person who takes control, and this is one vital area she certainly must watch.

Ten years ago, in Chet Flippo's cover interview with Dolly for *Rolling Stone*, she told him, "There is no top and no bottom to my career because once I accomplish the things I decide I'm going to, then I want to get into other things. I am a list maker. I like to write my goals and plans down and keep them in a secret place where people can't see them. You'd be *amazed* that even years ago the things I'd written down on my list, that I just mark 'em off as they come true and I think, boy, if that ain't proof that positive thinkin' is a marvelous thing. I practiced that all my life; that's what got me out of the mountains. Even as a little child, I daydreamed so strongly that I just saw these things happen and, sure enough, they would. We can be whatever we want to be, the Bible says that, that all things are possible, and it says that if you have faith even as a grain of mustard seed, then you shall move mountains and that nothing shall be impossible unto you."

So far, nothing seems to have been impossible unto Dolly Parton. What does the future hold? More of the same? A climb to even greater heights?

"Every seven years I sit down and make a new plan."

Among the new plans Dolly is making these days, besides her total involvement in her new ABC-TV variety show, are: a line of diet foods called Slim Pickin's at the same time that she wants to open a chain of restaurants to sell heavy, greasy country food like biscuits and gravy, fatback and greens—Aunt Granny's; a line of cosmetics—Dollyface; that motion picture which is to reunite Dolly, Lily, and Jane, but for which no final script has been approved. Will this take longer than Linda, Emmylou, and Dolly getting together to record Trio?; a Broadway musical about her life in east Tennessee, Wildflowers; self-help and inspirational books under her contract with Simon & Schuster; footwear, lingerie, songs, albums, the possibility of a tour with Emmylou Harris and Linda Ronstadt. Dolly Parton has enough irons in the fire to burn down a good-sized cabin.

What about this: Dolly Parton for President of the United States? Don't laugh. America laughed at the thought of Ronald Reagan. With Dolly as President, the budget would balance, we would be at peace with the rest of the world, and every day would start with a song. Besides, Dolly Parton has a rare integrity, matched with inner strength and a core of steel; she says that, while she never learned to harden her heart, she has learned to strengthen the muscles around it. She fasts and prays before every major decision. We should have more, much more, of that quality in our world leaders.

Dolly Parton's not afraid of growing old.

"I'll be a great old lady, lots of fun and busy and smarter," she told Cliff Jahr, "full of life and still foolin' around a little. If it's God's will that I'm healthy and I keep my mind, I can always sing, write for other people, manage, produce, do a talk show, a variety show, a TV series. I get these incredible offers all the time, but during this part of my career, I'm going for the bigger stuff—the movies, Dollywood, books I'm going to write, and helping to run my new film and TV production companies with my manager.

"I don't want people to think of me as someone who has not tasted enough of life to be an artist. I've had a *full* meal.

"When I sit back in my rocking chair someday," Dolly Parton says, smiling, "I want to be able to say I've done it all."

238